The Secret of Tamsworth Forest

A Fantasy Story

by

Kathleen B. Wilson

Published in Great Britain 2016 by Brighton NightWriters
Copyright © Kathleen B Wilson
Cover artwork and design Kathleen B Wilson
All characters and events in this publication are fictitious and any
resemblance to any person living or dead is purely coincidental.
All rights reserved.
No part of this publication may be reproduced or stored in a
retrieval system, or transmitted in any form or by any means
without the prior permission in writing of the publisher.
Printed by Create Space
ISBN: 9781535212007

CHARACTERS

In This World

Sue Dawson	Sister to Priscilla and Barry
Barry Dawson	Sue's younger brother
Priscilla Dawson	Sue's older sister
Aunt Moira	Aunt to Sue, Barry and Priscilla
Mrs Denton	Grandmother to Sue, Barry and Priscilla
Professor Harding	Searching for the other world
Cyril Grant	The Professor's assistant

In the Other World

Sonja	Sue's other identity
Raithe	Prince of the realm and Sonja's twin brother
Ruth	Queen of Therossa and mother of Sonja and Raithe
Thane	Hunter and tracker
White Hawk	Thane's wolf
Saturn	Thane's horse
Shaman	A gifted healer
Neela	The Shaman's assistant
Annalee	Thane's sister
Tansy	Tracker and friend of Annalee
Cailli	A tracker
Amos	Tracker, leader of his people and horse expert
Elina	Servant to the gypsies
Tug	Servant to the gypsies
Zuboarra	Chief of the gypsies
Jacques	A gypsy

CONTENTS

Prologue 1

Chapter 1	*The New Guests*	5
Chapter 2	*Thane of the Forest*	19
Chapter 3	*The White Wolf*	38
Chapter 4	*The Secret Place*	47
Chapter 5	*The Alien World*	65
Chapter 6	*People of Therossa*	80
Chapter 7	*Barry has a Plan*	102
Chapter 8	*Betrayal*	116
Chapter 9	*The Gypsies*	134
Chapter 10	*Searching for Sue*	151
Chapter 11	*Barry Meets the Girls*	165
Chapter 12	*Torture*	184
Chapter 13	*Making Friends*	203
Chapter 14	*Plans to Escape*	218
Chapter 15	*On the Trail*	235
Chapter 16	*Finding Sue*	250
Chapter 17	*Reunion with Barry*	262
Chapter 18	*The Sky Bridge*	278
Chapter 19	*The Hand of Friendship*	293
Chapter 20	*Ruth's Story*	310
Chapter 21	*Raithe Saves the Day*	326
Chapter 22	*Saying Goodbye*	342
Chapter 23	*One Way Only*	363

PROLOGUE

A chill winter wind teased the long velvet drapes hanging either side of the French windows. In the overcrowded, gloomy room a man and his daughter faced each other. The antagonism between them could be felt.

"Get out of my sight, I never want to set eyes on you again as long as I live," he told her.

The father had an advantage over her. He stood with his back to the window. She found it difficult to judge his expression. All she saw were cold eyes staring from his unyielding face. He had the posture of an upright man, which indicated he had served in the army. His military bearing stood him in good stead this day. He knew how to hide his feelings, especially from the enemy, and that was what she was.

Behind her stood three shadowy figures. They were frozen and incapable of speech. Too long had they lived under this man's dominance. It was more than they dared do to interrupt his tirade. Their sympathies were with the victim standing before him. Only she showed emotion. She held out one of her hands tentatively and did not let it drop when he ignored her attempt to bridge the gap between them.

"But my baby, Father!" Although her voice was choked, she endeavoured to keep her feelings under control. He abhorred any signs of weakness in his family. His expression never altered.

"There is nothing in this house belonging to you – now or ever. Let alone a baby."

She flinched. Her beautiful eyes clouded over. She could hardly see him through the blur of unshed tears. Her hand was nearly touching him now. "Father," her voice implored, "please, have you no compassion?"

"I am not your father." His voice was hard and cutting. "You have forfeited that right. You are nothing more than a fallen woman and I will not tolerate you living under my roof. Leave these premises at once and never return."

"Please!" This time she had the temerity to touch his arm and he jerked back as though stung. "Please – my baby!"

Her voice cracked under the emotional strain. Entreaty shone from her eyes, but it left him unmoved. His lips tightened. "My patience is wearing thin, woman."

She turned her face away so that he could not see the anguish on it. But she possessed her father's blood, and dignity came to her aid. Without another word she pushed past him and opened the French windows. The wind rushed in gustily, billowing out the curtains. They caught a valuable vase and it crashed to the ground. She heard a sharp intake of breath from the other side of the room and knew it came from her mother. Pride made her ignore it. She was hurt that no help had come from that quarter. As she stepped outside, her father's voice, curt as ever, cut across the silence.

"There is a carriage at the front steps to take you to the station. That is the last thing I am doing for you. After that you are on your own. You can go to the devil as far as I am concerned."

She ignored him and the offer of a carriage. Of what use was that to her where she was going? She crossed the lawn on unsteady legs, going in the direction of Tamsworth Forest.

At her going the plaintive cry of a baby echoed from somewhere in the house. No one in the room moved, with the exception of her father. They watched her go. When at last her slight figure disappeared among the trees, a wolf howled mournfully and a shiver of apprehension passed through the three watchers. Her father remained unmoved. His face was a rigid mask as he swallowed his ire. She had defied him to the bitter end – but she would be back. She had to come back. She could not survive on her own with no money. But deep down he knew he had lost, and much more than his favourite daughter. She was too like him. She would never return.

CHAPTER 1

THE NEW GUESTS

Summer arrived overnight in the forest after weeks of torrential rain. The Dawson family, minus their parents, piled out of the taxi and dutifully greeted their aunt who was waiting for them on the steps of the hotel. The grey-walled building was a blot on the landscape. It gave the impression of being an oversized folly, its architectural structure something between a castle and a large Victorian mansion. In spite of its grotesque façade, it was a popular place for visitors, mainly because it stood on the very edge of Tamsworth Forest, and looked as though it was about to be swallowed up by the surrounding trees which encroached onto its extensive grounds. The hotel was always full and had a long waiting list for vacancies. Perhaps because it was rumoured there were wolves in the forest.

Tall graceful fir trees were mixed with the deciduous oak, beech, birch and elm. The forest covered over two thousand acres. It was known for people to get lost when walking without a map. It was inhabited by many wild animals – but not wolves. In some parts of the forest ancient trees grew, standing as nature intended them to. Their girth was such that it would take twelve men with their arms outstretched and linked together to circle their trunks. Not many people set eyes on them.

Not many people knew they were there. Although marked trails crisscrossed the forest floor, and there were rangers to help guide people, many of these aged 'kings' were inaccessible.

Activities comprising of trekking, ornithology and fishing, were arranged by the hotel; the grounds were kept in immaculate condition, but there was little else to do. The hotel, although old fashioned, boasted of having a five star service. Most guests were happy in its family environment and returned year after year.

The Dawson family were regular visitors, but the eldest of them was not happy. They had been staying at this family-run hotel for too long. It was almost like a home from home. The tranquil atmosphere and unique layout of the place no longer moved or stimulated their imagination. It was all too familiar. Already four days of the holiday had elapsed. Priscilla chewed on her lower lip and glowered out of the window. Boredom was etched across her sharp features, making her look peevish. At eighteen she was a modern day miss – or so she liked to think.

"It's just not fair that we have to come here year after year for our holidays," she said, "We're not kids any longer. It's about time the parents realised that we're grown up. Moira doesn't need us under her feet. She's far too busy to bother about us and what we do. We can think for ourselves."

"Moira?" asked Barry, glancing up from his book about the lost city of Atlantis. "Do you mean our aunt?" The censure in his voice caught her on the raw. "You know damn well I do. Stop being such a fractious brat."

THE SECRET OF TAMSWORTH FOREST

The brat, a highly intelligent teenager, was about to retaliate with a scathing reply when he saw Sue watching him. Instead, he hunched down in his chair and contented himself with a scowl. Sue was the peacemaker. Stormy scenes distressed her, but she regarded her elder sister warily.

"Aunt Moira is getting concerned over Gran," she said. "None of us has been to see her for the last couple of days. I hope you haven't forgotten – but it's your turn today."

Priscilla shuddered delicately as though she had been given a distasteful mission to accomplish. She knew all the right actions, being an expert at getting her own way. "Please don't remind me," she grimaced.

Gran was the biggest bone of contention amongst them all. Their grandmother lived deep in the forest. No one could comprehend why she had decided to cut herself off from the world and live like a hermit, virtually existing with no other human nearby. It was not as though she were poor. This hotel belonged to her. Aunt Moira, and their own mother, Gaynor Dawson, had been raised here as children. In the early days there had been three sisters, but Aunt Ruth had left under a cloud of mystery. Little was known about her because no one ever spoke her name. It was one way of making Aunt Moira flustered by just mentioning it. Priscilla turned from the window, still talking about her grandmother.

"Can you wonder why I don't go? It's that disgusting old hovel she lives in that gets to me. No hot water – or cold come to that. You actually have to go

7

out into the garden and pump it up. The place is alive with spiders and most unhygienic." She gave a shiver for effect. "I think it's unreasonable of Mother to expect us to keep on visiting her. Why can't the old girl come back and live here like any normal person?"

"Because she doesn't like noise, motor cars and stupid people like you around her," retorted Barry, looking like an owl as he glowered over the rims of his spectacles. "Everyone I meet here thinks she's a wise old woman."

"I must say that's a great recommendation coming from you," snapped his sister tartly. "We all know the type of person you mix with. It's a wonder you're not making money by arranging excursions to her cottage. Why don't you display some placards, saying, 'come and see where the witch lives'?'

"I say, what a brilliant idea." Barry's eyes were shining enthusiastically. "Do you think you…"

"Shut up and be your age," Priscilla snapped, and turned her back on him. She looked towards her sister for support. They could be twins except one was dark and the other fair. "Sue," her voice became persuasive. "Do you think you could go ..."

"No," Sue cut her short. "She keeps asking for you. It wouldn't hurt you to make an effort. Besides it will get you out of here and you won't feel so bored."

"But you know I hate going there, whereas you love it. The forest gives me the creeps. Just go this once, sis."

THE SECRET OF TAMSWORTH FOREST

Sue ignored her, refusing to be drawn in. Priscilla's lips quivered and she tried to look pathetic – which was hard for her, being such a self-assured person.

"The forest isn't safe these days. People see weird lights and are saying they can hear strange noises coming from the trees. You know – like huntsmen blowing horns. Then there are the wolves."

"Poppycock," said Sue. "What d'you expect? Of course there are noises. There are animals in there. It's where they live. It's their home – and as for any howling, it comes from the rangers' Alsatians. Stop whining, Priscilla."

"But I've seen strange lights at night. Sue." Her voice became pleading, "you're so clear-headed and strong, you must realise how I feel. I know there are hostile things out there waiting to attack me."

Barry snorted rudely and flung his book down. "I've had enough of this. Of course things want to attack you, who wouldn't, I would myself if I had half a chance." His tone turned insulting. "How come no one else has seen these weird lights? You're a malingerer. Why don't you shut up and get off your fat..."

"Barry." Aunt Moira stood bristling in the doorway looking like an avenging angel. Barry had the grace to look ashamed. He admired his aunt and would never knowingly upset her, but this time he thought her timing lousy to arrive when she did. His keen eyes noticed how harassed and tired she looked. The hotel was hard work during the summer months.

"Sorry, Aunt," he mumbled, and bent to retrieve his book. Moira gave his head an absentminded pat as he scurried from the room. It did not seem to register with her that he had gone. Usually her appearance was immaculate. Today, however, found her smooth brow creased with an unbecoming frown. Something was on her mind. A lock of grey hair fell over her eyes. She pushed it back with a weary movement, and her gaze rested speculatively on Sue.

"Would you do me a favour, my dear? There are two guests waiting at reception who need to be checked in. I would not normally ask you, but I'm running behind schedule and I wish to have a word with Priscilla. Would you go straight away?"

Sue was the most compliant of the three. Her aunt's request filled her with apprehension. She slid from her perch on the window ledge and moved slowly to the door. Priscilla reverted back to the older sister routine by tartly murmuring, "As usual you get all the interesting jobs. Pity you haven't got a business-like mind."

Sue ignored her. She had worries of her own and was trying not to let her nervousness show. "Are you sure I'm capable? Maybe Priscilla would be a better choice. The guests like her."

Aunt Moira's eyes rested on Priscilla, but swivelled back to Sue.

"Of course you're capable of it. I happen to need Priscilla here. Remember to give these guests rooms that overlook the village and don't let them talk you out of it."

THE SECRET OF TAMSWORTH FOREST

Before Sue could utter another word, she was pushed quickly out into the passage and the door was closed firmly behind her.

*   *   *

Perplexed by her aunt's strange behaviour, Sue walked in a roundabout way to the hotel reception. Aunt Moira was excellent at receiving guests. The reception area was out of bounds to anyone unless she was there in person to supervise transactions. So how come she was allowing her young niece to do the job? Sue was filled with unease.

She descended via a back stairway, which at this time of day was shrouded in shadows. It was never used by guests or staff since it led off from the family's private apartments. To anyone unfamiliar with its uneven steps, the route was dangerous. To her and Barry it presented no problems. They often used it as an escape route when they wished to avoid detection. It traversed the edge of the tower and was camouflaged by the thick ivy which clung to the walls. Thus it was shielded from public view. On the way down, a spy-hole appeared in the greenery and gave uninterrupted views of the grounds and forest.

Sue intended to walk round the building and enter the hotel by the main entrance. This way she could get a good look at the guests waiting to be checked in. Maybe she would find out why this job had been passed on to her. For some unknown reason she knew her aunt had lied. She was not that busy.

11

All her life Sue had loved this old house with its mellowed walls and arched doorway. The lobby was old-fashioned, but in keeping with the rest of the building. An expanse of olive and white tiles covered the floor, where several comfortable armchairs were placed for the guests' benefit. Near to the antiquated lift, with gold coloured wrought iron gates, stood a majestic grandfather clock which had been in the family for years. It meticulously ticked away the hours and always kept the correct time. Either side of it were two large potted palms, and directly opposite stood the hotel's pride and joy, a highly polished mahogany reception desk. Sue would have admired it again, but the sight of the two guests standing nearby, sobered her up. Their expressions left much to be desired.

The elusive bellboy did not take long to locate. He was hiding round a corner wanting nothing to do with the newcomers. Her heart sank as she realised what this attitude must seem like to them. They had been left standing for ages without any attention. Or had the boy tried to help?

The fat one of the two, well past his first flush of youth, was constantly thumping the bell for service. His colleague, thin to the point of being gaunt, moved back and forth like a caged tiger. Neither endeared themselves to the watching girl. Sue inhaled deeply and failed to find anything amusing when the bellboy simulated cutting his throat. This was a job for Priscilla. She had a knack of charming any man.

The two men mistook Sue for a guest because she entered the lobby from the grounds. While the thin man glared up the main stairway, she approached silently from behind and said quietly: "Good afternoon. Can I help you, gentlemen?"

The taller one swung round and stared her up and down through hooded eyes. She had the uncomfortable feeling he could see right through her and classed her as a nonentity. The portly man was openly aggressive. There was a sneer on his red face.

"About time too," he said. "The service in this hotel is abominable." His fleshy jowls quivered with anger, and perspiration stood out like beads on his forehead. "We have been waiting for attention, in this draughty lobby, for nearly twenty minutes while you've been outside gallivanting. If the bell no longer works – why don't you do something about it? Is everyone deaf in this establishment?"

"No, sir – just busy." Sue kept her voice low and pleasant, sensing he wanted her to lose her temper and give him fuel to burn on his fire. Now he had to work up his own aggression.

"Don't you come lippy with me, young woman," his belligerent voice filled the lobby. "I've a good mind to report you to your employer. They never used to keep such slaphappy staff in the past. Actually, I've a good mind to cancel our reservations. See how you like that when you get the sack."

"That's your prerogative, sir," Sue answered sweetly. Her expression belied how mad she was, and she no longer intended to uphold her aunt's tradition of 'the customer is always right'.

Veins stood out on the portly man's face. He turned so red she thought he was about to have an attack of apoplexy. With an effort he got his breathing under control. "You are an impertinent little madam." Suppressed fury cracked his voice. "If I had you in my employment I would teach you a thing or two you wouldn't forget in a hurry. Look at me when I speak to you, damn you."

Sue walked past him. She could feel her hackles rise. What right had they got to speak to her like this? If they were that annoyed they could take it up with her aunt. Moving behind the desk with as much dignity as she could muster, she picked up the hotel register and thrust it under his nose. "I'm sorry for the inconvenience you have suffered, but the delay was unavoidable. Would you accept my apologies and please sign your name and address and I will book you in right now."

The fat man jabbed his podgy finger on the page. Ignoring the pen, he said loftily, "Hold your horses, woman. I haven't decided yet if we are staying here. I don't like the treatment you offer in this establishment."

"Then in that case don't waste my time." Sue's temper erupted. She slammed the book shut with unnecessary vigour, making him withdraw his finger smartly before it was crushed. She glared into his startled face. "Ring the bell again if and when you want attention."

She swung round to move off when unexpectedly the thin man leapt into action. Like a snake his arm shot over the desk and he caught hold of her just above the elbow. His claw-like fingers dug into her flesh like a vice – forcing her to stop. Sue glowered, but when her eyes met his, his expression sent a shiver down her spine. She felt the hairs rising on the back of her neck. He was an adversary to be reckoned with, unlike his companion. When he spoke, his voice fell like ice about her ears.

"My associate can do whatever he likes, but I expect my reservation to be honoured."

"Of course you do, sir." Sue's answer came through clenched teeth. She wrenched her arm free, resisting the temptation to rub the angry red marks which were appearing on her skin. Reopening the register, she pushed it under his hawk-like nose, her face burning with temper. The fat man smirked at her discomfort.

"That'll teach you to be a little more civil to your elders." His beady eyes appraised her insolently. "The Professor is used to respect from the likes of you, so jump to it, woman. We want our rooms on the first floor facing the forest."

"Then I suggest you go somewhere else," Sue snapped, not caring anymore. "We are fully booked for the more expensive rooms. The only ones left which meet your requirements are on the second floor, facing the village."

She was pleased to see how dissatisfied they looked. The Professor studied the slip of a girl before him and something about her struck a chord in his memory, the way she stood, the flashing eyes. He could not pin her down. He felt he should know her.

"You are not employed here, are you?" he hissed, leaning towards her threateningly.

Sue was tempted to say yes, but instead asked coolly, "Shall I book you both in?"

The Professor's face showed amusement, but the smile never reached his eyes. "When I made my reservation I expressly asked for rooms facing Tamsworth Forest and I was told I could have them. Since we are not going to get anywhere with you, I should like to speak to the hotel manager – or is that going to take another half hour?"

Sue turned resignedly and nodded to the watching bellboy. There was no need to explain to him what was wanted since he had been following the whole conversation with avid interest. With a curt, "Why don't you sit in an armchair while you're waiting," she quickly disappeared out of the front entrance before either man could stop her.

*   *   *

After aimlessly walking through the forest for a long time, Sue scaled a gnarled oak tree to survey her surroundings from a comfortable perch. Enclosed by leaves, she found her view restricted, but the breeze fanning her hot cheeks felt good. Resting back against the rough bark, Sue relaxed. After the harrowing experience with the two detestable men, this was just what she needed. She had no intention of returning to the hotel before nightfall.

THE SECRET OF TAMSWORTH FOREST

She had hoped to meet up with Thane. He had been her friend for many months. He looked like a gypsy, but she didn't think he was one, although gypsy encampments were commonplace in the forest. Then she realised she had wandered far off the beaten track into part of the forest unknown to her. Since Thane would only search on the paths leading to her grandmother's cottage, it was doubtful her wish would be granted.

Everywhere was quiet. By now the birds had roosted for the night and hotel guests long since returned after their day's trekking. She wondered dreamily where the path below her went. Thane would know. He knew the forest like the back of his hand. It was hunger that made Sue realise with a start she had a long way to go. She had lingered too long. The light was swiftly vanishing.

hen a howl rent the air, coming from nearby, Sue knew it was one of the rangers' Alsatians. But because it sounded so wolf-like, she understood why Priscilla was afraid. A sound of snuffling from the undergrowth reached her ears. She saw the dog lope out from between the trees, and stand directly beneath the one in which she was sitting. Then when it raised its head and gave another howl, a shiver ran down her spine. With dusk falling rapidly, in the half-light she could just make out the dog was white. It saw her at the same time as she saw it. Two amber eyes focused on her, shining like gold coins. Sue's mouth went dry. Normally she was not afraid of dogs, but something about this one gave her a premonition of danger. Its upper lip twitched and it bared its teeth. A growl

17

rumbled from deep in its throat. It had no intention of leaving and its eyes remained on her, unblinking. It was almost as though it was willing her to jump down.

Sue felt herself shaking. Why didn't the ranger appear? The dogs were never allowed out on their own, and if she remembered correctly, his dogs were black and tan and used to people. This one below her had a savage look about it. No way was she going to descend to the ground while it remained there, even if it meant she spent the night up this tree. Unexpectedly there came the sound of a huntsman's horn and she jumped violently. If that was not strange enough, the dog turned in the direction of the sound and bounded away.

For several minutes Sue didn't move. The forest was darker than she liked, but she knew her way home. Eventually she plucked up enough nerve to leave the tree and hastened off in the direction of the hotel.

CHAPTER 2

THANE OF THE FOREST

The sun filtered through the large window, giving the red velvet curtains the appearance of fire as they fell to the shiny wooden floor. Moira was sitting at a desk, her brow creased in a frown, and she wished more and more that her husband was with her. He would have known the best course of action to take. Gaynor's children had always been well behaved, so what had gone wrong this time? She tapped the envelope lying on top of her polished desk and gazed at it reflectively. Normally cool-headed, she had never found herself in a quandary like this before – but now this problem had come along and a lot was depending on the decision she made. After all this time, the past had reared its ugly head and she knew without a doubt that the wind of change was on the move.

Guilt weighed her down. She should never have exposed Sue to Professor Graham Harding and his obnoxious friend Cyril Grant. Sending Sue to them, instead of Pricilla, was like sending a lamb to the slaughter. They were now asking too many questions about her. Her niece might be unaware of it, but Professor Harding showed an unhealthy interest in her. Moira sighed. Trying to refuse the two men the rooms they wanted, had been the best way to inflame their curiosity. She had succeeded, but what had she gained? She just hoped none of the children would talk about their grandmother. Why did Sue, usually so docile, have to act out of character and bring attention to herself.

The answer to her problem came in a flash. With a decisive move, she snatched up the letter and stopped Priscilla from slipping out the main entrance. Dressed up to kill and no doubt going on some assignation with a young man, she was the ideal person to do what her aunt had in mind. Before Priscilla could disappear from sight, Moira called out to halt her.

"Wait, Priscilla. I should like you to deliver a letter for me."

Priscilla paused, furious that she was only two yards from freedom. The Professor and his friend pushed past her on their way out, with no word of greeting. She thought belatedly that she should have used the tower staircase if she wanted to get out unseen. But Priscilla disliked creeping around gloomy places and those uneven steps could easily break her ankles – especially with the high heels she was wearing. For her, Aunt Moira was definitely out of favour. Priscilla, still smarting from her last encounter with her aunt, looked down her pert nose.

"I hope you realise the last collection has gone. I'll do it in the morning, Moira."

Her aunt winced at the casual form of address. It was all right for Gaynor to feel proud that her eldest daughter had grown up to be sophisticated and was a delight to have around, but Moira was old fashioned

THE SECRET OF TAMSWORTH FOREST

and deplored the use of Christian names without a prefix. This time she was wise not to pursue the matter.

"I want this to be delivered by hand." Moira's voice was sharper than she intended. "You will have time to make the journey there and back before its dark if you hurry."

Her niece was incredulous. She felt her sinews tightening as she moved towards her aunt. "You're surely not expecting me to walk through the forest?" she asked in disbelief.

"It won't hurt you." Her aunt was unsympathetic. "Spare me your sob story. You haven't seen your grandmother for several days and this letter happens to be important. It's imperative she receives it today." Not wishing to get involved in another argument, Moira thrust the envelope into Priscilla's unwilling hand and turned away with the intention of heading for the stairs.

"Can't Sue take it?" Priscilla's voice rose to a hysterical wail. The older woman paused briefly and eyed her up and down.

"She is not here to do everything you choose not to undertake. Believe it or not, I would much rather you undertook the journey. On no account pass it on to Barry because he gets side-tracked. This letter has to be there tonight. If there should be an answer you can bring it to me in my quarters when you return."

As though that terminated the conversation, Moira turned and swept up the stairway without a backward glance. Priscilla compressed her lips and made a defiant gesture at her aunt's back. At this moment her face was not pretty, but distorted with anger. The temptation to ignore Aunt Moira's request was strong, but Priscilla knew it would make her own mother unhappy if she found out. Crumpling up the letter and stuffing it into her pocket, she flounced through the doorway.

Priscilla took a short cut across the lawn, swearing under her breath when the heels of her shoes sank into the earth. At the iron gate that marked the perimeter of the gardens, she passed through into Tamsworth Forest without even stopping. She was blissfully unaware that two men moved silently between the trees and started to stalk her.

In her present state of mind, Priscilla wouldn't see anything. She was smarting at being ordered around as though she were a child. She considered herself adult, and consoled herself that this was the last time she would come and stay here. The others could please themselves. In her fury, she forgot her fear of the forest. It was still daylight and there were several people still around. She was soon on the path which led straight to her grandmother's cottage.

Soon other people vanished from sight, going in different directions. Priscilla could not walk very fast in her unsuitable shoes. She put a hand into her pocket and withdrew the letter, where, metaphorically, it was burning a hole. Curiosity consumed her as she wondered what on earth could be so important that her grandmother must have it at once. Unthinking, she slowed down, and then stopped. She flattened the letter out to establish how well it was sealed. A quick glance showed there was no one to watch her. She could prise it open without feeling guilty about reading something

THE SECRET OF TAMSWORTH FOREST

that was not for her eyes. What secrets could there be between her grandmother and herself? The two stalkers also paused, debating their next move. It was obvious what their quarry was about to do and they required the letter to remain unopened.

Priscilla managed to get her fingers under the flap when someone came up softly behind her, and before she knew it, whisked the envelope from her hand. She stifled a scream. All the horrors of the forest were returning. Then she thought it was Barry creeping up on her to make her jump. It was the type of thing he would do, but when a voice spoke, it was not her brother's. It had a strange lilt to it. Priscilla spun round and glared at her assailant. She had never seen him before. He looked like a gypsy. His clothing was unusual. Twigs protruded from his garment as though he was camouflaged. She was convinced he was about to rob her.

"I'll deliver this for you, Miss Dawson," he remarked, placing the letter somewhere on his person. "I think it will be much safer out of your care."

Priscilla's eyes narrowed, realising she was being thwarted from reading her aunt's letter. How dare he purloin her possessions and use her name as though he knew her? She gave him her most withering look, which normally quelled people on the spot. "Give that letter back to me. It's not yours and it happens to be important." She stepped nearer to take it from him. "You don't even know where I'm going."

He laughed softly and the next moment she felt his arms enfold her rigid form. He held her so close, she

23

thought it was indecent. Her scream of protest came out as a squeak. "Let me go, you brute."

His smile vanished. He bent his head closer to her face. His expression was serious, but she heard him clearly as he hissed, "You were about to read it – but that's not the reason why I'm here. Haven't you realised yet that you are being followed by two men who also want your aunt's letter? They have been trailing you for quite a long time. No, don't scream, or I shall feel inclined to let them get you."

"How can I trust you?" Fear made her voice come out jerkily. "I've never seen you before in my life."

"I'm a friend of your grandmother, and your sister. Will that suffice?"

Priscilla exhaled. "Sue! That doesn't surprise me. She makes friends with lots of peculiar people." The derisive tone of her voice made him cringe, and his eyes hardened. "Do you mind letting me go" she went on. "You're hurting my arm and I bruise easily."

"I'm sorry about blemishing your skin – but no," he replied.

"I'll scream for help."

"Go ahead. Perhaps the men following you will come to your aid. Then you can go with them." His uncaring attitude silenced Priscilla long enough for him to finish speaking. "When I let you go, you will notice a pathway leading off to your right. It goes to the big house where you live. You will be safe if you walk fast enough." His glance was withering as he looked at her unsuitable shoes. "You can outdistance them if you hurry."

24

Priscilla had had enough. She hated the man's condescending manner and reversed her opinion that he was a gypsy. He sounded too educated. She tried to struggle free, but immediately his grip tightened.

"You're up to something," she said.

Very faintly she heard his mocking laughter. "No. I'm not. Just a good actor when the occasion calls for it – like it does now. We have got to make this meeting seem like a lover's tryst, my dear Priscilla – for the benefit of your pursuers. When I kiss you, you must run away and pretend to be heartbroken."

Before Priscilla could protest, she felt his lips brush her face and could not suppress the shudder of distaste. Her anger smouldered anew when she realised it amused him. She did not need to be told to go home. The sound of a wolf howling in the distance was better than any persuasion on his part. Directly he let go, she ran down the path he had indicated. The two men watching from a safe distance were full of chagrin. They had banked on getting that letter from her. Now she was returning to the hotel, instead of leading them to her previous destination. When they removed their eyes from her retreating figure, the young fellow had vanished.

*   *   *

Sue had no idea why she was prone to nightmares, but this one woke her in the middle of the night. Bathed in perspiration, and shivering, she tried to regain her bearings by sitting up. Her room was bathed in moonlight. She swung her legs to the floor and sat on the edge of her bed, vividly, recalling the nightmare. It was always the same, and this was not the first time she had had it. But why was this happening? What was the cause? It worried her.

Hugging herself more for comfort than warmth she relived the dream again in her mind. She saw the gloomy house where darkness prevailed and the only light came from a few flickering candles placed in sconces on the wall. Always, the same five people were grouped about a wicker basket containing a small wrapped bundle. Outside the wind howled mournfully as it swept round the building seeking a way in. It was the only sound to be heard because no one spoke in this place. The most alarming factor was that Sue felt she was part of this group of shrouded figures. The thought gave her a feeling of unbearable hurt.

She raked her fingers through the mass of tousled hair. She wished she could speak to someone without their thinking she was mad. Aunt Moira was kind, but so down to earth. She had a logical explanation for everything. She would no doubt say the nightmares were due to heavy suppers. If she approached Priscilla, her sister would twist the question round to suit herself and say this place was enough to give anyone nightmares. Barry, being a boy, would just laugh. The only person left to talk to was her grandmother. Well, tomorrow she would make an effort to see her. Decision made, she felt a lot better.

For a while she relaxed on her bed. Then an unreasonable urge made her want to look out of the

THE SECRET OF TAMSWORTH FOREST

window. She padded across the room and leant contentedly against the sill. Her eyes drank in the beauty of the hotel lawns which were glistening like silver as the moonlight touched them. The full moon brought out the best in everything. Sue loved this place. Already tranquillity stole over her.

It was only a small movement at the edge of the forest, but enough to draw her eyes in that direction. After observing for a few moments, she became aware of several shadowy figures slipping in and out of the trees. They were too far away for her to recognise anyone. Occasionally a light was seen, but she had the impression it was instantly dimmed because it vanished. Sue wondered what activity was going on. She was not aware of any night trekking excursions going on at the hotel.

The click of her bedroom door made her spin round guiltily, almost as though she was breaking every rule of the hotel by gazing at Tamsworth Forest. She exhaled in relief when she saw Barry. He sidled through and came to stand by her side, looking as usual as though he had never been to bed. His pyjamas were immaculate. Sue was not surprised to see him, he was a nocturnal boy. Even though it was dark, she was aware he looked excited. Barry was playing detective again.

"You can see them as well, can't you?" he whispered, his voice animated. "I've been watching them for ages and then thought I would wake you up. I wonder who they are and where they come from."

Sue realised she was privileged to receive Barry's confidence. He would never share it with Priscilla. But

27

there was no point in letting him get carried away with far-fetched ideas. Barry had a vivid imagination and seemed to live in a different world.

"They're rangers of course," she answered calmly, following his gaze to the trees. "I dare say they are preparing something for tomorrow."

"Don't be stupid. They wouldn't do that in the middle of the night." Barry's voice rose indignantly and he glared at her. That one unguarded moment of raising his voice made everything disappear. His boyish treble carried clearly on the still night air. Now there was nothing to see by the line of trees. Barry bit his lip in chagrin and Sue felt sorry for him. She tried to make amends by saying, unconvincingly,

"You're right of course. I dare say they were gypsies up to no good. You've succeeded in scaring them away. Let's forget them and go to bed."

"But gypsies don't keep company with wolves," Barry muttered. "I saw a white wolf with them a moment ago." He stared at her speculatively and Sue felt her throat tighten, remembering the large dog beneath the tree. Barry referred to it as a wolf. She wasn't happy with that explanation. She felt Barry touch her arm and saw concern in his eyes. Mistakenly he thought she was afraid.

"Don't worry, sis. I think that wolf is harmless. It didn't take any notice of me the last time I saw it."

"You've seen it before? Close up?" Sue's voice was incredulous.

"Well yes. I wander in the forest as well. He was like a playful dog."

Sue's smile was tight, thinking how savage the animal had appeared to her. Playful was not the description she had in mind. "How can you be so sure it's not a dog?"

"Because he told..." Barry stopped, clamped his mouth shut, and refused to look at her. Then he changed the conversation by adding, "Since you're awake, let's go to the tower. It's so much nearer to the trees and we still might see someone from there."

'Typical of Barry,' she thought, he did not wait for her to agree, because he swiftly moved out of the room. She wondered what he had been about to say as she followed. She felt like a schoolgirl on a midnight adventure. Barry's enthusiasm spilt over on to her and she crept along the passage way behind him. It was not too cold to be wandering about in their night attire, and the moon shed enough light for them to see where they were going. Had Aunt Moira appeared at that moment she would have had a fit. The house seemed silent and watchful. Sue felt it was marking their progress – as though this was meant to happen. She suppressed a smile. What with her dreams and talk of wolves, she was getting fanciful.

At the top of the tower they paused, waiting for their eyesight to adjust. Descending half a dozen paces down the cold steps, they reached the first opening. They pushed back the ivy to give themselves an unrestricted view across the lawn. They were now that much nearer the forest. A soft breeze fanned their cheeks as they wedged themselves into position, standing side by side. A faint noise reached their ears. The people were still there and this made their blood tingle with anticipation. Barry was not going to shout out a second time.

A streak of white flashed through the trees and headed straight for the tower. What at first looked like a huge white dog, slowly turned into something menacing. At the base of the tower, the ferocious animal raised its nose to the sky and started to howl. There could be no mistaking it was a wolf. Then it snarled and leapt up at them, even though it was a long way down. Sue was sure it could see them. Its howls of frustration once again filled the air.

"It doesn't seem very tame to me," Sue gasped. "I hope the door down below is shut otherwise that thing will be up here and tear us to shreds."

"I don't understand it." Barry looked confused. "It was docile the other day. You don't suppose it's because you're here?" he added unwisely.

Sue shivered. She wished Barry would keep his thoughts to himself. She moved away from the opening, not realising that the howling had stopped at her disappearance. But Barry did, and a thoughtful look came into his eyes.

"I've seen enough. I'm going to bed." Sue turned away and left her brother standing there. Even hearing the sound of the horn again failed to change her mind. For one night, she had had enough.

*   *   *

The majority of hotel guests were already out pursuing their various interests in the forest. But this didn't

THE SECRET OF TAMSWORTH FOREST

include the Dawson children. From the upper regions of the hotel were sounds of unrest as Moira shepherded her charges out. She was finding it difficult this year. Priscilla tried too hard to prove she was a young lady. Barry was misguided enough to think he knew his own mind and Sue was acting completely out of character. Moira sighed and brusquely shooed them along the corridor. She put it down to Professor Harding and Cyril Grant. Everything had gone wrong since they had taken up residence. Moira opened the lift gates for them all to enter. Its clanging vibrated in her head.

"Once and for all, Barry, will you please stop arguing and do something useful while you're here. It's giving me a headache trying to talk sense into you."

Barry, being the last one to enter, deftly shut the gates. Sue glanced at her aunt with sympathy. When Barry dug his heels in, he could be impossible. This morning he was bright and alert, showing no signs of his nocturnal activities. "You're not listening to me, Aunt. You never do," Barry grumbled as he pressed the button to set the lift in motion. He looked towards Sue for backup, and didn't get it. She shook her head. She was definitely with Moira all the way on this issue. "I'm still going," he added defiantly, and was prepared to leave things there.

The lift jerked and slowly started to descend. Too late Barry wished he had used the stairs to get away from all the women. The lift took forever to reach the lobby. He couldn't understand why, in the hotel brochure, this lift was listed as a special feature. It took ages to get anywhere, and conversation within its

31

confines was audible to everyone. 'The cage of doom' would be a more appropriate name for it.

Aunt Moira eyed her nephew askance. "I am in charge of you while you're here and I do not like your associating with the Professor or his companion. They are much too old for a boy of your age."

Barry wondered just how old he would have to be before his aunt stopped making his age an excuse to prohibit him from following his activities. He had his own reasons for cultivating Professor Harding's friendship, but he couldn't tell his aunt that. He thought it easier for her to think that he was being led astray. That idea appealed to him.

"If he's so bad, Aunt Moira, why have you allowed him to stay in this hotel?" Barry asked. "I find him great and he treats me like an adult. He is a very interesting man and I'm learning a lot from him."

"What sort of rubbish is he filling your head with?" asked Priscilla languidly, as she blew onto her nails to dry the ghastly-coloured nail varnish she was wearing. Moira averted her eyes from them. Barry saw this as an opportunity to sing the Professor's praises.

"He's looking for some ancient coins," he said, "which, when found, will show him the way to another world. I'm going to help him."

Priscilla laughed scornfully. "You're ridiculous if you believe that, little brother. I've never heard such a lot of tommyrot in all my life. He's seen you coming and you're too thick to see it. Wake up and forget the fairy tales."

Barry glowered at her behind his spectacles because he saw that Aunt Moira approved. "Who is the one who sees strange lights at night and weird things that want to attack her?" he flashed back. "You're the ignorant one with your hideous nails. Another world does exist. It's somewhere in this area and I'm going to help him find it."

No one noticed Moira's pallor. Barry's words held their attention. The lift grated to a standstill and Priscilla said rudely, "I didn't think I had such a naïve brother. How can you believe in that rubbish? Do you think Atlantis is suddenly going to appear in the middle of the forest? No – don't answer me. That man is using you. He wants your local knowledge. He's leading you..."

"That's why he takes no notice of you," flared Barry. "He knows..."

"Stop this arguing at once, all of you," Moira cut in grimly and she looked directly at her nephew. "I forbid it, Barry."

Their gazes locked. He would not back down and let her win. "You can't stop me. I'm interested in anything unusual. This is a great chance for me to do something interesting during these holidays."

'But not with him, Barry. I don't trust him,' Sue thought, but she never said it aloud. Moira opened the lift gates and they all rushed out, thankful to escape. As they entered the lobby they met Professor Harding who happened to be coming down the stairs. They all paused. Sue eyed him warily. His face was impassive but she knew he had heard everything said in the lift. In

33

fact, she would go as far as to say he stood and listened. She could feel animosity rising within her as she glanced at his sardonic face which had a fixed smile that did not reach his eyes. It galled her that he acted as though they were all the best of friends.

"Good morning, ladies," said the Professor. "How are you all today? It's really nice to see you on this lovely morning." His look embraced them all like a spider. Sue clenched her teeth to stop herself from speaking. Priscilla did not bother with niceties. She muttered something like 'creep' under her breath. For one horrible moment Sue thought he had heard her, because a nerve twitched violently in his cheek. His control was perfect. Moira nodded stiffly in his direction, showing just the barest acknowledgement. She pointedly ignored his presence by saying,

"Come into the office, girls. We have something to discuss."

"Are you not going to include Barry?" enquired the Professor, his tone razor-sharp. "I wouldn't leave him out here. I have the feeling you are worried about his welfare and have forbidden him to associate with me."

Moira glanced at him scathingly. "I would have done so if I had my way, but Barry is of an age to make up his own mind." She took a deep breath and considered her next words carefully. "You are a guest in this hotel, Professor Harding, but I should appreciate it if you refrained from disrupting my family. Whatever went on in the past is just that – the past. It has nothing at all to do with today. Kindly keep out of our affairs. Good day to you."

THE SECRET OF TAMSWORTH FOREST

Her speech was like water off a duck's back. His expression never altered. He lightly touched Barry's shoulder and much to the boy's consternation said, "We will forget our arrangements for today, boy. Your mother doesn't approve."

"Mother!" Barry's jaw dropped open, "Mother! You don't think she's my mother? That's Aunt Moira. Our mum and dad are abroad. That's why we're here."

Sue ground her teeth in despair and wished her brother could be struck dumb as she saw the flicker of curiosity race through the Professor's eyes. He now knew they were not the proprietor's children and this extra information was going to be stored in his mathematical brain. She was astute enough to know he was using Barry to get at Aunt Moira. But why? The Professor's acting was perfect. He knew exactly where he was going. Now he looked as though he found the fact that Moira was their aunt really interesting. He said with false joviality, not speaking to anyone in particular, "do you know – I'm a sentimental old fool. Years ago I met the three delightful sisters who lived here when I stayed here in old Mrs. Denton's time – so tell me," he turned like a snake and his piercing glance fell on Priscilla and Sue, "which one of them is your mother? Is it Ruth or Gaynor?"

At the mention of Ruth's name a hush fell, and eyes automatically focused on Moira. She appeared far more shaken than they would have expected. With an effort she tried to moisten her dry lips, but was incapable of speech. Seeing the strange look on his cynical face Sue rounded on him, her temper flaring.

35

"Our family affairs are private and no business of yours, Professor Harding," she stated coldly. Turning her back on him, she turned to her aunt and touched her arm gently. "Come on, Aunt Moira. The Professor is leaving." She attempted to lead her away and break up the conversation, but the Professor moved swiftly and deliberately barred her escape. His smile had gone. His eyes were no more than slits in his face. "If you don't mind my saying it – being a casual observer – I find it very strange that everyone here has got the Denton look except this firebrand who needs to be taught a lesson in manners." He stared pointedly at Sue. "Where does she fit in?"

Sue stiffened – hating him with an intensity she did not believe possible. Who did he think he was? What right had he got to cast aspersions just because she happened to be golden-haired? What devious path was he going along? Dislike for the Professor flared from her eyes.

"I look like my father," she snapped furiously, "and as I said before, it's no business of yours. I can't think why my aunt has lowered her standards to allow you to stay here. You are an odious man." With that she quickly side-stepped him and said over her shoulder to her aunt, "I'll see you later. I've got things to do."

"I'll have an apology from you, my girl," snarled the Professor, making a grab for her, but he spoke to thin air. Sue was gone – leaving them all staring at each other. For once the Professor looked rattled. He rounded on Moira, making her flinch away, but changed his mind about speaking. Ignoring Barry, he swept out of the lobby and met the podgy man coming in. The two of them vanished from sight, deep in conversation.

CHAPTER 3

THE WHITE WOLF

There were not many guests lingering in the grounds who saw the flight of the golden-haired girl before she disappeared into the forest, but curiosity made them wonder what had upset her. Normally they would have received a friendly greeting as she passed them. She was well liked.

Sue never saw anything. In her present state, all she wanted to do was get away. The greater the distance she put between herself and the hotel, the better. The sun was hot. Perspiration, mixed with tears, made her face look red and blotchy. But after a while the tranquillity of the forest made her headache disappear. She put Professor Harding firmly from her mind, until she thought of Moira.

It dismayed her that he seemed to have some sort of hold over her aunt. She clenched her teeth as she remembered his sadistic interest in their family affairs. The way his well-timed innuendos ruthlessly stripped off the veneer with which Aunt Moira protected herself. This left her vulnerable to his attacks. It had been the mention of Ruth that dismayed her most – and he knew it. He would play on it. Sue felt exasperated at not knowing what Aunt Ruth had to do with him.

THE SECRET OF TAMSWORTH FOREST

Sue pushed deeper into the forest, having her own route to her grandmother's cottage. It was certainly not one Priscilla would have taken. This one was wild and rarely used. She swung along the track, winding between thick trunks of beech trees. The sunlight filtered through a green canopy overhead and made dappled patterns on the ground at her feet. A soft breeze rustled the leaves and also lifted the golden curls from her forehead.

It would be good to see her grandmother again because she got on really well with her. The old lady had keen grey eyes and was by nature a shrewd woman. She did not suffer fools lightly. Her iron grey hair, cut short, had a 'no nonsense' look about its style. Her body was upright in carriage and she was not a lady to be trifled with. It would be years before she conformed to the storybook image of a grandmother, with bent back and croaking voice.

This thought brought a smile to her face, which vanished when she came to a tree blocking her way forward. Sue carefully manoeuvred her way round it and continued on her journey. But she hurried now because she did not want to be late in reaching the cottage. There were so many questions to ask to which she wanted answers, and she hoped her grandmother would be able to give them. Most of all, she wanted to know about Ruth. She was startled when a shadow blocked out the sun. It made her pause in her stride. The next moment someone dropped lightly to her side from a leafy bough above her head. It made the worry evaporate from her face as a young man greeted her

39

with a hug and his soft lilting voice said, "Hello, my pretty wood nymph. How are you?"

Relaxed, Sue walked by his side. "Better, now that I've seen you, Thane. I didn't expect to find you in this part of the forest?"

"I am not compelled to stay in any special part. The forest is my home as you know."

The way Thane dressed, it was hard to distinguish him from his surroundings. He blended in with the trees. He wasn't a gypsy and she accepted him as she found him. They had met for the first time last year when he told her he was on a mission looking for someone called Sonja. As far as she knew, he was still on that mission, but he never spoke about it and she never found out who or what Sonja was.

He was at least five years her senior, and there was something fey about him. Tall and slender, definitely good looking with his long dark hair framing his thin face as it fell to his shoulders. He wore a long-sleeved green shirt which was covered by a darker green sleeveless jerkin. This was pulled in by a belt round his waist. He always reminded her of Robin Hood because his brown trousers were slim fitting and tapered in at the ankles. As far as she knew, he lived in the forest. He had never taken her to his home, and she had never suggested that he should. She liked him as he was. He was her friend. He knew her grandmother. That made everything right in her eyes.

As they walked side by side, she matched her stride to his. This way they could walk in companionable silence for ages. Thane sensed her mood and kept

40

THE SECRET OF TAMSWORTH FOREST

glancing surreptitiously at her face. "What's up, Sue?" he asked casually. "There is a cloud covering your usual sunny disposition."

Sue shrugged, not wishing to air her grievances. Maybe she would, after speaking to her grandmother, but the least said about the Professor the better. "Oh – I was a bit down. I thought walking amongst the trees would calm me. You don't really want to hear about family squabbles. You're lucky, not getting caught up in such things. It must be fun running wild like you do."

She missed the strange expression that crossed Thane's face because she was staring straight ahead. But his demeanour changed and he became serious.

"We've known each other a long time, Sue," he answered carefully. "Yet there are many things concerning me you know nothing about. In the long run, that could be a good thing." He saw the look of surprise on her face as he in turn gave her a calculating stare. "If we reverse the situation, I could say you keep secrets from me, don't you?"

"No I don't." Her protest was immediate. "I tell you everything except the unimportant quarrels between Priscilla and Barry. They're boring. So what kind of secrets are you accusing me of keeping?"

Although she was still joking, she felt hurt. They had an understanding between them that neither would pry into the other's affairs. Anyway, he wouldn't be interested in their family matters like the Professor was. She knew Thane was staring at her intently. She could feel his eyes on her and she flushed. He, on the other

41

hand, realised she was not putting on an act for his benefit. She was totally out of her depth with this conversation. She had not got a clue to what he was hinting at.

He looked thoughtfully ahead, wishing he had never said a word. Mrs. Denton had warned him against doing so but he thought he was in the right. Now it struck him forcibly that he had opened up a hornet's nest and Sue was going to be the one to suffer.

"I suppose it's possible you don't know anything," he muttered resignedly. "Forget it, Sue."

"I can't." Sue halted, making him come to a standstill. "Once and for all, Thane, what are you on about?"

Because Thane was so annoyed with himself, he tugged at her arm to make her go forward. When she refused to move, he turned his back on her and started down the path on his own.

"Ask your grandmother," he answered enigmatically. "I take it that's where you are going."

"Thane… please don't go away."

He did not stop, his mind being elsewhere. What had he done? They would not be happy with him if he ruined all their careful planning, and the last person he wanted to upset was Sue.

*　　　　*　　　　*

With Thane walking off, the forest lost its appeal and it became dull and lifeless. Sue felt the whole world crumbling round her ears. He had triggered off thoughts

THE SECRET OF TAMSWORTH FOREST

which left her feeling bewildered. She wondered where this conversation with Thane had come from. What was wrong with everyone today, or in all fairness, was she to blame?

Sue stared after Thane pushing relentlessly ahead. She felt she was losing a friend. What had her grandmother got to do with it anyway? In all the weeks Sue had known him, this was the nearest they had ever come to arguing. The easy friendship she so cherished, seemed to be vanishing before her eyes and she didn't want that to happen. There were so many questions she wanted to ask him. Such as what did he know about the white wolf? He knew the forest like the back of his hand, so he was bound to know.

She started to follow him but he did not turn round. A few further steps and he would be out of sight. Pride stopped her from calling out. He disappeared round a bend and she felt devastated. This feeling immediately changed to a startled gasp of terror as something enormous flashed past her eyes. Her path was blocked by a massive white wolf. Its amber eyes smouldered balefully at her. The suddenness of its appearance gave her no time to escape. This time she was on her own to face it. There was no Barry beside her. It stood nearly as high as her shoulders. The carnivorous animal turned her legs to jelly. Petrified with fear, she watched it stealthily move forward a pace. She could feel its hot breath on her face. Backing away was not an option, her limbs refused to obey her.

The wolf drew back its top lip, exposing sharp pointed teeth. Saliva dripped from its maw. Nausea

43

flooded through Sue's body. Was it about to kill her? 'Scream for Thane' her mind told her, but her mouth was so dry she was incapable of speech and movement. What had Barry said last night? 'The wolf was like a playful dog'. Was he dreaming?

There was nothing friendly about the visitant before her. The rumbling growls vibrated through its body, the sound was very threatening. Sue could not look at it anymore or stop herself from trembling. She closed her eyes. How long before it sprang for her throat and bore her to the ground? Would it be quick when it killed her? With a snarl it crouched to spring. Something touched her shoulder and she screamed, waiting to feel its teeth in her flesh. All she heard was Thane's voice in her ear.

"Don't let it see your fear. Open your eyes and stare it down."

"I can't."

Thane's arm crept round her shoulders and he gave her a reassuring squeeze. "Yes you can – for me."

She was so relieved Thane had returned she automatically did as he bid. She felt safe with him, but soon discovered that staring at the wolf did not make it go away. It stood before her snarling in confusion, raking the ground with its huge paws. With Thane beside her she had enough courage to stare into those unblinking amber eyes. When he issued a sharp order, the wolf backed away uncertainly, but still glared from one to the other. Then it flexed its strong muscles and bounded effortlessly away and disappeared into the undergrowth.

THE SECRET OF TAMSWORTH FOREST

Sue knew she would laugh about this incident later, but it was a long time before she was fully composed. Thane did not rush her to speak and stood protectively by her side, but his expression was tight. For the first time Sue saw lines round his eyes and strain about his mouth. Without saying anything, she knew the wolf had come as a complete surprise to him. When she said "you knew that wolf" her voice was not accusing. She just stated a fact. Thane did not deny it. He offered no explanation either. She took hold of his hand to make him look at her, not prepared to let the subject drop.

"There are no wolves in Tamsworth Forest," she said carefully. "So where did it come from?"

Thane's jaw tightened perceptibly and he attempted to prevaricate. "It's not dangerous."

Sue's laugh was strained. "Two days ago I might have believed you. I always thought you told me the truth." By the expression on his face she knew the shaft had gone home. "Every time Barry meets the wolf he tries to tell me it is as playful as a puppy. Each time I see it" she pretended not to notice his start of surprise "I see a savage beast about to attack me. The first time it held me prisoner up a tree and last night it came to the hotel. If it had got in, I am sure it would have torn me to pieces."

"You've actually seen it before?" Thane's alarm was real and not assumed for her benefit. "How did you get away?"

Sue shrugged. "It obeyed the sound of a hunting horn – and that again does not exist in this forest.

45

You've got to tell me. Where does that wolf come from? A zoo?"

Thane looked confused. "Zoo – what is this zoo?"

Sue was exasperated. "Where do you come from, Thane? Is it another world?"

Thane drew himself up proudly. "We are moving away from the subject," he answered stiffly. "White Hawk is a friend but you should never have seen him. That was never planned. It just goes to prove to me that time is shorter than I thought. I told you ages ago that I was on a mission."

"Yes, I know."

"You were that mission, Sue."

Sue went cold at his words. He turned to her now and gazed steadily into her eyes. "There is something very important you should know, and only your grandmother can tell you. I think you're old enough to hear it. The trouble is… your grandmother does not want to tell you. We differ very strongly on the subject, but I can guarantee if she does not tell you today – she will tomorrow. Go to her now, Sue, and make her talk. The forest is becoming unsafe for you to wander round in on your own. I'm taking you to her right now and I will pick you up later and return you to the hotel. Just one thing. Please don't mention the wolf to her. She is an old lady living alone. You might make her feel afraid."

Taking Sue's hand firmly in his, Thane drew her off the path and into the actual forest.

CHAPTER 4

THE SECRET PLACE

Saying goodbye to Thane, Sue walked to her grandmother's broken-down wooden gate which looked the worse for wear. This was not surprising since for years it had been exposed to the elements. Going round it, she went along the overgrown pathway until she reached the cottage door. In a unique way, the garden was charming. It never received attention from anyone. Nature looked after it with an efficiency no gardener could ever equal. Rabbits kept the grass short. Evidence of their presence was everywhere. Only the strongest and most ruthless plants grew in a tangle which formed the flower beds. Except for a broken dividing fence, the garden could be called a continuation of the forest.

The cottage needed a lick of paint. It was run down and unkempt. Priscilla was correct in calling it a hovel. Scattered water butts were everywhere. The empty ones lying on their sides were now homes for rodents. Ivy grew indiscriminately over the roof, almost obliterating the chimney stack. It was a place that wouldn't attract any passer-by to stop and say 'hello'.

The inside of the cottage was spotless. Furniture shone from constant polishing. Curtains, crisp and clean, danced lazily in the draught of air blowing through the open windows. All around the snug interior an accumulation of rare treasures glowed dully in the subdued light. The windows were small, so to compensate the front door always stood wide open to let in extra sunlight.

Sue's grandmother welcome her, and she hugged the old lady without having the reservations Priscilla would have had. Her grandmother led her into her tiny living room, saying casually, "Did I see Thane outside? Why hasn't he come in with you?"

Sue walked in and made her way to the little kitchen at the rear. "He said he would come back later," she answered over her shoulder. "I'm going to make you a cup of tea, Gran."

"Bless you, child. You will need some water. The kettle is empty."

Sue whisked up the copper kettle and wandered out into the garden. While old Mrs Denton made herself comfortable in her favourite armchair, Sue pumped up water, splashing more on the ground than went into the kettle. Her mind was working out the best way to approach the older woman about the episodes on which she required information. The last thing she wanted to do was upset her.

Returning inside, Sue put the kettle on the hot coals, then without waiting for an invitation, propped herself on the wide arm of her grandmother's chair. This was usually the cue for her grandmother to regale her with stories about each of her treasures. They all made fascinating listening. Normally, she would be waiting

THE SECRET OF TAMSWORTH FOREST

expectantly, but today there was this tenseness about her of which the older woman was very much aware. She knew by experience that if Sue was asked a blunt question, she would prevaricate, so she asked lightly.

"What's new at the hotel, Sue? You seem uptight about something. Moira's not upsetting you, is she?"

Sue took a moment to steady her voice, before saying clearly, "I'm worried about her, Gran. We have a guest who has some hidden vendetta against her. He keeps asking about Ruth."

Her words left behind a silence and she could feel her grandmother stiffen. It was too late to recall them now. She pretended not to notice anything amiss. Keeping her eyes fixed on the open window she continued cautiously. "None of us know anything about Aunt Ruth. I wondered if you have any photographs of your daughters when they were young like us."

"My dear child – I did not think you were interested. Yes – of course I have. If you go over to that bottom drawer and open it there is a wooden box inside. Bring that over to me."

Sue relaxed. She wondered at her audacity for bringing up the subject, but she congratulated herself at the same time. It had been easier than she expected. Without showing her excitement, she fetched the box and placed it on Mrs Denton's knee. She could hardly wait to see what Aunt Ruth looked like. Gran was slow and Sue found it hard to contain herself as the old lady looked at each photograph and relived memories of long ago. It was ages before they were passed on to her.

49

Even so, the older woman's thin hands shook and her voice was full of emotion.

"That's Moira and me when we were coming home after a picnic," she murmured, thrusting the first one into Sue's hand. Then, "Look... Gaynor and Moira dressed for horse riding. Ah... now we have your grandfather with the two girls. He was such a handsome man."

Sue accepted them automatically and piled them up neatly. After nearly half an hour she realised she was being bamboozled. Never once had Ruth been mentioned – nor had there been a single photograph of her. The kettle was boiling on the coals, and to relieve the tension building up within her, Sue made the tea while her grandmother lovingly packed all the photos away in the box. This visit was rapidly coming to a close and Sue was getting desperate.

"Gran. Tell me," she blurted out. "Tell me about Ruth and what it is I should know."

Mrs Denton's expression was composed. Shadows masked her eyes and she said with unusual crispness, "There is nothing for you to know. All photographs of Ruth were destroyed when she left home."

"But why did she leave home? How old was she? I know nothing about her."

The old lady stood up abruptly. "Has Thane been speaking to you?" she asked, sounding annoyed.

Sue could honestly shake her head. "Not about Ruth. I shouldn't think he had ever heard of her. It's Priscilla, Barry and I who are interested. We want to know why the Professor keeps on about her."

Her grandmother walked to the door and inhaled the pure forest air. Sue thought the conversation had come to an end until her grandmother inquired, "What does this Professor look like? What is his name? Is he an archaeologist?"

"Professor Harding is forked-tongued, sarcastic, and looks almost like a living skeleton. I don't know about being an archaeologist, but he's kidding Barry he's looking for another world. The trouble is Barry believes him. Gran!" Sue moved to her side in alarm. "Are you all right?" Mrs Denton stumbled and spilt her tea. A sharp pain shot through her chest, but the old lady ignored it and waved Sue away.

"It was shock, dear. There's nothing to worry about. It came when you mentioned Graham." Her voice was full of distaste. "Promise me, Sue, you will never let him find me here, and you keep away from him as well. He's a nasty piece of work."

"But what about Ruth, Gran?" she pressed. "Why does… "

"Thane's outside," interrupted her grandmother, and Sue could have sworn she heard relief in her voice. Frustration made Sue feel like screaming, but since the old lady was already walking to the gate with the intention of saying 'hello' to Thane, she was forced to follow.

It took just a moment to say goodbye to her and before long the two of them were back in the forest. Thane knew without asking, when he looked into Sue's angry eyes – Mrs Denton had not told her anything.

The short curtains were pulled for privacy against the outside world. Moths fluttered around the many lamps. The lustrous glow from them made the old lady's treasures gleam. But Mrs Denton did not concern herself with her surroundings. She leant back in her armchair, her eyes fixed on her visitors. They were young and virile and in complete control of the situation. Had they wanted to, they could overpower her in seconds and show her who was in charge...but they did not. One stood silently by the open door and Thane was just in front of her.

He held himself erect, jaw clamped firmly. His eyes pierced the gloom and noticed her strained expression. He knew this was Sue's grandmother and he liked her, but events had gone too far for him to show any pity. She had had her chances many times and chosen to fritter them away. He still admired her proud and defiant stand. Her backbone was made of stuff not found in many people these days. But his voice was grim and he said in tones of finality, "Time is running out. You must make a decision tonight."

The old lady looked her age. She had known for ages this day was going to rear its ugly head, but it was easier to push thoughts of it away. Her tongue moistened her dry lips. "It's too difficult. I need more..."

"They know she is here," Thane cut in ruthlessly. "Either let me help her or let them take her. It's your choice."

THE SECRET OF TAMSWORTH FOREST

The silence could almost be felt. The sound of crickets from outside floated into the room. Mrs Denton sat in the chair and dropped her hands to her lap in despair. This agonizing decision was hard to make. "Give me until tomorrow," she pleaded, "I promise I will tell her then."

She stared up into Thane's eyes. "How did they find her after all these years?"

"They used the wolves," he replied.

The fight left her and she focused on a small figurine standing on her mantelpiece. A lady looking like a nymph, dressed in flimsy clothing and standing with wide open arms on a rock. The old lady's mind drifted back into the past, when the ornament had been given to her. It was a parting gift. They allowed her back to give it to her and she loved it. Thane knew he had lost her to her memories. He motioned to his companion and they both quietly took their leave. At least they had warned the old lady what to expect, they could do no more.

*   *   *

Sue and Priscilla crossed the hotel lobby, chatting away, blissfully unaware that Professor Harding had concealed himself behind a newspaper. The girls were looking forward to a relaxing day spent together without Barry tagging along. As they neared the open door Aunt Moira appeared. She stormed out of the office, a determined look on her face. These days she always appeared harassed. Not knowing why concerned

53

her two nieces. Today was no exception. She stood before them, causing them to halt. Sue was genuinely curious, wondering what was amiss. But Priscilla was immediately on her guard.

"Where are you two girls going?" Moira asked, a touch of crispness in her normal voice. "Everything has gone wrong this morning and I badly need help in the office. I need another pair of hands."

Her assertive attitude left the girls little hope of escaping, but when the challenge fell on Priscilla's ears, she was ready. "Then you will have to excuse me Moira," she returned sweetly. "I have already made other arrangements but I'm sure Sue will be able to give you some assistance." With that she gave them both a patronising smile and walked primly out of the front entrance, not giving her aunt a chance to reply.

Sue's lips twitched. She wished she had a little of her sister's aplomb. She waited for the explosion which usually followed Priscilla's remarks, but instead of a lecture on manners, Sue actually heard a chuckle. She stared at her aunt in amazement.

"Are you feeling alright Aunt Moira?"

"I'm sorry, Sue." Moira made an effort to control her feelings. "Do you know, I'm actually learning from your sister. I have found out how to become devious and feel quite proud of myself. But between the two of us, I did not want Priscilla here anyway. I had a message this morning from your grandmother and she wants to see you again."

The Professor's newspaper lowered and his inscrutable eyes were fixed on the two women.

THE SECRET OF TAMSWORTH FOREST

"But I only saw her yesterday," exclaimed Sue in surprise. "As far as I know, we didn't leave anything unsaid. Maybe ..." She hesitated, memory of her questions about Ruth returning to haunt her. "Maybe she didn't understand my question."

Moira studied her for a moment, wondering what on earth they had talked about. She said, "Well you know your grandmother better than any of us so she obviously thought of something new." Her voice became urgent. "You will go? I think it is important this time. The ranger who delivered the message said he did not like the way she looked. She was not her usual self. I'm worried. I cannot leave the hotel."

"She's not ill, is she?" Sue's face lost its colour. What had she said yesterday to upset her? She had only mentioned Ruth and the Professor. Was that it? No – the old lady seemed to be in control of the situation. It was Thane's fault. Why had she listened to what he told her? Unbidden, she recalled her grandmother stumbling.

The crackling of a newspaper being folded jerked both women's heads in that direction. They both saw the Professor rise from the armchair. It was obvious he had been listening to them. They greeted him with mixed feelings. Sue's anger, quick to rise, made her tense and immediately she hissed to her aunt, "Let's go into your office and finish this conversation there."

A *tut-tut* from the Professor inflamed her even more. "Now don't run away, ladies." His insidious voice grated, and he blatantly acknowledged having listened to their conversation by saying, "From what I heard, you have received some bad news. Now being a man of the world I have learned that in times of strife we should all help each other. I am offering my services to you, ladies. Now what can I do to help you?"

His footfalls were as silent as a hunting panther as he moved closer to them. The benevolent expression on his gaunt face gave the impression he was a guileless old man. Only those brooding eyes were at variance with his overall appearance and Sue could almost see the venom lurking in their depths. "You can't. Thank you. Stop poking your nose into our affairs. It's getting quite a habit with you," and before her aunt could say anything, she added, "Our conversation is private. You are extremely rude to have been listening."

Professor Harding uttered a false laugh, but his expression was tinged with ice as his glance swept over her. Inwardly he wanted to shake her, but he kept his feelings under control. Moira hastily pressed Sue's arm in silent warning, and dumbfounded everyone by saying, "Let's hear what the Professor has in mind, dear."

The supercilious smile on his loathsome face made Sue want to vomit. She clenched her teeth to stop herself saying anything that would distress her aunt. Aunt Moira was acting out of character. What had gotten into her? He was the last person they needed help from. He must have some ulterior motive. The Professor flexed his fingers and rubbed his chin, looking as though he was choosing his words carefully. To Moira he addressed his conversation.

"There are rumours going round that the forest is dangerous. You must have heard some of them, dear lady, running this hotel. It appears someone has released savage animals into the forest, wolves to be precise. Until they have been rounded up, you must see it's unsafe to travel in the forest alone – as your niece intends to do. As you know, I have not seen Mrs Denton for a great many years, her whereabouts being a great mystery up until now. I should dearly like to make her acquaintance again. As your niece is going to visit her grandmother, I thought I would offer her my protection and escort her through the forest. Mr Grant will be with me, so she will be perfectly safe, and Mrs Denton will receive a pleasant surprise at seeing me."

The smile on his face was far from sincere. It never reached his calculating eyes. Sue fumed at his audacity and could hardly contain herself. It was only the pressure from Moira's hand that kept her silent. The fingers pressed in deep, warning her to stay out of it. Her aunt gave the Professor a grateful smile.

"That is so kind of you, Professor Harding. I am sure Mrs Denton will be delighted to see you again and I know my niece will be pleased to have your company. She hates imposing on people but I am thankful she is not going alone. You did say wolves?" She gave a theatrical shudder which Priscilla would have found hard to copy. "Sue, my dear." She turned and looked directly into the girl's furious eyes. "Why don't you run upstairs and get your bag. The Professor and his friend will wait here in the lobby for you. Oh, and I should put on some sensible shoes so you don't trip on the steps."

Sue's face instantly changed. She gleaned her aunt's unsaid message. Keeping her poker-faced expression, she nodded curtly to the watching man and ran up the staircase to freedom. The Professor was in for a long wait.

*   *   *

Slipping down the tower stairway, Sue was unable to suppress the grin of devilment on her face. She felt a pang of gratitude towards her aunt who was more human than she gave her credit for. It had been unbelievably easy to fool the Professor. Sue would love to catch a glimpse of him pacing round the foyer, but it was too dangerous to get near the lobby. She closed the tower door, concealed it with ivy, then sped across the lawn and disappeared into the forest.

Professor Harding happened to be on the hotel steps at that moment and saw her vanish amongst the trees. For one second he was speechless, then with a furious oath he called to Cyril Grant. Angrily, the two men followed her. Moira watched them go, a grim smile on her face. She was not worried. Sue had youth on her side. It was unlikely they would catch her up.

Sue was content on her own. She had no fear of meeting wolves at this time of day. The Professor had painted that lurid picture solely for her aunt's benefit. The sun felt really warm on her skin as it filtered through the trees. She would have enjoyed it had it not been for thoughts of her grandmother. Did this summons mean she had decided to speak of Ruth – or was she ill as the ranger suggested?

A twig cracked in the undergrowth, causing her to pause. Startled, she peered through the trees and caught sight of Cyril Grant before a bush concealed him from view. In dismay she realised the Professor was following her. Remembering what she had been told yesterday, she dared not lead them to her grandmother's cottage. Swiftly she branched off in the opposite direction and quickened her pace. This was new ground for her. She had no idea where she was heading. It did not worry her at first. The thrill of evading the two men kept her going. She jumped easily over a stream and climbed up an incline. When the path veered to the right she glanced over her shoulder and saw Professor Harding helping Cyril over the stream. They were very near. That sobered her up. They were moving faster than she expected. She had to lose them, and quickly. Then she realised she was lost. The forest was vast. Fear began to override her senses, but still she went deeper into the forest. Before long she paused, out of breath. Which way should she go? If she dithered for too long they would catch her.

"Sue!" The voice came from her right. She recognised with relief, it was Thane. "I'm being followed," she said, "So I can't stop," and pressed on.

Thane detained her with a firm hand. Without warning, he pulled her into the bushes. She had no time to feel alarmed and no breath to protest. Her lungs were almost bursting.

"Stand against that tree," he hissed, on hearing the pursuing footsteps. "Do not move under any circumstances. I shall stand in front of you and I guarantee they will not see either of us."

Knowing his ability to camouflage himself, Sue quite believed it and stood upright against the trunk, almost without breathing. Knots in the wood pressed into her back.

Hot in the face and with breath rasping, the two men blundered past. They made enough noise to alert the whole forest to their presence.

"Hurry up, Grant – move faster otherwise we shall lose her."

Cyril mopped his red face inadequately with a handkerchief. He was in a sorry state. Perspiration ran freely down his podgy face. He knew better than to ask for a rest, and the Professor was determined to catch Sue. Once they were out of earshot, Thane looked down on her with raised eyebrows.

"What a charming pair. They seem to like stalking young girls. Why are they following you?"

"They think I'm leading them to my grandmother. The trouble is I became a bit overambitious and now I'm lost myself."

"You're not fit to be left alone. You haven't got a scrap of woodman's lore in you." His eyes crinkled at the corners with laughter. "Come on. Follow me. I've got something special to show you."

Sue held back. "I should like to – but it's my Gran. I must see her because I think she's ill."

THE SECRET OF TAMSWORTH FOREST

Thane chewed on his lower lip and a shadow fell over his face. Sue missed it because she was too busy trying to see where the Professor was heading. Thane reached out and put an arm round her shoulders, urging her to move, and said cajolingly, "See what I've got to show you first, and I shall take you to Mrs Denton afterwards."

Sue readily went with him. For the best part of an hour he led her along ways which looked like pathways, but when looking back there was nothing to see. She had no idea how he knew where he was going. The forest was beautiful, but all the trees and bushes looked alike and then she realised they were growing closer together. It was now looking like a forest one read about in story books. Not much sun came through the canopy above, but high up, the birds sang merrily to each other. Drowsiness fell over her because of the lack of air. Unexpectedly, they broke free of the undergrowth and burst out into a clearing. She wondered what it was that Thane wished to show her. Maybe it was his home since she had never seen it. They stopped at the edge of the trees and a gasp of astonishment escaped her lips. She stood motionless, gazing at huge trees which had a girth of colossal proportions; fourteen men with hands linked together would only just get round the trunk. The spectacle of them was awesome to behold. It was a magnificent sight.

Sue should not have been surprised, having heard of their existence from some very old rangers now pensioned off. Living in their tied cottages they had

61

nothing else to do but talk, and Sue listened. Up until now she had thought their stories exaggerated, but the massive trees really existed. Overhead their huge branches stretched out and entwined with others from different trees. These were the size of a normal tree trunk. It looked as though they formed a roadway overhead, one that could be walked on. She had an irresistible urge to do just that. Her eyes sparkled with longing and Thane recognised the look. "Want to climb up?" he asked, unnecessarily.

Sue contemplated the trunks. They seemed easy enough to scale. Thoughts of visiting her grandmother had taken a back seat. Eager to start and show off in front of Thane, she went up to the nearest trunk and searched for some reliable notches to give her a firm foothold. Unasked, he pointed out the way she should go, then laughed at her inadequate attempts to get her feet off the ground. Quietly fuming, she knew she could do it if only he wasn't around giving helpful hints. He put her off. Pride made her reject his help. She continued doggedly to try until she was completely out of breath and flushed in the face. She gave up. Thane swung himself up easily and had the audacity to grin down at her. 'Just like a man,' she thought grumpily. He leaned down and held out his arms. "Give me your hand and I will pull you up."

"You can't," retorted Sue ungraciously. "I'm too heavy."

"I know you are, but you can help me with your feet. Just dig them in and I shall pull."

THE SECRET OF TAMSWORTH FOREST

Reluctantly, Sue reached up to grasp his hands. His grip on her wrists was strong. Blood raced to his face with the strain, and veins stood out in his neck as he pulled. She tried to help by placing her feet in any small crevice she saw. At the last moment, with an acceleration of strength on Thane's part, he hauled her up the tree and she landed in an exhausted heap by his side. She soon regained her breath, and was looking around. For the first time disappointment filled her. The leaves up here were so thick there was no view to be seen, only a network of branches. Thane scrambled to his feet and held her steady. He pointed towards the nearest branch which led off in the direction of another tree.

"We shall go along there. Think you can manage it?"

Sue nodded, and waited for him to start. She had none of his expertise, but followed gingerly, needing all her concentration to watch where she put her feet. It did not help when every so often she caught a glimpse of the ground down below. Feelings of nausea swept over her. She reached the next tree after an unexplained surge forward and Thane held out his hands to steady her. The girth of this tree was even greater, but it appeared to be hollow. Looking inside the hollow trunk was like staring down into a dark pit. From her position it seemed to be bottomless and for some reason she wanted to get away from it. Nearby a wolf started to howl.

She shivered. "Is that White Hawk?" she asked pensively.

63

Thane's face was serious. He stared in every direction. Eventually he shook his head. "I doubt it. Just keep silent for a moment. I don't like this. The wolf howls only when someone is near."

Sue was already scared, wishing she wasn't standing so precariously on the edge of this hole. The howl was not repeated, but something else was heard. Masculine voices were coming towards them. Her blood froze in disbelief. There was no mistaking the supercilious sound of the Professor. He was still following her and was only a stone's throw away. Thane touched her arm to get her attention.

"He must be an expert at tracking," he hissed. "He's the last person I want to see right now. Jump down there, Sue." He pointed to the hole. "It's not deep. Trust me. It's only about three feet. He must not see you here."

Sue instinctively recoiled away from the edge, pressing against Thane because of the lack of space. "I can't – it's too dark. I will break a..."

Thane clamped a hand over her mouth and gripped her round the waist with the other.

"Sorry, Sue," he muttered in her ear as she started to struggle against him. "There is no other way," and he jumped into the void, taking her with him. Fear alone turned everything black.

CHAPTER 5

AN ALIEN WORLD

Moira returned to her private sitting room, having observed her niece disappearing into the forest. She had no qualms about the Professor catching up with her. Sue was bright enough to outwit him long before she reached her grandmother. Thankful to get away from it all, she pushed open her door and halted abruptly, not exactly pleased at seeing Barry comfortably installed in one of her armchairs. Her opportunity to relax disappeared fast. She closed the door and surveyed him warily, knowing full well her nephew usually had an ulterior motive to the one he would give.

"What are you doing here, Barry?" she asked firmly, hoping to stop him from saying something stupid.

"Homework."

"Homework," echoed Moira suspiciously. "In my room. This is supposed to be your holiday."

"I know." Barry smiled easily. "There is no fooling you, is there? Actually – it is not exactly homework, more like a holiday project for next term. Since it involves family structure and activities, the holiday is obviously the best time to do it. I just need to ask you some questions. Is that all right, Aunt?"

He looked at her so beguilingly that her defences dropped. Anything that would keep him away from the

65

Professor was welcome. Picking up her needlework, she nodded to him. Barry pondered for some time, studying the book perched on his knee. He hoped he looked studious. Taking a deep breath, he blurted out, "I want to ask you about Aunt Ruth."

"No one speaks about her," answered Moira.

"Well that's the trouble. If no one speaks about her, no one knows anything. Surely you can talk about your sister," Barry retorted, accusingly.

"She's dead."

Barry frowned at that answer. Then Moira swore softly under her breath as her needle snapped between her fingers. Although Barry was concerned about the amount of blood welling from such a small wound, he was still interested in pursuing the subject of Aunt Ruth. "What did she die of?" he asked.

"Barry – this is old history. Leave it alone. Why all these questions?"

"It's my school project," he replied. "We are studying genealogy. Mr Hubbard said we should learn a lot if we studied our own family structure. So you see… Aunt Ruth might have had some awful disease that has been passed on to me."

"Well she didn't." Moira's voice was tight. "It was influenza and you're in no danger."

Silence reigned in the small room for a few more moments while Moira found a plaster to stop the bleeding. Palpitations started up in her chest and she felt the need for fresh air. It seemed a good idea to escape while her nephew was occupied, but one movement from her and Barry raised his head. "Did Aunt Ruth have golden hair?" he asked.

Moira halted. She had waited for that question to crop up. "No," she replied.

"That's strange." Barry twirled his pen round. He looked as though he was deep in thought. He gazed out of the window. Moira was becoming anxious. She willed herself to remain motionless. It would be best to answer his questions calmly, to stop him from delving too deeply.

"What is strange about it?" she asked carefully.

"Well – all the Dawsons are brunettes with the exception of Sue. So I thought she must have Aunt Ruth's genes. But you say she didn't have golden hair."

"She was a brunette, Barry. Have you any more questions before I go?"

"Yes. Was Granddad golden-haired?"

"No, he wasn't. Sue could have inherited her hair from an ancestor. It does happen you know."

Barry looked owlish behind his glasses but his mind was working furiously. He sensed his aunt's reluctance to answer his questions and wanted to ferret out some more information. He wondered how far to press his luck on such a dodgy subject. He made the pretence of studying his book again before asking casually, "What blood group are you, Aunt Moira?"

Moira reached the point where she had had enough of this questioning. She pushed her work away and got to her feet, looking at him sternly. "Offhand I would not know. I think I shall phone Mr Hubbard and tell him I think his project is very intrusive. Now I have more pressing affairs to see about." Without another word she moved out of the room.

Barry heaved a sigh and glanced down at his book, *Fossils In The S.W.* Snapping it shut, he hoped she had not seen the devilish smile on his face. It had been worth trying to get information out of her. He might not have succeeded today, but there was always another time. He intended to uncover the mystery surrounding Aunt Ruth. There was no chance of Aunt Moira getting in touch with his tutor. He was enjoying a holiday in China, blissfully unaware of having given Barry a project to accomplish.

* * *

Sue opened her eyes, and her first thought was Thane. She was piqued at the way he had forced her to leap into the black hole. She would much rather have faced the Professor than have experienced the feeling of falling into nothingness. Where was Thane? He wasn't beside her. She was on her own, lying on a bed of thick moss. Her fingers dug deeply into it as she struggled to sit up.

When she looked up, she expected to see the rim of the hole she had fallen down, but overhead was a dark roof made up of intertwining roots. It made a perfect ceiling, but it filled her with unease. Where was the outside world? Her nose twitched at the musty smell around her. This place gave the impression it was hardly used. How did she get here and where was Thane? Why had he left her alone in a strange place?

THE SECRET OF TAMSWORTH FOREST

The height of the cave was deceptive. When she stood up she could stretch with ease. She hadn't been injured in the jump so her one thought was to find Thane, but with or without him, she must make tracks to see her grandmother. A lot of time had been wasted admiring those trees. Her eyes were attracted to where light was filtering into the cave. Hanging ferns framed an opening and bright sunshine beckoned her outside. She moved slowly in that direction, and stood for a moment in the dappled sunlight, being careful in case Professor Harding was in the vicinity. It was because of him she now found herself in this predicament.

Sue's ears pricked up on hearing voices. Relief swept over her knowing she was not completely alone and the voices were certainly not those of the Professor or Grant. Thane was outside with friends. Although Sue felt annoyed at the way he had abandoned her, her pleasure at seeing him took precedence and she burst out of the cave, only to come to an abrupt halt. Two people who were walking by spun round to stare at her in open astonishment. From the expression on their faces, Sue felt she must look as though she had just crawled out from beneath a rock. The air was electric and a stalemate situation arose as they sized each other up. No one seemed inclined to speak and the silence became unnerving.

Sue observed the tall golden-haired youth and slim dark-haired woman with plaits hanging far below her waist. By the way they were dressed she thought that perhaps they were going to a fancy dress party. Then something struck a chord in her memory. Their dress

69

sense was similar to that of Thane, except that both of them carried bows and arrows over their shoulders. They must be friends or family of his.

She hastily changed her expression to a smile, but the strangers showed no sign of friendliness. In fact, their gaze could be described as hostile. The air crackled with animosity. Sue stepped towards them tentatively, not wishing to upset anyone.

"I'm sorry to bother you, but can you tell me where I can find Thane?"

As her words died away, a hostile silence took over and Sue felt uncomfortable. The dark-haired woman's eyes swept over her, showing an insolence that even Priscilla would have had difficulty in competing with. It undermined Sue's confidence and she felt that unwittingly she had committed some unpardonable faux pas. Their lack of response to her overture made her hackles rise, and with it her temper. She could see no reason for their attitude.

"If you can't help me then have the decency to say so, and I'll find someone else to ask," she snapped, and turned away. They made no attempt to answer and angrily Sue started to walk in the opposite direction. She had taken just two steps when she heard the soft twang of a bow string and an arrow whizzed past one of her ears – so closely it moved her hair. Before her startled eyes, it ended up in front of her, quivering from the trunk of a nearby tree.

A shiver ran down her spine. She lifted a hand to rub her stinging ear. Her anger had reached boiling point. She was hardly aware of the imperious voice that said

THE SECRET OF TAMSWORTH FOREST

harshly, "How dare you turn your back on me? I did not give you leave to go."

Sue clenched her teeth, refusing to give way to fear. She waited a few seconds to calm herself down, and then she turned to face them again, showing none of the disquiet she felt. This time though, she kept her distance and studied the pair. There was something vaguely familiar about them both, but especially the youth, although at this moment his face was distorted with fury as he looked down at her. The woman gave the impression she found the incident amusing. She twirled another arrow between her fingers and stroked the flight feathers as though she was itching to shoot it. Since neither of them seemed disposed to make further conversation, Sue said evenly,

"I have no idea who you are – and to be perfectly honest, I don't want to know you. Normal people would be polite and answer my question and not use me for target practice. Since you don't know Thane, I see no point in remaining here. Are you going to shoot me again when I walk away?"

"Never heard the name," the woman answered contemptuously and turned her back on Sue. She whispered something in the youth's ear. His rage subsided, but there was still hostility in his bearing. He pushed back his long flopping hair from his pale face, and surveyed Sue through half-closed eyes.

"What manner of dress are you wearing, woman?" he asked insultingly. "You do not belong to our world, that is obvious. Is Thane the name of the place you come from?"

71

For the first time a niggling fear touched Sue. What on earth was he saying? Surely this was Tamsworth Forest. She looked round and studied the trees closely, but after all, trees were just trees, except now she noticed the massive ones seemed to have disappeared. She could not be in another world, just in a different place. Thane could have carried her here. What the youth was saying was not feasible – yet these two people were like no others she had ever seen before. Furthermore, where was Thane? He certainly wasn't here with her. Could she possibly have slipped through a time barrier when she jumped? Barry had said something about another world, and the Professor was looking for it. All these possibilities seethed through her brain but none of them helped her in her present predicament. Sue had no idea how long she stood there, under the scrutiny of the two pairs of unfriendly eyes. Lost in the confusion of her thoughts, she was suddenly jolted back to awareness by noticing the woman and youth were starting to walk away. On impulse she ran after them.

"Wait," she shouted out. "Please stop. Tell me where I am."

She might as well have saved her breath. All she heard was mocking laughter, but neither of them so much as stopped or turned to look at her. Soon they would be out of sight and Sue had no intention of letting that happen. If she had to follow them, then she would. They must live somewhere around here.

"Tell me," she gasped, nearly catching up with them. "Is this Tamsworth Forest?"

THE SECRET OF TAMSWORTH FOREST

At last the woman hesitated, turned and stared into Sue's distraught eyes. For a moment she wavered and a fleeting look of compassion crossed her beautiful face – but it soon vanished, dashing Sue's hopes. The youth pulled the woman roughly away with a scowl.

"Come on. Leave her to the wolves. She is nothing but a serf."

Although the woman shook his hand away, her aggressive voice said to Sue, "Go back to the cave. It's safe there and you will be found," after which she swung round and continued on her way.

*　　　*　　　*

Sue watched them disappear. Even after their silhouettes were swallowed up by overhanging branches, she still stood staring. The temptation to follow in their wake was strong, but she had a healthy respect for the woman's ability to shoot an arrow. She did not want to become a human pin cushion for her gratification.

Flies buzzed round her head, getting entangled in her hair. She decided to retrace her steps back to the cave. Here, she ignored the musty smell within. At least she was no longer plagued with insects. After contemplating her surroundings, Sue decided the outlook was no different from looking at Tamsworth Forest. She hoped to get back home before she was missed, especially with her grandmother not being well and asking for her. But which way should she go? Looking right or left made little difference. If this was

73

another world, there must be a door or tunnel back. The problem was – where did one find it?

From amongst the surrounding trees an animal howled. This made her apprehensive. Before long the howl was answered by a screech in another direction and it was not a cry she could identify. In spite of the sun, she shivered. She noticed it was well on its way to setting. She peered into the darkness where shadows were lengthening amongst the foliage and felt anxious; so when the undergrowth rustled nearby, her attention immediately focused to that spot. The howl was repeated. Sue's fingers curled into a tight ball. The premonition of danger pressed down on her. Two glittering red eyes stared straight at her from the forest. Hair prickled on her arms and legs and she bit back a scream. Self-preservation made her move backwards to stand in what shadow the cave offered. The move was a bad mistake. Hitherto the animal, which up until now had been wary, emerged from the trees and moved towards her. Her eyes widened with horror when it came fully into view and she could see the hideous creature clearly. As well as red eyes, it had pointed teeth, scaly leathery wings and four huge feet which ended in claws.

Sue could not think what to do to save herself. There was nowhere to go and she couldn't climb. Not that that it would have helped because the creature was huge and had strong wings. It showed them to her by stretching them out to their fullest extent and uttering a raucous cry as it edged nearer. Whatever species of animal it was, she broke out in a hot sweat and felt a trickle of coldness down her spine. Never before had she felt so alone and helpless.

More howls came from the trees. Other creatures were drawing near. Gazing around in desperation, Sue saw a jagged stone which might serve as a weapon. It was better than nothing at all. She stooped to pick it up when a voice said,

"Stand perfectly still."

Sue was immobilised. It was also the downfall of the predator who was about to attack her. It jerked its head in the direction of the sound. An arrow flew past her head and pierced the creature in its eye. Its raucous cry of pain had barely died away when it was hit by another arrow in the other eye. With an unearthly shriek the scaled body went into spasms and fell to the ground where it twitched for several seconds. Then it was still. The nightmare was over for Sue who, in a dazed state, took a step forward and saw the arrows protruding from the dead body. She thought she recognised one of the arrows as being similar to the one the woman had shot at her earlier. It had to be a coincidence! She sincerely hoped that the pair she met earlier had not returned. Her legs threatened to give way. She moved back to the cave and leant against the wall for support, closing her eyes to blot out the nauseating sight of the dead body. All was silent now. The other predators had slunk away.

Before long she heard the crunch of footsteps become louder and then they stopped in front of her.

"Sue!"

Sue's eyes flew open. She was filled with incredulous joy. "Thane!" She stumbled towards him and he steadied her by putting his arms round her shaking body. Unashamedly a few tears spilled down her cheeks. When the paroxysm passed, she lifted watery eyes and looked over his shoulder at the woman standing a few feet away. Although her heart sank on seeing her, she had to remember that the woman's arrow had saved her life.

The beautiful face was composed, the dark eyes inscrutable as they surveyed her. Sue glanced beyond the spot where she stood and realised thankfully that the sullen youth was not with her.

"I'm sorry, Sue!" Thane's voice, full of remorse, drew her attention back to him. "I should never have left you alone. The Professor proved more difficult to get rid of than I thought, but I did it with White Hawk's help. That is not a good reason for leaving you here in danger, but I did think someone would be around to help you." He released Sue and his glance went to the woman. "This wasn't the introduction to my world I wanted to give you, to be attacked by one of our numerous reptiles. But let's not dwell on that. You're safe now. I want you to meet my sister, Annalee. She was anxious to come along and see you, and I've been looking forward to this moment for ages. I hope both of you will become good friends. My sister is very good with a bow and arrow. I am proud of her. I know she will look after you when I'm not around."

Sue's heart plummeted. How could she tell him they had already met, and his sister was not at all friendly?

THE SECRET OF TAMSWORTH FOREST

She looked at the other woman accusingly. Annalee made her own decision and solved the problem by saying carelessly,

"I'm sorry I was not here earlier to greet you. I could have saved you from the horrors of that reptilian creature."

Sue remained unconvinced, but Thane looked pleased. He tweaked one of his sister's plaits in an act of brotherly love.

"You saved her life just now. It was a perfect shot. Mine was obviously redundant." As he spoke he retrieved both arrows from the dead animal's eyes and wiped their tips on the grass. He put his own carefully away in the quiver and handed Annalee hers. His eyes strayed beyond her to the edge of the trees. "I didn't realise you shot two arrows. It's unlike you to miss."

He did not wait for Annalee's mumbled reply and she bit her lip as she watched him walk up to the tree, cursing herself for leaving the arrow there. He snatched it out and examined the tip thoroughly as she knew he would, and he said questioningly, "You shot this, Annalee?" He sounded almost accusing but at the same time, made it appear to be a question. Annalee was obviously expecting it.

"You know I didn't," she retorted defiantly. "I passed this way earlier on with Raithe. We were having a game and he said I couldn't hit a tree from way back, so I proved him wrong. What does it matter, Thane? Why don't you leave me alone?"

"What about Sue if you were here earlier?"

77

A flush touched her cheeks and she looked decidedly uncomfortable. She knew her brother was not convinced. He would go on now like a dog with a bone, worrying about the incident. She knew bringing this woman from the other world was going to be trouble. Raithe was right. Hate welled up within her against the unfortunate victim.

"We were here very early. Stop treating me like a little girl." With a careless laugh she snatched her arrow from her brother's hand and stalked off along the path. Stunned, Sue stared after her. No matter what good impressions Thane had of his sister, she knew without a doubt, Annalee was her enemy.

"I'm sorry about her," he apologised. "Her friendship with Raithe is something I've been trying to break."

"Isn't she a little old for you to be choosing her friends?"

"You don't understand, but you will when you get to know Raithe," was his dry retort.

"I'm not likely to. I'm going to see my grandmother, remember?" Sue returned, and moved away from him. "Which way do we go?"

Thane stared at her, undecided. Then taking the bull by the horns, said, "We can't go now. It's too late. And we're not in Tamsworth Forest. You've passed into my world. It all happened because of the Professor following us. I'll take you back in the morning if you want, but meanwhile, let me show you something of where I live."

"But Aunt Moira will miss me..."

"No she won't," Thane interrupted, "She'll think you're with your grandmother. Please, Sue, come and meet my people."

The temptation was too great for Sue to resist. She wanted to see this other world that her Aunt Ruth had vanished to and she wanted to tell Barry where she had been. She turned to Thane. "Lead the way."

CHAPTER 6

PEOPLE OF THEROSSA

For Sue it had been an emotional day and the confused impressions she had of this alien world were hard to take in. It was the place in which Thane grew up but she was painfully aware of not belonging. Thane was not very talkative as they walked along. She felt he was holding something back from her. Feelings between them were becoming somewhat strained, and this was a new experience for both of them.

The paths were easy to negotiate and as dusk fell Thane deviated in his direction and swung round unexpectedly to the left. He halted abruptly and Sue was forced to a standstill. A welcomed standstill, because after the endless tramping along grassy tracks her feet were aching. She swallowed to ease her dry throat and decided to ask how much further they were going to walk when Thane held up his hand to silence her.

They heard voices from somewhere in front, and Sue was consumed with curiosity. At last she was going to meet the inhabitants of this strange world. She pushed past Thane and stopped in her tracks, catching her breath. Before her was a wide open expanse of rough grassland. The trees that had been her constant

THE SECRET OF TAMSWORTH FOREST

companions for at least an hour now fell away on both sides. In the vista beyond the clearing reared rugged mountains which seemed to go on forever, some so high they were capped with snow. They looked majestic, their peaks catching the last rays of the setting sun in a rosy glow. The scene was so spectacular it brought tears to her eyes, and the howl of a wolf went by unnoticed. She was completely lost to her surroundings. The breeze, more conspicuous now they were standing at the edge of the trees, lifted her hair away from her forehead. She turned to Thane, her eyes bright. "What is this place called?" she asked softly.

Thane relaxed for the first time since they'd started on their journey. He half closed his eyes and stared into the distance. The shadows became deeper as darkness swept out from the forest. Overhead leaves rustled and the dry grass whispered the answers to her questions, if only she understood. He placed his arm round her shoulders and said,

"In front of you are the Blue Lake Mountains, they look very awe-inspiring and beautiful. Many a traveller has been enticed to wander there – never to return. They are treacherous and unforgiving. They can be crossed – but only with a guide who knows the way."

"But this is so strange, Thane. I feel a strong pull towards them," Sue whispered. "It's as though I've seen them before in my dreams. Do you think I'm mad?"

For a moment her companion was silent as he drank in the view of the fast disappearing mountains. 'No,' he thought angrily, 'you are not mad, but you soon will be

81

if no one tells you the truth'. He felt his resolve harden and rage at her grandmother filled his mouth with bile. Further caution was pointless. It was time she was told, even if it meant he lost her friendship.

"Sue!" He paused, and she stared at him expectantly, waiting for him to continue. Thane had difficulty in choosing the right words. "Sue – would you like to know what it was your grandmother failed to tell you?"

"How do you know? She will tell me in her own time," Sue answered carelessly, "maybe when I get back to her. I wish she knew I was here with you. She wouldn't worry, you see, she trusts you."

The naïve simplicity of her words made him squirm. His voice was rougher than he intended when he said, "Your grandmother failed to tell you I was hired to abduct you." He heard Sue's gasp of astonishment and felt her pull away. He ignored it. "She also failed to tell you that your mother lives in this land of Therossa and I'm the one to take you to her. Your mother wants to see you."

This time Sue did pull away from him. Her face was white and her lips quivered with emotion. Then fury shone from her eyes and tinged her voice. "Are you telling me you planned this? What are you trying to do to me?" she asked. "My mother is in India and my brother and sister are staying with Aunt Moira. Tell me honestly why I've been brought here. Are you after slaves?"

Thane was now angry. He shook her roughly. Sue felt her head snap back. "Stop being an idiot. You will

THE SECRET OF TAMSWORTH FOREST

be hysterical in a minute. I've told you the truth. Priscilla and Barry are not your siblings."

With a superhuman strength, Sue pushed him away. Tears poured down her face. Her breathing became laboured.

"It's a lie – a filthy lie and I hate you." Before he realised her intention, she dashed back into the cover of the trees. There was a sudden vicious roar which shattered the quietness of the night, followed immediately by an agonising scream. Thane was at her side in a flash, and so were several other people. They found Sue in a crumpled heap, her arm bleeding profusely. Her assailant was nowhere to be seen. Someone quickly bound her arm and Thane picked up her limp body.

"Take her to the Shaman," he ordered.

*   *   *

Sue was in her nightmare again, underground and shivering with terror. The same people were present, their faces indecipherable in the gloom. Their incantations were drawing her back. The candles had burnt low and were spitting. Before long, the small amount of light they gave would fizzle out and then there would be darkness. She must be gone before then. But there was something wrong in the atmosphere and she moved nearer to them. The shrouded figures moved to one side and she saw the wicker basket was empty. They saw her, and in one movement surged in her direction. Their hollow wailing voices called out in unison,

"Come back. Come back. Come back."

Sue fled, stumbling along the dark passage. She knew it was imperative to get away. They must not catch her. The voices were becoming fainter and she doubled over with pain as she stumbled and one arm caught the wall. Her breathing came in short gasps. Unexpectedly someone called out, "The damage has been done. She should not have been told yet."

The voice was stern and sounded right beside her. Sue screamed.

"Go away! Leave me alone! What do you want of me?"

A cool hand touched her forehead with gentle pressure and a soft voice whispered, "Go to sleep. You will feel better when the drug wears off. It is better this way."

The hand remained there and Sue relaxed. Everything faded in her mind.

*   *   *

Drizzle covered the countryside. Every aspect of the land looked depressing. The constant sound of dripping water filled the air. Back in the Shaman's cave Thane was keyed up and paced two and fro like a caged animal, every so often glaring at the nondescript man bending over some charts which were laid out on the table.

THE SECRET OF TAMSWORTH FOREST

The thin man had a highly intellectual face which was wizened with age. His chin was devoid of hair but a few wispy strands adorned the sides of his head. The dome- shaped skull, pink and shiny, gave the impression it was polished each day. A small pair of spectacles balanced on his bulbous nose through which a pair of watery eyes peered. At this moment they were intent on his charts, otherwise he would have admonish Thane for being so irritating.

The Shaman was the greatest healer and philosopher in the entire kingdom and the wisest of all men, who could read a person's destiny in the stars. The small expedition was lucky to have him in the party and he was there only because the sovereign had dictated he must be.

Thane decided enough was enough. Helpers of the Shaman kept him at a respectable distance whenever he tried to see Sue, but no one thought of denying him his right to seek an audience with the healer. However, since he was not making any headway, he decided to take matters into his own hands, knowing Sue was lying in the next cave. He cast another exasperated look at the Shaman, who said without lifting his head,

"Do not disturb her, son."

Thane cursed him under his breath. He strode back to the old man's table and planted himself in front of him.

"I want to see her," he growled. "I want her to know I am still her friend. Do you know it has been three days you've had her here?"

85

This time the Shaman lifted his wise old eyes and studied him intently. "Have you not done enough damage to her already?"

Thane opened his mouth to protest, but the old man stopped him by raising his hand.

"You were told not to hurry things. People like to hear dramatic news gently. She was not ready. You, my son, were heard by half the camp. If you want my advice, leave her to find her own feet. Think about it. What you have told her must have traumatised her greatly. If she still considers herself your friend after all that, she will ask for you. Her health is not in any danger and her arm is almost healed. The mountain cat has been hunted down and killed. It attacked, but was disturbed by the presence of a wolf, so the damage was not too bad. No doubt the wolf was White Hawk as he shadows you everywhere. Now leave me, Thane. Go and join your companions outside."

Having dismissed him, he called to a young girl sitting silently at the back of his cave. She had listened intently to the conversation. "Neela – how is our patient today?"

Thane had just reached the cave entrance, but paused on hearing those words, and waited to hear what she said. Neela came forward noiselessly, an aura of restfulness about her. She was a bright girl of fourteen. Her large, expressive eyes were lowered as she passed Thane and went to stand by her master. As an apprentice to the Shaman, she loved her work for which she had a natural flair; she was by far the most apt pupil he had ever trained. Slender as a reed and dressed in her brown fringed tunic top and pants, she was completely deprived of adornments. What the Shaman liked about her was that she had the unusual quality of knowing when to remain silent.

With her eyes still lowered, she said softly, "She is about to wake up. I have prepared another potion to give to her if she is still distraught. What else would you have me do, master?"

He waved her away and at the same time saw Thane disappearing. He sighed heavily. "Go and see to her, child."

Neela slipped through an opening behind the Shaman's chair where only a hanging tapestry concealed it from sight. She entered another cave which was larger than the Shaman's but devoid of furnishings. It held only the necessities required in a sick bay. Three low camp beds were covered with green cloth. On one of these lay Sue. She had not moved since Neela saw her last, but her breathing was easy. A healthy colour stained her cheeks. This had been absent the last two days. Neela sat down beside the bed and waited. From another entrance at the back of the sick bay, Thane walked silently in and stared down at Sue. Neela looked up in alarm, awed that Thane could so blatantly disregard the Shaman's orders. He just ruffled up her hair and whispered,

"I won't tell him if you don't. Call me if you want anything. I'll be sitting outside."

*   *   *

Later that morning, Sue broke out of the induced sleep which overzealous carers had unintentionally forced on her. Slowly she opened her eyes. They felt very heavy. Some inner instinct made her remain perfectly still. She was acutely aware of not being in her own world. Even in her few moments of lucidity, she had been so traumatised, she was quite sure they had given her something to make her sleep. She was determined that was not going to happen again.

The atmosphere of the room was silent. She mistakenly thought she was alone. Concentrating on the ceiling above, she saw that it was rough stone and realised she was in another cave. The people of this land seemed to live in caves. Her fingers curled round the soft material covering her body. It was lightweight but full of warmth. The whole place was bright and airy and a cooling breeze fanned her cheeks. Carefully she turned her head in the direction from which it came and focused on the fine gossamer drapes hanging over the opening to the outside world. They were so flimsy, she could see green foliage beyond, but no matter how long or how hard she looked, no one ever passed the entrance.

It was the tiniest of movement, but it made Sue turn the other way, and she found herself gazing into Neela's calm face; such a beautiful face, she caught her breath and had difficulty in believing Neela was real. Neela blinked and leant towards her. She touched her forehead with a gentle hand. With a shock, Sue recalled having felt that touch before.

"How are you feeling today?"

THE SECRET OF TAMSWORTH FOREST

Sue remembered that voice as well. In fact, as memory came flooding back to swamp her, she struggled into a sitting position and the gentle hands which were also amazingly strong, helped her. She was thankful there was no repetition of headaches or faintness. "Where am I?"

Watching Neela smile was like watching the sun coming out. "In the sick bay," she replied. "Our Shaman has made you well and I have been looking after you." The young girl surveyed Sue anxiously. "Do you remember what happened to you?"

Sue glanced down at her arm, vividly recalling a fierce-looking animal and sharp pain before unconsciousness blotted everything out. Only two faint scratches showed where the animal had clawed her. It was not physically possible to heal so soon, she thought, unless she had been lying here for weeks. Her stupefaction made Neela smile.

"The Shaman has great powers," she explained simply. "And Thane took you to him swiftly."

Thane! Sue could not blot him out anymore. Neither could she forget their last conversation. At the very mention of his name, hot colour flooded her face. She had accused him of lying. No matter how much she suspected things were not as she believed, it had come as an unpleasant shock to have him tell her the truth. Trying to think rationally, she asked herself if she would have felt any better had it come to her from her grandmother? She doubted it very much. Her grandmother would have had a plausible explanation. Even so, nothing was going to convince her that Barry and Priscilla were not her brother and sister, regardless of what he said. Also, it was not her mother he was taking her to. She had too much love for Gaynor to believe that. Her real mother was in India, and Thane had to believe that. Her immediate embarrassment stemmed from when she recalled the hasty words she had said to Thane, telling him how much she hated him and never wanted to see him again. Memory made her clench her teeth. How could she ever annihilate those hurtful words? What must he think of her? She would be lucky if she ever saw him again and a lump came up in her throat at the thought. She shivered as misery swamped her. Neela became alarmed and Sue did not realise how clearly her feelings showed up on her face. Neela put out her arm to hold her and give some comfort, and at the same time reached for the potion, made up earlier, and pressed it to Sue's lips.

"Drink this," Neela coaxed. "It will make you rest."

"No." Sue pushed it away violently, causing the younger girl to draw back. "I don't want it and I don't want to sleep anymore. I want to see Thane." Even as the words were spilt from her mouth, she was shocked. Did she really want to see him? Did he want to see her? Her mortification was complete when a masculine voice asked, "Did I hear my name mentioned?

Thane came slowly from the shadows and stood at the foot of her bed.

Neela moved swiftly towards the tapestry separating the caves, and hoped the Shaman had not heard him. Sue flashed a quick look at his face. His eyes swept over her with clinical detachment and she felt herself

THE SECRET OF TAMSWORTH FOREST

go cold. Lowering her eyes, she concentrated on her clenched hands and waited for him to speak again. But Thane remained silent. As the silence built up between them, Sue became edgy. His attitude spoke volumes. In the end it was she who broke the stalemate.

"When can you take me home?" she asked dully.

"Home?" questioned Thane. He came to stand by her bed and his answer was impartial. "Where is home?"

"Tamsworth Forest," Sue replied. Her face was burning with humiliation and still she would not look at him.

"No." At the one syllable Sue's head jerked up in astonishment and it was the one answer to snap her out of the self-pity which engulfed her. Her whole demeanour turned to bewilderment. "But you've got to. I didn't ask to come here. You kidnapped me."

Thane glanced at her quizzically with the suspicion of a smile touching the corners of his mouth. "Kidnapped? What manner of word is that? I must learn more of your language." Uninvited, he sat down on her bed and stretching out, took hold of her hands and stared into her startled eyes. "Sue, I know you hate me and I don't blame you. Can you forgive me for my clumsiness? I should not have said what I did. Can we make a pact and start again?"

She nodded her head, emotion rendering her speechless. He was still her friend.

"If you promise me you will visit your... I mean, this lady who has gone to so much trouble to get you here, I will take you home afterwards."

91

Sue couldn't stop the tear which ran down her cheek. Her face lit up with a tremendous smile. Suddenly the world was a good place to be in. Thane gave her a hug and then pushing his luck, said, "Promise me you will never run off again. You nearly got yourself killed. Just thank your lucky stars White Hawk was there." It was not what he wanted to say – but it put Sue back on an even keel.

"I'm such an idiot," she murmured contritely. "I must try and make amends to your wolf. Had he been following us?"

"Yes. All the time. He stays hidden when he is not sure of someone." Thane eyed her seriously. "You're right about one thing. You must be introduced as Barry was…" He ended abruptly, suddenly realising he was treading on dangerous ground, but Sue caught up with him.

"I know. Barry told me he had patted a white wolf and I didn't believe him. The animal was far from friendly when I saw him…" Her voice trailed away.

Thane squeezed her limp hand to make sure he had her attention.

"Sue – White Hawk is not the only white wolf. The army of Therossa trains white wolves as trackers and silent killers. They obey commands without hesitation. White Hawk was the runt of a litter and he was given to me to dispose of as I wished. When I was very young I hung about the garrison all day, hoping to be a soldier. The soldiers gave me the wolf to get rid of me. I have trained White Hawk myself. He will do anything I ask of him, he is now my bodyguard and will guard any of

THE SECRET OF TAMSWORTH FOREST

my friends as well. You have got to meet him. How are you on your feet?"

Sue slowly threw off the green cover, thankful to find she was still attired in her shorts – crumpled though they might be. With Thane's steadying hand she stood upright and gingerly took a step forward, stumbling as vertigo overcame her. For a moment she remained still then, encouraged by Thane, started again. Before long she felt she could walk unaided. She laughed into his face with pure happiness. Thane joined in until a discreet cough behind them made the pair spin round. The Shaman stood by the tapestry, regarding them both with raised eyebrows.

"I am glad you are well, young lady," he said gravely. "And have such a persistent young man as your friend. You can leave here now as I see you are very capable of helping yourself. Neela will be pleased to be relieved of her duties. Take Sue outside Thane to meet the rest of our party, but leave White Hawk until last."

Without giving Sue a chance to say thank you, both he and Neela were gone.

*   *   *

Sue didn't realise how many tunnels had to be negotiated before she reached fresh air. They were dry to the point of being dusty, and illuminated at strategic points with flaring torches. But wherever she looked, everything seemed repetitive. Clattering down numerous well-worn steps, she was beginning to feel disoriented. Already she knew it was impossible to remember the way back to the cave she had been in. She had to trust Thane knew the way out, but she still asked. Under his breath she heard him mutter, "The long way out." That oblique remark made her wonder what the short way could possibly be, but she never caught up with him to ask.

At last they broke out from the claustrophobic passages into fresh air. She paused, happy to feel the fresh breeze against her face; and it took a little while before she noticed the scenery around her. Her eyes opened wide, taking in the spectacular view. The mountains were so much closer, giving the impression it would be easy to walk to them. They loomed ahead, their imposing peaks rearing above the racing clouds. Today though, they were dark and sinister and did not look very inviting. Nearer to hand, the trees swayed in the wind, their leaves sparkling from the early morning rain. The constant sound of dripping water filled her ears and the air smelled sweet and pure.

Sue looked up as they emerged from the tunnels. She had the feeling of something pressing down on her. Behind where she stood towered a wall of rock, almost eclipsing the sky. The rough granite soared hundreds of feet above her head, honeycombed with cave openings. They appeared like dark watching eyes. The ground at her feet sloped downwards, and very near the cliff face were two enormous trees. Very much like those in Tamsworth Forest. Yet these had a subtle difference. They were really ancient and their rough trunks were overrun with ivy. They towered upwards, competing with the height of the cliff, and many of their massive branches and secondary limbs reached out and touched with the rock face. To Sue's amazement, these branches were used by the local inhabitants as a means of access to the ground. With superb agility and the use of rope ladders, they swarmed up and down the trees to enter the cave openings. Then it hit her that it must be the quick way out that Thane mentioned. No wonder no one ever passed the cave she was confined in. She was pleased Thane never suggested bringing her out that way.

Thane allowed her to speculate for a while because he loved to watch the different expressions flit across her face. At last he drew her away reluctantly from the sight.

Voices, coupled with mouth-watering aromas of cooking, floated on the air. Hunger more than anything else made her go with him without protest. It was not until they suddenly branched off that she came face to face with the inhabitants of Therossa and felt the first qualms of nervousness. Her legs started to feel wobbly after her enforced stay in bed.

The glen came as an unexpected surprise. It was a spacious area surrounded by trees, shielding its occupants from the worst of the weather, mainly wind. From where they entered was a picket line of horses, tethered to several stout posts. They were well groomed healthy animals with glossy coats and bright eyes. One or two snickered a greeting but Thane quickly restrained Sue from approaching them.

"Not yet," he said quietly. "Let me introduce you first to my people."

The centre of the glen was taken up by a fiercely burning fire. Its glow touched the foliage of the trees around the perimeter, and they shimmered under a heat haze. No chairs, but logs were strategically placed for people to sit. There were many of them there. A good few were sitting, but most deep in conversation. The huge spit caught her attention. The body of an animal was slowly rotating. Two young boys were basting the meat from a tray and the delicious smell from it made her mouth water. She licked her lips, and at the same time felt sorry for the lads whose bodies were covered in a film of perspiration.

No one had noticed her yet so Sue surreptitiously examined the people, noticing they all dressed the same way as Thane, their sombre-coloured garments acted as a camouflage helping them merge into their surroundings. It was hard to distinguish men from women. Suddenly she had no more time because someone in the group looked up and saw her standing there with Thane. The people converged towards her. She fought a sudden impulse to hide. So many strangers all at once overwhelmed her. She knew if Thane had not placed a restraining hand on her arm, she would have run away.

The tallest man amongst them came right up to her and grasped her hands, engulfing them with his own. The pressure was firm and strong. His rugged face held a pair of twinkling eyes and his long dark hair tended to curl at the ends. This was held in place by a red band

THE SECRET OF TAMSWORTH FOREST

worn round his forehead. Sue felt herself smiling until he spoke. "I am pleased to meet you, Sonja, and I speak for all the people here. We have waited a long time for your coming, but Thane was in charge and we played the game the way he dictated. Just between you and me, the Queen has great faith in his judgement. Well, now you're here at last, Sonja. What do you think of our country?"

Sue stood, feeling completely lost, her hand still held by the newcomer. She glanced at Thane but he gave her no help. People were pushing closer, anxious to hear her answer. She was at a disadvantage because they all knew her. Swallowing nervously, she gasped faintly "Who is Sonja?"

The man looked surprised. Reluctantly, he released her hands and turned to Thane. "Doesn't she know anything?" he inquired in consternation. "I would not have said what I did had I known. She must think me all kinds of a fool."

"We haven't delved into names yet," Thane answered, "so if you don't mind, she only knows that her mother has asked for her. Sue!" He turned and looked her squarely in the face, deliberately changing the conversation, "This man you have just met is my best friend, Cailli. He will always be on hand to help you should I not be around."

"Like your sister?" Sue asked, thinking of the unfriendly Annalee.

She had the satisfaction of seeing his face darken. Cailli chuckled. "So you have met the delightful

97

Annalee. Now, I take it that your name is Sue? We might have a bit of difficulty over that."

"Why? I've been Sue all my life." Sue suddenly broke off, her attention drawn to an older man who was watching proceedings through shrewd eyes. He stood apart from everyone else; standing erect with ear-length wispy white hair and straggly beard. He became aware of her eyes on him and his leathery face broke out into a smile. He pushed forward. The wiry hand that grasped hers felt rough. He was obviously a worker in this land.

"I am very pleased to see you here at last, Sonja," he said gruffly. "You must not worry about a thing. I know it is going to be hard, but I will get you to the Queen if it's the last thing I do. No, Thane. I will not stop," he added as Thane opened his mouth. "You stay out of this. She may as well know right now that everyone in this land knows her as Sonja. Why are you trying to hide it from her?"

"Because my name is Sue," she cut in, alarm filling her. "I've always been Sue, it's what my mother named me. I am only sorry you have got me muddled up with someone else."

"You listen to me, Miss," retorted the old man dryly. "Your Ma, begging your pardon, sir," he said with a sly look at Thane, "Your Ma called you Sonja and that's the end to it. No more arguing in front of me."

Sue gave up and the old man saluted her and ambled away in the direction of the horses. They surged round him and he was soon lost from sight. She watched him go with mixed feelings. He looked the epitome of the grandfather she never had. A strange feeling of affiliation took her by surprise. Cailli, on the other hand, scowled after his retreating figure and she noticed for the first time the lines of weakness around his mouth. "That man takes liberties, you know," he said. "He thinks age allows him to say anything. You're too soft on him even if he is…"

"It's all right, Cailli. Amos is the least of my worries," Thane cut in, and a cold edge touched his voice. "What I want to know is – where is Raithe? He should be here to welcome Sue. It's what we all came here to do."

As he spoke, he peered amongst the people gathered round the fire. Not only was he annoyed at Raithe not being there, but also peeved his own sister chose to absent herself as well. Sue edged back and tried to make herself inconspicuous, not keen to be reunited with the youth who was Annalee's friend. She wondered if she might plead tiredness and get away from there. Her glance fell longingly on the tree trunks, but in fairness to Thane she remained passively beside him. Someone shouted, "The Prince comes," and she felt her sinews tightening. The Prince swaggered from the trees and headed straight for the group of people, wanting to see what was going on, wondering if he was being left out of something. Annalee followed on his heels.

"It's about time too," Thane admonished curtly, eyeing the Prince askance. "I want you to meet Sue."

The expression on the newcomer's face was unreadable. "I've never heard of her." To everyone's horror he laughed insultingly and looked her up and down. "I'm not surprised, looking like she does," he sneered contemptuously. "Anyone could forget such a mundane name. Don't we have a serf called that back home?" He looked towards Annalee for backup, and Annalee reddened slightly as she felt the eyes of her brother glowering at her. Thane wanted to strike the Prince but kept his smouldering fury in check. He had expected trouble, but not open warfare in front of his own people, and Sue especially. "I think you have forgotten who you are, and the oath you took before making this journey," he said.

Man and youth locked eyes. The younger lad was full of bravado but Thane stared him down and his eyes hardened. Yet Raithe was not put out. He broke the contact and waved carelessly at the people. They instantly moved back a step. Sue could not decide if it was out of respect, or for some other reason.

"I have not forgotten my oath," retorted Raithe imperiously. "We haven't seen any wolves, but I swore to protect her from them. I've abided by that and I don't have to do anything else. Do you mind moving out of my way?"

"Not until you've welcomed Sue here," Thane said between clenched teeth and some of the watching people nodded their heads in agreement.

"What on earth for?" Raithe drew himself up haughtily. "We don't need foreigners here. It would be a mistake to welcome them. Before long they will breed and swarm all over us like the vermin they are. You have my permission to remove her from my presence."

His thin face looked spiteful. His flippancy concealed a hidden warning. Shock silenced the watching people. It was broken by the neighing of a horse. Only a few turned their heads to look. Raithe stared at Sue, his eyes full of loathing. Sue was dumbfounded. She tried to stop herself from trembling. Thane and Cailli were momentarily frozen with indecision, but not Amos. No one saw him approaching. Like a snake his whip lashed through the air and curled viciously round the young lad's shoulders. Raithe howled with rage as he clawed at the lash.

The old man stood directly in front of him. The watchers had parted to let him through.

"That's the way we treat wayward dogs," he snarled. "Your manners bring shame to Therossa. You are nothing better than an insignificant parasite. You are not the Prince of the Realm yet, my lad, so do not act as though you are. Sonja has not come a moment too soon. I shall be having words with the Queen when we return." He turned away to go back to his beloved horses, but first he stopped in front of Thane. His voice was grim.

"It's about time you admonished that cub and kept him on a shorter leash. Mark my words – he is trouble. He should never have been allowed to come here."

CHAPTER 7

BARRY HAS A PLAN

It didn't take long for the news to spread that a young lady had vanished in Tamsworth Forest. The hotel became flooded with more visitors than it could handle. Unhappily, most of them were on the lookout for a morbid story. It was with difficulty that Moira showed polite interest when asked questions, but inwardly she was fuming. Her life of tranquillity had been shattered. Priscilla, surprisingly, missed her sister and openly accused the Professor of having had something to do with her disappearance. She ignored her aunt telling her that Sue would come to no harm and turn up like a bad penny. Mrs Denton had sent her on an important errand. It did not convince Priscilla and she told Barry as much. She, above everyone else, knew there were strange beings in the forest and maybe they had spirited Sue away. She would not investigate these suspicions herself in case they took her as well. The trouble started when the boys in blue arrived in their cars and caused a stir. Moira was furious. When she discovered Professor Harding had, on his own initiative, informed the police of Sue's disappearance, she forgot he was a paying guest and to the astonishment of Priscilla and Barry, told him in an icy voice he could now inform the police he had made a mistake. The expression on his gaunt

102

features belied what his real thoughts were on hearing her words. A muscle twitched near his tight lips, but he said in an expressionless voice,

"I will gladly do that if you tell me where your niece is."

"Where my niece is has nothing to do with you. I can assure you, Professor Harding, that if the police are still here tomorrow, I shall terminate your stay in this hotel."

He stilled his rage and stared at her as though she was something obnoxious that had crawled out of the woodwork. His eyes glittered. "You are in charge, Madam. It will be as you request." He turned abruptly and his smouldering gaze rested on the gawking Priscilla and Barry. Ignoring them, he walked out of the hotel.

"Phew," muttered Barry, removing his glasses and polishing them on his shirt. "He's a nasty piece of work."

"Don't tell me you've just noticed that," Priscilla snapped, and she swung round to her aunt. "Moira, where is Sue?"

Moira became uncertain under her probing eye. She turned in a fluster and made a point of studying her watch. "Dear me, is it this time already? I'm sorry, my dears – I've got to leave you."

"Where's Sue?" repeated Priscilla, deliberately standing in front of her, and Barry gave her ten out of ten for persistence. Moira paused, and looked at them both flatly.

"Ask your grandmother." With that she pushed past the astonished Priscilla and mounted the stairs.

*   *   *

The next day Priscilla did exactly what her aunt suggested. A group of trekkers happened to be going in the same direction as she was, so she tagged along with them until they reached the cottage. However, when she manoeuvred the conversation round to Sue and spoke about her disappearance, her grandmother slumped into her favourite armchair and muttered, "Why didn't I tell her when she asked?" No matter how much Priscilla pressed her for more information, she never said another word except to tell her off for being so inquisitive.

That evening she told Barry what had happened, and his eyes gleamed. So much was falling into place that he had the urge to put his thoughts into practice. He turned to his sister and said in a low conspiratorial voice,

"Sis, if ever I'm suddenly missing one day, tell everyone I've followed Sue."

Of course Priscilla, being Priscilla, wanted to know more, but Barry annoyingly put his finger to his lips and moved swiftly away from her.

The following morning Barry started on his reconnaissance of the forest, and his many trips, which he made no effort to hide, ignited the curiosity of the Professor and Cyril, just as he hoped. Furtively they commenced to track him and Barry led them a merry dance. He deliberately kept off paths to make it difficult. Now and again he would stop and pretend to be reading instructions, then continue on his way, pushing through gorse and shrubbery and tunnelling underneath impregnable thickets. The Professor might get through, but Cyril, being well endowed with flesh, would have difficulty. To stretch his legs he climbed trees and swung himself over brambles knowing full well it was the only way to get to the spot where he wanted to land. After studiously studying the outer wrapper of his sandwiches, he plunged through some waist-high stinging nettles and crossed a small enclosed lake by stepping precariously on some dead wood which was half submerged in the water. Then he walked up a slight incline, sat down on a hillock concealed behind a bush and took a well-earned rest. He waited to see if the Professor and Cyril were still following.

A grin spread over his face when he saw them negotiating the logs. One began to sink under Cyril's weight and he frantically caught hold of the Professor, nearly ducking the pair of them. It was obvious Cyril had given up on this reconnaissance and would gladly return to the hotel. He was sweating profusely and his companion looked grim. Barry waited a few seconds before letting himself be seen sauntering along the path. Without warning, he swung up into an old oak tree. He wished he could see the expressions on their faces. Carefully he crawled along a branch and crossed over on to the limb of a beech tree. Then he climbed up like an agile monkey to where a rope was tied to the tree.

Grasping this he pushed off with his feet, swung out over a patch of marshy ground and landed on another path. He walked down the path until he was out of sight, and then sat down on a log and started to eat his sandwiches. Quite a time elapsed before the sound of their voices reached his ears. Hot and dishevelled, the two men came along the path. Barry, with what he hoped was surprise, looked up at them.

"Hello, Professor Harding, fancy seeing you here. Are you enjoying the forest as well?" he called out, a guileless look on his face, "I couldn't get Priscilla to come with me, which is a shame. I say – would either of you like a sandwich?"

Cyril acted spontaneously and snatched one. He sat down with a thud as he hit the log and started munching ravenously. His face was a bright red and flies were buzzing round his head. The Professor glared at him, refusing both sandwich and seat. He could contain himself no longer. "What the hell are you supposed to be doing? Can't you walk in a straight line, boy?"

"I beg your pardon." Barry deliberately looked confused. "Have I done something wrong?"

The older man realised he had nearly given himself away, and asked politely, "Why are you climbing trees and swinging on ropes? Are you trying to break your neck?"

"Oh that." Barry looked relaxed, but he was chuffed the Professor had fallen unwittingly into his trap. "Have you seen me? Do you think I'm good? I'm training to be a soldier. I have worked out my own hazardous routes and try to do one in the morning and one in the

THE SECRET OF TAMSWORTH FOREST

afternoon. It helps to keep me fit and in good shape. You should try it, sir – perhaps we could go together?" The Professor nearly burst a blood vessel but Barry did not give him a chance to answer. Instead he went on urgently, "Tomorrow I'm going to try and do the whole course with a full pack. That will show how good I am. What do you reckon are my chances?"

He looked at the older man earnestly as though he really wanted his opinion. Professor Harding had a strong desire to shake him after having had a wasted day.

"If you want to be an idiot, go ahead," he snarled. Then turning to Cyril he snapped, "Come on – it's time to be moving."

Cyril reluctantly heaved himself up from the log. Barry also stood and brushed the crumbs away, and said, "I know what you two are doing." He hastily held back a smile as the older man stiffened. But suddenly he was like a dangerous animal.

"Are you going to share your knowledge with us?" he asked sarcastically.

"You're looking for that lost world, aren't you, have you found it yet?"

The Professor's teeth snapped together and his eyes were like stone. A shiver coursed down Barry's spine. He wondered if he had gone too far. The Professor resisted the urge to throttle him. Instead he put his face close up to the boy's and replied, "not yet, sonny, but if we found that sister of yours – she would tell us its location."

107

Barry tried to keep a bright smile on his face. "I don't think so," he contradicted, purposely misunderstanding him. "Priscilla's not interested in things like that. The forest scares her."

"Are you being deliberately obtuse, boy? I'm not talking about that neurotic female at the hotel. I'm talking about your sister Sue."

Barry started to feel out of his depth. He took a step backwards. "No – you're mistaken..." He got no further, the Professor interrupted him and at the same time he took a step forward.

"Don't tell me I'm wrong, lad. I've seen her with my own eyes, fraternizing with the strange people who come from that other world."

Barry shrugged that off. "Sue will talk to anyone, that doesn't mean a thing. Well, I've got to get back home for tea. Enjoy the rest of your day, sir."

Like a shot, Barry was off along the path. Cyril attempted to stop him but he was too slow. He stared at the Professor obliquely, and said, "Are we still following?"

"No, but that one is getting too big for his boots."

*　　　*　　　*

It was early in the morning. Barry stealthily crept into the hotel kitchen and raided the enormous larder for food. He knew the kitchen staff were having breakfast in the adjoining room, because the smell of bacon wafted through the door. This was a good time to be here. Having worked out in advance what he wanted,

THE SECRET OF TAMSWORTH FOREST

the boy quickly filled his rucksack, and left as silently as he had entered. He saw his aunt at the reception desk. This was an unforeseen blow to his plans. She could, and properly would, ask awkward questions. He paused to deliberate for a moment, when the telephone rang. Her conversation was brief, but it had the desired effect. She retired into the office. Barry exhaled and moved noiselessly across the foyer. He was lifting his hand to open the door when an imperious voice asked sharply,

"Where are you sneaking off to so early, son?"

Barry cursed softly under his breath. Was his day going to be blighted with a lot of holdups? Forcing a smile, he turned, saying. "Hello, Professor – I'm just off to navigate my hazardous course again. I told you about it yesterday. I've got a full pack this time. I say, are you down here because you are coming with me?"

His bravado was nearly his undoing as the Professor rose from the armchair and walked over to him. Taking the rucksack from Barry's hand, he weighed it by moving it up and down. His expression was incredulous as he looked at the boy. "A bit heavy, isn't it. What on earth have you got in there? Some bricks?"

Barry's mouth felt dry. With an effort he tried to appear unconcerned. Inwardly he was desperately trying to find words which would reassure the Professor and keep him from becoming suspicious. "Not bricks," he answered with a grin, "a few stones perhaps and some books, plus a little refreshment." Then a flicker of daredevil made him add, "There is enough for two in

109

there. Come on, sir! Be a sport and do the course with me."

Professor Harding thrust the bag back at him. "I am not in the mood for little boy games," he said disparagingly. "Just take my word for it. You won't make it with that weight."

Something clinked in the bag during its transaction and Barry went cold, but the Professor obviously had not heard it because he returned to his armchair. With relief Barry clasped the rucksack firmly, and with a cheery, "Goodbye, sir," quickly left the hotel.

The Professor forgot all about him and resumed his scan of the newspapers. He had lots of time before anyone disturbed him, being a man who did not partake of breakfast. After a lengthy time had elapsed, the foyer became busy. Moira returned to the desk to deal with petty complaints. With undisguised relief he saw Cyril approaching him.

Folding up the newspaper into its original creases, he laid it carefully on the arm of his chair as he stood up. Cyril reached his side as a man rushed in. Judging by the way he was dressed, he was a chef, and breathing heavily, he stopped in front of Moira. Not waiting to be asked what he wanted, he blurted out,

"We have had a thief in the kitchen. He has taken all sorts of things, tins, packets, bottles and my best tin-opener. I want something done about it at once before I get accused of being light-fingered."

He had everyone's attention. The Professor did not wait to hear what followed or Moira's response. Something exploded in his head and he was filled with malevolence. With sudden clarity he knew he had been duped by a boy. Fury raged through him. He grabbed the startled Cyril and pulled him down the hotel steps.

"Brace yourself, man," he snarled, "we've got some serious tracking to do and I want no whining out of you."

*   *   *

Barry paused and gasped for breath, gaping at a hedge made up from an assortment of plants. It was also very tall, hiding effectively what was on the other side. It was an impregnable barrier. This setback was unforeseen. Obviously there was no way through it.

No, that's wrong, he thought logically. There has to be a way. It's just that I can't see it.

He had been here with White Hawk and Thane many a time, and it was near here they had always vanished, but where? He looked up at the nearby trees. He quickly erased the idea that they went that way. The wolf couldn't climb trees. But then he thought they may have tunnelled through. No, Thane never looked as though he had just squeezed through a hole. Barry walked back and forth along the hundred-yard stretch, diligently searching for a way through. He wondered how much time he had before the Professor was on his trail. To go over the top was impossible, to crawl underneath was not feasible, it was too matted. So what way? Frustration built up in him. He knew beyond doubt he was near the entrance to the other world, but he had come to a dead end.

Barry gave up his aimless wandering and contemplated the greenery, looking for something that was slightly different and might be the way through. Noises of the forest went on about him without his awareness – then two things happened at once. Admittedly, it was in the distance, but he heard Cyril's voice complaining. Barry went cold. To think they were that near. Maybe he hadn't been as clever as he thought. The other thing was the whine and movement by his feet. Beside him was the wolf.

"White Hawk!" he breathed, and bent down to fondle his ears, receiving a wet tongue on his hand in return. "Am I pleased to have you here. I'm in trouble. It's a pity you can't speak or you would tell me the way. I want to get through there." He pointed to the hedge and straightened up. White Hawk stood up with him and gently took his hand in his muzzle and gave a small tug. Then he let go, walked a few paces away and looked back. The boy was bright enough to know the wolf wanted him to follow, but the wolf didn't know where he wanted to go. Still, what choice had he, with the Professor on his heels, so hoisting up his bag onto his back, he let the wolf lead him.

To Barry's utmost surprise, the wolf walked in the opposite direction – away from the fence of green. It needed great concentration to keep him in sight because the animal moved swiftly, going through places where Barry had to fall on his hands and knees and crawl. Occasionally White Hawk would be waiting for him at the other end of a tunnel, sitting on his hind quarters with his long tongue hanging over the sides of his jaw.

THE SECRET OF TAMSWORTH FOREST

It was when he leapt over a fissure that Barry had trouble. The rucksack proved to be a great hindrance. In the end, he had to take it off and throw it over, hoping the contents were not harmed when it landed. Then he took a run and jumped. Swiftly he picked up the bag again because the wolf was off almost at once. Once again, Barry was forced to his hands and knees. He received severe stings to his hands and face when White Hawk went through a bed of nettles.

Barry started to get uncomfortably warm and he wondered fleetingly if God was paying him back for what he did to the Professor and Cyril. A smile crossed his face at that thought, until he noticed the wolf had jumped into a gully which had running water at the bottom. White Hawk did not wait for him. He went paddling up the stream.

Oh hang it, Barry thought, and jumped in after him. If he did not succeed in getting to the other world, Moira would tear strips off him for getting everything wet. Walking up the gully was OK. It cooled his feet. But then the wolf went through a tunnel of greenery. Before long Barry had to bend and revert to his hands and knees. By now – no matter how careful he was – he was soaked. Darkness was setting in. Above him was a solid roof. The journey was getting scary. He had no idea what was before him, so he stopped moving. After a while, he nerved himself to move forward and feel out for the bank. No matter how hard he stretched, it was not there. Barry wondered if he should turn back. He had forgotten to bring a torch, which was very foolish. In fact – this whole venture had turned out to be foolhardy. He could not even see White Hawk.

Carefully he manoeuvred himself to turn round and keep the rucksack dry at the same time. In the darkness, he did not know how far round he had turned. He was in a worse mess now than ever. His hands and knees were getting cold and the anti-climax came when one of his knees pressed down on a piece of flint. He yelped out and his voice echoed back to him, which meant he must be in a vast cavern. It was not easy to scare Barry, but right now he was getting jittery. Straining his eyes he peered into the darkness. Above the plopping sound of unseen amphibians came the sound of a hunting horn. Gritting his teeth together, he made to move in the direction of the sound. The water was hindering his movement. After slowly crawling, with fronds of something tickling his head from above, he realised the water was getting shallower. Sand could be felt by his probing hands. Then he was out of the water. Barry stopped. His heart thumped to the extent it nearly deafened him. He was still blind in the darkness, but at least he was on solid ground. He attempted to stand up. Very gingerly he stretched and to his relief he found he could stand upright.

The horn sounded again in two short blasts, much nearer now. Barry started off in that direction, wary in case he came upon unforeseen obstacles. The one thing he did not expect was the passing of a pack of wolves. A score or more of what seemed to be amber lights raced past him and were gone. Barry still pushed ahead and suddenly saw a glimmer of light. It became brighter with every step until he was standing beneath tall trees. It looked like Tamsworth Forest, but Barry knew it was not. There was a subtle difference. He had reached the other world.

CHAPTER 8

BETRAYAL

Sue soon settled into camp life. The majority of people she came into contact with showed her a respect which began to make her feel embarrassed. They treated her almost like royalty; whereas Raithe and Annalee did the exact opposite. Thankfully, she did not see much of them. Cailli, however, disturbed her. She could not make her mind about him. He would have monopolised all her time had Amos not been on hand to direct him elsewhere. She could not fault him on anything specific, but something about his character disturbed her when he was near. Yet to all purposes, he was Thane's friend. Amos received respect without even trying. She wondered who he really was. Not a groom, although the horses loved him. Since his plain speaking that made Raithe look ridiculous before his people, he had melted into the background.

Raithe kept well away from most people, and if Sue ever met him, he treated her with the minimal amount of courtesy that etiquette required. He was always with Annalee. They could be seen with their heads together, no doubt plotting and planning her downfall. She wondered uneasily why they hated her. What had she ever done to them? She never knew they existed until she landed in this world. Her biggest bugbear was no one would explain about Sonja, who or what she really was. When she tried to unearth any information about the Queen, the people closed ranks. Not just a few of them – everyone, even to Neela this subject was taboo. In Neela's company she learnt how to swarm up the huge tree in safety and make her way to the small cave which had been allotted her. It was little more than a cell, but was made comfortable with a rattan mat on the hard floor, a small but adequate camp bed with a straw-stuffed mattress and some colourful tapestry hanging over the cave entrance. It was a place only for sleeping. All meals were a communal affair, around the camp fire.

Today Neela was with the Shaman, so Sue escaped to the solitude of her cave where she knew she would not be disturbed. She sat on the lip of rock with her feet dangling down the cliff face and the sun bathing her with its warmth. Trouble was brewing in some other part of the community, so Thane and several men were absent. The remaining ones were guards posted at strategic points. She wondered why. Thane did not seem to be in any danger as far as she could see. Sue would have liked to have gone with him because activity stopped her from brooding, but on this occasion women were not allowed. They were now probably preparing food for the evening, so instead of being with them, she preferred her own company and thought about home.

Someone was climbing up the tree. Sue squinted for a while because the sun dazzled her vision. She gave up and contemplated how long it might be before Thane

117

showed her the way back home. She could afford to pander to his whims because she knew this woman he was taking her to was not her mother. She was not in any great hurry. There was no real danger here other than animals, and it was quite an adventure. Something Barry would be envious of when she eventually told him about it. The person climbing up was very near to her now and, staring intently, she saw it was Annalee. To her amazement, Annalee was heading straight for her cave. She wondered whether or not to look away and feign surprise, but Annalee hailed her.

"Sue! Why are you sitting up here by yourself? I've been looking for you everywhere. Would you like to do some hunting with us?"

Sue's heart leapt, seeing no more than the hand of friendship being offered. Annalee was likeable when she was not with Raithe and for the moment she did not speculate about the 'us'.

"I'd love to but I'm no hunter. I'm not even good with a bow and arrow," she responded.

Annalee landed beside her with a smile on her face. She made no attempt to sit down, however, but balanced precariously on the edge of the drop. "Then we will teach you. You will enjoy that. Of course, we shall have to ride out into the hills to do so. Oh dear, I forgot, can you ride a horse?"

Sue thought her concern was touching. It was a nice experience to see Thane's sister full of solicitude, so much so she actually laughed. "Of course I can. There have always been horses in our family – but if it's all

THE SECRET OF TAMSWORTH FOREST

the same to you. I should like something docile rather than frisky. I haven't ridden for a long time."

A strange smile touched Annalee's face but Sue missed it, on account of the sun. "We can easily manage that," she answered briskly. "Come on, lazybones. Race you down the tree." She had started off before she finished speaking and Sue shouted out belatedly, "Does Raithe mind my coming along?"

"It was his idea." Annalee's voice floated back because she was already some distance away. Sue scrambled to her feet and followed as hastily as she dared. Was this going to be the beginning of something new?

* * *

There were only three horses at the picket line. The others had obviously been taken by the men. Annalee and Raithe had already picked out their mounts, leaving behind a wicked looking black stallion for Sue to ride. Eyeing him dubiously, she reserved judgement on this one being docile. The other two informed her that his name was Saturn and by the glint in his wild eyes, he looked decidedly devilish. Annalee and Raithe leapt easily into their saddles and controlled their mounts with expertise. They watched Sue. Saturn was skittish and would not stand still. Every time Sue took a step towards him, he flattened his ears and backed away. It was a stalemate that could go on all day and she was conscious of her mocking audience.

119

"Can you ride a horse in those clothes?" Annalee's voice was insulting and the only sound to break the silence. She stared down derisively from her lofty perch and added, "I mean to say – have you thought – it may be your appearance that's putting him off." Then her laugh filled the air.

Sue's face was burning and Raithe's sneer made her determined to get on this horse even if it killed her. Too late she realised these two had an ulterior motive for getting her here. Friendship had nothing to do with it.

"You seem to forget the horse and I are strangers to each other. I have to make friends with him first." It took all Sue's self-control to keep her voice on an even keel. She would not give them the satisfaction of knowing they were getting to her. "I'll not keep you long."

"That I'll believe when I see it."

Raithe turned away from the scene, bored, but Sue could detect he was edgy over something and wanted to leave quickly. His eyes were darting in all directions. Maybe he was keeping a look out for Amos. None of this would be happening if he was around.

Sue caught hold of the bridle and reached out to pat the horse's nose. His nostrils flared at her impudence in touching him. He lifted his head with a whinny. Undeterred, she whispered to him gently and pressed her advantage by stroking his neck. Saturn quivered and stood still, but his calculating eyes were fixed on her – daring her to go further. Sue's hand wandered to the blanket draped over his back beneath the saddle. Her sensitive fingers felt an unexplained bulge and the

THE SECRET OF TAMSWORTH FOREST

slight pressure she put on it caused the horse to round on her with bared teeth. Beads of perspiration formed on her brow. She knew for a certainty what was wrong with him now. He would have acted this way no matter who had approached him. It was the type of malicious trick the kids at the stable played when they wanted to unseat a rider. Completely ignoring both Annalee and Raithe, she kept up a low monotone talking to Saturn, all the time working her hand under the blanket and removing the burs she had found. Feeling the pressure vanish, Saturn lowered his head and blew in her face. The tension left Sue but she angrily threw the burs to the ground. Looking over her shoulder at the other two riders, Sue glared at them accusingly. "Was that your idea of a joke?" she asked but they did not have the grace to look ashamed. All Annalee said was, "we are going to gallop for a while, so keep up otherwise you will lose us." They were off without another word.

Having quickly decided that whatever the circumstances, a good gallop would be worth it, Sue sprang lightly on to the stallion's back and picked up the reins. With pressure from her knee she took control of the horse, gave him his head and chased after the other two.

*   *   *

Sue was exhilarated, travelling crouched over Saturn's withers with the wind blowing through her hair. Doing something positive made her feel good. The countryside flashed by, but to her eyes it was little more than a blur. Saturn's long legs ate up the miles easily, and she was enjoying the feel of a horse beneath her. Before long the trees were left behind and there was no cover from the relentless sun. The land was parched. Saturn's hooves pounded over the rough grass and small hillocks, he was very sure-footed. But still the two ahead of Sue were pulling away, looking like moving specs on the horizon. Yet they could not outdistance the stallion Sue rode. She kept them in sight. The landscape was slowly changing, grassland becoming sandy and interspersed with rocky boulders. The air started to become colder as the panoramic scene became more mountainous. She barely noticed with the speed the stallion was travelling. Occasionally the ground at his feet fell away, making some of the drops on one side of them sheer. She had the impression they were riding along the edge of mist-shrouded ravines.

The stallion began to slow down and Sue became aware Annalee and Raithe had stopped. They turned their horses slowly to face her, sitting stiffly in their saddles like a couple of warriors. Their bows were slung over slim shoulders. As she slowly trotted up, the look on their faces was ludicrous. She knew intuitively they had not expected her to keep up with them, but Annalee had invited her to hunt so she was deliberately obtuse. She reined up and slid off Saturn's back, allowing him a moment to cool off. He took advantage of it. He wandered off and found some succulent tufts of grass to chomp away at. She walked up to the heaving horse Annalee sat on and patted his neck. She was acutely aware of the unfriendly eyes watching her

THE SECRET OF TAMSWORTH FOREST

every movement. Purposely misunderstanding the situation, Sue said gaily, "That was really a great race, but I have to admit, you two won easily. You know, we should do it more often, don't you think? Only next time it would be fairer if we all started off together." She paused before adding briskly, "What now? Is this where you teach me to hunt?"

Annalee jerked her head. "We suddenly remembered we forgot to bring a bow for you." She shifted on her horse, her eyes inscrutable. Raithe swung himself out of the saddle, his face expressionless. Sue was still wary of him, especially when he came to stand by her side. They were very much alike in build, except that he was a couple of inches taller. It was their hair that was so remarkable. They both had a mop of red gold curls. She had never met another person with her hair colouring until now. He looked up at Annalee and something unspoken passed between them. Sue would have given anything to know what it was because she gave a slight nod.

He gripped Sue's arm, which made her jump, and led her a few feet away. Here, the ground fell away, but not sharply. All the same, she would not want to fall over the edge and she backed away. There was quite a drop to the valley floor below. Starting from her feet was a twisting path that hugged the side of the hill and wended its way downwards. In parts it was six foot across, covered with loose scree. Other than that it looked perfectly safe. But after a hundred yards, the path disappeared round a bend, not reappearing until a long way down. Then the track turned back on itself.

123

Raithe explained all details of the track, Sue followed it with her eyes and noticed where it emerged to ascend back to where they were standing. She looked at him enquiringly, wondering what all that narrative was about.

"Do you fancy a race?" he asked casually. "This happens to be our own private track."

"A race? You mean all of us?" she enquired.

"No I don't. It's too narrow for three horses." His look implied she had no sense. "When we race, if you agree, one goes one way and the other down the return track. Somewhere down at the bottom we pass each other. I cannot say where exactly, depends on who is moving the quickest. I have this feeling you don't like me and would love to have the opportunity of beating me. Well, I'm a sport. I'm giving you the chance to try it now. What do you say?"

His eyes never left her face. They were almost compelling her to race. She looked at the path doubtfully. A foot put down unwisely could cause a nasty accident. Annalee was still on her horse and had not moved. She looked like a stone statue. Sue moved back another step. "Wouldn't it be better to have the race up here where there is more room?"

Raithe snorted in disgust. "If you kept your eyes open you would have seen how treacherous the ground is up here, it's full of potholes and easy for a horse to break a leg. It's this track or nothing. Or are you too much of a coward?"

Sue looked back at the drop, still undecided. Raithe turned away in exasperation. His dark eyes smouldered as he looked at Annalee. He was expecting a little help from her.

"I always knew you would be gutless," he sneered at Sue, and she spun round to say, "You're on."

She knew she was being rash, but he had been egging her on, and right now she did not care. He had riled her for the last time. She was looking forward to showing him she knew a lot more about horses than he imagined. Ignoring the pair of them, she walked over to where Saturn was still cropping. Behind her back, Annalee came out of her trance. She gazed into Raithe's jubilant face and hissed in an undertone,

"Don't do this, Raithe." His smile was sinister. "We've got to do it. It's all going as planned. It's like taking milk from a baby. If you're squeamish all of a sudden – look the other way." He had already remounted by the time Sue trotted back sitting on Saturn. It was a little unnerving because the black stallion was becoming frisky. Raithe thought this was favourable to his plan. He pointed to the path.

"You stand by this track and I shall stand by the other. Annalee will tell us when to start. Sure you're all right with this?"

"Yes." Sue's answer came between clenched teeth.

"Right. Then may the best man win."

She nodded curtly and stood on the edge of the decline. A cold wind blew up from the valley where fingers of mist were floating along. She watched Raithe take up his position and wondered why she was bothering. He looked so sure of himself. She bent over and patted Saturn's neck to calm him down. Then Annalee shouted, "Go."

She was off, pushing Saturn down the track as fast as she dared. It was more scary than it seemed from the top, and needed all her concentration. It never occurred to her to turn her head and see how Raithe was making out, otherwise she would have seen him still at the top, watching her. He slowly drew out his bow and slotted in an arrow. When Sue reached the bend he took aim and deliberately let the arrow go. Its flight was accurate and deadly as it caught Saturn on his haunch. A shrill snort came from the stallion. He reared in terror before he bolted out of sight with Sue clinging for dear life to his neck.

Annalee's breath came out jerkily. Her throat restricted the air flow. Then a flush of indignation rose up in her as she watched Raithe calmly put his bow back over his shoulder.

"You hit the horse," she accused him.

Raithe's smile was cold and cruel. "Would you rather I hit her? Cheer up Annalee. It went perfectly. He's not hurt. I only nicked him and he will make his own way home."

"But what about…" Annalee was choked, unable to say Sue's name.

Raithe pulled her away from the edge. "She won't come back," he said roughly. "We are rid of her now. Our mission has been accomplished. Her friends will put it down as a nasty accident when they miss her. For goodness sake cheer up. We've got to make tracks back home."

"But what if she comes back?" asked Annalee.

Raithe's smile was mocking. "No one has ever come back from down there alive. You know as well as I do what's in that valley. Now for goodness sake start galloping."

*   *   *

With his ears flattened against his head, Saturn careered down the rough track in disarray. The acute discomfort he felt from the arrow wound made him arch his back continuously. He bucked powerfully to unseat his rider. Sue clung on to his mane like a limpet, hardly noticing that her surroundings had taken on a much wilder aspect. Having traversed the bend in the path, she knew she was now out of sight of Annalee. Already the reins had slipped from her fingers and she was terrified. She dug her nails into Saturn's neck to get a better grip. The stallion was completely mad. In his frenzied race to get rid of the weight on his back, and trying to alleviate the pain pulsating through his flank, he kicked out wildly. An enormous shadow loomed ahead and he baulked. In doing so, his rear end struck the rocky wall and the force of the blow knocked the arrow from his flesh.

In searing pain he reared almost upright, giving a savage whinny. Sue screamed out as she lost her hold and fell to the hard ground. Her head glanced off the rocky wall. Saturn galloped on, leaving her behind him in a dazed and shaken state. She remained where she had fallen, aware of a sharp pain in her head. Then fuzziness blotted out daylight and she floundered in a twilight world. The pain extended to her ears and a dull throbbing made her think her head would burst. She coughed – it was like a knife searing through her brain. She was vaguely aware of smoke that almost suffocated her and she gulped. Shadowy figures began moving around. As the roaring in her head increased, a rancid smell wafted over her. She was filled with repugnance but could not move away. Her limbs refused to obey her. In horror, she realised she could not even feel them.

Something very solid was prodded into her side and a voice spoke harshly above her. She flinched as hot smelly breath fanned her cheeks. The voice was guttural and made no sense whatsoever to her. The prod was repeated. Not so gentle the second time and caused unnecessary pain in her ribs. She wanted to speak, yell out to whoever was there, but she could not manage it. All her bodily functions were disorientated. Sue struggled to raise her head and felt something trickle down her face. Fear assailed her when she realised her eyes were not focusing properly.

The guttural voice was joined by another even harsher one. A big rough hand grasped a handful of her hair and jerked her head back with brutal force. She screamed out as agonising pain shot through her eyes. Her scream echoed all round the valley, reverberating off the rocky walls. Darkness took over her world as unconsciousness mercifully relieved her of all pain.

*   *   *

THE SECRET OF TAMSWORTH FOREST

Raithe and Annalee were galloping along the edge of the ravine, looking as though they were out for an evening canter. Before long, it was obvious Annalee had no heart for keeping up with her companion. She started to lag behind. They could be seen from quite a distance because their silhouettes were etched sharply against the backdrop of sky. The sun had started its descent in a mauve coloured sky and the shadows were beginning to lengthen. At their feet, down in the valley, mist was thickly forming, obliterating everything. In parts it looked like clouds. Raithe pulled up his mount, irritation showing on his sharp features. He waited for Annalee to catch up.

"Will you hurry yourself, woman," he snapped in annoyance as she came slowly abreast and halted. "You know it's essential for us to get back to the camp before we are missed. If you're going to delay me much more, I shall begin to wish you had never come."

Annalee's face was white and drawn. She suddenly looked old for her years. "I wish I hadn't," she retorted spiritedly. "I am not happy at what we have done, Raithe. It was rather callous when Sue was new to our world. There were other ways we could have got rid of her." Raithe opened his mouth to speak, but she quickly continued, "When we first planned this, our idea seemed all right, but now I don't think so. I've had second thoughts."

Raithe's glare was baleful. His face twisted with malevolence. Normally he had a willing accomplice in Annalee. She followed him uncomplainingly and he liked to feel the power he wielded. Yet since the

129

coming of this stranger who had been thrust into their midst, Annalee had changed.

"That's a bit late – isn't it? Just remember, once a thing is planned – it goes ahead. You know as well as I do I have every right to dispose of her," Raithe snapped. "I'm next in line to the throne, and people have to obey me." His tone also implied, 'And that goes for you too'.

Annalee answered him without thinking. "What will people say when they find out what you have done?"

"Are you going to tell them?" he asked. His face became ugly. "You are in this as much as I am. Just be careful what you tell that brother of yours when he starts asking questions."

"I think Thane has already guessed that I do not feel friendly towards her." Annalee was feeling apprehensive. "But you should be careful, Raithe. You've made your feelings known. When they find she is missing…"

"You won't say a word," Raithe spat out, "they have got nothing to go on that will lead them back to us."

"Let's go back to her," Annalee pleaded. "There is still time to…"

"Shut up and be silent," he interrupted furiously, "there is a rider heading this way and he has seen us. Now remember to back me up in whatever I say. We have got to be in union with each other otherwise he will think we are hiding something."

They both turned and stared in the direction of the newcomer. With hands shading their eyes against the setting sun, they saw the approaching rider was Amos.

THE SECRET OF TAMSWORTH FOREST

He was the last person they wanted to see. His horse thundered up to them and slid to a halt as he reined in sharply. His weathered face was inscrutable and he eyed them suspiciously. It was hard to tell if this meeting was accidental or planned. Raithe waited for him to speak, which was not very long in coming.

"What are you doing this far out from camp and at this time of day?" he asked. Breathing heavily he dismounted and fixed them with his searching eyes. "It will be getting dark soon and you know better than anyone this place is off limits because of the danger here."

"Can't think why anyone made that stupid rule," retorted Raithe coolly. "The air and scenery up here are great. Anyway, there's no need for you to get in a flap, old man. We can look after ourselves. We are on our way back as you can see, so leave us now."

"Are you presuming to give me orders?" Amos's voice was tight.

"I don't like being followed by you," retorted Raithe.

The way he said it was insulting. He was still feeling sore at the reprimand he had been given the other day. Amos stiffened. His colour rose but it went unnoticed under his tanned wrinkled skin. But his eyes became glacial and as he opened his mouth to berate the lad, a woman's scream travelled up the valley, making the hair stand up on his neck. The scream was not repeated and nothing stirred in the stillness around them. However, Annalee made a choking sound and her face looked ghastly. She swayed as if she were about to fall.

131

Raithe leapt off his horse and went to her, giving an admirable impression of being concerned. He caught hold of her wrist in a grip of steel. His words belied the look he cast at her.

"Are you feeling unwell, Annalee? There is nothing to be frightened of. You've got two men here to protect you. Come on – brace yourself and we'll get you home."

Annalee was trembling. She could hardly speak. From between stiff lips they both heard her say, "That scream was..." but before she could finish her sentence, Raithe cut her short and turned to the watching man, at the same time digging his nails viciously into her skin to shut her up. "Amos, can you help? That scream has made her feel faint. Those gypsies should be forcibly removed from this area. They are nothing better than scum. The way they ill-treat each other, and especially their treatment of women, is barbaric. Come on, Annalee – snap out of it for me."

Annalee moaned. Amos's face hardened. "Then it's a pity you decided to come this way," he snapped. For a few seconds he was bemused, as Raithe could be very convincing. Then he nodded curtly. There was nothing to be gained by arguing with him.

"You two get along – but first have you by any chance seen Saturn in your travels?"

"Saturn," echoed Raithe as he climbed back on his horse. His face was the picture of innocence as he looked at the older man. "The last time I saw him was at the picket line when we left earlier."

Amos turned to Annalee for confirmation and she just nodded without looking at him. She allowed Raithe to pick up her reins and lead her away. The old man was suspicious. He did not trust Raithe further than he could throw him. He had not missed the lad's spiteful action when he deliberately suppressed Annalee. He looked at her thoughtfully. He had never known her to be so subdued. They were up to something and he intended to watch them carefully. At the moment he had nothing to go on.

CHAPTER 9

THE GYPSIES

Sue opened her eyes and everything was dark. Her first thought was that she was blind. An obnoxious smell assailed her nose. It was all around her, cloying the air. A thudding pain hammered in her head and she felt nauseous. Maybe it would help if she were to be sick. At the moment, she just wished she was dead.

Her body was being jerked up and down and it was most uncomfortable because there was nothing she could do to stop it. She did not even know what was causing it. It felt as though someone was deliberately shaking her all over. A rattling noise added to the mayhem and echoed in her ears. Her head felt like an empty drum as the sounds bounced around. Then she heard the snort of a horse. It was followed by silence. Even the shaking stopped, which was a relief. So she was travelling somewhere. She had to get away – but from what – and how? She could not move on her own.

All hell suddenly broke loose. Raucous voices were shouting in a language she couldn't understand. Pain was all she was aware of. When the movement started up again, the pain accelerated. She was sick. She retched, out of control, and lay gasping, her face wet and sticky. Her first reaction was to wipe herself, but she was unable to lift her arms.

THE SECRET OF TAMSWORTH FOREST

She was pulled roughly upright. There was nothing gentle about the person doing it. The world swayed. She felt herself falling and there was nothing to stop her. Sue seemed to be hurtling so much that it pushed her back into oblivion.

*   *   *

The sun had already set over the camp when the men returned from their day's work. They had strengthened the gateway between the two worlds. It had been prophesied by the Shaman that the hold between would grow weaker and before long the link would break. The mission of Sonja had been completed. She was now with them. Visitors were not welcomed to Therossa but sometimes, unwittingly, they crossed the border. It had come to their notice that two strangers persistently tried to find the way through. Hopefully, that had been stopped.

Thane was happy and content as they ambled home. He now looked forward to relaxing around the fire with a mug of ale. It had been an interesting day for them, thwarting that couple of men who were getting too near to their boundaries. White Hawk became the hero of the day because he was efficient in doing his job. Thane smiled when he thought about what he had done. It would be a long time before those two men returned to interfere again.

As they neared the camp, Thane scanned the area for White Hawk, but he had vanished as was his wont. The wolf was a law unto himself as he wandered the

135

countryside, hunting as he pleased. Thane knew that a call from him and the wolf would be by his side in an instant. He was the most obedient of all the wolves. By the time they reached the settlement, Raithe and Annalee were already mingling with the people. Raithe was in high spirits, making himself indispensable to the women, who could be forgiven for thinking he was marvellous. When he put himself out, Raithe could be very charming. Annalee sat a little apart, brooding as she made patterns in the earth with a twig. She was not in a sociable mood and most people acceded to her wish to be alone. Her beautiful face held a pensive look. For the first time in her life she wondered about Raithe. Was he really so cold-hearted as he appeared? The communal meal was already well underway and a crowd of people were gathered around the fire. A huge stag was roasting on the spit. Pots of all sizes were placed around, and the aroma coming from it all was mouth-watering.

Annalee looked towards the picket line where the men were busy grooming their horses. It was a job of top priority to them. Horses were the mainstay of the community. Everyone looked after the horse they rode, it was an unwritten law, but Annalee felt no qualms that she had passed that job onto a young boy who would do anything for her. Raithe as usual stalked off and expected the boy to do his work without asking or saying thank you.

Annalee felt her stomach knot as Thane came towards her, but he only ruffled her hair and passed on, saying pleasantly, "What kind of a day have you had?"

THE SECRET OF TAMSWORTH FOREST

Annalee sighed in relief and watched him go up to another man. Raithe took this opportunity to sidle up to her, and hissed in her ear.

"You had better start looking happy before someone begins asking awkward questions and wants to know what is wrong with you. Thought of any plausible answers?"

Annalee kept her eyes fixed firmly to the ground and clenched her teeth. "They are going to find out that Saturn is missing before long. Have you thought up any answers yourself?" she snapped back.

Raithe glowered at her, annoyed she dare speak to him like that. He would have said more but he happened to catch the eye of a woman looking at him and quickly changed his scowl to a charming smile. He swaggered away until he caught sight of Amos approaching Annalee. Filled with anxiety, he quickly changed direction. He intended moving back to her when, to his dismay, he saw Thane heading that way as well. He arrived just in time to hear Amos say dryly, "Feeling better now, Annalee?"

Annalee stared at him blankly for a moment and then nodded her head. "Did you find Saturn?" she asked politely, ignoring his question.

That alerted Thane directly, Saturn being his horse. He had left him behind today to rest him. "What's the matter with Saturn?" he interrupted, and turned to his sister with accusing eyes. "Have you taken him out?"

Before she had a chance to defend herself, Amos said smoothly, "Sorry, Thane. Saturn seems to have run off and I have been searching for him this last hour or so. I happened to meet Raithe and your sister way down in the valley, but I couldn't ask them much because your sister was feeling unwell and Raithe saw her home." It was the truth, but not the way Raithe would have put it and certainly not the way Thane saw it. He was livid. "What the hell were you doing going that way?" he thundered, his voice carrying over the whole encampment. It caused people to pause in their conversation and raise their heads. "You've been told time and time again not to go near that place. I suppose you took Saturn because I wasn't around. What did he do – run off?"

"I haven't seen or touched him." Annalee, her eyes blazing with defiance, glared at him. "And we told Amos so."

"True," added Amos in an ominous voice, "and I still have not found him."

"Well you can't blame us," Raithe cut in smoothly, and added sarcastically to Amos, "I thought you were supposed to be a tracker."

Amos did not rise to the bait, but he quivered with silent rage. Thane thought it was anger and tried to calm the old man before he exploded. "How do you know Saturn went towards the valley?" he asked.

"Someone told me," Amos answered sourly.

Annalee looked alarmed and Thane considered the implications of that remark. Raithe crossed the clearing in two strides. Thane just managed to stop him from grabbing hold of the old man. Raithe shook him off and shouted, "Don't you try to make trouble because of your incompetence! Tell us by whom, man? Speak up and stop dithering." He moved closer to Annalee and appraised Amos, his face haughty, hoping to make the man appear small, but Amos did not cower or move back; he returned the look with a steely glint in his eyes and said,

"One of the guards on watch saw him gallop off."

He had the satisfaction of now seeing fear in the young prince's face. Food was forgotten for the moment. Every able-bodied person had turned to watch them. Amos looked like the cat who had stolen the cream. His lips tightened. He knew he was right in suspecting foul play and felt really delighted in adding, "There was a rider on his back."

A gasp came from the onlookers. Thane became suddenly anxious because he had not found Sue. He felt his blood running cold. "Did he know who it was?" he asked crisply.

Amos paused to get the desired effect. Without taking his eyes off Raithe, who was now staring at him like a mesmerised rabbit, he said clearly, "The watch was not sure of her name, but by the way she was dressed, it was Sue. She chased after two other riders who were ahead of her."

The silence was explosive. Only the crackling of the fire and the fat spitting from the roast made a noise. Annalee did not know how she stayed upright. Thane was consumed with fury; he needed no second guess as to who the other riders were. Raithe laughed callously as he quickly regained his composure.

"Do you presume to think Annalee and I knew she was following us? We are not in the habit of looking

139

over our shoulders for serfs. In any case, it would not have crossed our minds that she, being so lowborn, could ride a horse. If any of you had any common sense, you would realise she could have turned off in many directions. It doesn't take much more sense to work out she must have fallen off him."

Thane's look could have killed him. He would love to wipe that smirk off his arrogant face, but right now there were more pressing things to do. He swung round and shouted to his men,

"Forget your food. I want a search party out right now."

"Wait, lad," said Amos, "I know you're worried, but it's dark. Wait until dawn. Saturn and his rider are no doubt lost, but they may come back in the night, Saturn knows his way home. Just keep an extra watch with plenty of guiding lights. It will turn out for the best – you'll see."

Then Amos glanced down at Annalee and saw the wound on the back of her hand. He doubted very much that Sue would return and he smelt treachery. He remembered that scream which had really upset her. Tonight was not the time to tell Thane of his suspicions.

*   *   *

Cailli poured a hot brew containing special herbs, procured by Neela, into a hip flask. Picking it up he went over to the log where Thane sat with his head bowed. The light of the fire was comforting, giving an illusion of warmth, but it was also unkind as it threw shadows over his drawn face. Most of the camp had discreetly retired to their caves, realising there was nothing they could do that would be of any help tonight. The fact that Sue was missing cast a damper over the community. Cailli thrust the flask into his friend's hands and sat beside him, carefully choosing his words.

"You should rest like everyone else. If you go on at this rate you will not be fit for anything tomorrow. It's then you are going to need all your faculties working."

Thane knew he was correct, but he blamed himself bitterly for leaving Sue on her own for so long. If he was honest, she had not entered his mind during the excitement of the day's activities, and he had been gone all day. How could he blame her for riding off on his horse? Raithe, with his sly digs, was not being any help. He could at least show a little friendship towards her for his mother's sake. Thane raised his hand and gripped the flask so tightly his knuckles gleamed white.

"I can't understand why she went off on her own," he muttered distraughtly. "She has no idea of the dangers this land holds. It's nothing like her world. Anyone here would willingly have gone with her had she only asked."

Cailli chewed thoughtfully on his lower lip. "I don't think she went alone," he said at length.

"You mean Raithe and Annalee were with her?"

Cailli nodded reluctantly, realising he was incriminating Thane's sister. "But I don't think for a moment that they would harm her," he added hastily. "I dare say they thought it might be fun to get her lost. Surely you noticed how surprised they both were that Sue and Saturn had not returned."

Thane's jaw tightened. He had noticed, and didn't believe them. Amos was right in saying Raithe needed to be watched. He gulped down his drink with a grimace and jumped to his feet, unable to sit still any longer. He would find Amos, whom he felt was hiding something from him. He had only taken only one pace when a distraction from the picket line held his attention. Several voices were shouting at once above the unearthly noise which came from the horses. Then above it all was the shrill whinnying of one particular horse – Saturn. Thane and Cailli dashed to the scene, hoping to see that both Saturn and Sue had returned.

The men were hanging on to Saturn who was rearing and jumping with fear. He bucked wildly with his hooves flaying the air. If they approached him from the rear he rounded on them with nostrils flaring and showing his teeth. A quick glance showed that Sue was nowhere to be seen, which, taking the horse's condition into consideration, meant she must have been thrown and was lying hurt somewhere.

Amos approached the frightened stallion, showing no fear. He caught hold of his bridle and spoke softly to the frenzied animal. The men watched in admiration. Amos was good with horses. Slowly the wild look left his eyes. He quivered at first, then gradually quietened down and stood passive while Amos stroked his foam-flecked neck. His sides were heaving, a sure sign he had been galloping for a long time.

THE SECRET OF TAMSWORTH FOREST

Thane and Cailli drew nearer. It was not that they were frightened of the stallion, but it was best that only one person handled him while he was in such a nervous state. Thane cast a critical eye over his horse and they both saw the wound on his haunch. It had been bleeding profusely. The grass was dark around his stamping feet.

"My God – he's lame," Cailli exclaimed in shocked surprise and Thane, who bent closer, staring at the torn leg, added grimly, "That's an arrow wound he's got."

The implications of that were serious. Someone had deliberately shot him, most likely the gypsies. But somehow that did not ring true, the gypsies thought more of horses than people. Thane stood up and blew the horn hanging from his belt. Men ranging over the near vicinity were soon gathered about him. In one of the caves, Annalee shuddered and tried to cover her ears from the sound. Thane looked over the gathered men with a face that seemed carved from granite.

"Tomorrow we search for Sue. I want all the best trackers assembled here by dawn. She must be found before the Queen hears anything about her being missing. In the meantime, double the guard tonight. There is no telling what trouble there is out there."

*   *   *

In the confined place where she was, Sue stirred. It was still dark. An inky blackness surrounded her which successfully kept out all light and the rancid smell about her kept out fresh air as well. Her breathing was

143

becoming shallower by the minute. It was an effort to make her lungs work. Sue was burning up with fever. She felt there was a fire somewhere beneath her that was continuously being stoked up. Rivulets of sweat ran down her body and she was lying in a pool of water. Even that was hot and was making her sweat all the more. Her head seemed to be enclosed in bands of iron and with her every laboured breath a hammer seemed to strike in her skull. She wondered what was happening. Why had no one found her and released her from this hell? What had happened to Raithe and Annalee? They must have seen what happened to her – or looked for her when she did not turn up.

Sue attempted to lift an arm but nothing moved. Maybe she had not got arms anymore – or they were tied down. She tried her legs, they would not move either. Were her feet dead – or were they tied down as well? She gingerly turned her head and the effort affected her eyes. She closed them for protection and to clear away the wetness. By now her breath was rasping – hurting. Where was she? Why could she not see? The effort was getting too much for her so she gave up trying and drifted back into her dark world. It was safe there. Nothing hurt her. She would not bother anymore.

*   *   *

A sudden draught of cold air caused Sue's eyes to open with a snap. It was still dark, nothing had changed. Her whole existence seemed to be swathed in darkness. Maybe she was underground in some horrible sunless

THE SECRET OF TAMSWORTH FOREST

cave – alone and forgotten. But no, this air was fresh. A door was open nearby. She peered into the blackness, concentrating and trying to get her eyes used to it. As the air caressed her skin she made herself face the direction from which it came. After what seemed an interminable time, it became easier to distinguish between two different shades of black. She was sure there was an opening before her. It was like a square framed in black and in the middle unsubstantial shadows were moving.

Sue willed her eyes to stay open and not succumb to sleep. It was imperative to find out all she could about where she was while she could. The unaccustomed strain of keeping her neck raised was making it ache. She was rewarded by seeing a glimmer of red. It told her beyond all doubt that a fire burnt somewhere outside. She must be among a community of travelling people. Yet why didn't they show any concern about her? The stark thought came to her that she may be a prisoner. It made her go cold. Common sense told her that if that was the case, they would not have left the door open.

Escape? Sue's nerves tingled. Why didn't she try to? She focused on herself for the first time and attempted to move. Disappointment was so great she nearly cried, every part of her body was securely fastened to something she thought was a bed. It became obvious now that she was a prisoner. Sue licked her lips and found they were swollen, dry. She tried to swallow. Her throat was parched and her tongue swollen. With sudden clarity she knew her health was at a low ebb

145

and she knew she had to get out of there if she ever wanted to get better. Helplessness engulfed her. Why had no one tried to find her? Both Annalee and Raithe must know what had happened to her. All sorts of possibilities occurred to her but she shied away from them in disbelief. They would never abandon her. Then she thought of Saturn. Was he here or had he galloped off to freedom? If he was here, maybe she could escape on him – that's if she ever got free of her shackles. The dilemma she found herself in made her head ache and she did not notice that someone had entered her prison.

The first she knew about whoever it was, was that person's laboured breathing on her. They bent down and shook her roughly. A blinding pain shot through her eyes and seared through her head and she gasped weakly. A guttural voice spoke to her. This time it was the voice of a woman but her conversation was still unintelligible. Sue tried to speak to let the woman know she was aware of her, but no words came. The woman put two brawny arms round her, releasing something that allowed her to be pulled into a sitting position. The stench coming from her body was nauseating and Sue tried to cringe away. This action was greeted with hostility. Then she felt the rim of a drinking vessel thrust to her lips and a liquid was forced in. The vile taste of whatever it was made her retch and automatically spit it out. The large woman straightened and with a foul oath she struck Sue round the head. The brutal force of it made her see stars. Then the woman said something that did not sound very complimentary

THE SECRET OF TAMSWORTH FOREST

and shoved Sue back down on the bed. Cursing, she lumbered away, taking the bowl with her.

Sue lay where she had fallen, dazed, and her spirit broken. Whatever the liquid had been that was forced into her mouth, was still there. The bitterness of its aftertaste made her shudder, and the hopelessness of her situation caused despair to flood over her. How was it ever going to be possible to escape – she was trapped.

Then she realised that the woman had not re-shackled her. Gritting her teeth she attempted to raise herself up, but in her weakened condition it was hard work and beads of sweat formed on her forehead. By the time she attained a sitting position her exhaustion was complete, so for several minutes she remained motionless, then she gathered strength and started looking for all the other gadgets that kept her shackled down.

An explosive noise came from the outside. Although the words spoken were foreign, she was sufficiently aware to realise they were arguing – and violently at that. She debated whether or not to lie down again, in case someone else walked in. She had not come into contact with anyone yet who was not brutal. However, the decision was not hers to make. Bright light suddenly illuminated her prison, making her eyes flinch. A flaring light was held aloft by a brawny arm. It came straight towards her. She could not see the person who held the torch because the unaccustomed light dazzled her eyes, but at the same time the glare from the flames left his face in obscurity and caused shadows to dance on the walls.

Sue shrank back as far as she could get, pressing against the woodwork until it dug into her shoulders. Her eyes stung, she kept blinking. Fear was evident on her face and she wondered what fate was about to befall her now. Although they were indistinguishable to her, there were several people gathered behind this man. They were silent watchers. The cruel light showed up the disfigurement on her face with a clarity that would have dismayed her could she have seen it.

For a moment the man with the torch just stood and studied her. Sue was keyed up, waiting for the first blow to fall. Maybe he could read her thoughts because without moving he snapped out an order. Someone quickly came forward and took the torch out of his hand, leaving him free. Then Sue's terrified eyes could see his face. He was dark skinned and swarthy, with tight curly black hair and bushy eyebrows which met above his hawk-like nose. Large ornate gold earrings dangled from his earlobes and reached his shoulders. His open-necked shirt exposed a chest with matted dark hair. He reached out with a large hand and it terrified her. She closed her eyes tightly. It touched her face and stayed there. Surprisingly, it was gentle. Then he spoke in a grating voice.

"Open your eyes please?"

It sounded more like an order and she automatically obeyed him before she realised he had spoken in her own language. He smiled, showing a mouth full of teeth, many of them were gold and matched his earrings.

"Why are you so afraid?" he asked.

THE SECRET OF TAMSWORTH FOREST

Sue stared into his almost black eyes, unable to say that the treatment she had received here was brutal. He was obviously a person of importance amongst them and the truth could do more harm than good. He was waiting for an answer and he would not wait forever. She swallowed and tried to speak, but ended up croaking. For the first time in her life she was pleased she was unable to answer.

His lips thinned as he touched her mouth and fingered it gently. Without her realising what he was doing, he unobtrusively parted her lips and looked into her mouth. He stood up and angrily surveyed his people clustered behind him. Ruthlessly he slated them, his guttural voice austere. Sue wished she knew what he was saying, but after a while all the people except two vanished, a woman who looked very gaunt and a young boy. The man turned to Sue after he had placed the burning torch in a bracket on the wall. His manner was abrupt. She quickly realised he was not a man to cross. He pushed the woman forward with unnecessary roughness, causing her to stumble, but she uttered no complaint, her face was expressionless.

"This woman is Elina," he said, "and the skinny rat with her is someone she looks after. They are going to help you recover. I shall speak to you after I have made a journey, but hear me clearly, woman. Do not try to escape from here. If I find you gone it will be this boy who will suffer my anger. I shall flay him with my whip until it reaches his bone."

149

There was a sort of relish in his voice and with an evil smile he turned and walked away, leaving her staring after him in stupefaction.

CHAPTER 10

SEARCHING FOR SUE

The night passed without any further interruptions. Burning torches were everywhere. A haze of light lit up the sky. There were two reasons for this. One was just in case Sue returned and the other was to deter evil forces. Tension in the camp was palpable, but the men closest to Thane knew this was not caused by Saturn's misfortunes. They accepted Thane as their leader, unconditionally, and being loyal they kept watch without asking questions. By morning, the whole camp had heard of Saturn's misfortune. The news split their loyalties. Half wanted to leave the area at once and return over the mountains for home before more disaster assailed them. It was the Shaman's firm hand which stayed them.

Amos had been to see their spiritual leader, and whatever had passed between them would never be known. The Shaman did not often get himself involved in the everyday living of the camp, but on this occasion the men found him unexpectedly in their midst. With a strong voice he berated them for their lack of courage. "There are enemies of the Queen at work here amongst you," he said, "you would be better employed finding out what caused harm to befall the horse and its rider, an innocent rider I might add who was a guest in our midst."

Most of the hunters and trackers rallied to Thane's call and were assembled that morning in the clearing, mounted on their horses and raring to go. The sun shone above the horizon to greet the new day. It gave the promise of a fine morning, which pleased them all. They were grouped in two separate parties, men and women together. Thane was disappointed Annalee had not bothered to volunteer, as she was one of their best trackers. At Thane's command they turned the horses to leave but suddenly a yell halted the group. Red in the face Raithe rode up indignantly, his whole demeanour displaying outrage "Did you deliberately forget me?" he asked acidly. "I am the Prince of your realm and you should wait for me."

His head was lifted arrogantly as though expecting an apology but none came, so he continued. "Furthermore, I am the best tracker you have. You must all know that I think it important to find this Sue woman without delay."

Several of the women winced at his choice of words. To call her 'this Sue woman' was almost as though he classed her as a piece of baggage.

"We know that alright," growled Amos in a voice that belied what he really thought, "and we didn't forget you. After your long excursion yesterday we imagined you would much rather rest today."

"Then stop thinking, my good man, and do what is important," said Raithe, sneering condescendingly. "No one rests when a horse is lame. Now," he continued,

THE SECRET OF TAMSWORTH FOREST

"where are we looking first?" He glared from one to the other.

"Where you suggested yesterday," retorted Amos grimly. "You said the horse and girl probably went into the hills, and we know what dangers lurk there. You can join Cailli's party who are searching that area."

A scowl crossed Raithe's face but Amos did not bat an eyelid. He kept up the pressure by adding, "Do you find something wrong with that decision, lad?"

"Lad." The word swirled round in his head. Raithe had a malicious desire to hit the old man, but he swallowed it and answered petulantly, "I wish to search the top of the ravine. I will not take orders from you, Amos. I will go with Thane's party and that's that."

Thane, who had no wish to join in this fight, stiffened. He pushed his way through the group to Raithe, his eyes betraying the rage he felt. He rode right up to the prince until their faces were level. It pleased him to see the boy retreat slightly. "Just remember where you are and why. Your mother, our Queen, wants a man returned to her, not an undisciplined boy with the attributes of a stable-hand. An order is an order. You heard what Amos said. Obey it or stay behind and help with the cooking."

"That's woman's work. Who does he think he is, giving orders?" spluttered Raithe, glaring at the old man.

"Do you wish me to remind you what to do?" asked Thane icily, "and while we are clearing the air, why is my sister not with you?"

153

At the mention of Annalee, Raithe decided to calm down and not lie about her absence. With smouldering eyes he turned to Cailli without another word. He had the satisfaction of knowing they would not find anything along the ridge. That trail had gone cold by now. He smirked at how clever he had been, and Cailli – noting it – wondered what it meant. For the second time the group moved off but they had not gone very far when one of the riders said in surprise,

"There's another rider coming after us."

Even though everyone heard, Cailli's group continued onwards, but Thane stopped and looked back towards the camp. Pleasure flooded through him when he recognised his sister heading their way. He was really pleased she had made it and showed interest in tracking Sue. It felt like old times. Then he caught sight of Raithe's face as he turned in his saddle to see who was coming to join them. There was a shocked expression and it was full of anger and something else; fear. It was obvious he had not expected Thane's sister to put in an appearance.

Annalee came up to the group. She looked strained, her face was pale and her lips were compressed in a straight line. Swollen eyes told their own tale. Her smile was absent when she looked towards her brother. In a clipped voice she said,

"If I have delayed you then I'm sorry, but I'm here now."

Raithe fell back from his team and moved towards her, but Thane quickly put his horse between them,

THE SECRET OF TAMSWORTH FOREST

stopping contact. If Annalee noticed, she did not show it.

"You had better keep up with Cailli before you lose him," he said evenly. "You don't want to waste time."

"Annalee is coming with me," Raithe glowered.

"I think not," said Thane with expressionless eyes, "she is coming with us. Annalee – go to the head with Amos. Oh – I beg your pardon. You want to say something else, Raithe?"

Raithe breathed heavily, wondering why he put his faith in women. His smouldering eyes bored into Annalee, but she never looked in his direction. He shrugged his shoulders and with a sour expression on his face, turned back to Cailli. She would not let him down, he thought savagely, or would she? He was left wondering.

*   *   *

The eight people trotting along the ridge were in harmony with each other; except for Annalee, there was good comradeship amongst them. Tansy gave as good as she got. With her short-cropped hair and masculine look, no one dared to make the mistake of treating her as a girl, unless they wanted to find themselves pinned against a tree with arrows. She was a wizard with the bow. The men treated her as an equal and their light-hearted banter did not lessen the seriousness of their mission this day. A little way along the ridge they fanned out, looking meticulously for signs of hoof prints. It was not a well-used area, being off-limits to

155

KATHLEEN B. WILSON

people from the camp, so there was no guarantee they would find any.

As the group made its way slowly along the treeless ridge, no one looked down into the valley which was still thickly shrouded with mist. Where they were, the early morning mist had evaporated and the sun was beginning to be felt. The day dragged on and conversation petered out. Searching became hot work. Once the mist had been burnt up, the views from their elevated height were stunning. At the bottom of the drop, water flowed rapidly in miniature streams and churned as it rushed over boulders and down waterfalls. The trackers did not have time to admire the scenery. Thane was a hard task-master. On the type of ground they were covering, tracks were hard to find. Because of this, they were now leading the horses. At a patch of sandy soil, Amos squatted down and studied the ground intently.

"It's obvious that two horses were travelling together at this point," he said, "if you look over here, you can see a third horse came along. That was Saturn by the way."

He stood up and stretched the old bones in his back for a brief respite. The others gathered round to look. This was the first evidence they had that Saturn actually came this way.

"Are you sure of that?" asked Thane, looking up.

"Aye, there is a peculiar mark on one of his back hooves. I would recognise it anywhere," was the response.

156

THE SECRET OF TAMSWORTH FOREST

"Would he have thrown Sue by now?" asked Tansy, "because I have not seen any signs of it having happened."

Amos grunted, "at this point she was obviously still on his back and the other two riders must have seen her." He glared pointedly across at Annalee who was aimlessly leading her horse and taking no interest in proceedings. "Are you helping us, Miss?" he asked sarcastically in her direction.

It was as though she never heard a word – or did not want to. Annalee was shut away in a world of her own. The others, not surprisingly, were fed up with her, wondering why she had bothered to come with them. So far, she had not uttered one word. Had she been anyone else other than Thane's sister, they would have got rid of her. She kept close to the edge of the drop, too near for safety, and stared down into the valley. At least she was keeping out of their way, but it worried Thane; every so often he gazed at her surreptitiously. Amos touched his arm and said gruffly,

"We can't worry about her. There is still a long way to go."

Thane nodded unwillingly, but her attitude annoyed him, he could not worry about his sister right now. There would be time to have things out with her later. Sue was his concern now. The band of trackers moved on, and eyes diligently scanned the ground for clues. Silence was at last broken by one man shouting out, "There are more tracks over here – but they're going in the wrong direction. Do they count?"

157

Thane and Amos went over to look while everyone else took a well-earned break to ease their aching backs. One or two cast dark looks at Thane's sister.

"So they all returned from along this way." Thane felt relief sweep over him until Amos replied grimly, "The tracks indicate the exact opposite. They did not all return. These tracks belong to Raithe, Annalee and myself. I'm sorry, but not Saturn, Thane, we must push further ahead. We have got to find out where he went if we want to find Sue. It's just a pity your sister won't help us."

"Well she doesn't know," Thane began – but stopped at the cynical expression on Amos's face and closed his mouth with a snap. Amos said just the right thing to get everyone moving. It took another two hours of tedious tracking before they reached the spot where only yesterday Amos had met the other two. No one had found any signs of Saturn coming this way. They decided to stop for a break. Some carried a pouch of food and others a flask of water. They shared it out amongst themselves. Thane felt the food would choke him. He stared moodily ahead. This stop was very much against his will. Time was precious if they hoped to find out what happened to Sue.

Annalee looked distraught – not that many of them noticed, or cared come to that. She let go of her mount and stood perilously near the edge of the drop, as though she was debating about whether or not to jump over. Her eyes were fixed unblinkingly on the floor of the valley. The wind ruffled her clothes. Her unresponsiveness had started to get at everyone. Tansy deliberated for a moment, watching her, before she made up her mind and walked to her side.

There was a time when she and Annalee were inseparable and known as the terrible twins. It was a game to them to test their skills against each other in friendly rivalry. No one ever saw that their friendship would come to an end. It was Raithe who came between them. His interference put an end to everything. He wanted Annalee all to himself. Tansy would never give him the pleasure of knowing how much he had hurt her.

She stood quietly for a moment watching Annalee, knowing better than to touch her standing where she was. One false move and she would topple over the edge. In a very matter of fact voice, she said pleasantly,

"It's strange, you know. I've always been tempted to go down to that valley. It's so beautiful, and looks the picture of tranquillity."

Annalee never moved or acknowledged her presence. From her throat came a stifled sob. Tansy turned to her in surprise, and with dismay noticed tears streaming down her pallid face. She couldn't ever remember having seen Annalee cry. Instinctively she put an arm round her old friend's shoulder, attempting to draw her away from the edge.

"What's wrong, Annalee?" she asked. "Tell me. You know I will help you if I can. I hate seeing you like this."

Just for a second, Annalee was passive. Then she violently flung off Tansy's arm and glared at her. "You don't want to know. None of you do – go away from me." Her choked voice wavered on another sob, and her eyes dilated. "You can't help me. Nobody can. It's... it's too late, because... because I was implicated in what happened. Did you hear me? I'm part of what happened to Sue." She could not control her sobs, heedless of the fact that everyone was listening. "No – don't come any nearer to me," she warned as Tansy made to move forward again, Annalee took a step back and nearly lost her footing, hysteria rapidly taking control of her. "Sue, she didn't find it was tranquil when she screamed; and do you know what?" Her eyes glazed. She was not focusing anymore. "We didn't care and rode away."

Before Tansy could figure out what her next move would be, Annalee ran to her horse, sprang on his back, and immediately galloped off, back the way they had just come. The 'soldier' in Tansy came to her aid. Without thinking of the consequences, she whistled to her own mount and gave chase. The men watched them both go in amazement and Thane hastily rallied them together, saying grimly,

"We can't worry about them. There is still a lot to be done and we are two trackers short. Let's get on with it."

"Aye – let's do that," said Amos in a satisfied voice. He thought grimly that Tansy might break down her defences when she caught up with Annalee. If that happened, then Raithe would not have a leg to stand on.

*   *   *

THE SECRET OF TAMSWORTH FOREST

The men toiled over the uneven ground, determined not to give in. In places, the ground was sandy and they were rewarded with evidence that Saturn had come this far. Surprisingly, they missed the extra pair of eyes that were Tansy's. The sun was just on the point of going down when the search changed. They were faced with a jumble of tracks which converged on each other from which two sets emerged. Saturn's and another set. They both went straight to the edge of the cliff, but only one set went over. They stared in stunned silence, and gathered round to study them. Amos said through his teeth,

"Saturn went down that pathway we see before us and judging by the depths of his tracks – he still had his rider on his back. What madness made her go down there? The others did not follow. Surely they would have told her of the dangers as she was new to this place."

A feeling of disquiet fell over everyone. Thane's face was ashen. To go down there meant danger of death from the people who lived in the valley. Tribes of nomadic gypsies. From time to time they inhabited the place. They were brutal and ruthless. Their numbers vast – so many it was impossible to keep track of their movements. If Sue was in their hands: he shuddered and felt his gall rising at the thought. Sue would never have gone down there willingly, he was sure of that. She must have been deliberately fooled. No wonder Annalee was off-colour coming back this way. He would wring the truth out of her when he got his hands on her. He knew now for certain, they had been plotting

161

to do her harm – but his sister! Why had he ignored Amos? He realised this could be the reason why she had galloped off.

"If she went down there," Thane could hardly speak for the dread he was feeling, "then I'm following."

"Don't be daft, man," one of the trackers said vehemently, "are you trying to get yourself killed?"

"Thane's right," agreed Amos. "We shall all go down there except you, Orma. Numbers make for safety. You look after the horses up here. Now, let's see what tracks we can pick up by following him."

Five men followed the path down, swearing as they slithered on the loose rock. Hoof prints were hard to find, but every so often, one was visible. When they reached the bend, it was noticeable that the earth was churned up and part of the outer edge of the cliff had fallen away. Amos swore and said, "Saturn reared up here for some reason."

Thane paled, thinking how far Sue would have fallen if she had gone over the edge. He bent down, touching something dark on the earth. He was balancing on the very brink of the drop, and his voice was disbelieving when he said, "This is blood."

The men stared at each other, realising how vulnerable they were in the spot where they stood. If the gypsies decided to attack them, they stood no chance whatsoever of defending themselves. Foreboding was building up. Amos scratched his head, looking puzzled.

"How could Saturn have been shot just here? This is an unlikely place for an ambush."

THE SECRET OF TAMSWORTH FOREST

"Do you think that's Sue's blood?" asked another tracker unwisely.

Thane felt helpless, but he had no intention of giving up. Without looking at the others he continued to go further down the track, which narrowed considerably. The others followed, their eyes alert. Apart from the occasional cry of a bird, only silence prevailed around them. That told them there were no gypsies nearby. A soft wind blew in their face, there was no sign of smoke, and no smells assailed their nostrils. If there had been anyone here, they were long gone by now. It seemed as though they had been scrambling for hours when Amos halted them, with a whistle of astonishment escaping through his teeth.

"Here is the evidence we need, men. There is more blood scattered around here. I would say Saturn threw his rider at this point."

Thane stared bleakly at the scene before him. There was no sign of Sue lying unconscious anywhere and if he was honest with himself, he did not expect to find her. Someone had taken her and it could only be one of the many bands of gypsies who travelled these parts. It was useless to go any further because gypsies knew the art of covering their tracks and would be miles away by now. The whole situation smelt of foul play.

The group of rescuers noted Saturn still went on without his rider. They had achieved all that they could today, and nothing had helped in the search for Sue. The nomadic tribes were well known for their depraved way of life. People like themselves were of no consequence to them, but they valued horses, so Saturn

163

was lucky to get away. Yet it appeared they had shot him. That did not make sense. In the next few seconds that all became clear.

One of the trackers shouted, "I've found the arrow which was shot at Saturn." He held it aloft – but it did not cause any jubilation and his expression was unreadable. Thane snatched the arrow from him – not believing what he saw. Rage took over. He was furious because he had been so blind.

"This belongs to Raithe," he exclaimed vehemently. The others looked startled. Thane examined the arrow with its royal markings and breathed deeply, saying, "What was the point of making the horse lame?"

Amos took the arrow from his hand and placed it carefully in his quiver. "If you don't know by now I shall not spell it out. Raithe shot from the ridge-top when Saturn first reared. He wanted Sue to be thrown. I don't expect for one minute he meant any real harm to the horse."

Thane clenched his fists as he thought back on all of Amos's warnings. "But he meant to harm Sue," he groaned. "Why? Why, in God's name?"

No one answered him. They all found something to occupy themselves with but everyone present knew why. Thane was too close to the situation to think clearly, and in his frame of mind – it boded ill for Annalee and Raithe.

CHAPTER 11

BARRY MEETS THE GIRLS

Barry manfully tried to ignore his painful knee and decided for safety's sake to keep off all paths. He must remain hidden until he found out if the people living here were as friendly as Thane. He pushed his way through the thick greenery, searching for a sheltered spot where he could sit down in private and sort himself out. Someone must live nearby, and if he was lucky, he or she might just help him. First though, he had to remove some of his clothing. He was soaking wet, and even though the sun was hot, he was shivering. But he was sure that the way he entered this world was not the way he was supposed to. White Hawk had brought him the only way he knew. The way the wolves came.

Where was White Hawk now? He hoped the wolf would return and find him. With the wolf beside him he would feel safe, because he could lead him to where he wanted to go. After all, he was linked to Thane. Somehow, Barry had the feeling this was not going to happen.

He pushed on with the determination of youth, going in what he hoped was the right direction. Every so often he was slapped in the face by obstinate branches. Flies were thick about his head, landing on him to suck up

165

the moisture gathered on his forehead. He did not mind that, but it was hard to stomach the persistent buzzing and the overzealous ones getting into his eyes. He knew if he was a girl he would be crying by now. It's a good job he hadn't included Priscilla in this venture. The thickness of the shrubbery was stifling. Were the bushes ever going to thin out and give him some space? They couldn't remain as thick as this forever. A branch made a nasty gash right across his face. He smeared blood all over his cheek when he lifted a hand to rub the sore place. The flies zoomed in on him, settled on the cut. Barry's nerves were reaching breaking point. He bit his lip to stop himself from shouting out, and determinedly kept going.

With foliage forever brushing over him, the flies had difficulty in making a meal out of his flesh. They were swept away as the branches continuously moved around his head, and twice they nearly removed his glasses. He gave no thought to the time. He pushed onwards until he realised the sun was sinking and he had no wish to spend a night out in the open. Anything could live in this terrain, it was like a jungle. He knew for a fact that wolves ran wild.

Thinking of them triggered his imagination. He was sure he heard a howl. His ears pricked up. Could that be White Hawk? When a few more howls joined in, Barry knew there must be a pack. Near at hand, something slithered past his feet. He stopped momentarily to regain his breath and gazed about for anything that wasn't trees. His heart leapt. A few yards more and he would be out in the open, ahead of him were barren

THE SECRET OF TAMSWORTH FOREST

hills. Barry surged forward. In his haste and in the half-light, he did not see the hole and went crashing to the ground. A searing pain shot through his ankle and he used language that would have made Aunt Moira curl up in horror.

It was the last straw as far as he was concerned. His exploring fingers told him his ankle was swelling. Common sense restrained him from removing his shoe as that would give some sort of support. Of all the bad luck! He could not stay here. A place was needed to hide for the night and more than anything else, he needed the use of his legs if he was going to find Sue.

For a few minutes, pain made him rest. Thank goodness the flies had gone. He was about to remove his pack when a growl sounded nearby. Barry changed his mind and thought of moving on. He found it impossible to walk without aid so started to crawl instead through the long grass. Directly his knees touched the ground he knew that was a bad idea. After crawling through an underground tunnel for most of the day, his knees were still sore from the experience, and also very bruised. He had chosen a very painful way to move forward.

Doggedly he kept on, trying to pretend the Professor was behind him to keep himself going. The weight of the rucksack put extra pressure on his shoulders and now they hurt, as well as his knees. The wind blew through his wet clothes. In spite of all these setbacks, he still went ahead. The exertion did nothing for him. He was still shivering.

167

It was becoming a losing battle. The light deteriorated fast. He could not see much at ground level because the grass was above his head. He gritted his teeth and raised himself up on his knees, and a whiff of smoke assailed his nostrils. In the distance there was a red glow. As he strained to look, he could make out two people and some horses in the flickering light.

Barry gulped. He was beyond caring if they were friendly or not, he needed assistance. It was almost impossible to drag himself to his feet, so he shouted out, "Help me," before he wondered if these people spoke his language.

*   *   *

To escape from her torment was the only thought uppermost in Annalee's head. She fled from the valley, not caring where she went. Her awareness of everyday things had dropped to zero as madness goaded her to ride the horse almost beyond its limits. The wind rushed through her hair at the speed she was doing, but it did little to invigorate her. The sense of guilt pressed too heavily upon her shoulders. Above all things, Annalee knew she had to escape, from herself, from Raithe, from everyone she knew. Speed was the only thing that could help her. Her knuckles showed up white as her fingers clutched the reins.

Trees and bushes flashed by. Tears blurred her eyes, obscuring her view, but in spite of it all, Thane's face seemed to be continuously floating before her. His accusing eyes seemed to cut deep into her soul, emphasising that she had let him down. How he must hate her! But he couldn't hate her as much as she hated herself. She screwed up her eyes tightly to blot him out, but the vision remained. Never in a million years was she going to escape from him or the thoughts of what she had helped to do to Sue.

Above the rush of air came the pounding hooves of a horse galloping behind her. She tried to increase her own speed. No one must catch her. With sudden clarity she knew exactly what she must do. The same awareness made her realise her own horse was covered in lather from excessive exertion. He could not keep up his present speed indefinitely without harming himself. Annalee had no idea where she was, but Flash was tiring. The person behind her still relentlessly followed. With a sickening lurch she realised it had to be Thane. She would have to face him, but whatever the outcome of this meeting, she was not going to let him stop her from what she intended to do. With her last ounce of strength she pulled hard on the reins and the horse slithered to a standstill. The poor animal was almost dead on its feet. Guilt flooded over her as she noticed his sides heaving, the posture of his hanging head and the flecks of foam on his drooping neck. She slid off his back and gave him a belated pat. The rider behind thundered to a standstill and swiftly dismounted. Annalee controlled her shaking and waited for his fury to lash out at her. Since no one spoke, she nerved herself to turn round and saw with mixed feelings, not her brother, but Tansy standing there. She did not know whether to be pleased or disappointed.

169

Tansy seemed completely at ease with the situation. She stretched her legs and ran a hand through her short hair. Studiously ignoring the red and blotchy face of her companion, she said, "I must say that was some gallop. You came a long way to get whatever it was out of your system. Flash looks fit to drop, but you – are you feeling better now?"

"Why did you follow me?" was all Annalee said.

Tansy raised her eyebrows in surprise. There was nothing wrong with Annalee now, as far as she could see. She was more like the girl she used to know. Tansy pushed her own mount towards the other horse and said lightly, "I was concerned. You seemed rather overwrought in the valley. I left the men and came after you. I thought if you spoke to me it might help."

Annalee turned away from her and watched the two horses happily cropping together. A sudden longing for their old friendship returned. But she had forfeited her right to that long ago when she allowed Raithe to monopolise her life.

"Nothing can help me," she muttered.

Annalee's apathy came as a shock and alarm bells started to ring in Tansy's head. Being soft with her was not the right approach. She had to be stung into some sort of reaction. Almost as though she were not bothered, she wandered off to sit on a flat slab of rock and patted the space beside her invitingly.

"Try me – and come and sit here." It was several minutes before the other girl sat morosely on the rock. Tansy removed her water bottle and offered Annalee a drink but it was refused. She took a draught herself and felt her resolve harden.

"Suppose we stop beating about the bush and you tell me why things have soured between you and Raithe. Is it the coming of Sue?" she enquired. Receiving no reply, her eyes flickered over the other's pensive face. "Oh, come on, Annalee. Since when have you found it hard to confide your thoughts to me? We used to know each other's closest secrets. It's plain to all of us what is going on. I had hoped you would come clean with me. Then we could put it all behind us and resume our old friendship. So Sue is missing – tell me more. What have you and Raithe done?"

Annalee shuddered. What hadn't they done? She intended to clear her conscience no matter what the outcome. It would be great to be able to hold her head high again. Averting her face from Tansy, she blurted out, "if you hate me after this I will understand, but I can assure you I shall hate myself much more." With a tremor in her voice she told of how they had enticed Sue to ride into the valley where she was captured by the gypsies. Tansy was stunned at the cold-blooded plan, but refrained from interrupting. She allowed the other girl to empty her heart and was surprised to see a glimmer of a smile touch her lips as she reminisced.

"She rode a horse much better than Raithe expected, but I was shocked when he shot Saturn. The horse did not deserve that."

Tansy tightened her lips. "So you worried more about the horse than you did about Sue's life?"

171

Annalee shook her head. She was finding it hard to go on. "At first – yes," she said, "but I was not thinking straight, and when I heard her scream ….." Her eyes dilated at the memory. She drew in a ragged breath. "I realised what I had been part of. I wanted Raithe to go back and look for her, but… but…" the tears ran down her cheeks unhindered, "he laughed at me and threatened me if I told anyone."

"So why have you told me?" asked Tansy grimly.

"Because I trust you to do the right thing," replied Annalee. "I want you to tell every…"

"Oh no – you stop right there," Tansy interrupted swiftly and she backed away. "You will tell everyone yourself. I'm not doing it. Directly the horses have rested we must return to the camp. The sun is already going down and we've got a fair way to go, thanks to you. Did you have to gallop so far?"

The other girl did not answer. Her hands fluttered nervously. With bleak eyes she returned the tracker's look and said, "I'm not going back with you."

"Of course you are. What do you think you are going to do?"

"I've got to find Sue," Annalee said starkly. "It's the only way."

Tansy felt a wave of fear creeping over her. She had made a mistake, Annalee was still overwrought. There was no way she – a mere girl – could find Sue on her own. It needed a team of men for the fighting that it would involve. Yet looking at her, she could see the determination on Annalee's face.

THE SECRET OF TAMSWORTH FOREST

"Don't be silly. You've no idea where she is now," she retorted brusquely. "Be sensible and come home with me."

"No," Annalee replied, jumping to her feet, unable to hide her agitation. She had got to be firm with Tansy and make her understand. "I have to go. Call it my penance or whatever you like. It's the only way I can truly make amends to my brother, and Sue, who trusted me. It's going to be useless tracking the gypsies, but I have a good idea of where they are heading – and you're not going to stop me."

Tansy shook her head. "You should tell Thane and Amos."

Annalee laughed humourlessly. "By the time they decide I might have some useful information and acted on it – the gypsies will be even farther away. Tansy," her voice was pleading now. "Please don't stop me."

Tansy looked thoughtful and fingered her bow. "I could shoot you," she murmured softly.

A ghost of a smile touched Annalee's lips. She withdrew an arrow from her own quiver. "I could also shoot you," she returned swiftly. "Look, go back and say you lost me."

Their eyes met and they both laughed. The tension between them evaporated. It was like it used to be before Raithe split them up. Tansy got to her feet and walked over to her mount. She patted his neck and jumped nimbly on to his back. From her elevated position she looked down on Annalee and grinned.

"What are we waiting for?" she asked cheerfully. "You don't think I'm letting you go alone, do you?

173

We've got to hunt for some food before it gets too dark and find a place to camp for the night. Well, don't look so astonished. Buck your ideas up, girl."

Annalee made one final attempt at resisting. Walking over to Tansy she caught hold of the bridle, her eyes full of anxiety, and insisted, "Tansy, have you thought this through? We are not really equipped to make this journey on our own. It's foolhardy. We have no weapons other than our bows and arrows and there will be chaos at the camp when we don't turn up. You must change your mind."

"But you're still going," the other girl replied sharply, "so that means me as well."

Annalee flushed and tried again. "That's different. I'm the one who caused this situation. A word from me and it could all have been avoided. I'm prepared to face danger. It's my choice. You realise we could be killed?"

"Save your breath," Tansy retorted, "you are making it sound better all the time. I'm a soldier. Things like this happen to soldiers sometimes. For goodness sake shut up, Annalee, and get yourself mounted on Flash. It's time we got moving," and with that she started to trot away.

*   *   *

The flames from the fire the two girls lit roared high into the sky throwing a shower of sparks in all directions. It gave off a comforting warmth. Annalee banked the sides of the fire with dry wood and dead

THE SECRET OF TAMSWORTH FOREST

grass. When all was completed, she sat back on her heels staring deeply into its heart. The blaze pleased her. Fire-making was not one of her better accomplishments. The two horses were tethered on long ropes so they had ample space to wander and crop the grass. Annalee allowed herself to daydream while she waited for the return of Tansy, who had gone foraging for their supper. A rumbling stomach was a reminder of how long it had been since she had last eaten.

Night fell and the air became chilly, although there was only a slight breeze. Stars shone in the heavens. No cloud marred the velvet darkness. They were lucky that it was dry, as camping tonight was going to be out in the open. They had set out on this journey with only the bare necessities. To have any kind of shelter would mean their going towards the forest, and that was not a wise move. It was not safe amongst the trees after dark.

Annalee heard Tansy call out and saw her shadowy form trudging through the long grass with something dangling from her hands. Annalee smiled. Well, rabbit was better than nothing. She drew a knife from her sheath at the waist, waiting to skin it. Tansy was apologetic for its small size as she threw it down on the ground.

"It's the only thing I saw move. It was too late to do any proper hunting. Sorry it's a bit scrawny. Do you think it will be enough?"

"It will have to be," answered Annalee as she slit open its belly. "Look, while you've been gone I have collected some large leaves. We can wrap the meat up

175

and push it in the hot ash. Thane taught me how to do this trick ages ago. Give it an hour and it should be ready to eat."

Annalee prepared the rabbit and then Tansy wrapped it in leaves. Peace reigned as they worked together, both reminiscing about the past, when it seemed quite normal for them to go camping for several days and no one worried about their welfare. Hunger made them impatient and Annalee kept prodding the meat, hoping to make it cook faster. They were so famished it was hard to wait. Nothing could be heard except the sizzling of the rabbit and the occasional crackling of wood. Their mouths started to water. An appetizing smell filled the air. They stared into the fire, mesmerised by the flames, waiting for the moment when they could satisfy their hunger. The noise, when it came so unexpectedly, made them both jump. Annalee clutched her stick as though it were a weapon.

"What was that?" she gasped in alarm? "Did you hear it?"

They both scrambled to their feet, expecting something awful to happen, like being attacked by gypsies – or maybe a lizard. One glance at the horses showed they were untroubled, so there was no predatory animal creeping up on them. When the sound was not repeated, they ceased to be anxious and Tansy laughed, remarking, "We're too tense. We must toughen ourselves up a little. I dare say it was a rabbit that got away. No people live in this area."

THE SECRET OF TAMSWORTH FOREST

No sooner had the words left her mouth than the cry was repeated. This time the words were heard distinctly and the distress of the caller became obvious.

"Help me. Please help me."

The girls looked in all directions. Every nerve in their bodies was tense. This could be a ploy to separate them. Anyone or anything could be out there, lurking in the shadows ready to pounce. They were not about to take any chances. Tansy strained her eyes, trying to pierce the gloom and pointing, said, "It came from over there." She strained her eyes looking towards the forest where the tall trees stood outlined against the backdrop of the night sky. "You stay here and I will investigate."

She drew her bow and prepared it in readiness, going forward very carefully. Annalee followed her example but remained with the horses. There was no point in leaving them unguarded and encouraging trouble. With her body primed for action, Tansy moved stealthily towards where the sound came from. Once the brightness of the fire was left behind she could see better and pick out movement in the long grass. The fronds were thrashing violently side to side. She paused and stared warily at the spot, wondering who on earth was in there and why so agitated.

"Who are you? Come out and show yourself," her husky voice demanded sharply.

"I can't. I mean I'm here but I can't walk."

The voice came from almost under her feet. Warily, she stepped one pace closer and perceived a dark bundle on the ground. It was hard to work out what it could be as it writhed around. The light was too bad to

177

see clearly. From its size – it certainly was not a man. In fact, Tansy thought the voice sounded very juvenile. Still on her guard, she bent down and aimed her arrow at the moving mass, and tentatively touched what she thought was its back. In shocked surprise, her hand came into contact with something cold and clammy. She realised whatever it was that was there, it was very wet. Her fingers did an exploratory search. She felt the bundle shiver – at the same time she caught sight of a face that looked up at her. She knew she had seen it before on one of the occasions she had visited the other world with Thane. The distant glow from the fire reflected off his glasses. How on earth had he got here – getting past all the guard wolves? At the moment though, that could wait. The most important thing was to help him.

"Annalee," she yelled out. "Come here and give me a hand."

Between the two of them, they supported the unknown boy, almost dragging him to their camp. He clenched his teeth tightly, trying to suppress his cries of pain because making the noise embarrassed him. Boys were supposed to be tough. They did not make a fuss in front of girls. He would never live this down if he showed weakness in front of them although neither looked like Priscilla. He soon discovered they stood for no nonsense. Also, they seemed to be alone in this place and he was literally at their mercy. They did not ask for explanations. He had no time to wonder why and they dealt with him as though he could not speak. Annalee deprived him of his rucksack, and the weight of it came as a surprise to her. Then in spite of his half-hearted objections, she stripped off his top clothing. Tansy removed his shoes, feeling his ankle with firm but gentle fingers. Barry felt too exhausted to protest about this treatment. The heat from the fire reached him at last and he edged as near to it as he dared.

Whoever these women were, they knew exactly what they were about. One put a cold compress on his foot and bound it up tightly while the other laid all his clothes out to dry on the grass. Then he was offered a drink. His suspicion was aroused and he studied the liquid carefully, feeling a complete fool when he realised it was water. He was sure he saw the glimmer of a smile on the face of the girl with the flask. Not until everything was done to their satisfaction, did the girls sit back and look at him. For the first time in his life Barry felt awkward, feeling their eyes examining him. It was an experience he did not like. The one with the short hair had a mischievous smile on her lips.

"Well, you will live to see another day, boy, suppose you tell us where you hail from?" Tansy asked carefully. "You must be a long way from home. What are you doing here?"

Barry almost shrank under her inscrutable stare. How did he explain his presence? The pair of them looked so capable he knew they would detect a lie if he fabricated a story. He decided to prevaricate instead by saying,

"I did not expect you to speak my language."

"This is not our language," they replied. "We speak this way in deference to our Queen who comes from your world."

Barry could not describe the overwhelming relief that went through him. He felt the tension leave him. "So you know where I come from?"

"Come from – yes, but why – we don't know." Annalee laughed lightly, joining in the conversation. "We have had quite an influx of your people just lately," she said, "so the opening between the two worlds is now heavily guarded. It's a wonder you got through. The wolves guard it extremely well and attack the people first. I wonder if you realise how lucky you are."

"But it was White Hawk who showed me the way," he protested without thinking. The two women dissolved into gales of laughter. Barry felt uncomfortable and thought it wisest not to ask questions. He failed to find anything funny in what he said. Tansy recovered first and she wiped her eyes, saying, "So you know Thane?"

"No. Never heard of – of – of whoever you are talking about," he replied.

"Of course you haven't, boy," stuck in Annalee, thinking immediately of Sue, "But if you know White Hawk, you know Thane." Her eyes suddenly became serious but she had great delight in saying, "you travelled down the wolves' tunnel. That's why you're so wet. Do you mind if I make a guess as to why you have come here?"

"Go ahead," he replied.

Annalee paused before saying, "You are looking for Sue?"

Barry's mouth opened like a fish, and the girls' eyes gleamed. "What is she to you?" she asked.

For some reason warning bells sounded in Barry's head. The atmosphere had subtly altered. The first tinge of worry touched him and he wondered what was amiss, but there was no hesitation in his voice as he said proudly, "she's my sister."

He was aware of the silence which fell at his words. The two girls stared at him in dismay. Barry shifted uneasily when they did not speak. What had he said to upset them? Did they not have brothers and sisters in this world? On the other hand – maybe they knew Sue and something had happened to her. Sudden fear clutched at him and it showed in his face. "What's wrong?" he demanded gruffly. "Is Sue all right? Has she had an accident? Tell me. I want to know. Don't stare at me like that."

They could find no words to reassure him and calm his agitation. He was not to know he had caught them completely unprepared. They had not thought it necessary to think up a story about Sue. Fate played cruel tricks sometimes. The last thing they expected was to have her brother turn up and ask questions. Annalee took it upon herself to do the talking. She reached out, and much to Barry's embarrassment, took hold of his hand as though he was a child in need of consoling.

"Now you look like an intelligent person," she murmured carefully, "so I'm going to tell you about your sister. The trouble is – she is not with us at the moment. A band of gypsies has captured her and that's the reason you have found us here. We are following them. We want to get her back and it is dangerous work. The journey we are undertaking is perilous. The gypsies are not to be trusted boy. Never forget that. They are – look, just what is your name? We can't keep calling you boy."

"Barry," he replied.

"Well, Barry," said Annalee, "now that we have found you, which looks like a good omen, you have two choices. We can show you the way to find Thane and White Hawk. Or – " she glanced quickly at Tansy and received a nod, "or – you can come with us."

As far as Barry was concerned, he did not have a choice, he wanted to find Sue and told them both so emphatically. They did not ask what his reasons were because relief flooded over them. The last thing they wanted was for him to meet Raithe. Anyway, a third pair of eyes was always useful, and on hearing this, he felt a lot better. A shower of sparks jumped out of the fire and Barry quickly moved back a little. It was then he smelt the meat cooking and licked his lips hungrily. Watching the action, Annalee groaned in despair.

"Are you hungry?" she asked begrudgingly, thinking of their meagre supper.

"I'm starving," declared Barry. "Have you got some food to spare?"

"You can share what we've got, but we've only a small rabbit."

THE SECRET OF TAMSWORTH FOREST

"Oh." Barry stared at them apologetically, suddenly aware of the situation. "I am sorry. I did not realise you hadn't got much. I thought it would be nice to have something hot." The wistfulness in his voice made Annalee feel like a heel. "I've got some food in my bag," he added hopefully. "I can share that with you."

The girls' faces lit up like magic and Tansy thrust his bag under his nose. With them scrutinising every move, he removed a packet of ham and some bread rolls which had to be used before they went stale. Annalee shared out the ham and Tansy divided up the rabbit pieces. It was an excellent meal eaten in companionable silence. The night breeze blew the smoke away and sometime later, when the fire was banked up for the night, all three lay close together for warmth. They had only two blankets which they purloined from the horses. The moon sailed majestically through the heavens, shining down on their sleeping forms.

CHAPTER 12

TORTURE

Lying on the hard bed, Sue watched the emaciated woman named Elina untie the thong which bit deeply into her legs. Elina never acknowledged Sue or smiled. Her thin lips were pressed firmly together as she concentrated on the knots. She was so thin she looked ill and such a contrast to the heavy burly women she had come into contact with. Her long greyish hair was drawn back in the most unflattering way from her gaunt face. It made her cheekbones prominent and threw dark shadows beneath her sunken eyes. It was hard to gauge her age. Elina gave the impression she did not want to talk, which made Sue automatically look for the boy. A quick look round the small space showed that he had vanished.

Sue felt frustrated because she was unable to speak with a swollen tongue and cracked lips. Her throat constricted with the effort. As a last resort she tried to communicate with sign language but Elina showed no inclination of wanting to understand. In the end, Sue sank into despondency and waited patiently until the last thong had been released. Then she made an attempt to move. The woman spun round on her with the first signs of animation and a red tinge touched her sallow cheeks.

"No," she said.

With just one word she pushed Sue's legs back with more strength than her appearance gave her credit for. Sheer astonishment made Sue obey. Elina did not look at Sue. She concentrated on her legs and pressed her hard, calloused hands on them as she started to massage. She worked methodically on both with an even pressure. As the blood flowed through her legs, they started to hurt, but Sue clenched her teeth, putting up with the discomfort. The pain became so bad at one point she found it hard to refrain from crying out. Then the hands were removed. Sue looked up and saw Elina standing with her hands on her hips, watching her. Sue gave a weak smile, not knowing what else to do. Elina jerked her head and said, "Move," pointing to the floor.

Not waiting to be asked twice, Sue swung her legs down to the floor. They felt like lumps of meat and very heavy. It was not until she attempted to stand that a wave of nausea swept over her. The woman was by her side in an instant, being more of a support than Sue would have expected. She held onto the young girl until her equilibrium was restored. Sue took a couple of tentative steps, eager to move after so long on her back. From Elina's grunt of approval she had obviously done something right. The woman touched her clothing. An expression of amazement on her face, and her nose twitched like a rabbit. Sue knew her clothes were appalling, dirty, soiled and screwed up, but she was unprepared when Elina seized her wrist in a vice-like grip and drew her unresisting to the opening door.

The night air enveloped her and she took in some deep breaths. Never had anything smelt so sweet and fresh before. For the first time Sue saw the huge fire burning on her right and silhouettes of people gathered around it. The glow from the flames picked out several caravans parked nearby. Above the sounds of raucous laughter, harsh voices and children screaming, another more compelling noise reached her ears; a continuous roar which vibrated through the air. She was not allowed time to speculate. Elina tugged at her elbow to help her down the wooden steps – showing the first signs of impatience when she stumbled. It was not as easy as Sue first thought. After being tied up for so long, her knees refused to bend as though such an action was foreign to them. At last her feet touched the hard ground. Elina relinquished the hold on her arm, her face indecipherable in the darkness. She turned her gaunt form and her eyes pierced the darkness in all directions. Sue relaxed, endeavouring to take notice of her surroundings, which she soon found was impossible. She could see only the glow of the fire.

From the darkness a group of weirdly dressed women appeared. Instead of passing by, they swiftly surrounded Sue and Elina. The bulk of their bodies was overpowering and cut out what little light there was. Sue felt alarmed. There was something threatening about their attitude. She wanted to push them away. An evil smell made her feel claustrophobic, and then she caught sight of their heavy coarse faces and dark glittering eyes. Instinct told her they were far from friendly. Elina may have been sparing with her words when she spoke to her, but to these swarthy women she became voluble. What was said during their exchange of words was lost on Sue, but Elina stood protectively in front like a guard. The women circled round them until they were both confined in the middle, with no hope of escaping. Two of them seized Elina and held her captive while the rest grabbed hold of Sue, their nails digging cruelly into her flesh. Her reaction was to fight and call out, but she failed miserably on both accounts. She ended up by kicking viciously at her tormentors. Her struggles were ineffective, and without any trouble they whisked her away to be swallowed up in the darkness.

Sue tried to make things difficult by refusing to walk which was an unwise move because she lacked her normal strength. They dragged her callously over the rough ground, not caring if they hurt her. All she heard was jeering guttural voices. The more she struggled, the more excited her captors became. With their leader away, she was unexpected sport. Sue could feel pressure building up in her head and was petrified, wondering what their intentions were towards her.

Even had she wanted to walk and save herself unnecessary pain, she was not given the opportunity now. They hauled her along like a sack, disregarding rocks and brambles. All the time their harsh laughter passed over her head.

Then unexpectedly they stopped, but Sue barely noticed. Her body was on fire and she felt sick, but her captors did not relinquish their hold. The roaring sound was very loud here and something wet splashed her face. Terror of the unknown filled her mind. Her eyes could just make out the fast moving water below her feet. Ruthless hands stripped off her clothes, even her sandals. Her struggles were ineffectual against so many brutal women. Goose pimples covered her bare skin. She thought they might leave her there – as they had a warped sense of humour – but the next moment, several hands pushed her roughly over the edge of the bank. As their cheers of delight rent the air, she fell screaming into the water below. Her scream was cut short as icy water closed over her head.

Choking, Sue surfaced. The fast moving water tugged at her limbs. She wondered what would happened if she couldn't swim. The gypsy women hadn't cared or hung around to find out. The roar of the water was so deafening. In the darkness, Sue attempted to reach out for the bank, but already the current was carrying her away. She was at the mercy of the river. The sound of falling water thundered in her ears. She realised she was about to go over a waterfall. Her movements became frenzied. Feverishly she lashed out with her arms but it made no difference, she was like a cork bobbing around. The coldness of the water numbed her flesh. She had never known such fear.

A sob caught in her throat; she thought of Thane, Barry and Priscilla. She would never see them again. In some ways she was glad it was dark so that the horror ahead of her was out of sight. A large wave went over her head and filled her mouth. She coughed and spluttered, and one hand struck against something hard and unmoving. She caught hold of it desperately, it represented safety to her. Her breath was rasping in her throat – she knew she could not hold on much longer, her fingers were already slipping and the pull of the water was too strong. Above the roar she heard a strange high-pitched voice calling. Was she already hallucinating? She closed her eyes but the voice came again, calling.

"Lady! Lady!"

Without really realising what she was saying, Sue answered it as she fought against the current. "Who – who's there?" she spluttered.

"Lady – let go of the rock."

"You... you're joking." Sue clung on tighter than ever, not realising she had spoken. She was not yet ready to drown. She ignored it.

"Lady," the strange voice pleaded, "please let go."

Another wave of water doused her and Sue regained her senses. What was she thinking of? This was not one of those gypsy women calling to her. She could understand what was being said.

"I – I – c- can't," she gasped, but her numb fingers were slipping.

"Lady – let go. I will save you," shouted her would-be rescuer.

A few more yards and she would be overwhelmed by the water. What choice had she? She must trust this person or die. As her fingers slipped from the rock, the water greedily sucked her away with more speed than she expected. Sue lashed out in terror. As she was spun around something caught in her hair and jerked her head up; now she was being pulled two ways. The current relentlessly gripped her body but something else unceremoniously dragged her towards the bank. Her rescuer was fighting against the mighty pull of the water. Whatever held her hair, transferred its grip to her shoulders – then claw-like hands hauled her out. She fell on the bank, shivering uncontrollably and gasping as she coughed up water. A blanket was thrown over her and someone started to rub her down briskly. The warmth that followed was comforting, but still her teeth chattered. Then the rubbing stopped and Sue heard a sharp command. Her blanket was whisked away. Almost immediately another one took its place. This was much more voluminous and covered her completely. After a while Sue struggled to her feet and hugged it closely around her naked body then she looked around to see who was with her. A small hand tugged at the blanket.

"Come, lady, follow me," said the voice.

Startled, Sue peered through the darkness and saw the earnest face of a young boy. His enormous eyes were very expressive. There was no way he could have dragged her from the river. She looked round to see if there was anyone else who could have helped with her rescue, but she and the boy were alone. She concluded this was the boy she had seen earlier in the caravan, and who had been speaking to her just recently from the river bank. She must be going mad.

"Come," he said again, and Sue had no option but to follow him. She winced in pain directly her feet started to move, and her bare skin encountered thistles and brambles. They were not used to treading on such unfriendly surfaces. Walking became slow and painful. After a while her feet were cut and bleeding. Things could not get much worse. Her guide waited patiently by her side. He waited while she struggled along at her own pace, but before long she reached the point when her feet did not even want to touch the ground. At long last, when she felt fit to drop, her eyes saw the glow from the fire of a gypsy encampment. Her heart missed a beat and she halted. A huge lump came up in her throat, nearly choking her. No way was she going back there. She had got to escape while it was dark. Yet how far would she get in her present condition with no clothes, and feet that could barely touch the ground? The boy tugged her blanket urgently and she suddenly remembered the beating he would get if she should escape.

"Must come with me, lady," he pleaded. "Elina, she have clothes for you and shoes for your feet."

"You don't understand," Sue retorted bitterly, "these people tried to kill me."

He protested at once, "no, lady. They not touch you now unless you upset them, you have been washed."

"Washed," echoed Sue in surprise. "Washed! They could have drowned me." The last words were said indignantly. "In fact, I'm not so sure that wasn't their intention."

The boy just shrugged and walked ahead, indicating she should follow. "You were lucky," he said in a matter-of-fact voice. "Elina saved you, like she did to me once. They will now treat you with caution. The women will leave you alone."

Good, thought Sue bleakly and stumbled after him, not wanting to be left on her own – but at the back of her mind she had a disturbing thought. What about the men?

*   *   *

As they approached the caravans the gypsies were celebrating. Raucous laughter came from them as they congregated around the blaze. The light from their fire made the shadows denser around the perimeter. Sue's progress past their unsuspecting backs was painfully slow. She was petrified one of them would turn and see her slinking by.

Elina met Sue at the top of the wooden steps, which were illuminated by the flaming torch within; she gave no greeting, but pushed Sue roughly on to the bed, now cleaned and giving off a fragrance of wild herbs. A few sharp words were directed towards the boy who followed her in, and he disappeared from sight. Elina studied Sue carefully, not showing any sign of her earlier activities. What had happened earlier was something she had no wish to speak about. But the grimace etched on Sue's face drew her attention to her feet hanging over the bed, swinging just a few inches off the floor. They were badly bruised and bleeding. The girl found it hard to bear the touch of Elina's hands as they gently lifted them up for inspection. The older woman's grunt was noncommittal. She rummaged in a sack and produced a container filled with a thick dark paste. In spite of Sue's quick intake of breath, Elina spread the paste evenly over Sue's feet and was satisfied when she noticed its soothing effect take away the edge of pain. Sue's face relaxed slightly, yet fear still lurked in her eyes. The older woman's attitude softened. She held out her hands for the blanket. Not fully comprehending what was about to happen, Sue hugged it tighter to her naked body. Her action immediately renewed the bad feeling between them. Exasperated by the language barrier, Elina snatched at a pile of garments from the end of the bed and thrust them at Sue none too gently. At the same time, her thin fingers curled possessively round the edge of the blanket and tugged.

"Give," she ordered in a voice that dared Sue to refuse.

Reluctantly she relinquished her hold, shivering as the cold air touched her bare flesh. She fingered the clothes uncertainly. They were unfamiliar garments of gypsy origin, not her own, which were no doubt miles away, floating down the river.

"Dress," instructed Elina, breaking in on Sue's thoughts, and she turned to look out of the open doorway to give her some degree of privacy. The frigid atmosphere within the caravan goaded Sue into action. Hastily she donned the low-cut blouse which laced up the front with black ribbon, then quickly slipped on a long petticoat and voluminous green skirt edged with a fringe. A long piece of red material caused her to look bewildered until Elina took it from her hands and tied it with expertise round her waist. After that, sandals were fitted to her sore feet. They were made of rush and kept in place by a long thong crossing her ankles and lower leg.

Elina straightened her back and looked down on Sue's tousled hair. She grunted, but at that moment the boy returned, coming up the steps with several items in his arms. The older woman spoke to him in the common language of the gypsies. Their conversation lasted several minutes, at the end of which, Elina left the caravan. The boy dumped everything he was carrying onto the bed with the carelessness of youth, then glanced at Sue. The eyes that appraised her were not those of a boy, and for the second time, Sue started to wonder about him.

"Except for the colour of your hair and skin, you look like one of us," he said. "Zuboarra will be pleased, lady."

"Well, before you go any further, just tell me a few things." Sue's voice was full of annoyance. She swung round on him and said, "Will you please tell me what your name is, and who on earth is this… this Zuboarra you've mentioned – and while you're at it – why doesn't Elina ever say much?"

The boy shook his head sadly. "You are like women of the tribe," he replied, speaking to her as though she were the child and he the adult. "They always ask questions and give orders to keep me busy. Lady, my name is Tug. It is what everyone calls me. I was found years ago by Zuboarra wandering in the forest. He took me with him and gave me to Elina so that she could look after me."

"You're not a gypsy then?" Sue interrupted.

THE SECRET OF TAMSWORTH FOREST

"I do not know who I am," he retorted. "I have no memory. I shall live with Elina until she goes." He paused because Sue gasped, but he added sadly, "Elina is dying. She does not know your speech, only what I or Zuboarra have taught her. But, never forget this, she understands a lot. You must never show you feel sorry for her." His face was suddenly fierce and he almost glared at her.

Sue sat back, stunned, realising all too clearly why Elina looked so gaunt. How on earth did she have the strength to pull her out of the water? No, the boy had got it wrong. She was just ill. Maybe she was going away. Tug touched her to regain her attention. "Do not be sad, lady. Zuboarra is our chief – he will give me to someone else to work for when the time comes. Tomorrow the tribe moves on, the next time we stop Zuboarra will have returned. Now look – I have got food for you."

"Thanks, Tug." Sue smiled. "Now please, will you do something for me?"

Tug put his head on one side, and enquired, "What might that be, lady?"

"For goodness sake stop calling me lady. I'm Sue."

"Then, Sue – let's eat," and so saying he started to lay the food out on the bed. Sue was too hungry to resist – no matter what it was.

*   *   *

That night Sue was locked up in the caravan. Maybe it was for her own good but being a prisoner again after having tasted freedom made her frustrated.

Elina had inspected the caravan to make sure Sue had everything, and Tug found himself ejected. A surly man barred the wooden door with sadistic enjoyment. The expression in his eyes made her cringe. It was as well she did not suffer from claustrophobia, as the wooden door was the only opening in this cell-like place. At least she had the comfort of a light, although it was flickering and wouldn't last the night.

She lay on the bed and stared at the roof, thinking up ways of escaping, that would not bring down the wrath of their chief on Tug. She was not going to be the cause of him getting a beating.

Surely by now Thane would be searching for her. He would hear the truth from Annalee and Raithe about what happened. But would they tell him when Raithe hated her so much? Why did they hate her so when she was a stranger to them? Her mind became more confused as the hours flashed by. The torch eventually went out. The last thing she remembered hearing was the creaking of wheels and feeling the room sway.

*   *   *

The shutters were flung back with a bang and the caravan door opened. The refreshing smell of rain-soaked earth drifted in. Sue sat up with a start to see who was there. When no one entered, she made her way to the steps and looked out.

THE SECRET OF TAMSWORTH FOREST

An invigorating breeze caught playfully at her skirt. Soft misty rain touched her face. Sue took in a deep breath; it was like nectar from heaven. Before her, an awe-inspiring scene of mountains met her eyes. They were looming over her head, their tops lost in low swirling cloud. In ordinary circumstances the scenery would have enchanted her. The land around the area where the gypsies camped was very rocky, with little evidence of greenery. A lake nearby was surrounded by reed-like grass. Not enough to be of any use. She wondered how the horses were fed and suddenly thought – where were the horses?

It might have been a foul day, but the gypsies were congregating in groups and working near their caravans. They were mostly women. This was the first time Sue had seen the spectacular, colourful caravans in daylight. They had large painted wheels, the vibrant colours of the painted wood vying with the clothes they wore. The communal fire was missing, but to make up for its absence, several of the small chimneys protruding through the caravan roofs were smoking indicating other sources of heat. One or two of the women glowered as Sue stood surveying them, but no move was made towards her. She was left well alone.

She looked round the wet campsite for Elina or Tug, but neither were to be seen. The outdoors beckoned and Sue could not resist its call. She made up her mind to explore. Surely no one would think she was trying to escape. Where would she go in a place like this? If they had wanted to stop her they would have kept the door locked. In trepidation, she descended the steps and

KATHLEEN B. WILSON

started walking away in the opposite direction to the women. The way she chose was devoid of people, the only drawback being, there were still several caravans to pass.

The rush sandals were soon soaked – so were her clothes. The feeling of soft rain on her skin was wonderful, especially on her hair. Just as she was passing the last caravan, a man came down the steps with a purposeful tread. She gritted her teeth and kept going. The man cried out in a thunderous voice, "Stop, woman," causing her to jump. In spite of herself she shuddered. Her steps faltered for a moment but then she determinedly carried on as though he had not spoken. A hand fell heavily on her shoulders, fingers digging into her flesh. She stopped and looked up defiantly, not liking what she saw. The man's long greasy hair fell round his thick neck. He wore no top garments, only red baggy trousers pulled in at the ankles. Rings of many sizes adorned his ears. Bare feet, which were hardened to the rough terrain, stood astride and took up the stance of authority. He towered above her, being a big man and she felt like an ant waiting to be squashed.

Sue stiffened, immediately remembering the treatment handed out by the women and tried to suppress her thumping heart. She looked at the burly man, keeping her face expressionless. Hopefully this would disguise her fear. He shoved a large cumbersome wooden bucket at her and snarled.

"Get some water, woman."

None too gently, he swung her round to face the lake. Sue stood transfixed. His meaning was perfectly clear, as was his speech. Her mouth went dry. She hovered on the verge of rebellion.

"What about the water?" she jerked out.

His dark brows drew together in a scowl and he removed a whip which was hidden by his voluminous trousers. Sue's eyes dilated. He bent his head and leered at her – showing stained teeth.

"So you try to make a fool of me," he said, his voice low deadly, "a big mistake, lady."

He straightened his back and whistled. Immediately another man lumbered down the steps. In his brawny hand he carried another bucket and came abreast of her. Sue felt the hairs prickle on her arms and legs. He grabbed her hands and forcibly put a bucket in each, squeezing her fingers viciously over the handles. She bit her lip hard to refrain from shouting.

"Now get water," he said in a grating voice. "We are waiting for it."

A red flush of anger tinged her cheeks and she retorted, "Then get it yourself. Where I come from men get their own water – not the women."

The words were no sooner out than the whip landed on her back. The sting of the lash felt through her blouse was something she had never experienced before and made her scream. She was about to say something else but the whip fell again. Weals erupted on her skin, burning like fire. The two men regarded her impassively, showing no remorse. They towered above her shrinking form aggressively. The one with the whip stroked it lovingly, but the other bellowed out in his guttural voice, "Would you like to feel her caress again?"

Realising the hopelessness of her position, Sue started to walk towards the lake, her humiliation complete as she passed the women and received jeering rancour from them. The rain falling on her face disguised the tears she had no control over. At the edge of the water Sue sank to her knees. Her back was smarting. She could feel the wetness of the blood. It was enough to remind her not to antagonise the men any further.

Very slowly she filled the first bucket from the clear water and took a hasty drink at the same time. Then she realised it was impossible to lift. Glancing over her shoulder she noticed everyone was still watching her. Resentment turned almost to hate that they had nothing better to do. Working sluggishly she halved the quantity of water and poured it into the other bucket – deciding that two half-filled would be easier to carry. Even so, it was quite a shock when she tried to lift them and found she could hardly manage to get them off the ground.

Determination made her pick them both up and start walking. They were extremely heavy and the strain on her shoulders was agonizing. Her return journey was far slower. She knew if she put the buckets down to rest she would never pick them up again. Her blood boiled to see everyone watching her struggle. Before long, the rough handles rubbed the palms of her hands and their stinging added to the physical anguish she was

THE SECRET OF TAMSWORTH FOREST

suffering. Before long the blisters broke open, making her hands raw.

Panting with exhaustion, Sue at last approached the two men who stood waiting for her. She did not put the buckets down – they fell from her almost numb hands. She had no control over them, one landed fair and square – the other toppled over, spilling its contents over the rocky outcrop. She was not aware of the whip until she felt it across her face. Then she screamed out again in agony, her hands flying to the wound. Someone pulled her hands away and an evil pair of eyes held her like a mesmerized rabbit.

"Go back and fill that bucket, woman," the man hissed venomously, "otherwise you will feel this whip again. All the time you are here – you are our slave and you will be treated like a slave."

Sue felt sick and dispirited. She forced her body round to face the lake. A dull throbbing started up in her head as she wiped blood from her cheek. The bleakness of her surroundings did little to encourage her fight for survival. What sort of a place was this? Slowly she started to walk back to the lake, working out how she could escape this type of life. She meant nothing at all to these people. A haze formed over her eyes. She was unaware of whom she passed. She turned her mind to going straight forward, until she bumped into something solid, then two hands steadied her and Sue muttered, "Elina." But it was not Elina who answered; another person with a gravelly voice said, "I shall speak with you in my caravan. Elina – clean her up and bring her to me now."

Then the hands let go of her and she swayed – unable to keep her balance. She was suddenly aware she stood with Elina and Tug. Walking away from her was the black curly-haired giant she had seen only once before, Zuboarra. He was making his way to the two men who had whipped Sue.

CHAPTER 13

MAKING FRIENDS

The gypsy women were annoyed their sport had ended so abruptly. They watched in sullen silence as Elina and Tug helped Sue stumble back to the caravan. A sheen of perspiration showed up on Elina's face, but she still ordered Tug around in her own language. Behind her back, Tug shrugged and pulled a face. Sue happened to see the incident and was instantly swamped with nostalgia. It reminded her of Barry.

Elina shooed him out of the caravan and turned her attention to Sue. She soon had the girl dressed in dry clothes and her hair combed out, which was a very painful experience for Sue. She sat passively while the dark cream which had worked so well on her feet was now massaged into her hands. For some reason it was not applied to her face or the angry wheals down her back. Tug crept back into the caravan, but stayed out of sight. Elina did not see him until she stood back a pace to survey Sue. The results of her handiwork pleased her. The glimmer of a smile touched her mouth. For the first time, Sue warmed towards her for all the trouble she had taken for her well-being. Impulsively she sprang forward to demonstrate her feelings with a hug when, without warning, Elina doubled over, and an agonising cry escaped from her lips. Thin skeletal arms clutched tightly at her chest. Panic shot through Sue. She caught hold of the older woman, folding her arms tightly round her to give support. She was shocked, there was nothing of Elina. Her body seemed to have no flesh and might snap at any moment. She noticed the waxen tinge of her skin and could not control her alarm. Elina's lips trembled; she tried to get away from Sue.

"Go," she gasped painfully. "He waits."

Tug sprang forward, not looking the least bit put out. He shook his head at Sue as though admonishing her. Sue was not to know he had seen Elina collapse like this on many occasions.

"We put her on the bed and make her comfortable," he ordered.

Sue used what strength she had to ease Elina onto her bed. Although her body was of no weight, it made Sue wince. Tug helped by lifting her legs and placing them out flat. He pushed Sue out of the way, and bending over Elina's inert form, spoke to her urgently. Whatever she mumbled in return was inaudible. Sue watched, feeling utterly useless, unable to join in the conversation because she had no idea what was being said. All she knew was that Elina was ill. Tug turned to face her. He only confirmed her worst fears by saying,

"Elina is not feeling well enough to take you to Zuboarra. She asks me to go with you instead. Please remember, Sue, not to say anything about her being ill. He must not know. Do you understand?"

"But we can't leave her like this. I'll go later," Sue protested quickly.

THE SECRET OF TAMSWORTH FOREST

Tug was aghast. "You must come right now. Big trouble if Zuboarra is not obeyed. Elina will soon be up. This happens many times. Please come now, Sue."

He walked to the steps and looked back almost pleadingly. Sue took one last look at Elina and followed him, she was loath to leave the old lady. The gypsies, still sitting in the rain, watched them go in baleful silence. Sue averted her eyes, trying to ignore them. The buckets, she noticed, were still where she had dropped them. They had no need of the water. She was grateful to Tug for being with her. He might be small, but at least the gypsies deferred to him as he was a protégé of Zuboarra.

The light rain turned to a heavy downpour. Before long Sue was wet again. She squelched along dispiritedly. The distance to Zuboarra's living quarters was not all that far. It stood apart from the rest of the camp, hidden behind an outcrop of rock. His caravan was of lavish proportions, standing in a small space where sparse grass appeared in clumps. Two stunted trees actually grew there and a stallion and a mare were doing their best to graze, not looking contented. Sue studied the caravan. It was a palace compared to her prison. Large windows gave a good view of the lake. Nothing in this camp went on without his knowledge.

Sue felt Tug's fingers press warningly on her arm. He indicated that she was to go in and he would wait outside. Sue nerved herself to mount the steps; there was nothing to fear, she told herself. The last time she met Zuboarra he had shown her kindness. She hovered on the top step and peered into the interior where

205

several lamps lit the room. Cushions were heaped about the floor and Zuboarra sat in a chair. On seeing Sue hesitating at the entrance, he beckoned her in and said, "Please sit down".

Sue sank awkwardly on to a cushion and sat watching him stiffly. A strong smell of incense caught at her throat and she coughed. The long gold earrings glinted in the light of the lamps as he moved his head, and his dark inscrutable eyes stared fixedly in her direction. Nothing about her was missed. He started the conversation by saying, "What do you call yourself, woman?"

"Sue."

He stiffened his massive form slightly and his eyes closed almost to slits. "Since you can now speak, woman, tell me something. Why do you not use your correct name?" he enquired.

Sue was dumbfounded at the question and hoped her surprise did not show on her face. She was suddenly uneasy. He was not a man to take liberties with so he would not take kindly to being corrected.

"I have," she answered truthfully, her lips going dry. As she expected, Zuboarra became angry. He looked dangerous and suddenly seemed much taller in his seat.

"Are you ashamed of who you are – or could it be you are trying to make a fool out of me?" he demanded in an aggressive tone. The air seemed full of electricity. Sue looked at his hard face and swallowed nervously. Drawing in a deep breath she said clearly,

"Where I come from my name is Sue." Her voice sounded almost defiant to her ears.

THE SECRET OF TAMSWORTH FOREST

"Ah," he grunted, and unexpectedly the man's face broke into an evil smile. He looked at her insultingly. "So you try to be clever. You think yourself better than I am. You, from the other race, take me to be some kind of an idiot. If you think that, then you are a stupid foolish woman. You were recognised the first time I set eyes on you. The whole camp knows you are Sonja and they hate you. The bad news for you is that I can never let you go free. You will remain my prisoner and stay here surrounded by their hate."

"But I'm not Sonja," retorted Sue and, white to the lips, she scrambled to her feet. She was beginning to feel real fear. "Why does no one believe me? What do I have to do? I don't even know who Sonja is. You have made a mistake. My name is Sue. I am a guest in this land. Very soon — "

"Enough, woman," interrupted Zuboarra with a roar and he stood up, towering over her. "You dare to argue with me? I – Zuboarra who knows everything. If you wish to be beaten within an inch of your life – go ahead. Stop these lies at once," he thundered. "They make me furious. I beat people for them – and that includes you, woman. Think carefully before you say any more. You came to us on a royal horse and now you have the audacity to say you are not Sonja. Only she would ride such a beast." His face was contorted with rage. It was as though a madness was gripping him. Sue cowered back, but he went on relentlessly. "You have many enemies, woman. People from your own race who planned for us to capture you – ah – you did not know that," he taunted as he noticed her start of surprise. "It was the biggest disappointment of my life that the stallion escaped – but we have got you, and you are going to be sold for much gold and shipped away. No one will see you again."

Sue felt her world crashing down around her. She was confused and bewildered. All this time Sonja had been she. If it were true – then why had not Thane told her, explained it all? She still did not know who Sonja was, someone royal if Zuboarra was to be believed, and royal, was something she definitely was not. Her future, if she had one, was looking decidedly precarious. She was treading a hazardous path and did not know why. Zuboarra was a barbarian and would never believe she had no idea of what he was on about. Unless something drastic happened, it seemed she would never see her home again. Her legs gave out and she sank back on the cushions. The gypsy chief sat himself down and contemplated her. He studied the weal on her face which stood out red and angry. He saw the others on her shoulder.

"Are my people giving you a hard time?" he asked casually, and his tone was very deceptive. Was he trying to catch her out? Sue was wise enough not to complain.

"Elina and Tug have been good to me," she muttered, feeling her face dampen with perspiration.

His thick eyebrows rose inquiringly. It was obviously not the answer he had expected. "Yet you have been whipped?" he questioned, leading her on.

Sue licked her lips. "That is because they said I am a slave." Further caution on her part seemed pointless

THE SECRET OF TAMSWORTH FOREST

now. Zuboarra was enjoying himself. He gave a shout of laughter. There was not an ounce of remorse in him.

"That is because you are one. We are a proud people of nomadic origin. We have no time or love for your race and will tolerate you only as slaves. If slaves want to eat then slaves have to work, otherwise we get rid of them and they are never heard of again. It is surprising how many fatal accidents we have." He paused, aware of Sue's pallor. "Now in your case," he continued briskly, "we keep you because there is a market for you and we shall get much gold when we sell you. That is the reason you have been put in the care of Elina. Now a word of warning, woman, and you would do well to listen. If you keep wandering around on your own as you do – and believe me, I am not stopping you – you can expect more of the treatment you received today. After all, you're only a slave and that's what happens to slaves. So now, woman. Have you any questions?"

He looked supercilious as he waited, but his meaning was perfectly clear. She would receive no help from him. With a supreme effort on her part, she gave off an air of nonchalance. Looking at him steadily, she said with quiet dignity,

"May I go now?" And she was rewarded with a nod of approval.

*   *   *

The morning felt chilly. Mist swirled around the sleeping boy. Barry opened his eyes, suddenly aware the two girls were breaking camp. Tansy was checking

209

KATHLEEN B. WILSON

the horses, while Annalee was unashamedly going through his rucksack; trying to find out what they could eat that would save early morning hunting. The array of tins baffled her. Seeing he was awake, she looked towards him with inquiring eyes, showing no embarrassment at being caught in the act of riffling through his belongings, and held up a tin.

"That's salmon," he said, crawling up to her side. "Shall I open it for you?"

"Salmon? What is this, salmon?"

"Fish," he retorted, "and it's ready to eat."

"But fish swim in water. It is not found in tins." Annalee was obviously out of her depth.

Barry drew forth the tin opener from his pocket. Leaning forward, he took the tin from her hand. "Sometimes it is, where I come from." He proceeded to remove the top and drain away the liquid. Annalee took it back and sniffed the contents. An exploratory finger prised out a chunk which she put in her mouth.

"This is good," she exclaimed. "I hope you have more of it. Tansy, come and taste this."

Tansy left the horses, allowing them to wander, and joined Annalee and Barry. Before long the tin was empty and Annalee was looking for something else. Barry realised he needed to show his authority otherwise his stock of food would soon vanish. He pulled the rucksack towards himself and ignored Annalee's hurt expression.

"We must keep something for later," he said. "Let me help you instead."

210

"Not yet, young man," interrupted Tansy, "wait until you can walk. You will rest that foot and ride behind me on my horse. Annalee, for goodness sake put all that stuff back. It's time we made a move. Someone like Raithe might decide to follow us. He's rather good at tracking."

Barry refrained from asking who Raithe was. It took all his energy to scramble to his feet. His limbs were surprisingly stiff. The fire was soon extinguished and the blankets replaced on the horses. Tansy leapt up and when Barry stumbled over to her, Annalee gave him a leg up, then with a lithe movement she mounted the other horse. They moved steadily in the direction of the mountains, heading for a place called Thunder Falls. According to Annalee, it was a place where the gypsies congregated. This sounded very exciting to Barry and he thanked his lucky stars he had found these two girls instead of someone hostile. But his hopes of finding Thane faded. He wondered what Thane would have thought of these two girls. It was all exhilarating and he meant to enjoy every minute of this adventure. Before long he would be with Sue again and that made everything worthwhile. He did not envisage any trouble.

Barry's ankle improved rapidly. By the end of their second day, he was well enough to put his full weight on it. The bandage was removed, and he could help the girls. Tansy gave him lessons on how to shoot with a bow and arrow and he was astute enough to grasp the rudiments of their use. Barry was keen and had an accurate eye. Trees became easy targets, but a moving animal was another thing. To his mortification Tansy laughed when his arrows went wide of the target. She pretended not to notice, and to his disgust made him forage for wild potatoes to go with the bird Annalee had brought down earlier. It was now cooking on their small fire and the seductive odour coming from it wafted tantalizingly on the evening air. With their arms full of potatoes, they joined Annalee, who looked uneasy. Periodically she glanced over her shoulder towards the undergrowth and frowned. Normally she was not the type of girl to worry.

"I feel I am being watched," she said, and Tansy immediately dumped the potatoes and said, "Stay here. I'll have a look round."

Tansy disappeared before Barry realised what was happening. He made a move to follow her, but Annalee detained him by catching his arm. "Leave her. You will make too much noise amongst the trees."

"She might need help."

"She might, Barry, but certainly not yours. There is an art in moving silently which you haven't got, my boy. Come and help me with these potatoes. After all, you did dig them up," she added.

Barry begrudgingly consented. He was rather annoyed at being criticized. He knew he wasn't an experienced hunter. She didn't have to rub it in. Then a howl rent the air. The hairs on the back of his arm stood up. He thought Tansy was in danger, which amused Annalee.

"What was that?" he asked, peering anxiously through the trees. The dappled sunlight mingled with

THE SECRET OF TAMSWORTH FOREST

the approaching dusk. It threw many shadows on the ground, making it difficult for him to discern anything. Annalee grinned at his discomfiture and murmured with relish, "a wolf."

To his astonishment she threw back her head and mimicked the call they both had heard. Barry felt foolish, realising it was a signal between the two girls, but he was unprepared when something crashed through the undergrowth and a white wolf sprang at them and slithered to a stop. Barry's first flash of fear vanished. Delight filled his eyes and he made a move towards the wolf.

"White Hawk," he cried, putting out a hand to pat the large head. Annalee screamed, pulling him back. At the same time the wolf's lips drew back, showing his pointed sharp teeth.

"Never do that, Barry," she hissed angrily. "Let the wolf make the first move."

"But White Hawk knows me," he protested, wondering what all the fuss was about. His voice trailed away because the wolf showed no sign of recognition. Now Barry looked uncertain. Annalee said, "Maybe, but you must remember White Hawk is a savage animal. He is trained to obey only one person and that person is not here. What makes you think it is White Hawk anyway? We have many white wolves in our army. They all look alike."

Barry wanted to say 'intuition' but remained silent. He appraised the animal before him, still sure it was White Hawk, but the wolf came no closer. His fur bristled and he took up a threatening stance. Unblinking

213

amber eyes fixed them steadily to the spot. Barry's urge to touch him, won. He moved only one arm a fraction and the wolf snarled.

"I'm glad to see you listen to your superiors," said a clipped voice.

Someone emerged from the tree line with Tansy following silently in their wake. The wolf turned its head and a small whine came from his throat. As the travel-stained man drew nearer, White Hawk rolled over on his back in an act of submission. The doubts that had been forming in Barry's head vanished. He leapt up with a cry of welcome.

"Thane! You don't know how great it is to see you again. I bet you're surprised to see me here?"

"Not really." Thane's glance passed over his sister to give the boy a grin. "I'm glad you got here OK."

Barry's mouth fell open with surprise. "But how did you know I'd be here?"

"Because I'm the one who helped you." Thane flopped down on the ground and ran his fingers through the thick ruff of the ecstatic wolf. Immediately White Hawk licked his face with a long rough tongue. "I sent the wolf to help you when I noticed you were having trouble with Professor Harding. Once I knew you were safe, I dealt with the Professor. He's the last person we want in this land. I must say you're very enterprising. I see you have found yourself some decent company." He turned his gaze to the girls, but this time it rested on Annalee, and his voice was noticeably grimmer. "Have you told him yet what you've done to Sue?"

214

THE SECRET OF TAMSWORTH FOREST

Annalee, having got over her sudden shock of seeing him, bit her lower lip. She could tell by just looking at her brother how deeply she had hurt him. "I know Barry is Sue's brother." She waited, expecting to hear some berating remarks, but none came.

Thane said gravely, "I take it you haven't told him. So I'll ask another question. Why are you doing this foolhardy thing?"

Barry's mouth fell open in surprise. No way would he believe Annalee had harmed Sue, but she had obviously upset Thane and he wasn't going to let things rest.

Thane's glance was calculating as it rested on his sister. He wondered how she had explained the whereabouts of Sue. Annalee returned his look without flinching.

"Because it's my fault Sue walked into a trap. It's up to me to help her escape."

Thane lifted his eyebrows slightly, saying, "That's rather a strong opinion you've got. You see yourself as the only guilty party?"

"No – but I could have done something about it at the time. I – I thought Raithe would back down at the last minute." Her voice wavered and she wished her brother would lose his temper, she could handle that. Taking a deep breath, she said courageously, "Please don't try to stop me if that's why you've come here."

"I wouldn't dream of it," he answered, "It was my intention that the two of us should do exactly what you're doing now. Before you start to thank me" – he paused warningly as Annalee sprang to her feet – "I

215

KATHLEEN B. WILSON

want you to know I have not forgiven Raithe for what he did. My intention is to keep you and him apart. That way I might break the hold he has over you."

"I'm my own master," Annalee retorted defensively. "No one has a hold over me. Thane." Her eyes pleaded with him. "Raithe is not really bad. He is just scared of what Sue's presence here means. He had no idea she existed until his mother told him. The opposition have been filling his head with a lot of lies."

Thane listened to her impassively. "There is more to it than that," he retorted grimly. "He happens to hate her – or have you forgotten? We can't blame the opposition for everything. He has done everything in his power to make her feel unwelcome."

"But Raithe.."

"Don't Raithe me, Annalee. I want no excuses for his behaviour. You had better know right now that we found the arrow he shot at Saturn. It has his fletch on it."

"Does he know?" Annalee queried.

"We haven't told him. The silly idiot thinks he has been smart. This way we shall catch him out. I suggest you fill Barry in on all your misdeeds. He is dying to know who Raithe is."

Barry was listening to the conversation – his eyes looking owlish as he tried to make sense of it all. Tansy stepped forward, her eyes hard as she glared at Thane. "You can't tell Barry that, even Sue doesn't know," she said.

"Do you want to bet?" Thane laughed harshly. "I should think the gypsies have told her by now.

216

THE SECRET OF TAMSWORTH FOREST

Anyway, enough of this speculation." He looked back at his sister. "Tansy tells me you are heading for Thunder Falls."

Annalee nodded, eyeing him warily. "Good." Thane's face broke into a smile. "If you have no objection, I am going to travel with you. Between the four of us and White Hawk we make a formidable team."

CHAPTER 14

PLANS TO ESCAPE

The weather took a turn for the worse and they were unable to continue. Thane worked with dogged determination to lash up a temporary shelter to give them all some protection against the rain. Tying several boughs to each other, he bent them over forming an arch. Abundant with thick foliage, it kept out the worst of the rain. Near the entrance, three horses huddled together, heads lowered and looking dejected. At the other end, an indentation in the rocky face helped to keep them dry.

Annalee stared moodily at the heavy clouds as they scudded across the sky. Rain plastered her long hair down the sides of her face. Things were not going very well. The day was not progressing the way she hoped. Tansy tried to coax a few twigs to burn while Thane taught Barry how to put points on arrows. Barry was absorbed with the task and was unaware of the tension building up because of the deteriorating weather.

It rained incessantly all morning. High winds made it impossible to travel. Paths were slick with mud and unsafe for the horses. They had to safeguard them from becoming lame. They cursed the delay. It not only gave the gypsies a chance to widen the gap, but also washed

218

THE SECRET OF TAMSWORTH FOREST

away their tracks. Everything depended on following them through this hostile land.

Annalee was unable to sit still. She knew Barry was expecting to meet up with Sue. She loved having Thane with them, but felt under pressure. Barry convinced himself they would soon be meeting up with Sue. She hadn't the heart to explain to him what a depraved life the nomadic people lived. Not many of their prisoners were ever seen again. Hating her thoughts, she moved towards the horses, and this made them skittish. She raised her face, looking up at the sky to see if it was getting any brighter. The rain stung her cheeks. Trees were bending as the high wind caught their foliage. Without the sun the day was chilly.

"I've done it!" Tansy's jubilant cry made everyone look at her. A small fire was burning merrily and already a sense of comfort filled the shelter. Annalee returned and crouched beside her, holding her hands to the warmth. Thane and Barry joined them. "This can't last much longer," Thane grumbled. "Once it stops we can make some headway and maybe reach the Falls by early evening."

"It doesn't give me the impression it's ever going to stop." Barry was pessimistic. "Looks like it's set in for the day."

Tansy gave him a shove, nearly knocking him backwards. "Oh ye of little faith. Look on the bright side. Cheer up, will you."

An hour later the rain stopped. A watery sun broke through the clouds and with its appearance, the wind subsided. They extinguished the fire and were off.

Barry rode behind Thane on Saturn. He was by far the most powerful horse they had and was now healed of his arrow wound.

The earth smelt sweet and fresh. Everything looked clean and sparkling. The drops of rain on leaves glittered as rays from the sun caught them. Dark clouds still gathered in the distance. They looked threatening but were speeding away, having done their worst over the land. Above them the sky turned blue.

Thunder Falls could be heard long before they got there. They quickened their pace, and turning a bend, saw the Falls below. They were eager to arrive, excitement stirring within them. The thunderous noise of the Falls filled their ears. Heavy rain had made the water swell to a dangerous level. They left the horses behind, and drew near on foot, standing on a rocky outcrop. The river surged fiercely through a deep gorge below them, boiling and churning over rocks as it crashed against the sides, making white-water rapids. Then the fast flowing waters thundered over the lip of the Falls, crashing down onto the rocks below. It was breath-taking to watch, a magnificent sight. The vision of the falling water was compelling – almost hypnotic to the watchers, it disappeared from sight behind the trees, and in the thick mist caused by the spray, a hundred rainbows danced.

The beauty of it could not hold them forever. They turned away, the place was deserted. There was not a gypsy or caravan to be seen; not even any litter. Bitter disappointment swept over Thane as he cast his eyes over the area, and Annalee pressed his arm sympathetically. Signs of the last communal camp fire were barely visible and the ruts made by caravan wheels were filled with water. The gypsies had long since gone. There was nothing to show which direction the caravans had taken when they left.

Separately they wandered around with little idea of what they were looking for. Barry thought a view from high up might be an advantage, so he tested his ankle by climbing a tree. White Hawk had already vanished into the undergrowth looking for his supper, and Tansy was drawn back to the water. Only Thane stood in deep meditation beside the grazing horses. He seemed to be indifferent to what was going on around them. Annalee was loath to leave him. She could almost feel his hurt and frustration, but the expression on his face made her wary.

"I'm so sorry, Thane," she burst out. "Maybe it was a mistake coming here, but I thought we would learn something. This being one of the gypsies' watering holes, all tribes come here to fill up."

Her words made Thane snap out of his meditation. His face brightened up. "That's it, Annalee. You've solved our problem." He was suddenly animated. "We don't need any tracks to follow. Where is the next river or lake they go to from here?"

"I don't know." Annalee felt awful. "There are so many lakes. They could go to any of them."

Her brother swung away to hide the bleak look in his eyes, but not fast enough. Annalee had already noticed. Before she could bring herself to say more, Barry's voice floated down to them from his high perch. "There

221

is a string of caravans approaching from the east," he said, "twenty at least. I think the gypsies are heading back here."

Thane tensed. It wouldn't do for them to be found here on a gypsy camp site. They would be hopelessly outnumbered. He had to get the girls and Barry away. His voice was curt. "Get down here at once, lad," he called, "we need to be moving." He raised the horn to his lips and sent a warning out to Tansy, who immediately hurried in their direction. At the same time White Hawk burst from the bushes with an object hanging from his jaws. This was bad timing. They had not got time to bother with him, but Barry was amused and remarked,

"What a strange supper he's got. Shouldn't think he could eat that. What on earth is it?"

Whatever it was, White Hawk was not prepared to hand it over. The powerful young animal pricked up his ears and bounded away a few yards, thinking maybe he could make a game of this. Thane ignored him, anxious to be away. He urged everyone to mount the horses, and before long, they were trotting briskly in the opposite direction. Tansy tried to lighten the situation a little. "White Hawk has been digging around at the top of the Falls. There was some rubbish there which I dare say the gypsies forgot. I shouldn't think he's found any food. They don't leave that sort of thing strewn around."

"Looks like an old shoe to me," observed Annalee, grinning, "in which case he can't be hungry."

THE SECRET OF TAMSWORTH FOREST

Her remark made them all stare down at the wolf as he bounded along by their side, still carrying his find. Something like a strap dangled from one side of his jaw, flapping with the movement of his body. Its shape niggled Thane. He had the feeling he had seen it before. White Hawk's actions were completely out of character. When Thane decided they had put enough distance between them and the oncoming gypsies, he pulled to a halt. Thane leapt nimbly from Saturn and approached the wolf. White Hawk looked ready to dash off at the slightest provocation.

"Drop it," ordered Thane.

The order was curt and White Hawk knew it had to be obeyed. Reluctantly he let the object fall to the ground where everyone could see it but he did not back off, he stood over it, his posture threatening. Thane became immobilised by shock. Barry leant forward to see what was wrong and fell off his horse. He dashed forward and picked up the slimy object. At the same time a deep snarl came from the wolf. In normal circumstances he would have sprung at the boy, but with Thane watching, obedience made him remain still. He contented himself with hard-to-miss warning sounds.

It was Barry's turn to be stricken with horror. He stared at the article in his hand and blood drained from his face. His lips moved, but no sound issued from them. This was a nightmare facing him, not a game. For the first time he realised what they were doing was in deadly earnest. He held the dirty object up and turned to Thane. "It's Sue's sandal," he choked, his

223

voice full of misery, "what's it doing here? She would never go anywhere barefoot."

No one could think of anything to say. Apprehension filled every face at this macabre turn of events. Barry's lips quivered, much to his annoyance. "She's dead. You all think she's dead – don't you?" he yelled, out of control. "The gypsies must have killed her." A sob escaped his throat. His whole body shuddered. Turning swiftly, he fled into the trees. The others sat in stunned horror, unable to speak. Finding the sandal put a different aspect on things. Raithe was in more trouble than he knew. Tansy slid silently from her horse and followed the distraught boy.

*   *   *

Sue walked slowly from Zuboarra's caravan, taking a deep breath. She followed Tug without speaking as he guided her back to Elina. The meeting had not turned out as she had hoped. The realisation that Raithe had deliberately led her into a trap, made it clear no one would try and find her. He held all the cards and could tell his people anything he liked. But would Annalee contradict him?

The name Sonja kept recurring. It gnawed at her like a rat. Just who was Sonja? Zuboarra hinted she had royal connections, which was utterly stupid. Yet Raithe was a prince. Could that be why he hated her? The whole thing was farcical. There was nothing royal about her. She was plain Sue Dawson who had the misfortune to look like someone else. She could not

THE SECRET OF TAMSWORTH FOREST

blame these people because even Thane was under the same impression.

Sue's mind was in such a turmoil she was not looking where she was going. She thought of Zuboarra, and her first encounter with him. The gypsy chief had been kind. Was that why she expected protection from him now? He had shown her clearly that that was not going to happen. He was as callous as the rest of them, the only difference being, he was educated.

A well-aimed clod of earth caught the side of her head. It had been thrown with considerable force. Jeering laughter and lots of cackles came from the group of women sitting nearby. Sue made to stop but Tug pulled at her arm, saying, "Do not look at them Sue. Pretend they are not there. Keep walking with me."

Sue's face was smarting. Every fibre in her body wanted to retaliate. With an effort she respected the boy's wishes and did as he bid. He must know his people better than she did. Another clod of earth, bigger than the first and impregnated with stones and chippings of rock, hit her in the small of her back. She tried not to call out, but her temper started to rise.

Stopping abruptly in her tracks, she ignored Tug's urgent warning and glared angrily at the ruthless women who found baiting her so very funny. Without thinking of the consequences, she bent and picked up the stony lump at her feet and threw it back with all her strength. It caught one of the gypsies on her shoulder and a piece of stone flew off at a tangent and hit another one in her eye. With shrieks of rage the women

225

charged at Sue; she stood rooted to the spot, stunned at what damage her throw had done, but she didn't regretted it.

There was no escape for her. They pushed Tug away like a discarded leaf and fell as one on her. They were all big blousy women with hard faces and murderous expressions in their eyes. One grabbed, and held her locked in an iron grip while another one, with blood running down her cheek, smeared wet earth on Sue's face, with rough, calloused hands. She even tried to rub it in roughly and force it into her mouth. A vicious bite from the captive ensured that the treatment was not repeated.

Using her legs to her best advantage, Sue kicked out wildly, making contact with many of them. She could hardly see, as loose grit entered her eyes. Tears of rage came as a blessing in disguise, because they flushed out her eyes and saved her from permanent damage. The more she struggled the worse it became. The gypsies derived pleasure from her anger. As someone's nails raked her skin, someone else used a knife to hack at her hair. Then, without warning, she was swamped in a hot oily liquid which was tipped over her head. It ran all the way down her body and the smell of it made her gag. The next moment a hefty push sent her to the ground. Sue's head made contact with the hard earth and she decided to play dead. Her attackers stood over her and callously kicked, to see if she moved – then receiving no reaction, they moved off muttering under their breath and watched from a safe distance.

THE SECRET OF TAMSWORTH FOREST

Tug crept back to Sue and gently touched her face, just as a roar filled the air and vibrated from rock to rock. Zuboarra came striding over the land shaking his massive fists at the women. His fury could not be ignored and his raucous voice was full of venom. It penetrated sharply to every corner of the camp. He spoke at great length. Tug crouched over Sue, wincing at the words he heard as he helped her to regain her feet. The women slunk out of sight.

Breathing heavily, the gypsy chief turned his attention to Sue. He stood with hands on hips and legs apart, glaring at her from beneath his bushy eyebrows. She felt and smelt like a sewer rat, and looked at anything except him. This is how she came to see her hair on the ground. With a cry of horror her hands flew to her head, frantically feeling to find out what damage had been done. He dragged her hands away ruthlessly.

"You have got what you deserve, woman," he roared furiously. "Why did you anger my people? You are nobody important. Now look at you. I have seen better things crawl out of holes. Already your price has fallen with hair looking like that." As he spoke, he scooped up the hair and thrust it in her face. She backed away, trembling. "This cannot be stuck back so the rest must come off." He grabbed a handful of what hair she had left.

"No," she gasped, "you can't."

"Yes," he snarled, "I can. Tug – fetch Elina to my caravan."

He did not wait for the boy's answer. When he ordered something it was done. A fleshy hand caught

227

Sue's arm in a ruthless grip and he dragged her back, protesting, to his caravan.

*   *   *

They waited for Elina to come. Fear smote Sue as she watched the old lady approach. Elina moved slowly, her face expressionless, and Tug watched her anxiously. Meanwhile, Sue gazed at the world through unseeing eyes. Nothing meant anything to her anymore.

Zuboarra spoke sharply, telling Elina what he wanted done, and strode away. Sue slumped against the caravan wall, looking morose. Elina almost shook her in despair as she tried to attract her attention. The last two hours had callously stripped away all hopes of escaping for the girl. There was no fight left in her as she mutely stood before Elina. Tug went on errands that would keep him out the way while Elina stripped the young girl of the foul-smelling clothes. She used the gypsy chief's personal bathtub to scrub her down thoroughly. Then, with an ivory comb and sharp knife, set about rearranging what was left of Sue's head of curls. A mass of hair fell to the floor, the sight of which brought tears to her eyes. Elina grunted unhappily. She did not like this job that had been thrust upon her. "It grow," she muttered, trying to cheer Sue up, but her remark fell on deaf ears.

Sue barely registered anything. She wondered what the point of this was. Why go on? She was never going to see her home again. No one was going to rescue her from this hell. Everyone here hated her with the

THE SECRET OF TAMSWORTH FOREST

exception of Elina and Tug. She just wanted to be left alone.

More clothes were found to dress her in. This time it was boy's breeches at Zuboarra's orders. With a cotton shirt that completed the outfit. Soft, calf-length boots, which were of good quality, were added and she did not dare to speculate from where they came. Having covered the scratches on her arms, she now looked more like a youth. Elina stood back and surveyed her. A look of wonder spread over her gaunt face. If only she could know what the outcome of all this was going to be.

Tug chose that moment to creep back into the caravan. His gasp of surprise made her aware of his presence. Elina quickly thrust the dirty clothes into his arms and in their own lingo, ordered him to remove them. She knew her time was short. The pain never left her chest now. She had to rouse Sue somehow from her apathy. On the spur of the moment, she picked up Zuboarra's hand mirror from a shelf and handed it to the girl. "Look," she ordered tersely, the effort making her hold the table for support.

Sue remained motionless, not complying at all. The older woman moved closer.

"Fight! You must fight." A strange urgency in her voice made Sue feel vaguely uneasy and forced her to look up.

"Fight? Why?" She wanted Elina to leave her alone. But that was not Elina's intention. She gave Sue a small shake.

229

"Escape," she hissed, frustration beginning to show in her actions.

Sue looked at her blankly. "Escape, why? Let them sell me. They will soon realise their mistake when they find out I am not really this Sonja."

Vexation showed clearly in Elina's face. She was annoyed she did not know enough of the language to say what she wanted. She thrust the mirror at Sue again and almost shouted, "Look. Look."

This time Sue did and Elina had the satisfaction of seeing her body stiffen. Confusion now filled the girl's eyes and suddenly she was no longer sure of anything. Her reflection mocked her. Elina had made a good job of her hair. It was a lot shorter and barely reached her ears. It was not so curly either. It altered her appearance dramatically, but it was all wrong. It was not her face looking back at her, but Raithe's. Bewilderment flooded her mind. She looked mutely at Elina for explanation and the older woman took pity on her. "You are Sonja. You, you," she whispered urgently, and Sue recoiled, uttering a sharp, "No."

"Yes. Not stay here," Elina cut in relentlessly. "You are Sonja, sister to Prince…"

She stopped short as a shadow fell over them. Zuboarra lumbered up the steps of his caravan and she hastily moved out of the way. He had not heard anything. His eyes immediately fell on Sue and they glinted with approval. He rubbed his massive hands together and looked very expectant. Good humour quickly restored, he grabbed her chin and lifted her face to the light.

THE SECRET OF TAMSWORTH FOREST

"Your short hair has proven your identity beyond doubt. I cannot afford any more mishaps occurring to you. Tonight we move from here and tomorrow with some of my men I take you to the ships and collect the gold you will bring me. No more harm must befall you before then. Take her away, Elina, and make sure the caravan is securely locked."

Sue did not remember being escorted back to her prison. No one accosted her this time. She slumped on the bed. Nothing made sense anymore. She could not deny Raithe looked almost like her twin, yet to say that he was her brother was impossible. Even now, with the likeness staring her in the eyes, she could not admit to it because he looked nothing at all like Priscilla and Barry. *But then* – a little voice said in her mind – *neither do you.*

It was not until they were back in the caravan and Tug started to speak to Elina, that Sue realised what a terrific strain had been put on the older woman. Pain was etched sharply on the contours of her face. Mortified, she jumped up, insisting that Elina rest on her bed. Elina gave no argument this time. She complied thankfully, wiping moisture from her upper lip. Her feverish eyes sought the boy's and she said,

"Speak, Tug. Tell her."

Tug went to the door to make sure no one was outside, listening. He turned to Sue, looking very grown up. Not for the first time did she wonder how old he was, and his words made her go cold. "Elina wants you to escape tonight because it is your only chance."

231

Shock made her say, "Don't be silly, I shall be locked in here."

"But I'm prepared for that." Tug smiled as though he were humouring her and revealed a bar of iron which looked remarkably like a burglar's jemmy. "I know you will be locked in by Elina. What you don't know is that I shall be in here with you. Tonight the caravan will start moving and making much noise. It is then that I remove some of the floor with this." He flourished the tool in his hand. "Much later – in the darkness, Elina will become ill and that will stop the caravans moving."

Sue looked sharply at the older woman, wondering what she was planning, but her face was blank. Her gaze switched back to Tug. Unease was creeping through her. If escaping was this easy, why hadn't she tried it before? "And I suppose I slip through the hole you've made and run away without being seen." She found it hard not to be sarcastic. "Think of something better than that! Whoever was in the caravan following mine, would see me. I don't know this land. I'd soon be caught."

"I'll explain," Tug said calmly. "We will be following the base of the mountains. It will be easy to hide in the confusion Elina will make."

Sue breathed in deeply, refusing to let her hopes rise. "I wouldn't know which way to turn. I don't even know the language. I don't stand a chance." So instead she became practical. "I suppose it hasn't occurred to you that I don't know this land. I wouldn't know where to go. They would soon catch me."

THE SECRET OF TAMSWORTH FOREST

"No they wouldn't, because I shall be with you." Tug's simple statement took her breath away. He made it sound so easy. "It's all been arranged. I shall have food and I know exactly what to do. The terrain is marshy but I can guide you through it. They will not be expecting you to escape when you are locked up in here. You must take this chance, Sue. If they get you to the ships, all will be lost. You will never see your friends again – and if you keep on insisting you are not Sonja they will kill you for the trouble you have caused."

Shakily, Sue sat down by Elina. One of Elina's thin hands touched one of hers and held it fast. Her dull eyes held hers for a moment before looking away.

"There will be much trouble for you if I escape," Sue said softly, "I can't let you do this, Elina. You are my friend. There must be some other way."

Elina's eyes glazed over. Unexpectedly she gathered Sue in her arms and held her tightly. Sue heard the rasping of her breath. "I die," she whispered huskily, "time short. Take Tug. He must go with you. Not stay here."

Tears rose unbidden to Sue's eyes. The older woman was a barrier between her and the gypsies. It was through her intervention she was saved from drowning. Her presence made life bearable. It was all a lie. Elina could not be dying. Sue tightened her grip, trying to hold back the darkness looming ahead. The touch of Elina's clammy skin and feverish heat told its own tale. With an effort Elina pushed her away and walked upright to the door. For several minutes she stood there

233

looking back at Sue and Tug as though committing their faces to memory, then she said something rapidly to Tug and turned to Sue, hardly seeing her and said, "goodbye, Sue."

Elina swung the shutters together with a bang and shot the bolts on the outside. The noise made several men look in her direction and she was satisfied. The little caravan became shrouded in darkness. Tug and Sue did not hear her move away but they were aware of men's voices as they stopped outside and tried the door. Even Elina was not trusted.

CHAPTER 15

ON THE TRAIL

From the area surrounding the gypsy camp came the howl of wolves. The men were superstitious and became uneasy. These were normally tough, brutal men, but the nearness of the wolves changed them dramatically, especially when they couldn't be seen. For Zuboarra, it was the last straw. He needed to reach the ships and he cracked his whip down to get them moving. He was hardened against any form of superstition, but it was unusual to have predators so near the mountains. He strode amongst them, gold earrings swinging wildly against his swarthy face. More howls rent the air. The horses' eyes rolled in their heads, showing the whites. They were getting skittish at the closeness of the wolves.

"Get those horses harnessed up," his guttural voice roared and he glared through the shadows at the confusion surrounding him. "Make sure nothing is left behind to attract the scavengers. It just means there are a lot of hungry wolves out there. Has anyone seen that good for nothing boy yet?"

The two brawny men standing near him shook their heads. If they couldn't see Tug, there was no point in answering. Zuboarra scowled. Since having that girl in their midst the men had become belligerent.

"What about Elina?" he asked harshly.

Jacques spat onto the ground, not bothering to stop what he was doing. "She's in 'er caravan. Been there all day and the kid's been running errands." It was not strictly true but Zuboarra was not to know that. "Want me to get 'er?"

Zuboarra ground his teeth. "It's not her I want…it's him. When you see that runt again, send him to me, and Jacques, I want you to drive the prisoners' caravan when we get started. Is it still locked up?"

"Yes. No one's been near it since you last saw her."

"Good." More howls pierced the air. The pack of wild wolves was getting nearer. This knowledge had the desired effect and spurred the men on. An apprehensive feeling settled over the camp. Everyone was careful; they never strayed beyond the light shed by the fixed flares. Children were forcibly kept in the caravans under strict surveillance and were told not to move. They harnessed up the horses and eased them between the shafts in record time. The smell of the predators made them skittish.

In next to no time the caravan train was underway and jostling through the rocky terrain. At the first jolt Sue's sinews knotted. Directly enough noise came from the rolling wagons, the boy extinguished their light and worked in the darkness. Sue peered through the gloom, excitement and apprehension warring inside her. Sitting rigid on the bed, she waited while Tug prised up part of the floor to make an opening big enough for them to slip through. At any moment she expected the door to open and Zuboarra to confront them. A cold draught of

THE SECRET OF TAMSWORTH FOREST

air rushed through the newly made hole and circulated in their prison. The sound of the hooves were now loud and vibrated in her eardrums as they clip-clopped along the rocky trail. The job done, Tug crept back to the bed and sat beside her. When Sue would have spoken, he placed a finger on her lips and whispered, "You can be heard outside now. Keep quiet."

They sat in silence for a time. Sue found the waiting frustrating. Something horrible was sure to happen and prevent her escape. Suppose Elina was unable to distract everyone's attention. Suppose she had another attack?

Above the clatter of the horses, Sue's keen ears heard a scream. Almost immediately they saw light reflecting on the ground and shadows of moving people as they walked past the caravan holding naked flames. Tug reached for a cloth bundle and motioned Sue to kneel on the edge of the hole. She was more than pleased to be wearing boy's clothes. The cold air blew up in her face and she nearly lost her balance when, with a violent oath, the driver of her prison jerked the horse to a standstill. He clambered down, muttering under his breath. Pandemonium had broken out everywhere. Zuboarra's voice could be heard shouting out orders. Footsteps continually ran past their caravan and then for a brief moment, there was silence.

Tug jumped out of the hole first, landing lightly, and he helped Sue as she gingerly felt for the ground below her dangling feet. She landed with an unexpected thud. People were passing by on either side again but Tug and Sue were not seen crouching between the wheels.

The flaring torches created more shadows which luckily hid them. The bellowing voices were now returning. Tug grabbed Sue's arm. "When I say run – head into the bushes that way."

He pointed to their left. Sue moved into a position that would aid her flight. Her trust in Tug was implicit. Zuboarra's voice roared out something and she felt the boy stiffen. "What's wrong?"

Tug steadied himself. "He wants your caravan searched to check that you are there. Go now. Quickly...run."

His hand helped her on her way with a sharp push. Keeping fingers crossed no one was looking in her direction, she sought refuge in the undergrowth growing thickly before her. Regardless of the brambles that pierced her skin, terror made her forge ahead. Deep scratches made her arms burn. In desperation born of terror, she forged ahead, going deeper and deeper into the hostile environment. They must not catch her. Suddenly the ground disappeared from beneath her feet and with a choking cry she fell.

*   *   *

Four hours earlier, Thane and his companions built a fire. The thick foliage of the trees growing along the ridge gave them cover. They were deep in gypsy territory and needed to stay alert. Annalee and Tansy were no longer feeling jubilant. This journey was not going as planned. After one night spent out in the open,

THE SECRET OF TAMSWORTH FOREST

they were still undecided as to what their next move was going to be.

The girls took their minds off what had happened by doing the cooking, and were both pleased Thane was with them. He spent his time sharpening all his weapons. The scrape of his blade was the only sound to be heard, but Barry remained idle, sitting alone by choice. He never spoke to them. He spent all his time staring bleakly towards the mountains, rebuffing anyone's overtures. He looked a lot older than the boy with a bad ankle they had rescued. With suspiciously bright eyes he studied the sandal in his hand. He would not let the others near. Only one person was not happy with this arrangement.

White Hawk's golden eyes were fixed on him with an unblinking stare, his breath fanning the boy's face. But Barry disregarded the wolf. His concentration was on the sandal. Unbidden, Sue's happy face flashed across his vision. Hastily he removed his glasses and made the pretence of polishing them, at the same time dabbing moisture from his eyes. Annalee pretended she never noticed.

White Hawk wriggled along on his stomach until he was beside the boy. He whined softly and pressed a wet nose on his neck. Barry turned to focus on him, wondering what he wanted. Almost taking liberties, the wolf's head came level with the sandal and he sniffed it. The boy allowed him that much leeway, but his grip tightened. The wolf nipped his hand gently then his powerful jaws closed over the shoe. Barry was about to tug it away, when for some inexplicable reason he let it

239

KATHLEEN B. WILSON

go. White Hawk bounded away with the object once more dangling from his mouth. His eyes glowed in the setting sun and settled on Barry's face. Pawing the ground, he moved off a few more paces. Barry scrambled to his feet when White Hawk once again turned his head. The boy said incredulously,

"He wants me to follow him." From being despondent he was suddenly excited. "He's got a scent from Sue's sandal."

Without thought of any implications, he pursued the wolf. The other three looked up, startled. Thane grasped the situation quicker than the girls and leapt to his feet, hastily sheathing his knives. "Hang on, Barry. I'm coming with you," he called.

"You can't," protested Annalee. "The food..."

Thane glanced at her. "Pack up the food and break camp," he said, not giving the girls a chance to protest. "I'll leave you a trail to follow." He whistled to Saturn and sprang onto his back, galloping off after the running boy.

*   *   *

Harsh guttural shouts filled the air. Sue lay where she had fallen, dazed and too scared to move. A cold sweat covered her body. The darkness was intense, even her own hands were invisible. Whatever was nearby was a mystery. Fear kept her in one position in case she fell any further. She could not rid herself of the feeling that she was suspended somewhere. Horror of being seen by the gypsies filled her. She could still hear them, but just

240

THE SECRET OF TAMSWORTH FOREST

how far away were they? She hoped no one would look down the hole into which she had fallen.

She was lying on something springy and prickly. If she gazed upwards, she could see the stars, and then, unwanted, there was a flicker of a light. The gypsies were searching for something. Their raucous voices seemed very close, and above her came another sound. It was like the thrashing of a whip. Sue trembled, because it went on for a long time. Was it something to do with Elina?

Then she began to wonder where Tug was, but had enough common sense not to shout out. When it was daylight she would be able to see for herself. The voice of Zuboarra was now directly over her head. She wished she could understand what he was saying. His voice sounded furious. He obviously knew they had both escaped. The light moved away and suddenly she heard the wheels of the caravan and the thud from the horses' hooves as they continued on their way. Something fell very near to her, causing a draught. She wondered what it was they had dumped.

Sue braced herself to lie still until dawn. Then she could assess her position. She fell into a fitful sleep and didn't wake until something fluttered by her face, almost touching her nose. Her eyes jerked open. She saw a huge bird, beautifully coloured but with a cruel beak, sitting on a branch above her head. Its glassy eyes were fixed on her. Its cry was harsh and grated on her ears. Sue eased herself up until she was sitting. Whatever was beneath her gave way, and her heart leapt into her mouth. Although her limbs felt stiff after

241

a night exposed to the elements, she reached out cautiously and caught hold of a stout branch for support. Once secure, Sue twisted her head round to view her whereabouts. Then she wished she had not bothered. A strangled gasp escaped her lips and her blood felt as though it had turned to ice. She had to be hallucinating after her fall. Directly below her was a sheer drop and when she looked upwards, towering cliffs loomed above her head. Petrified, she clung for dear life to the branch of the tree which had broken her fall; fortunately nature had woven the thick foliage into a sort of ledge. Somehow finding her voice, she croaked out,

"Tug! Can you hear me?"

The only answer she received was a squawk as the bird flew off. She tried to make her numb mind face up to her situation. If Tug had followed her, he could be at the bottom of this precipice. He obviously had not known this cliff was here or he had been misinformed. On the other hand, Zuboarra had threatened to thrash him to within an inch of his life if she escaped. This made her shiver again. She remembered hearing the whip being used and felt sick with horror. Was that Tug who had fallen past her in the dark?

It took a long time to gather up courage and overcome the fear which controlled her mind. The only way to safety was to climb up, unless by some miracle she sprouted wings. Her eyes followed the trunk of the twisted tree. Did it reached the top of the cliff. "No." Her nerve gave out as she realised the hopelessness of her position. Eventually self-preservation asserted

THE SECRET OF TAMSWORTH FOREST

itself. Her limbs were sore, badly scratched and stinging, but she was all in one piece. She called out Tug's name again, louder, but there was still no answer.

Tentatively Sue tested the strength of the branch before she put her full weight on it. It appeared to hold well and the trunk was even thicker. Gingerly she pulled herself into an upright position and gritted her teeth at the unexpected strain. Then she cried out as one foot sank through the leaves. Panting, she nerved herself to continue and slowly started to climb. There were many footholds at first and she blocked out thoughts of the yawning drop beneath. Her tattered clothes were wet through. The sun rose in the sky and before long beat down relentlessly on her back. Progress was slow. Every move she made needed her utmost concentration. It didn't take long before her strength began to fail. She could see the top but doubted she had the ability or stamina to reach it. She was already near the top of the tree trunk and the cliff face showed a daunting aspect. With a small sob she rested her hot face on the rock and wedged herself between trunk and cliff. If she did not move, she was safe for a while.

"Sue!" The voice came from above. She looked up at the face peering over the edge of the cliff in disbelief. A face blotched with dark marks and streaked with blood. One eye was completely closed. Horror flowed through her. Zuboarra had caught him.

"Tug. What happened to you?"

"Sue – don't move anymore. I will find help for you." And the face disappeared.

243

Sue began to wonder if she was hallucinating. She felt sick, and almost vomited. She remembered the swishing sound in the dark. They had beaten him senseless because of her. Tears of frustration ran down her cheeks at feeling so helpless. She needed to be up there to help him. Sue had never felt so full of despair as she did at that moment. How far would he have to go before he met anyone? If he ever did. Was he in a fit condition to do anything?

"Tug," she screamed, "Tug... come back." Suppose the gypsies were still up there? It was too late to think about that now. She had given herself away. Her scream faded away into silence. Her voice echoed back to her. He was gone and no one else looked over the cliff. She closed her eyes and sank into oblivion. The beautiful bird circled around. Only the tree kept her wedged there. He was content to wait.

*   *   *

"Stop, Barry! Get up here, lad."

Thane reined in his horse beside the running boy. Barry ignored him. There was a determined expression on his face and his eyes were fixed on White Hawk, streaking way ahead of him. He must not lose sight of the wolf. Thane cursed, but kept up with him. The boy gave him a cursory glance.

"I'm not coming back. I'm following White Hawk." His voice was defiant. He knew Thane would be furious and waited for him to explode. People always got mad when he took the law into his own hands, so Barry was deflated when Thane laughed softly.

"So am I. Wouldn't it be better if we went together? Wouldn't you find it easier riding with me? We could get along much faster sitting on Saturn, and then White Hawk won't be able to get away from us."

He patted the glossy neck of his horse as he spoke and Saturn tossed his head as though in agreement. This time Barry did pause.

"You mean to say you are still looking for Sue after what we have just found? You don't believe she's dead like the others do… " His voice trailed off. Something in Thane's expression stopped him from saying any more. He knew he had gone too far. Thane quickly swallowed his angry retort. How dare the lad even think he had abandoned Sue? But staring into Barry's distraught face, he relaxed. His face softened. The boy was not to know how he felt about his sister. He leaned over to give Barry a hand up, saying, "White Hawk moves with much speed. He's got four legs. You would never have kept up with him on foot."

"Oh, I don't know," Barry answered, settling himself comfortably behind him on the saddle. "He would have waited for me, you know."

Thane grunted. "Then he's not the wolf I trained."

After that they remained silent. Diligently they kept the wolf in sight, which no longer turned to see if they were following. He moved swiftly, his body low to the ground. He had been trained to move unobserved, but Saturn kept up with ease For some reason White Hawk led them back towards the gypsy encampment where a

245

smoke haze in the air showed clearly that the nomadic tribe were again in residence. Thane was not looking for a confrontation, but he wondered if it were possible Sue could still be here, because hiding places along the water's edge were numerous, and keeping a prisoner in a cave was certainly possible. However, his unease was not necessary. White Hawk skirted the camp and ploughed along a deeply rutted valley.

Soon habitation was left far behind. The area became rocky and harder to traverse. If caravans came this way then their drivers must be miracle workers to get them through the rocks. The barren landscape began to look forbidding. As the sun vanished behind the mountains, which were now close at hand, shadows fell heavily over the land. White Hawk stopped in his tracks, sniffing the air. Thane stared in all directions, not wanting to miss any vital clues. They both slid off Saturn's back to give the horse a rest. Some of Barry's colour returned to his cheeks, along with his appetite.

"I'm hungry," he stated, looking ruefully at all the desolation around them. The place was silent as the grave. Thane made up his mind swiftly. "Well, the girls will be following with the food. I suggest we make camp."

"Camp," echoed the boy, "you mean we are going to stop?" Barry was torn between finding Sue and his pressing hunger. Thane pointed out that they would not be able to follow White Hawk in the dark; he might see where he was going but the horse would have difficulties and they wanted to avoid making Saturn lame.

White Hawk was also going nowhere. He squatted on his hind quarters as though to say 'that settles matters'. Then he pointed his nose to the sky and emitted a howl. From somewhere further afield, an answering cry rent the air. Barry could not suppress his astonishment, but Thane watched the wolf intently. As though on cue, White Hawk howled again, and for longer. In return, several other wolves joined in the chorus.

"What on earth's he doing?" asked Barry, anxiously. "We shall soon be overrun with wolves if he goes on like that."

"Don't worry, son," Thane replied, "the pack will not come any closer. They are communicating with White Hawk. Telling him what is up ahead."

The cries went on for a long time. On a flat rock far in the distance, two wolves appeared, silhouetted against the darkening sky. One reared up on his hind legs as though saluting White Hawk, and then they vanished. Barry blinked, wondering if he had really seen them. A hush settled over the landscape. It was almost as though there had never been any wolves, and White Hawk was content. He wandered round, getting under their feet as Thane looked for a suitable place in which to bed down.

A long time elapsed before the girls cantered up. Greetings were kept to the minimum. Conversation was low and restricted because sound travelled in such an open area. By now it was completely dark, but Thane had managed to rummage around for material and lit a fire. It threw a warming glow over them all. Tansy produced some food, already cooked, and Annalee passed round her flask of water which she had managed to fill.

"Where did you find the water?" enquired Thane, pulling at a piece of tough meat with his teeth and glancing quizzically at her shadowed face.

"We missed your trail and went wrong," replied his sister carelessly. "But before you start telling me off and saying what a lousy tracker I am, let me tell you that we came across something interesting which you obviously missed."

"Like a lot of water," interposed Barry innocently.

"Oh – better than that," replied Tansy, and her voice rang with suppressed excitement, "we found traces of horses."

Thane stopped eating. The implication of her words was enormous. He tried not to get elated too soon and raise their hopes. His own journey today had not borne any fruit. "Tell me more."

The two girls were too excited to keep him in suspense. "We drove off a pack of wolves because we wanted water from the lake. It was then we saw the droppings. They were fresh, Thane. The gypsies could not have been gone long. Our guess is that they moved off as it got dark."

"We've caught them up," whooped Barry and he sprang to his feet, forgetting about food. "If Sue's with them we can get her back. Come on, let's get going."

"Hold it, son." Thane's voice had the effect of a douche of cold water and Barry stiffened. "There are three things you had better start considering right now.

THE SECRET OF TAMSWORTH FOREST

Firstly they may not be the same gypsies, this country has many thousands of them, secondly we cannot follow them in the dark, they have lights, we don't, and if we did, they would see us. Thirdly, we need more people with us, because they would overrun us in no time."

Barry could feel his temper rising; they were trying to obstruct him again. "In other words, as far as you are concerned, they can get away," he said. It was a bleak statement of fact. His voice was bitter. Tansy threw an arm round his shoulders, even though he tried to shrug it away. "It's nothing like that at all, Barry," she said kindly. "Directly it is light in the morning, you and Thane can start tracking them and see where they make camp. Then we can get reinforcements from our army, especially if you see your sister amongst them. Whatever else you may think, they are not getting away."

CHAPTER 16

FINDING SUE

An hour after dawn Saturn cantered along the dusty track. Fingers of mist curled round the mountains and thickened at their peaks. The sun had not yet risen high enough to illuminate the snow-covered summits. Down below shadows still enveloped the landscape giving it a purple cast in the early morning light.

Barry was like a coiled spring as he climbed up the rough track. He found it hard to sit back and let events take their course. With White Hawk racing ahead, the boy often had an urge to run with him. It was common sense, rather than Thane, which kept him sitting on the horse. He was not used to the altitude of this alien country.

The track wound higher. On their left the ground fell away. More often than not, the drop was obscured by trees and shrubbery. Brambles were also much in evidence. Barry tried to picture caravans travelling this same hazardous route, and failed. He realised very early on they were not going to see any gypsies. It was hard work to mask his disappointment. The emptiness of the area disenchanted him. It was deserted, except for the occasional bird of prey which would swoop by looking for food and, not finding any, glide easily down to the valley below.

THE SECRET OF TAMSWORTH FOREST

"What on earth do they find to eat up here? It's barren," he exclaimed.

"Oh, they find a rodent or two, sometimes a dead mountain cat."

"Would they attack us?" asked Barry, noticing their vicious beaks.

"Only if you're dead or just about to die, then you would make a tasty meal. Don't dwell on them, Barry." Thane did not add that seeing the bird worried him. It was a bad omen.

They toiled on. The sun rose higher as the morning progressed. Eventually Thane called a halt, saying, "Jump down, Barry. Let's stretch our legs and have a drink."

Thankfully Barry joined him, flexing his legs. He was sweating profusely. While Thane was searching for his water flask, the boy stared intently at the loose scree, puzzled that there were no tracks. Surely a string of caravans would have left evidence of their passing. Thane pushed back his damp hair as he handed the bottle to Barry.

"They cover their tracks extremely well," he explained, noticing what he was doing. "It keeps their destination a secret." The fact that Annalee and Tansy had found traces of the gypsy horses was a chance in a million. That was a bad mistake on their part. For some reason they must have been in a hurry to get away and he for one would like to know why.

"Do you think they know we are following them?" Barry asked.

251

"Not a chance. We would have been ambushed by now."

"And taken prisoner the same as Sue?"

Thane's features hardened. "Best you don't know. Finished with the water, lad?"

The change of conversation had the desired effect. Barry took a huge swig and placed it back in Thane's outstretched hand. It was packed away carefully for future use and Barry, as he stared up at the mountains, asked, "Are we crossing these?"

"I doubt it." Thane looked puzzled. "This is not a usual gypsy route. For some reason it has been changed. We are relying solely on White Hawk to follow the scent. So let's get going."

Barry looked behind him, surprised at the height they were already. He saw the girls far below and gave them a wave, unexpectedly chuffed when they returned the greeting. He felt they were watching out for him. They continued toiling up the steep track, their pace slow so as not to push the horses too much. Sometimes they gave them a complete rest by walking. When the ground levelled out they resumed their positions on the horses' backs.

White Hawk had given up bounding ahead and now walked a few yards in front. The sun was at its height and still they laboured on. Barry felt drowsy and the scenery had long since lost its novelty. Thane remained on the alert, and when White Hawk paused with ears erect, he tensed, even though a moment later the wolf shook his head and plodded on. After a few more bends in the path, he halted again; this time his fur bristled

THE SECRET OF TAMSWORTH FOREST

and a low warning growl rumbled from his throat. Thane sprang from Saturn's back, notching an arrow ready for aiming. He motioned Barry to stay behind but the boy produced a knife of his own. He had no intention of letting Thane face trouble alone.

A small and tattered figure stumbled into view. With a snarl the wolf flung himself forward, teeth flashing. He leapt, driving his huge body at the small figure, sending them both crashing to the ground. He was far bigger than his adversary, so had the advantage. With legs astride the unmoving body, he howled defiantly and lowered his jaws to close them round a thin arm. Barry broke free from the hypnotic stupor that held him immobilised and threw himself in front of the startled Thane, landing on White Hawk, and courageously pushing him away. His voice screamed, "leave him alone, you big brute. He's only a kid. You shan't kill him."

Thane's lips tightened into a thin line. He shouted out an order and the confused wolf backed away, looking uncertain. Thane, however, was incensed and his fury knew no bounds.

"What the hell do you think you are doing?" he yelled, flinging Barry aside. His eyes smouldered as they raked over him. "You could have got yourself killed, you silly idiot. He wasn't going to hurt whatever that is until I gave the order."

"Then you could have fooled me," Barry shouted back angrily. "He had his teeth in the boy's arm. Look… you can see the marks."

253

Blood oozed slowly from several wounds. Thane breathed heavily, still shaking with rage. "White Hawk is trained to be vicious. He is not a dog. He has to make his adversary afraid. How else do you think he can help us? Don't interfere in the future, Barry. You're lucky it's just one gypsy and not a band of them."

Barry contented himself by glowering, and knelt beside the inert form to see if whoever it was had a pulse. The sight made him feel sick. Thane dropped down beside him, and he, a grown man, felt bile filling his mouth as he took in the extent of the boy's injuries. He did not look like a gypsy. He hadn't got that swarthy cast. Blood streaked his whole body, where angry weals were deep and open, attracting flies. The face was bruised and swollen, one eye completely closed. His attacker had been ruthless, showing no mercy. Whatever the boy had done, it did not warrant this sort of punishment.

"He's been abandoned here to die, and would have done if we hadn't come along."

There was uncertainty in Barry's eyes, which at Thane's words immediately turned to hope. "You're going to help him, aren't you?" He was not quite sure of Thane's reaction anymore.

Thane nodded curtly. "Try giving him some of this for now and keep those flies away." He thrust the water flask into Barry's hand. Then he realised White Hawk had gone. "The girls will catch up soon and help you. He might say something but I doubt you'll understand. The gypsies have a language of their own. Call me if he does. I must go and see where White Hawk has gone."

THE SECRET OF TAMSWORTH FOREST

Thane rose stiffly from his knees, still feeling utter revulsion. That child could not have walked to this remote spot with his injuries. After the gypsies had mutilated his body, they had cast him away. They must be the same gypsies who had Sue in their power. At that thought his throat constricted and a terrible anger burnt within him. He had to find her. Whether or not he was successful, Raithe was going to pay dearly for this.

Moving round yet another bend, he saw White Hawk tracking something which was invisible to him. He watched, and was on the verge of calling him back when the wolf pushed through a tangle of undergrowth. Thane went rigid, realising there was a sheer drop concealed behind those bushes. He raced to the spot just as the wolf howled. White Hawk stood on the edge of the precipice, feet firmly planted to the ground, ears erect and tail pointed. Thane took a moment, composing himself. So the boy he had just passed had a companion, the poor lad. He wondered grimly if he also had been beaten. At his master's approach the wolf fell silent, but he did not move and stared down with unblinking eyes.

Thane moved cautiously to the edge. There was not much hope for the other person; it was such a long way down. He did not expect to see anyone but as his eyes followed the cliff face down, he saw what he thought was the other boy wedged between a rock and a tree. This one was not a gypsy either, judging from the colour of the short hair. Blood stained his ripped shirt, but there was something familiar about this person hanging between life and death. Thane's breath hissed

255

sharply through his teeth as the 'boy' below became aware of being watched and looked up. Her curls had gone. She had changed beyond recognition. It was someone who must have been to hell and back again – but he knew her.

"Sue." The anguish in his voice reached down to her, "Oh my God. Sue – hang on. Don't you dare to move. I will get a rope and haul you up. Please, Sue – hang on." He moved back a pace and removed the horn from his waist. Putting it to his lips, he blew it three times. Barry looked up, startled. Annalee and Tansy kicked their horses to a gallop and from far off in the mountains, another horn sounded in answer to the signal.

*   *   *

With perspiration pouring down their faces, the girls slithered to a standstill. Springing from their lathered horses, they knelt on either side of the inert form on the ground. Through disbelieving eyes they studied the mutilated body. Tansy glanced from Barry's tight-lipped expression back to the boy, and gently moved some of his tattered garments. The exposed raw flesh of his wounds caused her to suck in her breath. "This must be very painful. I'm surprised he's still breathing. Any idea who he is?" she asked.

Barry hardly acknowledged her question. "He just appeared, and White Hawk attacked him." His harsh rejoinder made Annalee's eyes widen. Lifting one of

THE SECRET OF TAMSWORTH FOREST

the thin arms which clearly showed the puncture marks of teeth, she saw Barry's lips tighten.

"White Hawk is trained to apprehend strangers," she exclaimed calmly, at the same time wondering how Thane dealt with it. "He would never do this to anyone." Her head jerked towards the unconscious boy. "This lad has been brutally thrashed. Where is Thane, by the way?"

"Further up the track looking for – for the wolf." It was all Barry could do to refer to the unfortunate animal. "I decided to stay here."

"Very sensible of you," retorted Annalee dryly. She stood up, trying to understand why Barry felt such a sense of injustice. "Thane has called for help and a healer as you must have heard. The healer is obviously for the boy so that shows you he cares about what has happened to him. The help part – I'm not so sure why he wants that. Will you two be alright if I go and investigate further?"

"Go ahead," answered Tansy, not bothering to look up. "Have you got some water?" She turned to Barry, Annalee already forgotten.

Annalee moved off along the rocky track coming face to face with her brother. At first she did not recognise him. His face could have been carved from granite. The only movement was a muscle which twitched in his jaw, and the hand which was about to blow the horn again. He stared straight through her.

"Thane." Annalee sprang forward and caught his arm. "You can't blow that."

257

"Yes I can. Go away. They haven't answered my call and I need them now."

"But no one blows the horn twice unless..." Warning bells rang in Annalee's head. She scrutinised him through shrewd eyes. "OK, Thane – what is it that is so terribly wrong? Tansy is looking after the boy back there... but you have called for help. In fact – if I had not come along, you were just about to call again. What is so important?"

Her gaze scanned over the mountains and turned to the tangle of brambles on the other side. Seeing nothing untoward, she suddenly thought of the wolf. She pierced him with a questioning look. "Is it because you seem to have lost White Hawk?"

Thane clenched his fists to keep himself under control. She could see the whites of his knuckles. He gritted his teeth and growled. "Why haven't they got here yet?"

"Give them a chance. For goodness sake let me help you with whatever is so wrong."

"You can't. No one can – except those I have summoned."

Thane looked unexpectedly vulnerable and defenceless. In consternation Annalee stepped nearer to him. She was just about to lay a hand on his arm when she heard a faint cry. It alerted her to the presence of another person. In disbelief she turned towards the precipice on the other side of the brambles. Her heart lurched at what that implied. Things started to fall into place.

THE SECRET OF TAMSWORTH FOREST

"Is there another boy… down there?" Annalee's voice was incredulous. In a trice she stepped towards the edge. Her brother grabbed her elbow and shouted,

"Keep away, Annalee. You don't understand. The cry you have just heard… heard… was from Sue." His voice cracked with emotion and he fought to continue. "She's just hanging on down there and I can't do anything. If I distract her again she might fall. I wish whoever answered my call would hurry up and come. I need help to lift her up."

"Snap out of it, Thane. Where's your rope? We need it now," Annalee hissed. She gazed down at the horrific sight of Sue wedged between cliff and tree. For one moment a wave of dizziness assailed her. Although Sue looked up at the disturbance above her, it was doubtful if she recognised anyone. "The rope, Thane," she repeated.

"That's the trouble," he said through tight lips. "It's not strong enough to hold my weight, and hers. We would plummet down into the valley below."

"Maybe *you* would, but it will hold my weight and she needs help now."

"You are not going down there."

"Try and stop me, big brother," she answered defiantly.

For one second there was silence, and then her words mobilized him into action. Whistling sharply, he sent a call to Saturn. The horse trotted into sight – thankfully without Barry in attendance, he could not have coped with Barry at this moment. Thane quickly relieved him of the rope and tied one end to a flexible

259

tree, wound it round himself and attached the other end securely to his sister. He stared deeply into her dark eyes. "You know I can't pull you up until help arrives – don't you?"

Annalee swallowed her fear and forced a smile. "I know. I intend to stay down there with her and give my support. It's the least I can do. Thank you for not stopping me."

"Then don't look down," he warned. They stared at each other and he squeezed her hands, unable to express his gratitude – but she knew what he felt. Holding the rope firmly in his hands, he played it out slowly as she slid over the edge. His breath came out in short gasps while he took the strain. Thane was tense all the while she made her way down to where Sue was stranded, and it was not until Annalee found a small ledge that he relaxed. Annalee paused to gather her second wind. Then she reached out to the other girl. At her touch, Sue turned, amazed to see Annalee beside her. Annalee nearly lost her footing; the change in Sue's appearance made her stomach turn over and she knew she was partly to blame. The gypsies had left their mark on her. Sue would never forgive her, and neither would Thane. Annalee felt perspiration trickling down her back. She put her arms round the trembling girl.

"Oh, Sue, I'm so sorry," she choked. "This is my fault." How inadequate this sounded when she looked at the vivid scars clearly visible on Sue's pale skin. It was obvious she had shared the same fate as the boy

THE SECRET OF TAMSWORTH FOREST

lying up above with Tansy. Sue tried to smile. Her husky whisper was barely audible.

"You have come to help. Are you alone?"

"No. Your brother is with us," replied Annalee.

To her dismay she felt the tension run through Sue and she cringed away. "I'm not ready to meet Raithe. Please keep him away."

"I didn't mean…" But Sue swayed and closed her eyes.

Annalee bit her lips hard, realising Sue had learned a lot of facts. The shock eliminated Barry from her mind. This was not the time to put the mistake right because Sue closed her eyes and swayed. Annalee swiftly wound the rope round her thin body and secured her to herself. It was a safety harness until help arrived from up above. Sue was beyond further conversation.

261

CHAPTER 17

REUNION WITH BARRY

A dozen horses and riders were ready to move off. Everything was in readiness for their journey through the mountains and the men were keen to be away, each rider was armed for battle. The rest of the people were assembled nearby, waiting for the hunters and trackers who were leading them to Therossa. For several days the whole band of people had been camped together, waiting for some news from Thane about his search for Sonja. When the sound of the horn was heard being blown three times, they understood the signal and knew what they had to do. One half of the band was to go home and the other half would respond to the call.

But unexpectedly there was trouble from Raithe. While Thane was absent, Amos automatically took control. Raithe sat arrogantly on his horse at the head of the column waiting to ride off in answer to the call for help. He stared down superciliously from his elevated height, trying to impress the men behind him. Anyone less hardened than Amos and Cailli would have quailed on the spot. Not moving from his chosen position, Raithe said haughtily,

"Are we starting now or tomorrow, or could it be that you're not up to coping with the situation? I always said you were too old for the job."

THE SECRET OF TAMSWORTH FOREST

Amos's eyes flashed fire, his expression humourless. Raithe was at his best when he tried to belittle people and right now the old man knew Raithe wanted to impress. The watching people and waiting men could do nothing other than listen. Amos kept his emotions under control. A slanging match in front of the men was not advisable, no matter where their loyalties lay. For the last few days the Prince's behaviour had been impeccable, but Amos was not fooled. He knew Raithe thought he had been clever. Deep in his chest, anger seethed.

"You can turn about right now because you're not going in this direction. You're leading the people back to Therossa." His tone was clipped and Cailli added, "It is only right that the heir to the throne should lead his people home."

"As future King it is my place to answer a call for help," retorted Raithe, moving his horse forward and nearly flattening Amos, but the horse sidestepped, and much to his disgust, blew softly on the old man's head. Raithe tightened the reins, unable to conceal his fury.

"You take too much on yourself, Amos, but I suppose that is an old man's prerogative. You can lead the people home. You have my permission."

"Your mother is waiting for your return," cut in Cailli smoothly before Amos exploded, "and since she is your sovereign you had best obey her."

Raithe could feel himself burning up. Things were not going his way. How dare they treat him like a nonentity? He was so furious, he failed to notice that

263

two people had detached themselves from the group around him, and his mount was becoming skittish.

"You both forget yourselves. Do you realise to whom you are talking?" Raithe's tone was now patronising. "I am the one who gives the orders and I am going with these men while you two shepherd the people home, old man. Don't try to argue with me. I ask, just what good would you be in a fight?"

"Better than you, my Prince," cut in a new voice smoothly.

Silence fell over the assembled riders and two black apparitions glided into sight. Amos and Cailli respectfully fell back to leave the way clear for them to come forward, and with a slight incline of their heads they stood before the magnificent animal belonging to Raithe. The foremost one lifted a hand and placed it on the horse's neck. Immediately it calmed down. Raithe's fear was almost tangible. He was always wary of the Shaman, who seemed to know things before he was told. With a tight smile he soon reverted back to his swaggering ways and gave the newcomers an exaggerated bow. He could easily work their appearance to his advantage.

"Greetings, Shaman," he called out, "have you come to bless our journey?"

The black hood fell back from the face of the foremost rider and his watery eyes surveyed the assembled people. His bulbous nose was minus the small pair of spectacles which usually balanced there. Yet in spite of their absence, his keen gaze was penetrating and Raithe could feel his bravado slipping from him. "We are just going out to answer a mercy call," he blustered.

"But why are *you* going, son? That is a job for soldiers. Your place is back home with your people. The Queen has heard rumours and anxiously awaits your return. There are plenty of others who can answer the call."

With an effort Raithe kept his expression amicable. "But it is Thane who has called for help. Something is amiss and I must be there to give what assistance I can. My mother will understand. Please do not be concerned over me, Shaman."

"But I am not. There is no need to be. I have received news that Sonja has been found. Now that must make you very happy." He either didn't see or carefully ignored the disbelief that showed up on Raithe's face. "Your mother needs to be informed, since you were her emissary to escort Sonja safely to her – you must realise you have to go with the good news."

Everyone heard the Shaman's words, although they were spoken in a low voice. A hum of excitement filled the air, except from Raithe, who gave a violent start and forgot himself. "But that is impossible. She couldn't have been found?"

"Why not, my son?" enquired the Shaman.

"Because – because – " Raithe pulled himself up sharply realising he was letting his tongue run away with him. "Because the gypsies have her and no one ever escapes from them."

The Shaman eyed him sadly. "How can you be so sure the gypsies have her, my son? It has only been speculation up until now. We have no actual proof."

Raithe felt trapped, knowing every eye was focused on him.

"Annalee told me," he blustered, saying the first thing that came into his mind. "You ask her when you find her. She – she suggested it."

The Shaman's eyes turned to ice and an angry murmur came from some of the men. Annalee was well liked. "Suggested what?" he asked in a low voice.

Raithe felt Amos's and Cailli's eyes boring into his back, and the outrage around him. He opened his mouth to say something else when the Shaman said sternly, "Do not dig your pit any deeper, Prince, otherwise you may never escape from it."

A silence fell at his words and a murmur rustled through the ranks. A feeling of unease settled on Raithe as accusing eyes seemed to strip him of everything he stood for. The Shaman seemed to grow in stature. He held out his wizened hand and the person behind him handed over an arrow. A gasp escaped a few unguarded lips, but Raithe cringed as the Shaman held the arrow up high. All could see the coloured fletches which pronounced it as from the royal household. The Shaman forced him to meet his eyes.

"We did not take this from your quiver, Raithe, but from the horse Sonja was riding when she disappeared. You, my Prince, committed one of our worst crimes by endeavouring to make a horse lame." The Shaman turned his back on the boy and spoke to Amos.

"I want him to come with us," he said deliberately. "It is time he faced up to the suffering he has inflicted on others. I wish to introduce him to his sister unless she gets to him first and kills him. Come, Neela," he said as he turned to his companion. "We shall lead the way."

*   *   *

Sue felt suffocated; standing in a tunnel where the rocky walls were glistening with dampness. The flickering sconces illuminated pools of water lying on the uneven floor. She was being invited to step within, but Sue drew back. The same people were chanting to her in their mournful voices, "Come back, come back to us." She tried to blot them out, but they were so compelling.

Gritting her teeth, she put on an extra spurt. The lights were suddenly extinguished as though by a giant hand which forcibly brought her to a standstill. Now the darkness was complete and she knew her pursuers were gaining ground and closing the distance between them. With an effort, Sue moved forward. Although she was blind in the darkness, stumbling along unknown ways, she could still sense them getting closer.

"Come back. Come back to us," they continued calling.

With a start, Sue realised the voices were almost in her ear and she could feel the warmth of someone's breath on her face. She shrank back against the rocky wall, petrified. Something touched her shoulder, making her scream out in terror, and someone said,

"Wake up, Sue. You're dreaming. You are safe now. I am with you."

She knew that voice. Sue fought through the darkness to surface. Her eyes opened and then the nightmare was dismissed. For one brief moment she lay rigid, bathed in perspiration and she wondered where she was. Two lamps threw a soft glow around the area where she lay. Through the half-light she saw Thane. Her heart gave a lurch as her eyes made contact with him. He leaned forward with a smile of welcome spreading over his face and she felt his lips lightly brush her face.

"It is great to have you back again. How are you feeling, Sue?"

"Where am I? How did I get here?" She struggled to sit up and found herself fighting off a wave of nausea. "I was on the cliff. Did Annalee save me?"

"You remember Annalee?"

"A little. She was beside me. I think I passed out." She choked on the words. Her tongue felt swollen. The nausea rose up persistently. It made her feel heavy and drugged and pulled her back into darkness. As her eyes started to close she saw Thane disappear from her sigh. Panic engulfed her.

"Don't leave me, Thane," she gasped. It was a cry for help.

"It's all right, Sue. Don't try to speak yet." Thane turned his head anxiously as Neela glided out from the shadows and placed a cool hand on Sue's feverish brow. She pressed the rim of a bowl to her lips. Sue was suddenly transported back. Her body froze as she jerked her head away. She was back in the smelly caravan, completely at the mercy of her captors, and they were trying to poison her. How hot and stuffy the air was. She had to get away. Automatically her head thrashed to and fro, and she nerved herself for the blow to fall. They did not come but two hands firmly held her face still.

"Sue. Can you hear me?"

It was Thane. He had come back. She knew he would save her. Sue strove to focus on her surroundings. The blurred outline of two people filled her vision. Slowly they solidified, and she recognised Thane and Neela as the nausea subsided. Thane removed his hands and Neela once again held out the bowl. "Please drink this, Sue," she said, but Sue reacted violently and pushed it away. "No more drugs. I never want to sleep again."

"And we don't want you to," cut in Thane, softly. "You get too many nightmares. Just drink what Neela is offering you. It is only water."

Sue felt embarrassment sweep over her. What on earth was the matter with her? The nightmare had completely unsettled her way of thinking. This was not the gypsy camp. She had escaped that horror. They must think her very foolish. Giving a weak apologetic smile, she took the bowl from Neela and sipped the water gratefully. The cool liquid refreshed her burning throat. Thane gave Neela a slight nod and she slipped unobtrusively away. He waited patiently until the last drop had gone and sat on the bed. She looked a lot better now and had more colour in her cheeks. The fever was subsiding. Making himself comfortable, Thane put an arm casually round Sue's shoulders and felt her relax.

"It's good to have you back again, Sue. I have really missed you. Another day here and you'll be fine, I'm sure. The Shaman has healed all your bodily wounds of which there were many. The sight of them made my blood boil. Only time will heal your mind. When we found you, thanks to White Hawk – we also found a young boy who had been viciously beaten like you and…" He stopped, taken by surprise at her response.

"Tug," she interrupted. "How is he? I must go to him at once."

"Well, you can't. You must look after yourself. The Shaman is with Tug right now so stop worrying. He is in good hands."

"But you don't understand, Thane." Sue tried to pull away and get to her feet. "He was my only other friend beside Elina." Her lips trembled as she said the name and if Thane noticed, he made no comment. "He helped me escape and that's why he's been beaten. He put himself in danger for me." With determination Thane pushed Sue back, ignoring her struggles. "For the help he gave you I shall always be in his debt. So will everyone else. Forget him for a little while and leave him with our Shaman." He paused. "Outside this tent are many people who want to hear your story when you feel up to it." Now her dismay stopped him. "What's the matter?"

THE SECRET OF TAMSWORTH FOREST

"I can't speak about it, ever."

"I understand," he replied, "I gathered a lot from your delirium. What happened to you should never have occurred. No one is going to insist you speak about your ordeal."

"What do they want to know?" Sue looked decidedly apprehensive and clenched her hands tightly. The events of the last few days flashed through her mind and made her shudder. Elina's gaunt face hovered in her vision. It brought tears to her eyes. She looked imploringly at Thane. "I don't want to talk about it – now or ever. You would understand if you had been through it. Please make them go away."

He squeezed her hand reassuringly, to give her some comfort. "You don't have to – but Annalee insists on coming in. It was thanks to her we were nearby to help you both – and your brother is outside as well."

Sue's expression became remote as though a veil had dropped over her face. With blank eyes she looked at Thane. "I'm surprised you can mention him so calmly," she said. "I have no wish to meet him after what he's done to me. Just keep him away." Her usually soft voice was full of loathing.

"You are not surprised he is here?"

"Annalee had already told me, before I was rescued. I expressed the same sentiment when she mentioned him."

"Sue. She wasn't talking about Raithe," said Thane, trying to patient with her. It was not easy since she seemed determined to build up a barrier. With a rueful grimace he thought of Barry waiting to come in and

271

tried to explain. "You're making a mistake," he persisted, "I really think you should change your mind."

She glared at him, saying. "Why? I don't care if he were the King himself. Keep him away."

"But..." As his voice trailed into silence, Barry took the law into his own hands and shoved his way into the tent. He came straight to where Sue was sitting and stopped at the foot of her bed. His cheery grin faded as he gazed at her changed appearance in disbelief. This was the first time he had been allowed to see his sister since her disappearance. Under the Shaman's orders, the men had kept him away, giving feeble excuses such as she was asleep. Sue stared at him in stunned surprise, looking as though she had seen a ghost. Where on earth had he sprung from? Simultaneously, their eyes met, full of welcome for each other, then they were in each other's arms. Tears of joy wetted her cheeks.

"Oh, Barry – I'm so pleased to see you, little brother."

"Not so much of the little," retorted Barry gruffly, hugging her fiercely. They were both choked for words. Thane was forgotten and he felt a lump in his throat as he slowly moved away from them. Unnoticed, he left the tent, falling over Tansy and Annalee outside He said quietly, "She has the best possible medicine to make her feel better. We will come back later."

*   *   *

THE SECRET OF TAMSWORTH FOREST

Sue slipped away from her companions and made her way to the Shaman's tent where she knew Tug was still receiving treatment. Knowing the amazing powers the Shaman possessed, she thought by rights Tug should have been well and truly healed by now. Barry saw her creep away and followed like a shadow. He did not trust her out of his sight now that he had found her; and he was not the only one on guard. The alert eyes of a wolf watched their progress and padded along nearby, inconspicuous to the many people loitering around.

Outside the tent, Sue paused. Shadows from the people within flickered on the material. She needed courage to announce her presence. Would her visit be welcome since she had not been invited? The light escaping from around the edge of the opening enticed her nearer, but still she hesitated. Then Barry moved up, making her jump, and for the first time she became aware of him. Seeing her uncertainty, Barry touched her arm. His concern for her was genuine. He could not help wondering why she wanted to see the boy who had received such appalling injuries. "You don't have to do this, Sue. It's not a sight I'd recommend. Why don't you wait until he's better? You've only just got out of bed yourself."

Sue was grateful for his consideration, but shook her head. "I'm fine – and I'm hoping Tug is as well. I'll tell you one day what a good friend he was to me. I believe I heard that you found him."

Barry pursed his lips. "You could say that, I suppose. Actually I stopped White Hawk from killing him."

273

"Barry!" Filled with disbelief, Sue spun round on him. "White Hawk is not a killer. Why, you said yourself only a few weeks ago that he was as playful as a puppy. What's changed your mind?"

"Well you didn't see the way his teeth sank into the boy's arm. That wolf ..." His voice petered out as he saw two golden eyes fixed intently on him, and he thought White Hawk knew exactly what he was saying. The wolf drew nearer, hot breath from his mouth forming a mist. Barry was almost petrified when he lifted his muzzle and sniffed his hand. Then he watched White Hawk sit on his hindquarters. Barry's first inclination was to make a fuss of him, but when he thought of the boy's arm, he did not know whether to make a fuss or be angry. He ended up by appearing disinterested.

"Go away, you Judas," he muttered, and White Hawk pricked up his ears. Sue bent and ran her fingers through his thick ruff, earning herself a gentle nip on the hand in return.

"What are you doing here, boy?" she asked in a puzzled voice.

"Strange. I could ask you the same question."

The tent flap was pushed aside and Thane stepped out. He looked quizzically from brother to sister, not having expected to see either of them outside the Shaman's tent.

Sue smiled uncertainly. "I've come to see Tug."

"No one sent for you."

THE SECRET OF TAMSWORTH FOREST

"Do I need permission to visit my friend?" Sue was obviously nettled. "You know I'm worrying about him?"

"I told you he was in good hands."

Sue's frustration showed in her eyes. "I'm not worrying about his health. I want to know what is going to become of him. Because of me the gypsies have cast him aside."

Thane smiled annoyingly and reached out to ruffle her short hair. "Stop getting upset. Tug's future has all been worked out. The Shaman has seen to that and the boy is more than happy with the arrangement."

Sue stared at him doggedly. "I want to see him."

"Yes, of course." Thane stepped to one side, allowing her to enter the softly illuminated tent. Barry did not wait for an invitation but followed quickly on her heels. White Hawk bounded in after the pair of them. Before their astonished eyes the wolf flung himself at the small figure sitting on a pile of cushions. Barry drew in his breath sharply. He was about to rush angrily after the wolf when he felt himself clamped to the spot by Thane's hand.

"Leave it, lad," he said grimly. "The wolf is not that hungry."

The dull flush of indignation on Barry's face turned to scarlet as he heard the mockery in Thane's words. He knew then that he had heard his earlier words. The boy on the cushions was shrieking with delight at the presence of the wolf and he rolled over with the huge animal, White Hawk licking his face. Suddenly Tug was aware of Sue and he pushed the wolf

275

unceremoniously away. "Sue," he exclaimed in delight. "Come and sit here with me."

As Sue did as he bid, Barry's eyes goggled. There was no sign of Tug's former horrific injuries. The skin was as soft and clear as that of a new-born babe. How could he get well so fast? It made him curious as to what Sue looked like when they refused to let him see her. This land contained magic and he could feel excitement stirring within him. Now that his sister had been found, he had time for adventure.

White Hawk transferred his affections to Sue. All the time she scratched his fur he was content to remain docile. Seeing his envious face, Thane gave Barry a push saying, "Go and join them. Neela will throw you out in a moment. I need to see Amos."

He disappeared through the tent flap just as Tug announced importantly, "I am going to be trained as a healer. I am now an acolyte of the Shaman and will remain with Neela. Do you mind?" His grave face looked at Sue.

Sue smiled warmly. "I'm pleased for you."

For a moment Tug stared at her silently then he became serious and said earnestly, "Sue, you have your friends now and I see you are very happy – but never forget the gypsies. They have long memories, and until they find your body – Zuboarra will continue to search for you. They lost a lot of gold when you escaped. Take heed. Never...never go anywhere by yourself, even when you meet the Queen."

"Are you saying my sister is still in danger?" demanded Barry.

Tug regarded him seriously. "Are you saying you are another brother?"

"Not *another* brother. I'm her *only* brother." Barry was indignant.

"Ah…then you do not know she is also Sonja – who is sister to the Prince of the Realm." Barry opened and shut his mouth. Then he locked his eyes on Sue, who shrugged resignedly.

"You can't tell them anything," she murmured. "It's best just to go along with them. One day they will realise their mistake."

"But," interrupted Barry.

Sue patted his arm and said, "Just wait until you have met Raithe. Then I will listen to whatever you have to say."

CHAPTER 18

THE SKY BRIDGE

"Am I a prisoner?" Raithe's voice was full of outrage. He glared sullenly at the two men-at-arms sitting outside his tent. The game they were playing, widespread amongst their companions, included using stones of various sizes and throwing them into appropriate holes marked in the ground. To the casual observer they looked relaxed, but a more discerning person would notice they were fully armed and very much on the alert. "Just how much longer are you intending to sit there?"

The two men looked at each other, trying to give the impression they were surprised at the interruption. Then, ignoring him completely, returned to their game. So Raithe prodded one of them in the back with his foot, saying, "I asked you a question, moron."

"The way I see it, you asked two, and that tends to confuse simple fellows like us," the man he had kicked retorted nonchalantly. "Which one requires answering?"

Raithe sucked in his breath at what he thought was insolence. He looked beyond them, towards the tents assembled on the other side of the clearing where he caught sight of a strange boy and a wolf disappearing from sight amongst the rocks. People were ambling around, laughing, talking, and in general having a good time. Not one of them spared a thought for him. That hurt. He was their Prince. They should respect him. This ostracism had been caused by the Shaman and it galled him. Why should he stay here and put up with it? Let his mother deal with the situation.

With a muttered oath he pushed the two men aside, spinning their stones in all directions. He wished they would lash out so that he would have an excuse to retaliate – but they silently retrieved their stones as though this was an everyday occurrence. Raithe crossed the space, his objective being the large black tent which housed the Shaman and his acolytes. The two soldiers scrambled to their feet and followed him unobtrusively. Although he was irritated, Raithe disregarded the action, knowing only too well they were carrying out orders.

Outside the tent he paused. He had not thought about his next action. Why should he announce himself? He was not a commoner. He was the future King. They had no right to treat him this way. Straightening his shoulders, and with a resolute look, he stormed in.

The interior was austere. The Shaman turned in surprise at his unexpected visitor, and rose to his feet. He adjusted the glasses on the tip of his nose and stared at the Prince with a benign expression. Raithe ignored all primary greetings and came to the point at once.

"I wish to return to the Kingdom."

"Why, my son? What is the hurry when we all return tomorrow?" asked the Shaman, and overlooking the lack of etiquette, he waved Neela away lest her presence cause embarrassment. She backed into the shadows of the tent.

"I am not needed here." Raithe's eyes glittered dangerously.

The Shaman's countenance remained unmoved. "Have you spoken to your sister yet?"

A nerve twitched in Raithe's cheek. "Why should I?" he sneered. Then he saw the warning light in the old man's eyes, and added defiantly, "Chance would be a fine thing. I can't get near her."

"Who stops you?" asked the Shaman.

"She does."

"She?" The Shaman lifted his eyebrows in surprise, "Annalee, Tansy, who is she?"

Raithe choked on the name which he had no intention of saying. "That girl Thane brought over from the other world. She has no business to be here."

"Ah. So Sue does not appreciate your company. Can you wonder why? What does she do to keep you at arm's length?"

"Apart from you having her constantly protected, what on earth does it matter?" Raithe snarled. "The feeling is mutual."

The Shaman pressed his fingertips together and appraised the lad before him, then added, "I have never known you to be thwarted before, my Prince. Why do you not pursue her and offer your friendship instead of enmity?"

"Are you joking?" Raithe was finding it hard to stay calm. There was only so much he could take and the old man was asking the impossible of him. "She does not belong here." He gritted his teeth.

"Do you refuse to believe she is your sister?"

"Just as much as she refuses to believe I am her brother," retorted Raithe. "You cannot make me accept her. Send her home."

The Shaman shook his head sadly. What should have been an exciting time was going horribly wrong. "Your mother asked for her, my son," he continued, "after that it is Sue's decision as to what she does, but now that her other brother has arrived here, it is very possible you will get what you want. Listen to what I say. Look into your heart for a change. Why do you hate her? What are you afraid of?"

Raithe glowered. "Me – me – why is it always me?" he exclaimed. "She is beneath my contempt and I will not continue this conversation. I just need your permission to leave on my own."

He watched the old man turn away and call to Neela. When she came to his side, he gave her instructions. "Fetch Cailli. The Prince needs an escort. He is – "

"He's going alone," interrupted Raithe furiously. "I know my way and what dangers there are. I do not need to be cosseted by you."

So saying he swung round to leave, once again forgetting all etiquette. Regardless of people staring at him, he stormed over towards the horses and vaulted into the saddle of his own mount. With a vicious flick of the whip he went galloping off. The soldiers loitering outside, nodded to the watching Shaman, and saddled their own horses to follow.

KATHLEEN B. WILSON

*   *   *

A freezing wind surged through the icy pass, whipping cloaks away from the riders' shoulders as they made their way towards home. The mountain trail was dangerous. They passed grotesquely shaped, stunted trees encased in ice, keen to get through the narrow cutting before nightfall. On one side the cliff dropped perilously away with nothing to save them if they fell. It was getting colder. Their breath frosted on the air. The jingle of harnesses could barely be heard above the shriek of the wind. Noses and fingers were becoming numb.

Sue pressed herself against Thane's body for warmth. She was sitting in front of him on Saturn, enveloped in a large fur cloak. Normally heights did not bother her, but travelling on the edge of this ravine with its horrific drops caused her to have butterflies in her stomach. One step out of place could send anyone hurtling down over the shelves of rock. She wondered how Barry was faring, but so many cloaks were flapping like flags it was hard to see who was near.

A massive eagle swooped unexpectedly from the heights above and sailed over the head of someone close to her. A horse baulked and became skittish. Sue trembled to think of what might have happened if it had been Saturn. He was walking close to the outer edge. It took her a few moments to recover her composure.

Sharp grit hit her face, and it was some time before she realised it was frozen snow. Before long, the path before them wore a blanket of white. The sound of hooves was deadened and they were nowhere near the summit. The white world was a desolate place. She would hate to be here on her own. Fleetingly she wondered how Raithe had fared, travelling by himself.

A holdup came as a surprised. She wondered what had gone wrong up in front. Thane edged Saturn forward. "There's nothing to worry about, they are crossing the bridge up ahead," he explained. "Only one person can go at a time because of the weight on the bridge. I'll have to ride on another horse, but Saturn will take you across."

Sue pictured a flimsy bridge, high in the mountains, about to shatter when she stepped on it. She brushed the snow from her lashes. "Is it likely to collapse?" She kept her tone deliberately light, but inwardly she was terrified of being on her own.

His face was shadowed by his hood, but even so, he looked away from her as he explained. "There is a stone pathway which is the continuation of this track and leads to the bridge ahead. It shows no obvious means of support and crosses a deep gorge between two mountains. It is the only pass to our city. It's about fifteen yards long and one yard wide with a sheer drop on either side. The wind is violent and screams through the pass, trying its best to knock one off one's feet. One needs to have nerves of steel."

Sue's face had lost its colour. "If you're trying to make me nervous, you've made a good job of it."

"I'm being truthful," replied Thane. "Our people have crossed it for years."

As his words faded away she could feel her stomach turn over with fear. Hairs prickled on her arms and legs. She took a deep breath to steady her nerves. The prospect was frightening. "This bridge," she managed to jerk out. "Everyone here is going to cross it?"

"Yes," he said, "horses as well."

Her senses were screaming out in protest. This could not be happening. She asked hesitantly, "Could we possibly go over together?"

"No. Only one at a time because of the limited load-bearing weight."

The line of horses started to move, getting nearer to the crossing. She could feel that the temperature had plummeted, but already she was frozen with horror. Cailli came pushing his way towards them, all muffled up. He could see the fear on her face.

"Amos has suggested we blindfold her now," he said, his voice was cool. "Don't let her see anything until she reaches the other side."

Sue drew in her breath, annoyed at being treated like a child. "I don't want my eyes covered. I want to see where I'm going. I – I – I might fall over the edge."

"Sue." Thane leaned over and, gripping her shoulders so that she was forced to look at him, said reassuringly, "You will not fall. The horse will take you over automatically. Take my word for it. Cailli will be directly behind you and I will lead. It really is best you do not see because you could not help yourself. You would look down and suffer vertigo."

"But I must see," Sue insisted. "This horse needs to be controlled. I don't trust it. I've not bonded with it."

THE SECRET OF TAMSWORTH FOREST

"Well, Saturn's bonded with you. He will see that no harm befalls you." Thane removed himself from behind her just as Cailli came close with a black band in his hand. Sue backed away shouting, "No blindfold."

The people were moving ahead and Cailli said blandly, "Just try it, Sue, before we get there and find out how it feels. If it is too awful then we will remove it."

Thane nodded in agreement. "That sounds fair to me."

Sue acquiesced and the blindfold was tied on firmly, Saturn following the horse in front. Sue suffered a peculiar reaction. Seeing nothing at all made her feel claustrophobic. The wind rushed down the narrow gorge and her cloak whipped away from her shoulders. Every so often Thane whispered words of comfort and asked, "How is it going, Sue?"

She gritted her teeth. "I don't like it," she replied, "I feel terrible, as though I'm going to fall."

"Well, try holding on tighter. Grab a handful of Saturn's mane, he won't mind if you do and you will feel more secure," interrupted Cailli.

Thane's mouth tightened. He said softly in Sue's ear, "Just go on for a few more minutes, then I will take the blindfold off. It's been worth a try, hasn't it?"

As he spoke they turned a bend and the bridge was before them. It presented a picturesque scene of a winding path, seeming to go through the air, against a backdrop of white-tipped mountains. Huge icicles hung like swords from the edge of the bridge. The wind bit into the travellers' cheeks. Far below, the bottom of the

285

gorge was covered by a blue haze. Everything was in miniature. Thane stepped onto the rock, which was glacial and slippery and went steadily across. Cailli did not give Saturn a chance. Unthinkingly he slapped his rump in exactly the same place the arrow had entered. With a shrill scream of rage Saturn reared and plunged forward onto the bridge.

Sue swiftly pulled the black band away from her face while trying to hold on for dear life. Before her terrified eyes, it seemed as though Saturn had jumped out into space. She shrieked loudly. A roar filled her ears and her chest constricted. This was the end. Unless she sprouted wings, only a miracle could save her. Saturn was pulled to an abrupt halt by Amos and someone's arms lifted her from his back. A crowd of concerned people gathered round. Thane held her trembling body tightly in his arms and he glared at Cailli who rode sheepishly up to him. "What sort of insane idea entered your brain?" Thane snapped furiously. "She could have been killed."

"I didn't think," Cailli answered contritely. "Saturn has a long memory – but look at it this way – she's crossed over that bridge quicker than anyone else."

Sue twisted in Thane's arms and studied Cailli's face. He looked like a small boy being caught out in some misdemeanour. You could not stay mad with him for long. She smiled. "Forget it, Cailli. I'm safe and sound. I just hope there is nothing more like that to face as we progress."

The silence which fell was most unexpected. Nothing could be heard except the wind. Amos

THE SECRET OF TAMSWORTH FOREST

coughed and moved away. Cailli looked embarrassed. Sue felt her jaw dropping and a dreadful sense of unease filled her being. She stared at Thane, a question in her eyes, and in doing so missed the broad wink Cailli gave him. Thane tightened his grip on her.

"Whatever happens in the future, you're not leaving my side."

*   *   *

A blizzard hit them. They were forced to take cover until it blew itself out. Luckily they had all crossed the bridge before the worst of the weather descended upon them. Amos knew the mountains like the back of his hand, and knew where there was an extensive overhang which had room for the horses and everyone else. It went a long way into the mountain and gave them shelter from the icy wind. Always ready for an emergency, the trackers carried kindling and they lit several fires, all of which served as a place for cooking and a source for warmth. People automatically gathered in that area.

Everyone was busy doing their allotted jobs, and Sue, with nothing better to do, wandered off to the far end of the overhang and watched the swirling snow. Only one pair of eyes saw her go, and the watcher did not like to intrude on her thoughts, but kept an eye on her from a distance. Sue hugged her thick cloak round her body for warmth and soon became mesmerised by watching the falling snow.

The shriek of the wind and babble of voices faded into the background. She began to unwind. The first time she heard the noise she disregarded it. The second time she thought it was a voice and looked over her shoulder. There was no one near her. The third time she could no longer ignore it, and peered out into the vast white area before her. Visibility was not good, but someone was out there. Maybe a soldier or tracker was in difficulty. Then the muffled sound came again and seemed to come from overhead. Above her was rock, but when she poked her head outside, she knew that it was from up there that the source of the noise came.

Sue gazed back into the overhang. The trackers and soldiers were too far away to have heard anything, and too occupied to care. She stepped out into the snow and gasped when her feet sank in up to her ankles. She looked up, hearing the rattle of loose scree. There was a dark area above her head which was obviously another overhang or a cave. The noise had to come from an animal, although what lived in the mountains she could not guess. Not really thinking straight, she shouted out, "Is anyone there?"

Sue saw the blurred vision of a cave opening. She blinked her eyes furiously to clear them. No one answered her and she did not expect a response. If anyone had been up there they would not have understood her. Sue examined the area carefully from where she stood. The rocky wall of the mountain glistened with thick frost. No snow clung to it. The deep clefts were fairly visible. She decided she would climb up high enough to look into that cave and settle her mind. Sue had not expected the rock to be freezing. Halfway up, her fingers became so numb they adhered to the rock. She should go back down, but stupid though it was, she called out again.

"Hello. Is anyone up there?"

The noise came again, almost an answer. But it sounded like a groan of pain. Going back down now was not an option. Unexpectedly, someone answered her back in her own language, saying, "Get away from here while you can, you stupid fool."

Sue nearly fell when she recognised the voice. Raithe; what on earth was he doing up there? He had made his journey home a day before they had all started. Was he hurt? But why should she bother about him? He did not care about her. She had almost decided to climb back down when there came the rumbling noise of loose scree, and a snarl rent the air. Raithe was not alone, hence his warning. Sue heard his quick intake of breath and with grim determination climbed up further. Her fingers were almost dead. She reached the cavity and tumbled over the edge. Raithe was lying on the ground with his leg at a peculiar angle and a long thin knife clasped tightly in his hand. A few yards away, with hackles up, stood a bedraggled mountain cat. Its green-flecked eyes were fixed unblinkingly on the Prince. Her coming confused it for a moment. Then its feral eyes embraced them both. In spite of being afraid, Sue crawled slowly towards Raithe. He knew she was there, but he never moved his eyes off the cat. The eye contact must not be broken. That was a sign of weakness in the animal kingdom. However, Raithe could not restrain himself by saying sarcastically, "Playing the hero?"

"Not really," answered Sue evenly. "But I don't wish to see you torn to shreds in front of me and have nightmares over it. You're not worth it."

"Then what the hell did you come for? What good do you think you can do? You're only a girl. That cat's going to have us both now. You've acted like a fool coming here."

"I'm not the fool. That's you," Sue answered bluntly. "You're the one who can do everything on his own and can't move. I can jump down from this point and save myself. Then the cat can have you."

"Then damn well go," Raithe snapped.

The mountain cat advanced, its upper lip curled showing long pointed fangs. It snarled, keeping the two in its vision. It was lean and hungry looking – wounded on one of its legs. It looked as though it had not eaten any food for days. Sue slowly rose to her feet and unclasped her cloak. To Raithe's astonishment she flapped it wildly in the animal's face. The cat spat and backed away with a snarl. Sue stood watching, ready to wave her cloak again should it advance.

Raithe tried to move, but succeeded only in hurting himself. He ended up groaning, "Give it up, Sue. You will never win against that animal, just leave me and save yourself. I did try to warn you to keep away."

"I'm not going anywhere."

"Don't be so stupid," hissed Raithe, "I would leave you if the positions were reversed."

"I know you would – but I'm not you." Sue clenched her teeth. "So shut up."

Surprised, Raithe shut his mouth and really looked at her. From the corner of his eye he saw the cat crouch down and tense on its hindquarters. Before he could shout out a warning, it sprang at them. With quick reflexes, Sue flung her cloak at its head. The heavy material engulfed its face and extended claws. Not seeing anything, it veered the wrong way, landing between them and teetered on the edge of the cave. Immediately Sue pressed home her advantage, pushing hard on its hind quarters to send the cat crashing over the lip, but it was heavier than she expected. Her fingers sank into its fur but it did not move. Its feet seemed bolted to the ground. With a frenzied movement the cat ripped at the cloak and turned swiftly on to her, snarling and showing its sharp needle-like teeth. It sprang for her throat. Raithe threw his knife, exhibiting his good marksmanship but although the knife penetrated the cat's neck, it was not killed. From the cave entrance an arrow twanged through the air and pierced through its heart. Sue went down with a shriek, and the weight of the cat on top of her. The foul smell from its mouth made her gasp for air. She heard Raithe calling her name, then another voice shouted out, but she was unable to move. Her breath was being squeezed from her body.

"Sue." Annalee made short work of scaling the rock face, followed immediately by Tansy. They stood aghast at the sight before their eyes, Raithe sprawled on the ground and Sue struggling to get away from beneath the dead mountain cat. The lecture both girls were about to give her on the dangers of wandering off, died in their throats. Tansy leant over the Prince while Annalee went to Sue's aid. Once free of the heavy body, Sue started to tremble, mainly from the cold. Her cloak had gone and Annalee put her arms round her.

"What happened up here?" she asked. "We came this way only because Tug saw you climb the rock and was worried about you."

"Forget all that now." Tansy was instantly brisk with efficiency. "Raithe has got a broken leg and we need help." She stretched herself to peer over the lip of rock. Down below a boy was staring up with wide dark eyes, snow falling softly on his uncovered head. "Tug," she called, "will you fetch the Shaman and a few men for lifting? Tell them the Prince is hurt."

"Why do you all help me?" Raithe was trying to pull himself up into a sitting position. "This is my own fault and caused by my own stupid actions. I tried to get rid of the men following me by sending my horse on alone. He knew the way and they followed him but then I slipped and broke my leg. To cut my story short, the mountain cat must have smelt my scent and if Sue had not investigated the strange noises she had heard – I would not be here now." He paused and added quietly, "But I'm pleased I am."

It was the nearest thing to an apology anyone had ever heard from Raithe.

CHAPTER 19

THE HAND OF FRIENDSHIP

The blizzard blew itself out in the night while everyone slept peacefully near the fires. At the first sign of dawn preparations for departure began. Neela found the person she was seeking and gently touched her shoulder.

"Wake up, Sue. Someone wishes to speak with you."

She continued touching her until there was a response. Opening her eyes and seeing the acolyte, Sue struggled to her feet in alarm.

"What's wrong? What's happened? Is it Barry?" Then she realised it was night.

"It is the Prince. He is leaving before the rest of us."

"What again?" Sue replied automatically, then seeing Neela's shocked expression added, "Why can't he go quietly? What does he want me for?"

Neela chose not to answer. Sue felt her stomach lurch so her first reaction was to stay where she was, not feeling at all sure about Raithe. Such a lot of bad feeling had passed between them. In spite of what happened yesterday with the mountain cat, Raithe was still Raithe. There was no love lost between them.

Sue gazed round the smoke-filled area. Bodies were sleeping everywhere. Tansy, Annalee and several others she knew by sight were nearby and still lost in

293

their dreams. The menfolk were at the other end of the overhang. Thane and Barry were nowhere to be seen. Sue nodded to Neela and, gingerly stepping over the prone bodies, followed her to where the horses were tethered. They were stamping and snorting in the cold air. A vapour of mist rose above their heads like a small cloud. Half a dozen soldiers were busy fixing their harnesses. Sue waited and the Shaman approached her from the shadows. The old man took hold of Sue's hands in greeting.

"Thank you for coming, child," he said, "I did not think you would refuse. You are wise beyond your years. I want you to know this meeting was not designed by me. It came from Raithe. He insists on seeing you before he departs."

"What on earth for? Surely he's not fit to travel after his ordeal?"

The Shaman was amused and said gently, "You forget this is not your land, Sonja. Our way of life is different from yours. Raithe was healed last night. You will find him waiting for you outside on the ledge. Forgive me if I don't come with you. I have much to do." He gave her hand a squeeze and turned away. Sue walked to the opening. A blast of icy wind hit her. One of the soldiers handed her a cloak and said, "Put this on unless you want to freeze to death."

Sue smiled her thanks and took a few more steps forward. The snow had been cleared where she stood. It was early morning and the air fresh and clean. She gladly filled her lungs with it after the stuffy atmosphere inside. It felt good to be out here. Up above, the sky was tinged with pink and distant peaks reared their heads to the racing clouds. Everywhere was calm after the blizzard. The white world looked peaceful.

At first, she did not see Raithe; his cloak was white and blended in with the background. He watched her carefully for a few moments, and when he knew she had registered his presence, said stiffly, "I did not think you would come."

"Then you're not a bad judge of character," she replied. "Do you blame me?" The words were out before she could stop them.

Raithe scowled and bit his lower lip. He was offhand because he hated this meeting. "I ordered you to come," he said.

"Precisely, that's why I'm here."

"I thought you might have been curious about how I felt," he prompted.

"Why should I?"

The two of them stared at each other, neither of them giving an inch or showing the hand of friendship. They looked so alike, except for the way they were dressed. With Sue, now that her hair was short, it was hard to tell them apart. The silence between them grew longer and with it the antagonism increased. In the end, feeling exasperated and giving a little shiver, Sue snapped, "What did you want to see me for?"

Raithe jumped, realising he was the instigator of this meeting. Although his face revealed nothing of his thoughts, he said in a flat voice, "to say thank you for saving my life."

"Forget it." Sue turned away, although she was touched by his words. "I would have done the same for anyone. It just happened to be you. Anyway, Annalee killed the mountain cat."

Raithe digested that remark in silence. Then, seeing she really did mean to walk off, he shouted after her retreating figure, "I want you to travel with me this morning."

Sue stopped dead in her tracks, stunned. She turned round to stare at him. Her mind was telling her not to trust him. The last time she did, she ended up with the gypsies. Her face was more revealing than she knew, because he said in a softer tone,

"Please, Sue."

"Just you and me?" she asked.

Raithe stepped up to within inches of where she stood and the mockery returned to his voice. "I don't blame you for not trusting me, but if it is of any help, there will be others, soldiers, the Shaman, Neela, and of course, Thane."

"Then why not travel with everyone?"

Raithe drew himself up proudly. "Because I am the Prince. I do not travel anywhere with a crowd."

Sue was perceptive enough to realise it had cost him a lot of pride to invite her along. She was not one to hold grudges and decided friendship was always the best policy. After all, before long she would be returning home and none of this would matter. Furthermore, Thane would be with her.

"Thank you, Raithe, I will go and get myself ready."

THE SECRET OF TAMSWORTH FOREST

*   *   *

The small cavalcade set off before the camp was half awake. To Sue's acute embarrassment she was given a cloak of white ermine, almost identical to Raithe's. Her protests against such an expensive gift fell on deaf ears because Raithe as good as ordered her to accept it. "I can't have you walking with me wearing a soldier's cast-offs, and the mountain cat ripped yours to pieces. The least I can do is to replace it."

Although she thought uncharitably it was not any hardship to him, she buried her chin in the soft fur and appreciated its unique warmth. Six soldiers headed the group, on the alert in case trouble arose. The Prince demanded that Sue should ride by his side. She glanced appealingly at Thane but he shrugged and fell into place with Neela. With that arrangement she had to be content. The Shaman was nowhere to be seen but one could be sure his eye was on everything.

For the first few hours, the journey was tedious. The snow had made the track hazardous. Raithe was not inclined to make conversation. For all the companionship she got from him, she need not have been there. It did not take her long to deduce that she was by his side for appearance's sake only. At times, when it was only possible to travel in single file, Sue managed to get close to Thane, and this was the only time she felt safe. If Raithe noticed, he made no comment.

The day wore on and a brilliant sun set up a slow thaw of the top snow. The party picked their way

297

downwards, a constant sound of dripping filled the air. The horses' hooves threw up slush. The ermine cloak was getting dirty; it was also becoming hot. Sue pushed it back off her shoulders, and seeing the expression on Raithe's face, she knew she was going to be ordered to put it back on again. Thane cut in smoothly, "Would your Highness care to remove your cloak? You must be getting very hot."

Raithe raised his nose in the air. "I shall cool off with a gallop," he retorted, and urged his mount forward. At last Sue was alone with Thane. They stopped for food behind a sheltered shoulder of rock. It was only cold fare, but nourishing. Thane drew her to one side, away from the soldiers and murmured, "Before long the trees will start reappearing. This will be a sign that our trek is coming to an end. It is not the royal palace we are visiting. That is in the city. The Queen has a home in the forest, a very spectacular and beautiful place which I am sure you will love. She spends a lot of her time there since the King went away. There is a huge colony of people around her and they know Raithe was sent to escort you here. I know how you feel, but for that reason alone, you must be at Raithe's side when he enters the forest. They are eager to see you."

"That is all he cares about," retorted Sue bitterly. "He must have been indoctrinated with protocol as a baby. This is all wrong, Thane. I should not be here and you know it."

Thane stared at her. "Give me one good reason why."

THE SECRET OF TAMSWORTH FOREST

"I do not belong here. I'm nothing to do with him, or his mother. You know where I come from. It's not right to try and fool decent people with such a sham as this."

"Sham." Thane was exasperated. "Please keep an open mind. Do you honestly think, deep down, you are not connected with Raithe? You cannot blame the Queen. It's you that have been deceived all your life."

"No I haven't. This whole thing is ludicrous," declared Sue. "This is another world. No one is being deceived. I grant Raithe and I look alike, but no one in my family has ever visited this place. It does so happen that some people have doubles. This is pure coincidence."

Thane studied her strained face before saying, "I doubt if Barry would see it this way. He is more astute than you give him credit for."

Sue was saved from answering because the journey was resumed. Once again she was beside Raithe. As before, he ignored her. It was on the tip of her tongue to tell him she was going to ride with Thane, when the situation changed and apprehension silenced her. The track took a sudden steep turn and the gradient went down alarmingly. As the sure-footed horses picked their way along, Sue guided her mount as close to the rocky wall as she dared. The drop on the outer edge of the track fell away into a sea of green. Raithe's gaze in her direction was scornful. He tossed his head and cantered onwards with more bravado than any thoughts of safety. Thane came to her side and caught hold of her reins.

299

"Don't you dare to try to race with him. He's a fool."

"I can assure you that thought never entered my head," she replied and her stomach turned over as she looked down. It was a sight so unexpected. There was a strange aura coming from the growing trees. She tried to ignore the sensation.

"Do they grow out of the mountain?" she asked uncertainly. "They are not fir trees. I can't make out what they are."

"They actually grow from the valley floor," answered Thane nonchalantly, "They are sequoia. Lots of our people call them redwoods."

"But the valley is hundreds of feet down. It's not possible." Sue reined in her horse and went towards the edge of the track, looking down on the great giants. Their tops were moving gently in the wind. Birds of many colours hovered over hidden nests. A sensation to jump came over her so strongly that she pressed her feet down firmly on the ground. She forgot all about continuing down the track. The trees hypnotised her.

"How many of these redwoods are there?" she enquired.

"A forest full," said Thane.

Awe held her speechless. The sight captured her imagination. A dense forest of redwoods was unbelievable. Thane poked her in the ribs to get her attention.

"We must move on. You will see their magnificent splendour when we reach level ground."

THE SECRET OF TAMSWORTH FOREST

After negotiating the steep track, the rest of the journey down was uneventful. At the bottom the small group reassembled before proceeding along a wide pathway. Sue was enthralled with all she saw. She thought of the trees hidden in Tamsworth Forest which she thought were huge. Compared with what she was looking at now, they were only miniature. Surrounded by so many trees, Sue stood staring upwards and she felt like an ant. The trunks were vast, displaying doorways and windows cut into them. Steps ran up the side of several trees, and were railed for safety. These trees were obviously homes to the village people who lived here. Walkways interlocked overhead, crowded with people going about their daily business. Higher up there were more doors and windows. This was a town built in a forest. No matter in which direction she looked, there were tree houses, and their little windows had curtains and flower boxes.

The people dressed themselves in colourful clothes of long skirts and trousers with colourful baggy tops. From what she could see, their hair was long, even on the men, but the most remarkable thing, they all looked happy. Suddenly from high up, petals floated down and they surrounded her like snow. These people were paying homage to her and she felt she had no right to accept it. Voices called out, but only one word made any sense – Sonja. Sue's fixed smile hid the dismay which overwhelmed her. She had to get away. She spun round to confront Thane, but it was Raithe she came up against. His expression was inscrutable. Before she realised his intentions, he caught hold of one of her

301

hands, and bending forward, kissed it. The sensation she felt was like a searing pain on her skin. Regardless of the thunderous noise which came from above, Sue indignantly tried to wrench her hand away. Raithe anticipated the move. His grip became vice-like and his eyes glinted dangerously.

"You will dismount right now," he hissed through clenched teeth, "and you will walk with me to my mother's dwelling with a smile of welcome on your face. After that," he shrugged indifferently, "you can go to hell or back to Thane, since you like him so much."

Sue tried to pull away, but to no avail. "Let go of my hand." She was furious. "I can walk on my own. I don't need to be handcuffed to you."

Raithe's eyebrows rose. "Handcuffed? What strange word is that?"

She breathed heavily. "It means you are binding me to you by force. Just let me go right now."

"I understand your reasoning," replied Raithe, "I feel the same way about you, but for now – etiquette demands that I lead you to my mother's house. So, *dear sister*" – Sue felt a shiver go over her at his emphasis on the word 'sister' – "Will you please walk with me, smile and acknowledge my people?"

Sue swallowed hard and bit her tongue. Somehow she managed to keep a smile on her face and comply with his orders, hoping her hostility did not show. How dare he think she was subservient to him? She no longer tried to pull her hand away, but followed unresistingly wherever he led her.

THE SECRET OF TAMSWORTH FOREST

The rest of their party kept well back and watched them go. Thane's lips tightened. He wanted to shake the pair of them. Raithe smiled charmingly in all directions, giving a wave here and a bow there. The cheers from the spectators resounded through the trees. The people were so happy for their Queen and they intended to make her long-lost daughter feel welcome.

In spite of her innermost emotions, Sue gradually shed her antagonism towards the Prince, and her own smile became spontaneous. She could do no less, faced with such a reception. But she drew all the attention to herself. Before long, the people were coming out of the trees, trying to touch her. Too late did she notice the fury building up within Raithe. He turned to his people and rapped out a harsh order in his own language. There was sudden silence. The people fell back. Thane rode swiftly up the track with two horses. He sprang to the ground, thrust one towards the Prince and assisted Sue to mount the other. Before Raithe could say a word, he shouted out to the now silent spectators, and the response to his words was a thunderous salutation.

"Now get riding," Thane commanded, holding his temper in check. Raithe did not need to be told twice. He was off. Sue followed, feeling bewildered. Thane left a small gap between them and shadowed their footsteps. Before long the spectators faded away. The walkway became deserted. It was almost as though invisible barriers had been placed across them.

The pathway widened unexpectedly and one gigantic tree towered up in front of them. Its enormous size filled Sue's vision; the trunk was bigger than

303

anything she had seen already. The lower limbs branching off were larger in circumference than any tree growing in Tamsworth Forest and its thick top gave privacy to the walkways above. There was a tangible difference with this redwood. From what she could see there were no doors or windows – or even stairs leading upwards. Raithe leapt from his horse and said stiffly, "I am going to my mother, alone."

Thane did not deign to answer him but when servants appeared from some unseen source, he helped Sue down and gave her a grin, saying, "You did well under the circumstances. I'm proud of you. Come on – I will get you something to eat and before you know it all the others will be here."

Sue hesitated. "What about seeing the Queen?" she asked.

Thane tucked his arm in hers. "Don't give her another thought. She will send for you when she is ready."

*   *   *

From the ground, the room perched amongst the leafy boughs of a tree was almost invisible but when seen close to, the room was evidently a work of a pure genius. The actual limbs of the redwood tree formed the window and some of the lesser branches wove intricate patterns around its edge. Gossamer drapes fell on either side which were pulled across when the days were chilly. There was no glass in the structure so a soft breeze blew gently in through the leafy boughs. The

THE SECRET OF TAMSWORTH FOREST

view from this room over the forest was stunning. It spread for miles over the treetops to the distant horizon, which looked like a blue haze.

Because it belonged to the Queen, it was not overlooked. There were other rooms attached, but these were hidden behind woven drapes hanging from the walls, in colours of bronze, orange, red, green and yellow, to give the impression of living amongst the leaves. It was here the Queen conducted her business while the King was away.

Covering the doorway to this room hung a tapestry of exquisite design. As Sue approached it, still overawed by the massive size of the redwood, she came face to face with Raithe. She was overwhelmed with a feeling of trespass. This was his home and she was the interloper. It would have been awkward enough had they been friends, but their acquaintance had not reached that status. She gave him an uncertain smile – not quite knowing how to take him after the way he had left her earlier. Raithe had changed from his travelling clothes into a full-sleeved shirt of embellished silk and deep blue breeches. A cloak fell from his shoulders, clinging softly round his legs. He looked the epitome of the Prince he always professed to be.

Sue was pleased that earlier, Annalee and Tansy had taken her away from Thane to a private pool in a small dell hidden away amongst the redwoods, to bathe. Amidst much laughter, they made sure she removed the grime of travelling. Annalee dressed her in a clean fringed tunic and long pants, but Sue still clung to the boots acquired from the gypsies. Tansy brushed her

305

hair until it shone like burnished gold, yet still she felt grubby standing before Raithe in all his splendour. Raithe clicked the heels of his knee-length boots and afforded her a bow. He motioned those following behind her to stay where they were, and stepped back. His eyes watchful, he said in a dispassionate voice, "My mother is ready to see you. Would you please show her some respect with a curtsy."

"Raithe." A voice from within the room sounded exasperated. "You forget yourself. Just show her in."

Sue hadn't realised she was holding her breath until she let it out. The voice sounded normal enough, it was low and melodious. She entered in trepidation, wondering what the woman looked like who mistakenly believed she was about to meet her daughter. How she wished Barry was here beside her to give support and share this ordeal. But he had not been invited. It was a private occasion. Sue's eyes immediately went to the ottoman on which Raithe's mother sat, and she inhaled sharply. The light from the huge window shone directly on the Queen's face. For one incredible moment she thought she was looking at Aunt Moira. Sue quickly banished that thought. Of course it was not Moira, but the likeness was uncanny. The Queen was dressed in a way that would make her aunt shudder. Her dress, if that's what it was called, looked almost like a sheath and was held together on one shoulder with a golden clasp. The ivory colour of the material almost glowed and was a complete contrast to the long, dark braided hair that fell over her bare shoulders and did not look as though it had a grey hair in it.

Unlike Moira's flustered disposition, the person before her was poised and sophisticated. Their eyes met. The older woman's face was full of love, but in Sue there was uncertainty. Doubt still held her firmly in its grip. It was not easy to throw away a lifetime of thinking that Gaynor was her mother, Priscilla her sister and Barry her brother.

The elegant woman rose to her feet. She was taller than Moira. Sue reprimanded herself sternly; why did she keep comparing her to Moira? There was no connection between them. The woman then held out her graceful arms which were covered in bangles and grasped hold of Sue's limp ones and said,

"So you are Sue." Her voice sounded full of poignancy. "I have waited a lifetime for this meeting. I would have recognised you anywhere. You are so like my husband."

Episodes of conversation she had heard in the hotel came to the fore. With a great effort she said the first thing that entered her thoughts. "You're my Aunt Ruth?"

The lady smiled. She looked beautiful. "You are right about 'Ruth', my dear, but I am not your aunt." She paused, allowing Sue to relax. "I am your mother."

"No!" Sue cried out. She could not help herself, and noticed Raithe stiffen. He was not about to see his mother upset. Even with the facts staring her in the face, Sue clung to her old beliefs. "No! You're not. Gaynor is my mother."

307

"Gaynor brought you up," said the woman gently.

"No, you're wrong," insisted Sue, feeling desperate. "How can I be your daughter? Everyone has told me Sonja is Raithe's sister. I'm not Sonja, I am Sue, and Barry is my brother. He is somewhere down there on the ground. I'm sorry to disappoint you." In spite of herself, Sue felt tears glisten in her eye. "It's all a big mistake. I tried to tell Thane but…"

"Please stop right there, Sue," cut in the Queen. "You will make yourself ill."

A touch of authority entered the other woman's voice, but her arm crept up and snaked round the distressed girl's shoulders. Sue fought hard to get her emotions under control, and could not stop the involuntary stiffening at the Queen's touch. Ruth deemed it wise to ignore the gesture. "All females in the royal household are called Sonja – but you were not brought up here," she uttered with a strained laugh, and Sue realised what pressure she was under. Ruth then beckoned her son over and held him with the other arm.

"Look at you both," she declared. "Like peas from the same pod. I can assure you that you are blood brother and sister. However, I do not expect you to believe me or to like each other, come to that." Her listeners were suddenly aware she was very perceptive of the atmosphere. "Neither of you know the story of your heritage. I am to blame in respect of Raithe, but your grandmother is to blame for your ignorance, Sue. Only my husband, the Shaman, Amos and Thane know the truth and they were sworn to silence. Raithe has never told me so in words, but I know he resented your

THE SECRET OF TAMSWORTH FOREST

coming here. It is very hard to be suddenly asked to share a position you think is yours alone, but enough of this. I am not helping you very much."

"Whatever you say, Mother."

Ruth turned to Sue. "What about you, my daughter?"

Still confused, Sue managed a wan smile. "Can Barry hear it as well?" she queried.

Raithe opened and shut his mouth without saying anything, but his thoughts were perfectly clear. Ruth laughed happily. "Of course he can, my dear. He is, after all, family and Raithe's cousin."

CHAPTER 20

RUTH'S STORY

To Sue it seemed as though an army of white-clad servants waited on the Queen. At her command, food arrived in the room high up in the tree. Men and women were dressed alike in white silk tunic tops and white pants, with a royal insignia embellished on their shoulders. Everyone had their hair cut short, just below the ears and styled with a fringe, a custom which had been followed through all generations of servants.

Sue wondered how they kept such perfect balance and coped with the stairways. They seemed to float along the walkways, never dropping anything.

While preparations were proceeding, Ruth stared over the trees, reminiscing over forgotten years. She forgot Raithe and Sue existed. She was back in Tamsworth Forest, amongst the trees of her childhood, playing in landmarks she had forgotten. Her childhood had been happy, socialising with people she and her sisters met. She thought of her sisters wistfully, thinking how like Gaynor she was. They made friends easily. She was pleased Gaynor had brought up her daughter. Moira was a stick-in-the-mud.

*   *   *

When at last the food had been placed down on the white-covered trestle tables, the Queen waved her hand and the servants vanished. Sue was astonished at the speed and ease with which all this had been accomplished. The food she knew had come up from the ground, but where the trestles had materialised from was a mystery. All she could see when she looked around was thick foliage.

Several people entered the room and paid homage to Ruth. They were acknowledged politely and told to sit down. Sue found herself sitting between Thane and Barry. The food before her was mouth-watering and the aroma coming from it made her feel hungry. Barry was itching to get started, having an enormous appetite. He couldn't see any cutlery, so got the impression one picked the food up by hand to eat.

Sue sat opposite Ruth and she refused to make eye contact with her. Raithe was on the left of his mother and the Shaman, her right. Towards the further ends of the food-laden table were Cailli and Amos, Annalee and Tansy. Although still harbouring doubts about being Ruth's daughter, Sue felt pleased to have her friends nearby, especially Barry, but Thane was watchful.

A general hum of conversation passed between the guests, and at the Queen's request, they spoke in the language of their visitors. Ruth manipulated the topics with dexterity, steering them away from any undercurrents. Even so, little snippets got through. Sue made a big hole in the food, as did Barry. With no compunction, he tried everything within reach of the

311

length of his arm. Raithe, his eyes veiled, watched him covertly for a time, and then tried to make him feel small by asking in his sneering voice, "Is food hard to come by in your world? Is that why you eat so much?"

Thane stiffened, his eyes flashing a warning to the Prince, but it went unnoticed. Barry lifted his owl-like stare to the Prince and said gently, "Actually, where I come from we use a knife and fork. You wouldn't know about such things, would you? They keep the fingers clean when you eat. I wonder why you've not invented them?"

A hush fell over the company and all eyes flew to the Queen to see if she felt insulted. Sue could feel herself shrinking with humiliation, not daring to look at Barry. Ruth rose serenely to the occasion and, bestowing a smile on Barry, said carefully, "Things are done very differently here and we like to eat this way. You see, no one feels embarrassed at the amount they take, whereas if they piled it all on a plate they might become self-conscious." Her smiling countenance turned from Barry to Raithe, but it had perceptibly tightened. "I am so pleased you are making our guests feel at home."

Barry had turned red but an audible sigh of relief came from everyone else. The Shaman deemed it wise to rise to his feet. His gaze embraced everyone round the table and he said clearly, "You have all been invited to see and celebrate the reunion of our Queen with her long-lost daughter Sonja. Now the time has come for more personal details to be discussed privately, so on behalf of our sovereign, I thank you all for coming and

THE SECRET OF TAMSWORTH FOREST

would suggest that those of you not directly involved should now leave."

Cailli lumbered to his feet with good grace and the two girls followed suit. Amos lowered the curtain and placed himself on the outside to make sure those who remained behind would not be disturbed.

*   *   *

Night had fallen and the gossamer drapes had been pulled across the opening as a deterrent against flying insects. Through them a myriad of lights could be seen twinkling from other trees. A soft-footed servant brought in several lamps and placed them strategically round the room, filling it with a soft glow. A feeling of expectancy and comfort filled the air.

Ruth sat composedly on the low couch with Sue and Raithe on either side of her. Barry and Thane made themselves comfortable on the floor with the aid of a few cushions, and the Shaman had a chair specially brought for him to ease his aching limbs. Ruth's voice, low and melodious, filled the room.

"It is common knowledge that I came from the other world. I was born in a large house standing on the edge of Tamsworth Forest, the eldest of three girls. To the people living nearby, we were thought of as being privileged. To them it seemed as though we lived in the lap of luxury. There was not much difference in our ages, Gaynor being the middle one and Moira the youngest. As sisters, we were great friends and always stood together. Why people were envious of our way of

313

life, I have no idea. The one thing we lacked and I dare say they had, was love. Our father, a military man, ran his household like a barracks. He was strict, liberal with punishments and our mother was dominated by him. He treated us like soldiers. Servants were hard to keep. To get away from his reign of terror we would take our horses and gallop through the forest for hours, doing anything that would keep us away from his company. We had many friends away from the house. Workmen, gypsies, vagabonds. Whomever we met was better than our father.

"Our days of freedom could not last for ever. When we reached a certain age, life took on a bitter twist. We did not think it could get any worse. Being an army man, father's discipline bordered on the impossible and he expected us to marry high-ranking officers of his choice. Not for *our* sakes – but his. One had already been chosen for me. Captain Graham Harding."

Ruth paused because Sue gasped and drew in a startled breath. Barry whistled between his teeth. "Gosh, no wonder I always thought the Professor was in his dotage."

Ruth looked perplexed and said, "Does the name of this gentleman mean something to you?"

"You bet it does," Barry said before his sister could answer. "He's staying at the hotel right now and searching for another world. He nearly followed me here."

Ruth returned to her story. "He was a tall willowy man in those days," she reminisced. "Upright, frigid, with an eye open for opportunity, and he had already

THE SECRET OF TAMSWORTH FOREST

decided I was that opportunity. He wanted to marry me. When he put that ring on my finger, he would be on his first step up the military ladder. That meant everything to Graham because he was a snob.

"Under pressure from my father, mother made sure he received invitations to our house in the company of his fellow officers. The way he grovelled made me sick. Even if my heart had not already been given to someone else, I could never have married such a narrow-minded, soulless man as he. With Gaynor and Moira helping me, because they knew the true situation, we did our best to pull the wool over his eyes. Captain Harding was so full of himself, he never suspected us of anything. While my sisters kept him busy, I slipped away and met my true love in the forest; Tam."

It was now Raithe's turn to show surprise. "Did my father live in the other world?"

"Yes. I had been in love with him for a long time; but I knew nothing of his origins, what he did or where he came from. None of that mattered to me. I even accepted the wolf that followed him around like a dog. We were soul-mates and meant for each other. I remember the day I asked what his name was. When he said Tam, I laughed and said what a strange name it was. To which he answered, "What do you expect? I am King of the forest." He wanted to marry me and take me away to a beautiful place where I would be loved and have lots of freedom. It was very tempting. I decided to speak to my father. I was deluded enough to think I could change his mind about my marrying the Captain. He went berserk and nearly thrashed me for

315

having such an idea. Did I realise what an ungrateful daughter I was after he had put himself out to find me the perfect match? Was I misbehaving? He looked at me as though I could not be trusted. After that it became harder for me to slip away into the forest and meet Tam. My father's eyes were always on me, watching. When Gaynor became unwell and mother sent her away to stay with a distant relative, I had lost a friend and really missed my sister. Moira was not so good at keeping the Captain occupied. He showed displeasure with her company.

"Suddenly my father became suspicious. It could have been that Captain Harding was pushing for the marriage to be brought forward. Whatever the reason, preparations for the biggest society wedding the county had seen, went ahead. I was distraught. I was a prisoner in the house. It made me feel ill. I heard the wolf howl and the forest called to me. Graham gloated because he had been given promotion. Invitations went out and lavish arrangements made. Then I discovered I was having a baby. I still wonder how I had the courage to tell my parents.

"Father nearly killed the Captain until he found out the baby was nothing to do with him. Then he nearly killed me because I would not divulge who the real father was. He called me a tart and lots of other things. Hell was let loose. Then Captain Harding told him stiffly he no longer wished to marry me. He went – or was sent on – a secret mission. Whatever it was, he had been made a fool of. He could not face my shame. Actually, neither could my father. He accused me of

THE SECRET OF TAMSWORTH FOREST

ruining his life. He said he could no longer hold his head up in decent society, was I pleased with myself. As far as he was concerned, I was disowned. He would not even stay in the same house with me. He packed his bags and went to live in the officers' mess.

"For months I saw no one except my mother and Moira. Gaynor wanted to come home but my mother said a strange thing, something about my being a bad influence on my sisters. However, Tam risked everything to see me; after all he was the father of my child and appalled at the way I was being treated. He offered to take me away but I was in no condition to make what he said was a hazardous journey. I promised I would go with him directly the baby was born.

"A midwife was procured. She was a lady of mystery. No one seemed to know where she came from, but she looked after me well. Her whole attitude was supportive. I was her only concern. On the day she told my mother I was expecting twins, my mother nearly had a heart attack. I was devastated at her reaction. I thought mothers showed joy on such occasions, but she became worse than my father, especially when she told me in no uncertain terms that she could bring up only one child. The other would have to be adopted, perhaps by some farm labourer. I think my father put a curse on me. I had a very bad time in spite of being helped by the midwife. After several hours, when I cried out for Tam, my mother bent over me and said, "Your first born was a son, and he died." Moira told me afterwards the midwife was so furious she banned my mother from the room. There was no

317

time for tears, I screamed out in agony and the second baby arrived with lusty yells to let us know she had survived.

"It seemed a long time before I looked upon the face of my little girl. Her hair was as fair as Tam's. I believe my mother was surreptitiously trying to work out how many fair-haired men I knew. She would not speak about my son when I questioned her, but from the midwife I gleaned that he also had been fair. It was then my grief took over. They thought the midwife had upset me and as my mother never liked her, she was dismissed, but Moira said she walked out. Then Gaynor returned home, a shadow of her former self, and so did my father. Making sure my sisters were kept far from me, his first action was to throw me out the house. He declared it was no longer my home and he warned me not to try and return. I did not care. Tam would be waiting for me in the forest. Yet in my heart I was sad to be leaving with so much hatred in the air. The bitter blow came when my father refused to let me take my daughter. He enjoyed watching me squirm and plead. His last words were, 'You are not a fit person to bring up an innocent baby'."

Ruth's voice trailed away into silence. Sue felt tears gather in her eyes. At last she was moved to compassion and put a hand on her mother's arm. She believed her now. So much had fallen into place. She caught Raithe's eye and he said quietly, "She has more to say."

Ruth cleared her throat and caught hold of Sue's hand.

"I walked from the house of my childhood with tears streaming down my face. I refused to look back, it was what my father wanted me to do. As I reached the forest a wolf howled, and I knew Tam was there, waiting. He never spoke but I felt his compassion. He led me away from all my unhappiness. Just a few steps into the trees and out of sight of the house, we were confronted by a hooded figure. I recognised the midwife immediately – and when I saw the bundle she was carrying, my happiness engulfed me. She had smuggled my baby out of the nursery. But it was not you, Sue. It was my son. The midwife said, 'He did not die. Your mother wanted me to get rid of him – so I brought him to Tam in the forest and between us both, we have looked after him. Now you can go to your new home with at least one of your babies – and I will come with you to help'."

The silence was now poignant. Barry looked surreptitiously at the girl he had always thought of as his sister, and his heart beat fiercely. As far as he was concerned, she still was. Ruth took a sip of water, her eyes fixed on Sue.

"I hope you now understand why I sent people to bring you here. Before long our two worlds are going to part and no one really knows how severe the breach will be when it happens. It could be that we shall never see each other again. Thane has been my chosen emissary who has visited your grandmother on many occasions. Now you know why she lives deep in the forest. It was to save gossip and to hide the guilt she felt at the way she had treated me. When I learnt that my father had died, I returned to see her. She was full of remorse and promised that when you were old enough, you would be told the truth so that you could make up your own mind as to what you wanted to do. I returned back to Therossa feeling happy, but as the years went by and I heard nothing of you, I sent Thane to see where you were. It was then I realised she had failed to keep her promise. Nothing had ever been said to you, Sue, about your true origins. The situation could not go on because enemies of the state heard about you from someone or other, and your life was now in danger. After their wolves tracked you down I had to step in. Tam would have fetched you himself but a war in the far north of our country drew him away. I had to leave it to Thane. I feel sad that you will never meet your father if you return to Gaynor."

"That's blackmail," Barry said in an undertone and although Ruth appeared not to have heard, Thane eyed him speculatively. Ruth went on with her story.

"I do not know why your grandmother has such a horror of your visiting this land. She came herself once and was shown every consideration – but still she thought of us as barbaric." Ruth's eyes held her daughter's. "You may be too old now to change horses in mid-stream, but I would dearly love you to come and live with me."

Sue had no chance to answer. Barry flung himself at her with a choking cry, shouting, "No, Sue – no – you mustn't! You've got to come back home with me and Priscilla. Please don't listen to her!"

THE SECRET OF TAMSWORTH FOREST

Everyone looked at the boy and saw the fierce determination on his face. He was going to fight tooth and nail to keep his sister in his family.

*   *   *

The following morning Barry and Sue were dangling their feet in the crystal clear water of a pool. Sunlight played on their head and shoulders and to anyone passing that way, the scene looked tranquil. Yet there was tension between them. Barry didn't realise what a pain he was being, following Sue around like a shadow. He was scared she might get talked into staying in this country. He couldn't visualise life without her around.

Yet his sister was dreaming of the city where Ruth had a palace. Annalee had been describing the spires, cobbled lanes and extensive parkland, when Barry had rudely dragged her away, ignoring Annalee's astonished face.

Sue sighed, wriggled her toes around and made the surface of the water ripple, acutely aware of Barry's presence. What could she say that wouldn't hurt him, or intensify his resentment against Ruth and this new world?

Sue was attuned to this land. The forest was spectacular bathed in sunlight. A colourful sheen came from the many red trunks. The shimmering leaves moved gently in the slight breeze. It was an idyllic place. Insects droned lazily in the air and Sue was very near to sleep when the ground suddenly heaved violently. She and Barry were thrown into the pool.

321

Spluttering, they made for the bank and climbed out, expecting to see chaos around them. But to their surprise, everything was tranquil again. It was as though nothing had occurred. Sue pushed the wet hair from her eyes.

"I can't believe that just happened. What was it? Is someone playing games with us?"

"If they are," Barry answered sourly, "I don't think much of their sense of humour. Suppose I couldn't swim. I bet no one thought of that."

"Well you would not have drowned," cut in a new voice, "the pool is not very deep."

The tall willowy figure of Ruth glided from between the trees and stood before brother and sister. She was elegantly dressed in a green shift, looking as though she were part of the forest. A smile touched her lips, and her dark eyes embraced them. When she held out her arms, Barry stiffened.

"Come," she invited, "I want to get to know you both. You are my only daughter and my only nephew." Her voice was seductive and Barry became wary, but Sue went to her immediately. He frowned, and after the briefest hesitation, followed. Ruth drew them further into the forest. They reached a small secluded dell where an old trunk made a convenient seat. She sat down and drew Sue beside her, making room for Barry. He ignored the gesture and sat on the ground the other side of Sue. It amazed him that in such a busy forest there was no one else about. Maybe they had orders to stay away. To his surprise, the conversation they had was not about anything important. His suspicions were

THE SECRET OF TAMSWORTH FOREST

lulled, but he still thought Ruth had some ulterior motive. Sue watched the expressions flit across the Queen's face, and wished she felt a stronger bond to this lady who was her mother. Unexpectedly Ruth changed the subject, saying,

"Tell me about my sisters. It is a long time since I had any information about them."

"You don't want to know about Aunt Moira," Barry responded bluntly "She worries too much. It would have done her good to have had a few children. Maybe then we should not have been expected to stay with her year after year."

"So Moira never had any children? Then why did you keep going there if it has been so bad?" asked Ruth curiously.

"Because Mum and Dad travelled a lot," Sue answered, without thinking, "and we're expected to visit Gran. It's not that I minded because I liked the hotel and the forest. Priscilla is the one who thinks she is now too old to be told what to do. She is nearly eighteen."

"But she's younger than you. You were born before Priscilla." Ruth's face had suddenly gone still and there was shock in her eyes. She stared intently at them. Sue looked surprised.

"But I wasn't. There is not a lot of difference in our ages. People always thought we were twins, even though we don't look alike. Why do you seem astonished?"

"Because I am," Ruth said. "After all these years I have just found out why Gaynor was sent away. Their

323

veiled remarks of why I was a bad influence on my sisters. How could they be so cruel?" She gave herself a firm shake and pulled herself up. What good would it do now to dwell on ancient history? It was best forgotten. "Are you happy with Gaynor?" she asked eventually.

"Oh yes," said Sue, her face glowing, "she's been great to me. Nothing will ever change that." Then she realised what she had said and turned to Ruth. "Please forgive me. In my heart I know you are my true mother, but I have a great love for the family which brought me up. I look upon your sister Gaynor as my mother and Barry is more of a brother to me than Raithe will ever be. I have to go back to them. You see," she floundered a little, "I could never stay here unless I explained to them why, although I suppose they know the reason anyway. I find this land very beautiful and have experienced good and bad things here, but I promise you one thing. I will come back and see you again."

A tear glistened on Ruth's cheek but she left it there and enfolded Sue in her arms. "All I ever wanted was to see my daughter before the two worlds parted," she whispered softly. "I understand your feelings and your urge to return. I was always sorry I never felt that way – but then I did not leave with love behind me." She looked towards her nephew. "At least one of us is happy."

Barry flushed. "I think this is a great land," he retorted quickly, "and I would like to come back again sometime. I think you're great too, Aunt Ruth."

THE SECRET OF TAMSWORTH FOREST

Ruth stood up and put an arm round each of them, giving each a big hug. "Thank you, my dears – but once you leave, unless fate plays a strange trick, you will never return here. The two worlds are parting. The Shaman is worried. It has already started. The recent shaking of the earth was a warning. You must return at once if you want to get home, but for tonight we shall hold a party beneath the trees to say goodbye. The people expect it. Tomorrow – Thane and whoever else wants to go – will escort you both back over the mountains."

Sue could feel her own emotions building up at Ruth's words and suddenly realised it was not only Ruth to whom she was saying goodbye. She had made so many friends here and some were dearer than others. Barry's hand grasped hers behind the Queen's back and gave it a squeeze. She needed his support, and that made him feel better.

CHAPTER 21

RAITHE SAVES THE DAY

A myriad of lights festooned the forest. Each tree was decorated with the owner's personal touch. The whole redwood forest looked magical. In a special clearing kept for such an occasion as this party a huge fire blazed. Although no one attended it, it never died down. The flames gave out heat but Sue was convinced they would never burn the redwoods. The aroma of cooking drifted on the air. Dressed in their best outfits, the inhabitants of Therossa loved ceremonial parties and this one was special; even if it did mean they were going to lose Sonja so soon. For them, Sue was determined to show a happy face. She joined in everything she could. Some of the dances were strange to her but somehow she seemed to know the steps. There was magic in the music, although try as she might, she never caught sight of the musicians.

Her eyes glowed as she looked around the whirling figures. No one gave the impression of being tired. For a moment she paused to catch her breath, wondering where all her friends were. Barry was sitting beside his aunt. Wild horses would not get him dancing. Thane was standing nearby, and now and again bent down to add something of his own to the conversation. Of Annalee and Tansy there was no sign. Thane looked up

326

THE SECRET OF TAMSWORTH FOREST

and caught Sue's eye. Seeing her at a standstill, he moved towards her enquiring, "are you enjoying yourself?

Sue's face was flushed. He looked so elegant and he fitted in with his surroundings. "Very much; I shall never forget this moment. I want to gather together everything I can in my mind to take home with me."

Thane's face was unreadable in the flickering light. "You have definitely made up your mind to leave?"

Then a treacherous surge of emotion suddenly swamped her. Some of the sparkle surrounding her fell away and reality reared its ugly head. Thane wished his last remark had been left unsaid. He had no wish to spoil her enjoyment, so he held out his hand. "Let me take you to where the food is being served. You are normally hungry when I catch up with you."

Unexpectedly Sue drew back. "No, Thane. I want to be on my own." The spell had been broken. She wanted to escape from the party. She smiled to soften her refusal and added, "Is it permissible for me to wander off?"

Thane nodded, and in consternation watched her go. Before she disappeared from sight he whistled sharply and White Hawk came from the shadows to stand beside him. Thane pointed in Sue's direction.

"Follow and guard," he commanded curtly, and watched while the wolf threaded his way through the crowd. He soon disappeared amongst the redwoods. At least, thought Thane, Sue would be safe.

Sue wandered on through the forest, enjoying the silence. Everyone was revelling at the banquet but she had only the twinkling lights, which were suspended from the trees and looked like stars that had fallen from the sky, to surround her. She continued walking until she was able to come face to face with the trauma that was pulling her apart. Which was right? Going back home to her own world and leaving behind her mother, or staying here and shattering Barry's hopes of keeping his sister in the family? Then, unbidden, she thought of Thane. What about her feelings for him? He belonged in this world. This was the hardest decision of her life. She wondered, if Barry had not followed her here, would she have stayed?

The forest floor took an unexpected drop. She could hear the sound of running water. The lights in the trees had petered out, but that did not make any difference since a brilliant moon gave clear vision. Sue was isolated where she stood. She could have been the only person in the world. For a brief span of time she leant back against a trunk until a sharp twang echoed on the night air, followed by another. She was not the only person seeking solitude. Then she saw Raithe aiming arrows at a post. She watched unseen for a while and admitted to herself that he was an excellent shot. Just a pity his social behaviour left him wanting. Quietly she moved in his direction, but not silently enough. He spun round like a coiled spring, ready to shoot, his next arrow already notched and pointing at her heart. The speed of his movement made her falter, but determination kept her going until she was level with him. Raithe seemed reluctant to lower his bow.

THE SECRET OF TAMSWORTH FOREST

"Surely you should know that walking in the forest at this time of night is looking for trouble. Weren't you worried I might shoot you?" he asked coolly.

"No," lied Sue, almost too quickly to sound offhand. She hoped the tell-tale colour flooding her cheeks could not be seen. He smiled cynically, and loosening his arrow put it back in the quiver. "It's good to know my sister is not above fabricating the truth when she wants to. What are you doing here so far from the party being held in your honour? Surely you should still be there?"

"The same as you, I expect. I needed space to think," said Sue.

Raithe's eyes took in everything about her until she felt uncomfortable. "Ah yes, it's very easy for you to walk away from my mother, is it not? But not so easy to walk away from the almighty Thane and leave him behind."

He was so near the truth Sue caught her breath. Was she that transparent? It was the sneer that curved his mouth which made her temper rise and she rounded on him. "You have no idea of what you're talking about," she flared angrily. "I have explained to my, our mother," she quickly amended, "why I have decided to leave. Unlike you, I have a code of honour. I happen to love the people who brought me up from a baby, and for what it's worth, Barry is more of a brother to me than you will ever be."

Raithe did not look in the least put out. "I know. That's what you told my mother so prettily," he replied blandly. For a moment Sue was speechless.

329

"You were listening to my conversation," she retorted indignantly.

"So what if I was."

"Listeners never hear any good of themselves," she snapped. "I'm surprised you had nothing better to do than skulk amongst the trees."

The tension started to build up between them. No longer was the forest a peaceful place with their angry voices echoing through the trees. They drew sparks off each other every time their paths crossed. He did not appear to have heard a word she said, which infuriated her all the more.

"Why have you come here?" he asked tersely. "What is the attraction?"

She shook her head in confusion. "Raithe, whatever else you may think, I am not trying to score points off you. I am not trying to wean your subjects away from you either. I was pleased to find you here because I was looking for you. I wanted to say goodbye without anyone else around."

"You don't have to. I would have lived if you hadn't managed to do so." Raithe turned away from her abruptly.

Biting her lip, Sue tried again, saying, "I know you haven't wanted me here, and if it helps, I didn't want to come either. You could have saved yourself a lot of time and trouble when you tried to get rid of me." She saw him stiffen and she ignored the action. "However, now that I am here and I have met my, our mother, I am sad to be leaving, but you don't have to believe that."

He swung round. "But you're still going."

THE SECRET OF TAMSWORTH FOREST

"Yes," she replied, "even though I have great feelings for her. I know that the two worlds are going to part and that I shall never be able to return here. That upsets me more than I can say."

Her voice trailed away and she took a deep breath to steady herself. A tear rolled gently down her cheek, sparkling as the moonlight caught it. Raithe stared, fascinated. He put out a finger to her face and wiped it away. Another tear followed and Sue trembled under his scrutiny. "Sue..." Whatever else he was about to say came to an abrupt halt as an arrow narrowly missed the pair of them and thudded into a nearby tree. They spun round, startled. A grotesque shadow of a man detached itself from the forest and stood looking at them aggressively. His voice sounded evil as it snarled, "Stand back, Prince. We will take over from here."

Raithe was not one to succumb to threats, especially from an intruder. His eyes raked over the trespasser, and taking in his appearance, knew exactly what he was. Sue fell back a pace and felt the hairs prickle down her arms as her blood froze. The past came up and swamped her. She recognised that voice even though the person's features were indiscernible. She wondered if he was carrying a bucket which he wanted her to fill with water. All the horrors of the gypsy encampment flooded back. The gypsies had followed her and she was with the one who had betrayed her in the first place. Fear tightened her throat and she was unable to scream. Raithe, however, spoke in his most dismissive voice, which made most people quail.

331

"You are trespassing in the Queen's forest and I would suggest you leave while you have a chance, before I call the guards."

The man laugh was coarse. He moved forward with an insolent swagger. His earrings glittered in the light of the moon. A lethal dagger was clearly seen tucked in his baggy trousers, making it obvious he was not the man who shot the arrow. There were more of them hidden in the forest. Sue trembled, realising she was about to return to captivity. Raithe noticed and deliberately stood in front of her with some idea of protection.

The man approached with surprising stealth. "Just move out of our way, youngster. Our argument is not with you, but that vixen lurking behind you. We've come to collect her. She's caused our tribe a lot of trouble. Our chief was most upset when she escaped and he wants her back. Through her he's lost a lot of money. You run away like you did the last time and leave her to us. There's no need for you to get involved."

Raithe cursed that Sue heard his words. He was also unimpressed at being referred to as 'youngster', and drew himself up haughtily, hoping they hadn't detected his fear. The past could not be changed. The odds were against him. Gypsies never travelled anywhere on their own. They went around in bands. He wondered how many were skulking out of sight.

"Are you calling my sister, the princess, a vixen?" he said. "That is treason, man."

THE SECRET OF TAMSWORTH FOREST

"Come off it, you hypocrite," snarled the gypsy, "You don't care about her. You gave her to us once, or have you forgotten? Stop being heroic for her benefit or else you'll get hurt."

A threat underlined his words which could not be ignored. Raithe's answer was to draw his bow in one fluid movement. It was not what the gypsy expected and he paused warily, deciding not to come any closer. Instead, he watched his companion creeping up unseen towards the unsuspecting Sue. So did someone else, lurking in the bushes. His fur bristled, he snarled softly from his throat, and his upper lip drew back showing a row of powerful teeth.

"Put that plaything of yours down before you hurt someone," the gypsy ordered harshly. "You are outnumbered. You can't stop us from doing what we have come all this way to do. No one is going to help you. All your soldiers are enjoying the celebrations." He laughed raucously, feeling he had outwitted the Prince.

"There are always guards about. You won't get away." Raithe's show of calmness started to undermine the gypsy's confidence, but his eyes glittered with cunning as he watched his henchman getting closer to Sue through the trees. Not much longer to wait now. Suddenly a harsh voice shouted out, "Got you!"

Sue screamed as she was grabbed from behind. Struggling furiously, she kicked out. No way did she intend to be hauled away from the forest. A large grubby hand was placed roughly over her mouth, nearly suffocating her. A blur of white fur flashed out from the trees and jaws closed viciously round her assailant's arm. It was his turn to scream now. He let go of Sue, yelling out in terror as the wolf's teeth sank into his flesh.

"Get it off me. Kill it, Jacques, kill it. It's mad."

The other gypsy grabbed his knife to throw but Raithe was quicker. His arrow sang as it left his bow and found its mark in the man's chest. With a surprised look on his face, Jacques's hands came up as he crumpled to the ground. Raithe whipped out his horn and blew on it twice. Then he turned his attention to Sue. She stood petrified, unable to close her eyes. White Hawk had his teeth on the other gypsy's throat. His yells turned to a gurgle, then ceased, but the wolf continued to savage the man. Raithe put his arm firmly round Sue's shoulders and drew her forcibly away from the scene. But the sight of so much blood made her cling to him, horrified.

"You've got to stop him," she gasped. "White Hawk will kill him."

"I can't do anything," Raithe returned through clenched teeth, supporting her as she stumbled back through the forest. Her heart thudded against her chest. She went with Raithe, blindly, relying on him in her terror. A crashing noise came from up ahead and she nearly fainted, realising they were too late. The gypsies had circled round them and had chased them into a trap. Despair overwhelmed her senses. Footsteps charged up to where they stood and someone snatched her away from Raithe. With a scream of panic she looked up into Thane's face. He and several men surrounded them.

334

THE SECRET OF TAMSWORTH FOREST

"What has happened?" asked Thane, looking from her stricken face to the Prince. "You blew the warning – why?"

Raithe looked grim. For once in his life he acted normally. "Gypsies," he snapped. "They came for Sue tonight. They have been following us ever since she escaped from them. I shot one and White Hawk had another, but they are not alone. It's thanks to your wolf that we got away."

Thane turned to the soldiers behind him. "Spread out," he thundered, "I want them caught. I don't care if it takes us all night to do it."

He turned back to Raithe and gently passed Sue towards him. "Take her back to your mother," he said, his voice deepening with concern, but when his eyes held those of the Prince, they held respect. "I'm proud of you. You did well, Raithe. At last I can see your father in you. You are going to be a worthy successor."

He did not wait to see the pride which filled Raithe's eyes because he set off with his men, but Sue had seen another side of the Prince. They were standing now where the lights began, and music faintly reached their ears. Unexpectedly she turned and hugged him, making his face go red with embarrassment. "Thank you, brother," she breathed. "I owe you a lot."

A smile spread over his face and he remarked, "I should be careful what you say. You may regret it. You called me brother."

"You called me sister earlier," she replied.

He grinned. "Don't let's argue – just tell me. Do I come up to scratch with Barry?"

335

Sue's answer to that was to hug him again. "Yes, but in a different way." With a satisfied smile he tucked her hand in his arm and led her back to the festivities.

*   *   *

Although there were no casualties and no damage done, panic spread through the colony when, at dawn, the earth moved again. One or two saplings were uprooted but it was enough to make Amos put his decision into practice and prepare the men to make the crossing back over the mountains. He said that if they did not leave within the next two hours it would be too dangerous to attempt the journey. Sue and Barry might find themselves living in Therossa permanently. That made Barry eager to get started. Willingly he lent a hand wherever it was needed to reduce the waiting time, but Sue felt devastated now that the time to leave had actually come.

The biggest problem was that Thane had not returned from last night's foray with the gypsies. Nothing had been heard from him or his men since. She couldn't understand why no one was worried about them. All sorts of thoughts flashed through her mind, knowing the mentality of the gypsies. Had Thane been hurt? Was he a prisoner? Maybe he was trapped somewhere? How could she leave without knowing he was safe or saying goodbye to him?

Barry was at a total loss when he looked into her morose face. He had no such compunctions. He chatted endlessly about seeing Moira and Priscilla again. In the

THE SECRET OF TAMSWORTH FOREST

end Sue turned away from him. She hadn't the heart to dampen his spirits with her own feelings.

A small band of travellers assembled at the foot of the path leading over the mountains. It seemed like only yesterday that they had arrived here, Cailli was giving a last minute inspection to the horses, checking hooves and bridles and making sure everything was in pristine condition. Amos stood at the edge of the group, speaking with the Shaman. Both were waiting.

So were quite a lot of people, who had gathered to see their newly acquired Princess leave. Sadness covered their faces. They fell back when the Queen arrived to make a pathway for herself and Raithe. Quite a few people were obviously hoping the Queen would change Sue's mind. This was the penultimate moment. Sue was feeling wretched, standing a little apart from everyone, when Ruth walked up to her and put her arms around her. For a few moments neither of them moved. Sue swallowed a lump in her throat. After today her mother would be only a memory, like everything else here, like Thane. She closed her eyes tightly to stop the tears from welling up. Why, oh why had her grandmother left it so late telling her what she should have been told when a child?

Raithe touched his mother's arm and she reluctantly drew away. He took her place and held Sue tightly as though never wanting to let her go. He sensed her depression and said, "I've got something for you. It's a small trinket so that you will never forget me." He drew a ring from his hand and placed it on one of her fingers. Sue stared in disbelief at the green stone, which to her

337

looked like an emerald. The sun caught it, and green fire shone from its facets. It was too much for her to accept. She had nothing to give back. Embarrassment swamped over her.

"It's too precious, Raithe. Sister or not, I cannot take this from you. I've got nothing I can give in return."

"Yes you have. Your forgiveness for the way I have treated you, since you've been here."

Brother and sister stared into each other's eyes. There was not a trace of animosity between them. They had both discovered their innermost shortcomings and accepted each other. She gave him a gentle push, saying, "You didn't have to ask for that. I forgave you last night."

Raithe grinned. Ruth caught her breath, watching the two of them together. For the first time in her life she almost hated her mother for never letting Sue know of her true origins. Life would have been so different had Sue come to visit when she was younger, and it would have been good for Raithe. He would not have grown so selfish. Fate had been cruel in that she had never been blessed with any more children. Now her daughter was going away again. For a while she contemplated them both with a wistful look on her face. Then catching sight of Amos gathering together his group, she drew Raithe and Sue's attention to herself.

"I also have something to give." Slowly she drew a ring off her finger. Its quartz top was inscribed with a wolf's head. It was a beautifully crafted piece of jewellery. Sue had never seen anything so delicate. Ruth held it towards Raithe. "This belonged to your father. It is an heirloom of the royal household and was given to me not long after I first came to Therossa. I was a stranger in this land and really missed my family. I was told the ring was magical. With it in my possession I could get in touch with anyone I wanted to, provided there was enough love. All I had to do was to think of this person." She paused for a moment then added sadly, "but it did not work for me. Maybe it will for someone else."

"How do you know it didn't work?" asked Sue, who was really interested. "Who did you try to reach; Grandmother, Moira, Gaynor?"

Ruth shook her head, "When I think of all those years I wasted! It was only quite recently that the Shaman told me I was doing it all wrong. Evidently there is a right and wrong way to use the ring and I was never told. When he explained that I could harm the person I wanted to contact – I stopped trying to do so. That is why you were never aware of me. Maybe that was just as well because you are here now."

"You tried to contact me?" Sue's husky voice was barely audible. Her nightmares surged back, the group of hooded figures, the empty wicker basket. The floodgates opened as Ruth answered.

"Yes. I kept asking you to come back."

Sue felt faint. Whether it was from relief or horror she did not know. Those nightmares had terrified her, and her mother had been the cause of them! Ruth looked at her anxiously, noticing her pallor. "Are you feeling all right, Sue?" she enquired. "You never heard me – did you?"

339

Sue managed a weak smile, determined not to tell her, and said, "I am fine. Are you going to try again after I have left?"

"No," replied Ruth, looking at her son. "I am giving you the ring since you are now so close to your sister. The Shaman will tell you how it works, and no protests please, Raithe," she added as he tried to butt in. "It is yours by rights as you will be the next King. Now it seems as though you are about to go, Sue. The others are mounting the horses. Thank you for coming to see me, my dear. You will never know how happy you have made me."

There was a suspicion of wetness in her eyes as she kissed Sue on each cheek. To her stupefaction, so did Raithe and before he drew away he whispered in her ear, "Don't give up. Thane will come after you."

Sue felt colour flood her cheeks but Raithe turned away to Barry, who had come impatiently to find out what was holding up his sister.

"Goodbye, cousin," said Raithe. "Make sure you look after my – our – sister and take this as a memento of your visit here." He thrust a dagger encrusted with jewels into the boy's hand. Barry's eyes lit up with excitement. He weighed it with expertise in his hands, studied the intricate gold work and setting of blue stones, and removed the leather sheath which covered the blade and inspected that. Then he beamed happily.

"Gosh. Thanks, Raithe. You're a mate," he exclaimed. "I will make everyone jealous back home. Come on, Sue – they're waiting for us."

THE SECRET OF TAMSWORTH FOREST

Sue gave one long lasting look at her brother and mother, then turned to follow Barry. Their faces would be forever etched in her memory.

CHAPTER 22

SAYING GOODBYE

As the waves and cheers died away, so did Sue's smiles. She stared ahead miserably, with Annalee and Tansy riding on either side. She was pleased they were there but had no inclination to talk. What should have been an exciting moment was anything but. All she could think of was Thane. Where was he, she wondered? The two girls gave up on trying to speak to her and spoke amongst themselves. Sue could not control her actions, but kept turning back and looking along the deserted track until in the end Tansy declared if she did it again she would have to be blindfolded.

"Who on earth do you expect to see following us?" she asked.

"No one," Sue lied, and added, "I just wanted to find the place where I can see the redwoods again before they vanished."

"Well, you've a long way to go before that happens," said Annalee. "I'll give you a shout when we get there. There's a lot of hard climbing to be done before we reach that point."

For a while the two girls left her in peace and laughed together, leaving Sue engulfed in her own misery. Every step Sue's horse took forward was one taking her further from Thane. Raithe had been

THE SECRET OF TAMSWORTH FOREST

incorrect. There was no sign of his catching up, and the parting from her mother was harder than she expected. It made her wonder why she was doing this. Why didn't she turn round and retrace her steps? Then she thought of Barry and knew she couldn't desert him. Annalee sidled alongside and her dark eyes probed Sue's face. She asked what was wrong.

"Nothing." Sue's answer was abrupt, so Thane's sister trotted back to Tansy.

Left to her own thoughts Sue tried to concentrate on the journey. The going uphill was easier than it had been descending it. The weather was better and a lot of the snow had cleared. The invigorating breeze put a little colour into her pallid cheeks. The sun felt hot on her back even though the air was getting colder. She was glad Barry had decided it would be more interesting to travel up front with Amos and Cailli. After another hour of climbing, Annalee halted Sue and waved her arm at the scene behind her.

Sue turned slowly in the saddle and gazed at the panorama displayed below. The beautiful redwoods still looked enormous, yet they themselves were already standing at a great height above them. The track could be seen as a narrow thread of ribbon far below and winding between the huge trunks. The vista took her breath away.

Annalee screwed up her eyes as she peered downwards. "There is someone galloping hard down there," she remarked innocently. "They're certainly in a hurry to get somewhere."

343

Sue's heart gave a lurch. She squinted against the sun. Her eyes swept the landscape feverishly but she could not see a thing. A loud cracking noise came from above and swiftly the two girls grabbed the reins of Sue's horse. Before she knew it, they were all galloping ahead up the slope. A tremendous roar filled the air and the ground shook. Part of the mountainside tumbled down behind them. Sue choked in the dust-filled air. Tansy looked at her in concern. "Sorry about that. The mountain is unstable at the moment. We must push forward and catch up with the others."

Sue had no choice but to follow. The path behind her was now partially blocked. Cailli came galloping down and surveyed the landslide. "That was close. Are you girls all right? Keep up with us from now on. Amos wants to get over the bridge."

Resigned, Sue proceeded onwards, wondering who had been on the horse below. But it made no difference now. Then she saw Barry anxiously waiting for her, and felt contrite. Whatever happened now – she was going home.

Amos regarded them all seriously. "We must push ahead swiftly. No stopping for food. Crossing the bridge is vital. Should it collapse, our only other option would be very dangerous, but I doubt even then that we would be able to cross between the two worlds in time. Are there any questions?"

His rugged face held an expression that dared them to say anything adverse. Sue's acquiescence was obvious but Barry showed undisguised consternation. Getting home meant everything to him. He looked towards Sue and felt his heart sink. She must not change her mind at the last minute.

They continued on their journey. The horses dropped to a steady walk. It would not do for them to become lame at the crucial moment when they wanted speed. Although it was not snowing, there was enough snow around to make some parts hazardous underfoot.

Sue hunkered down in her cloak as the wind screamed through the high passes. Her cheeks felt numb. Shelves of rock reared above her, fringed with long sword-like icicles. Several rumblings were heard and the icicles quivered. Sue wondered if they were a danger to them as they passed below. She had never heard of anyone being stabbed by a piece of ice.

Towards mid-afternoon they passed the overhang, which today was dark and deserted. But Sue shivered. She knew what was ahead.

The bridge came into view all too soon. From the direction in which they were approaching, it looked daunting. The slender rock formation, straddling the breach between two mountains, gave the appearance of a fragile arch and looked a lot narrower than it did on her first crossing. Already butterflies were in Sue's stomach. Against her will she looked down. The sheer drop ended in a haze of grey and she felt dizzy.

Amos halted everyone to get them all together. A roar resounded through the air and a boulder crashed down into obscurity very near the bridge. It was followed by a shower of rock, snow and ice. Amos's lips tightened as he realised the incident could have ended their journey. He rode towards the edge of the precipice, as the others watched. Sue felt sick and her breathing became rapid. With an effort she tried to get it under control and concentrate on what Amos was saying.

"I will cross first," Amos announced, "and the next one will step onto the bridge as I leave it. I want that one to be either Barry or Sue. Then I think that you, Annalee, should follow while Tansy helps whichever one of our guests is left. I would much rather, Callie, that you came last in case of trouble. Now our time is precious and thankfully the bridge still holds. There is no time for blindfolds." His glance rested fleetingly on Sue. "You have all done it before anyway. So let's get going." Without waiting for an answer he stepped onto the bridge as though it were only six inches off the ground. The horse picked its way over with the utmost ease. Barry glanced sideways at his sister, who drew in a ragged breath. She did not speak, but just nodded her head for him to go next. Barry showed no fear. The wind buffeted his body and his confidence made her feel ashamed. Annalee came forward, tightening her hands on the reins. She glanced at Sue's white face in alarm and halted, asking if she were all right.

"Not really."

"Would you like to go next and get it over with?" asked Annalee.

"No." On both occasions her answer came through clenched teeth. Annalee caught Tansy's eye and nodded. The hunter set her foot on the narrow stretch of rock as Barry walked off, and gently urged her mount over the span.

THE SECRET OF TAMSWORTH FOREST

Annalee trotted up beside Sue and leant towards her. She was worried that Sue seemed incapable of doing anything. A sheen of sweat stood out on her face, and her expression was one of stark terror. Annalee touched one of her hands and spoke to her as though she were a child. "Now whatever you do, Sue – don't look down. Look up at the peaks or close your eyes. You did this perfectly well the last time," she lied, "so you can do it again. The horse knows what to do. He's done it many times before and he's never lost a rider yet." She put a little more pressure in her touch because she had caught sight of Amos's anxious face watching from the other side. "Now come on. It's your turn. Off you go."

Sue was transfixed – unable to carry out any orders. The thought of crossing that bridge petrified her. Another explosion shattered the air and the ground beneath their feet trembled as a massive piece of granite crashed down beside her. She felt the rush of air as it passed. The horse whinnied, flattening its ears. It sensed her fear and it looked as though it was going to bolt. Annalee compressed her lips as she saw Cailli coming forward. He was the last person Sue would want to see at that moment, so she swung off her own horse, slapped it on its rump to make it cross on its own, then vaulted up behind Sue. Disregarding the warning cry from Cailli, she leant forward, grabbed the reins from Sue's hands and urged the horse to accelerate. Before Sue realised what was happening, they were across and Barry was beside her, concern written all over his face.

347

From the other side of the bridge another horse galloped in view, coming at a dangerous speed. The rider thrust Cailli aside and crossed the span in front of him, followed by a blur of white. Cailli was about to cross himself, when suddenly the bridge shattered and fell hundreds of feet into the void. Dumbfounded, everyone looked across at Cailli who was now stranded. He shrugged resignedly and waved to them.

"Sorry about that, everyone," he shouted, "My journey has apparently come to an end. I will let the Queen know you all crossed over safely," and with a salute to them all, he turned his mount and retraced his steps.

*   *   *

Amos greeted Thane hastily and drew him quickly away from the others. Sue was dumbfounded to be ignored, even though at the last minute Thane glanced over his shoulder and said in passing, "Good job you got across the bridge before it collapsed."

What had she done wrong? Ever since meeting the gypsies in the forest, her mind had been confused. She needed to speak with him, and find out what had happened. Did any of his men get injured? Were the gypsies still after her?

For a short while the tremors in the mountains ceased, but everyone knew they would return. They had time to reach the camp in safety, where the people of Therossa lived in caves. But even here, Sue's hopes were dashed. Thane remained busy with the hunters

THE SECRET OF TAMSWORTH FOREST

and guards who protected the secret passage between the two worlds. She found herself in the company of Barry and the two girls. But now pride came to her aid and she deliberately avoided him.

Barry was in awe of the cliff face with its many caves. He wanted to climb the tree and visit the cave which had been allotted to her on her first visit. Tansy asked him laughingly if he wanted to stay after all. He was tempted. It was written all over his face. Then something must have crossed his mind because he laughed and said, "If there is another way back to your land you can bet your life I'll take it. After all, I've got relatives here now."

Sue was disappointed he had not said this at the beginning of their journey. But the sudden violent, shaking of the earth started all over again and made speech impossible. Amos stayed at the camp to keep his people calm. He ordered the rest of them to get going to the passage. He drew Sue to one side, his weather-beaten face serious, and said he was sorry she was returning to her old life. He had hoped for a different outcome – which didn't make Sue feel any better.

"If things were not so serious I would have returned," she said, averting her face from him before he could see the anguish in her eyes. But Amos was already walking in the opposite direction. Dejectedly, Sue went with the others. They left the horses behind and walked. She didn't realise at first that Thane had joined them because he preferred the company of his sister. Sue trailed behind, finding it a great effort to put one foot before the other. Barry, on the other hand, was

349

eager to make the crossing. He sensed he was nearly home.

They approached the cave opening, partially concealed by hanging ferns. It was almost hidden from view. A shower of earth and roots descended from above. The grit billowed out like a foggy cloud, making it unwise to venture within. They waited for it to subside, and nearly lost their balance as the ground shook beneath their feet. Thane immediately took charge of the situation. He ordered Annalee and Tansy to move away from the cave. It was quite the wrong thing to do because they argued with him at once. They pointed out that if it was dangerous for them to be there, it must also be dangerous for him. So they stayed. Thane's composure snapped.

"I have got to show them the way through," he said through clenched teeth. "There is no need for everyone to put their lives in jeopardy."

"We already have," Tansy answered, "by coming over the mountains. What difference does the cave make?"

"A great deal. You could get trapped in there and I don't want that to happen."

Sue looked on helplessly while they argued. Barry was impatient, and since it seemed they had been forgotten, Sue made up her mind. She surprised them all by grabbing hold of Barry and pulling him into the partially cleared cave, deciding to make the crossing by herself. The gloomy interior confused her and she asked Barry to lead. Barry looked at her with a start. "Me – you're joking. I thought *you* knew the way."

THE SECRET OF TAMSWORTH FOREST

Sue was desperately looking around. "I don't remember anything. Thane carried me here the last time. Come on, Barry, think. When you came, you came alone."

Her brother looked helpless. His eyes took in the earth wall and roots hanging out of the roof. "I didn't come this way," he answered ruefully. "I followed White Hawk."

Then Thane stormed into the cave, his outline almost filling the entrance. Although their vision was restricted, Sue and Barry saw that his lips were compressed in a straight line and his eyes were blazing at them from a furious face.

"Are you two trying to kill yourselves?" he demanded, his voice so full of anger it made Sue quail. "Doesn't anyone listen to me these days? Are you all so wise that you think you can do it yourselves?" His sarcasm was cutting and so unlike him.

"I thought..." began Sue, but she stopped with a splutter as another mass of earth fell from the roof and showered upon them. This time the falling earth had sharp edges and cut her skin. Thane caught hold of her savagely and at the same time pushed Barry further into the cave towards the back. "Stand by the wall – now," he thundered.

Sue found his overbearing attitude impossible. She pulled back, breaking free from his restraining grip, and her face burned with indignation. Before he could react she flared, "there's no way out at the back. I've been in this cave before. Remember?"

351

Thane's temper had reached boiling point. He caught hold of her again, none too gently and his fingers dug into her arms as he swung her round to face the back.

Sue gagged in the stale air and her eyes smarted as the flying grit got into them. Barry was already at the back, trying to keep out of trouble and desperately holding his own fear under control. The walls seemed to be alive – cracking and pinging every second. Unseen by either of them, Thane pulled on a lever which could easily have been mistaken for a root. A slab of rock moved inwards and sideways, revealing a cavity of total darkness. There was no time to ask questions. Thane pushed them both inside. The temperature plummeted once the stone closed behind them. The place was claustrophobic. Although she could not see, Sue frantically looked for a way out. From within the blackness, Thane spoke harshly.

"You are not safe yet. Just do as I say and we shall soon be out of here. Sue – come closer to me."

"Is that meant to be funny? I can't see you."

Thane exhaled sharply. "Then feel around, for God's sake. That's what you've got hands for."

Sue lifted her hands and waved them around in the dark until she made contact with Thane's shirt. He guided them to his belt and said, "Good. You hold on to that, and with your other hand grab Barry. Then we can get started. I'll lead you."

It was easier to comply than say anything else, but Sue had the childish urge to argue with him. Slowly they shuffled down a slope, having no idea where they

THE SECRET OF TAMSWORTH FOREST

were going. The darkness pressed down on them and Sue felt confused. A strange feeling came over her – she felt she was no longer in her body. Maybe the air was giving out. A constant roaring was heard, it resounded even down here in the bowels of the earth. Her head felt as if it were exploding. It was not just she who was experiencing this sensation, because Barry gripped her other hand tightly. To the relief of them both, the noise faded. The hard ground became soft and before long they were walking on a bed of something yielding. Thane stopped and she drew in a deep breath. To her joy a breeze fanned her cheeks. She let go of Barry.

"Sue." Thane turned her round to face him and caught hold of her hands. His grip was warm and firm, so different from his former treatment of her. She could not see his face but it felt very near to her own because his breath blew the hair from her temples. "Sue," he said again in a low voice, "this is the parting of the ways."

She stood very still. Her heart plummeted. Her first surge of joy was quickly dashed and taken over by desolation. It had come at last, the final time to say goodbye. She was not ready for it. Her lips quivered and tears gathered in her eyes. She was pleased he could not see her, but Thane's hands moved up to her arms and he held her.

"The choice is yours," he said softly. "Is it to be your world or mine?"

Before she could utter a word, Barry protested loudly, "That's not fair. She's coming home with me.

353

Priscilla is waiting for her and so is Aunt Moira and our grandmother. Tell him, Sue."

Sue was incapable of telling him anything. She was dumb with misery. The tears overflowed and were running in rivulets down her cheeks. Her breath caught on a sob and she leant against him. Thane's arms went round her and he held her tightly.

"I'm so sorry, Thane," she whispered in his ear. "I promised Barry I would go with him. I can't let him down."

Thane stiffened, but he felt the wetness of her tears. Gently he brushed them away and kissed her. "It's not what I wanted to hear, but I understand, Sue. You know your heart best."

The next moment he removed his arms and she was standing on her own. It felt like being abandoned. The next time Thane spoke, his voice was crisp and impersonal. He took hold of one of her hands and placed it on a wood and rope ladder, saying, "Climb up this and it will bring you to the spot where I made you jump." His voice was drowned by an ear-splitting roar. When the noise subsided he added grimly, "Go quickly now because time is short."

Sue started climbing automatically – mainly because she had to get away from him, not understanding what he wanted. Her fingers and feet felt for the rungs. She was numb and emotionally drained. Barry, behind her, pressured her to go faster. He was getting impatient. Just as they both reached daylight, the tree they found themselves climbing, shuddered. Sue crawled carefully

THE SECRET OF TAMSWORTH FOREST

onto one of the thick branches with her brother following.

"Where do we go?" he gasped.

"We must make for the next tree. We can get down from there."

Thick as the branch was they were crawling on, although nothing like the giant redwoods, it moved two and fro. A whole tree nearby toppled over, and another splendid tree was lost for ever.

"Do hurry up," said Barry. "We must get away from here."

She couldn't move. Barry took over. He chivvied her along and helped her down the other tree, almost sliding down the trunk himself. Not giving her any time to think, he pulled her along after him. They had no idea what direction to take but just pushed through the thick undergrowth.

"I think we're lost," Barry muttered angrily, "lost in our own forest. Doesn't it make you feel sick?"

Sue barely heard him. She still stumbled on and quite suddenly broke out into a clearing. Looking filthy and dishevelled, with a tear-stained face, she pulled up with a start, staring into the hawk-like eyes of Professor Harding.

*   *   *

"Well, what have we got here?" His icy regard flickered over her, staring dispassionately at Sue's white exhausted face and hunting clothes Annalee had given her Looking down his bony nose, he asked, "Just

355

returning home from a fancy dress party, are we? I must say your aunt will be surprised when she sees you. I would suggest you get washed first. It might take the shock off."

Sue had difficulty trying to collect her scattered wits. She knew she looked dirty, but he was the last person she expected to see.

Barry timed his entrance perfectly as he stumbled through the bushes behind her. Seeing the Professor gave him a nasty jolt, but his brain was a lot more active than his sister's. It should be easy to fob the Professor off.

The Professor's eyebrows raised a fraction at his appearance. Then his expression hardened as he remembered the boy's deception the last time they met. "As for you," he said, "I've got a few things to say about your behaviour." His voice became threatening and he advanced towards them. "Where did you go, boy, after you robbed your aunt?"

Barry swiftly looked around in case Cyril Grant was there. His absence gave the boy more courage. He deliberated on how far to push the Professor. He stared at him owlishly through rather dirty glasses. This usually annoyed adults because they either thought he was simple or making fun of them.

"I don't remember robbing Aunt Moira. This is awful. Do you think I've got amnesia?"

"You will have in a minute if you don't answer me."

"But this is serious," continued Barry. "When did it happen?" He turned to his sister, trying to make eye contact. "Did you hear what he said, Sue? Come on –

THE SECRET OF TAMSWORTH FOREST

best foot forward. We had better get back to the hotel. It appears someone has broken in."

He made to move but the Professor blocked his way. "Don't you think it's a little late in the day to show concern? You should have done that on the day you stole all the food. Where have you come from? There's nothing for you in this part of the forest."

"You should know if you've been here before," retorted Barry cheekily.

"I'm warning you. Don't be flippant with me, boy. Answer my question."

"But I can't. It's private, for family ears only." His smile was enigmatic. It caught the older man on the raw and he lashed out with his fist with the idea of teaching him a well-deserved lesson. Sue came to her senses with a jolt. She sprang at him, her eyes blazing with anger.

"Don't you touch him, you brutal man," she flared. "Where we've been or what we've done is none of your business. I'm surprised you're still here. I should have thought Aunt Moira would have thrown you out ages ago. Get out of our way. We're in a hurry."

The Professor's jaw tightened and his expression turned feral. He caught hold of her upper arm and shook her violently. Her head snapped back with a jerk. "I've had enough of your belligerence, girl," he snarled through clenched teeth. "If you know what's good for you, you'll answer my questions." He gave her another shake. "Look at the way you're dressed, for a start. That's not exactly the fashion around here. You've

357

come from the other world, haven't you?" and he gave her a third shaking.

Sue was so disorientated she could hardly speak, but she managed to jerk out, "mind your own business."

Her words made his thin bony fingers dig viciously into her arm. She winced. A savage push sent her sprawling into the thick undergrowth. As the ground came up and met her, the rough compost smothered her face and went into her mouth. She spat it out angrily, and gingerly moved her head. Sound seemed to come from a distance, but she heard Barry roar indignantly, "Take your hands off my sister."

Sue started to sit up, when something wet touched her out-flung hand. Her startled glance focused on a pair of amber eyes. She must be hallucinating, but the soft whine was real enough. Her heart went out to the wolf. White Hawk must have got himself trapped in this world. A groan from Barry made her realise the Professor had struck him and she saw red. She struggled to her feet, but his hand shot out with the swiftness of a snake and he caught her arm again. She cried out as he pulled her towards him.

"Stop wasting my time, girl, by sitting on the ground." His voice was harsh. The expression on his face sent shivers down her spine. "If you know what's good for you, you will…" He broke off in mid-stream. A low threatening growl reached his ears. He saw the wolf, its lip curled back to reveal a row of teeth. Incredulity shone from his eyes. "Did you bring that brute back here with you? I'll kill it."

THE SECRET OF TAMSWORTH FOREST

His hand moved to his pocket, but to get what, was never known. White Hawk sprang and sank his teeth into the Professor's arm, causing him to shriek out in pain. Barry struggled to his feet and watched in fascination. He thought, as his sister had, that the wolf was trapped here. For the first time in his life he felt sorry for the man, but could do nothing – even had he wanted to. Barry's eyes scanned the surrounding area. His jaw fell open in astonishment, yet he never said a word. Sue felt sick at what was happening again. She knew how deadly the wolf's attack could be and she had no wish to have Professor Harding's death on her conscience. Tentatively she touched the bristling White Hawk.

"Leave him, boy," she whispered, "he's not worth your effort."

Surprisingly, at the sound of her voice White Hawk relinquished his hold and stood by her side, contenting himself with threatening growls. But his unblinking eyes were fixed on the Professor. Blood poured from the Professor's arm and he glared balefully back at them.

"I'll see to it that he's shot," he spat out, venomously.

"The wolf was protecting me. You asked for what you got." And to the Professor's horror she crouched down by the wolf and put her arms round his thick neck and scratched him. White Hawk turned his head and licked her face, his wet tongue rasping against her skin.

"Don't make me laugh. That animal is a danger to the public. It's going to be your word against mine and

359

your word will not carry any weight." As the Professor backed away, he added, "I've got bites to prove my case. No one will listen to your stupid fairy tales, my girl."

"But maybe they will mine," cut in a new voice. "I've been watching you for a long time. I would have thought you had learnt your lesson by now and gone home."

Having been perfectly camouflaged, the newcomer stepped out into the open. The Professor recognised Thane immediately and his face contorted with rage. He saw his carefully laid schemes crashing down in ruins. Also he remembered their last conflict which ended with his companion, Cyril Grant, packing his bags and leaving.

"Don't think you've won. I mean it. That animal is as good as dead." With a muffled oath, he turned and stormed off, not wishing to prolong the conversation.

Barry flung himself at the newcomer and gripped his hand, his eyes alight with welcome. It was worth having a wallop just to see him again.

Thane ruffled his hair and said in a low tone, "Go and tell your family that Sue is home," and when Barry did not move, added, "Right now, lad!"

Barry knew he was being got rid of but did not care. He gave Thane a wink, which made the older man smile, and bounded off to see Priscilla and Aunt Moira. Sue stood where she was, not daring to believe what her eyes were telling her. White Hawk gently nipped at her hand to make her keep scratching. Thane moved to

THE SECRET OF TAMSWORTH FOREST

her side and touched her cheeks, which were smeared and dirty and still showed traces of earlier tears.

"Have you nothing to say?" he asked. "I thought you would be pleased to see me."

Sue swallowed. This was like a dream. First there was White Hawk and now Thane. She thought she was manipulating her feelings to go the way she wanted. Yet his touch was real. It sent a shiver of happiness through her. "Are... are... you trapped as well?"

Thane's eyes crinkled at the corners. "I'm not trapped," he said, sounding amused.

"You mean," she raised her face then, her eyes alight with hope, "you mean the way is still open?"

"No," he replied. "The way we came has gone for ever. It means I stayed behind deliberately because I could not leave you. When I asked which world – you chose this one. So here I am."

Sue's hands stole up to his shoulders. She could feel tears of joy brimming in her eyes. "But you didn't want to come with us."

"I had White Hawk to sort out. I could not leave him behind."

"Thane." This time Sue did hug him, tightly. Over the top of her head his eyes were thoughtful. He was still not sure if she really wanted to be here, but then, there was so much pressure on her. He had to be sure before he did anything else.

"Are you happy, Sue?" he asked, stroking her hair. "I mean, really happy?"

"Yes, now that you're here." She lifted a radiant face to him, but his probing eyes saw the shadow before she

361

added, "I wish the way was still open. I would love to see my mother again and all my friends."

He took hold of her both hands. "Sue, I'm being serious now. Will you do me a favour? If by some remarkable chance of fate, you were able to cross back over again, would you really be happy to go, and mean it?"

She nodded at once without really thinking, but he went on steadily, "will you promise me that you won't go, unless you really mean to stay there forever?"

Sue opened her mouth but he did not wait for her answer, because he added, "It would not be fair to your mother or anyone else. Now – brighten up that solemn face and I will take you to your grandmother's cottage. I will leave you there while I scout around."

He had already started to walk her away, not giving her the chance to question him. He thought he knew the answer anyway, but he still had to make sure.

CHAPTER 23

ONE WAY ONLY

For her, it was always known as the best time of day. When the sun started to sink and shadows lengthened to touch the cottage. They touched Mrs Denton now, where she sat in her favourite armchair, with an open album of photographs on her lap. Not the ones she had shown Sue all those weeks ago, but family ones she usually kept well hidden. There was no need to hide them now.

Ever since Sue had been taken away, because she failed to keep her part of a bargain, she looked at them every day. Ruth's face smiled up at her from the open page. When this picture was taken she had not as been old as Sue was now. The old lady drew her breath in sharply and closed the album with a snap. Looking at it made her emotional. Ruth had given her so much pleasure and joy before her father introduced Captain Harding into the family. Nothing was the same after that odious man frequented the house with his disreputable fellow officers. One of whom had made Gaynor pregnant. The abhorrent feeling she felt then, was still with her now. Time and time again she mulled over it. Suppose she had acted differently. Would things have changed? At that time, her only thought had been to get Gaynor away before her puritanical father guessed the truth. So when Ruth dropped her own bombshell, she did not stand a chance.

Mrs Denton was feeling her age and thinking of returning to the hotel. She had come to this cottage to escape her guilt and memories – but they had insidiously followed. Sue had been her last hope of normality, being so like her mother – but now Sue had gone, just like her daughter before her.

A noise coming from the outside made her stare in that direction. A shadow filled the doorway and a young lady stood there in the last rays of the sun, which turned her hair into a halo of gold. Mrs Denton's eyes opened wide. Joy touched her old face. Things had turned out for the best after all.

In a trice Sue was inside, giving her grandmother a bear hug. Even as her arms went round the her she was shaken to realise that the old lady seemed much thinner and less sprightly. The grey eyes were not as sharp either. She had aged.

Her grandmother extricated herself from Sue's arms and sat back in her chair. She looked at the shorn locks for a moment and nodded her head in approval. They made her granddaughter look elfin. But there was also something different. Suddenly she realised Sue was not a child anymore. In her absence something had happened to make her grow up. Seeing Sue perched on the arm of the armchair made the old lady reminisce about bygone days. Then she enquired, "Have you been to see Moira?"

"Not yet," replied Sue. "I've only just got here. Barry has gone on ahead to break the news to her."

THE SECRET OF TAMSWORTH FOREST

"So Barry was the reason you came home. Not your mother?" remarked Mrs Denton, and she snapped her jaws shut as though surprised at what she had said.

Sue did not pretend to misunderstand. The brightness went from her eyes and she looked at her grandmother. It made Mrs Denton feel unbelievably sad and she lowered her eyes, bracing herself for what Sue might say.

"Why was it I was never told about my family, when even Professor Harding knew?" Sue asked quietly. The old lady shrank from explaining. What could she say other than that she had been a selfish old woman who thought she could manipulate everyone to get her own way?

"I did not want to lose you." The words were true, but rasped in her throat and Sue steeled herself against any emotion.

"But you led me to believe Gaynor was my mother. You deliberately kept me away from Ruth, and she loved me."

"I'm sorry, child," said the old lady.

Sue jumped to her feet and looked down on her grandmother. "You have a lot to answer for, Gran." Her eyes thoughtfully searched the face before her. She missed seeing the shadowy form which slipped unobtrusively into the room. "I have been through so much because you allowed me to grow up with the wrong ideas. Not just me, but Barry, and Priscilla as well. It was the hardest thing I ever did, coming back here, and I came only because of Barry." She paused for a moment. "I want you to know, Gran, that now I

365

am here I am pleased. Pleased because I realise I have only come back to say goodbye."

"What do you mean?" Her grandmother's voice was querulous. Alarm made her struggle to get to her feet. "Please don't go back to that heathen place again. I am not proud of the way I have manipulated your life. It has been lonely here without your coming to visit me."

Sue bent forward and pushed the old lady back in her seat, but still held her with strong arms and studied her face intently. "Why don't you go back to the hotel and live with Moira?" she asked. "There is no need to stay here and be lonely. Ruth is never coming back."

The old lady's eyes misted over. Her lips quivered. "Would you come back for a visit if you left, Sue?" Her voice was barely audible.

"Gran, I'm not that hard. If it is at all possible, of course you'll see me again. But I haven't gone yet so don't start upsetting yourself. I still have Moira and Priscilla to see."

"Please take care, child. That Professor is still around, he – oh – bless me. What's that?"

The shadowy form materialised, and White Hawk came forward. He looked enquiringly from one to the other. Although to Sue he represented a friend, to her grandmother the wolf was something to be wary of. Sue gave her gran a reassuring squeeze as the old lady whispered in alarm, "Are they back in the forest again?"

"No, it's only Thane. He guided me back. This is his wolf, White Hawk, and my protector. He has already had an encounter with the Professor so I'm not likely to bump into him again."

Mrs Denton eyed the animal suspiciously. "How can you trust it? It's a savage beast."

"Not to friends," replied Sue, bending over and patting his head while the wolf growled contentedly. "He has come to escort me to the hotel. Take care, Gran, and think about moving house. I must go and see Aunt Moira now."

*   *   *

Moira was vague and gave Sue a peck on the cheek. Sue did not think the greeting was offhand because her aunt was not very good at showing her feelings. When she said something to the effect of, "nice to see you again – how long are you staying?" Sue felt the greeting was uttered for the sake of politeness. Her aunt continued with her hotel business. One look at Sue's despondent expression after such a casual greeting made Thane, who had escorted her, vanish. He had already attracted more than his fair share of curious looks from the residents.

Sue watched him disappear into the forest. She felt uneasy with everything. Thane was not going to fit in very well, and White Hawk was definitely a problem. She should have listened to her heart instead of Barry, and stayed in Therossa. How many people had she unwittingly made sad because of her decision to come home? Keyed up and tense, she had allowed her emotions to overcome common sense. She would look for Barry. Maybe from him and her sister she could get the solace she badly needed. She moved out of the hotel lobby.

Barry proved to be elusive, and Sue had the feeling he was deliberately avoiding her. But why? After a fruitless search she thought that maybe their private sitting room would be a good place to look. Rather than risk coming into contact with any more hotel guests the way she was dressed, Sue made her way outside and up the stairs of the tower. At the door of the sitting room she paused. Conversation floated out from within. Two people were speaking angrily. Barry was protesting furiously about something Priscilla had said and his boyish voice carried clearly to her ears.

"Well, you can do what you please. I feel like a heel, dragging Sue home to this. If I had known beforehand what had happened, I wouldn't have been so insistent that she came home."

"You're being absolutely stupid," Priscilla said. "It's not your mother over there. What would you get out of it had you stayed? It wouldn't have been your family."

"Yes it would," Barry snapped back. "There would be Aunt Ruth, who is a Queen and er...er Uncle Tam, and my cousin Raithe. Then there..." He broke off because he was interrupted by a mocking laugh.

"Uncle Tam? Is he as peculiar as his name?" asked Priscilla disparagingly, and Sue decided to walk in on them and break up whatever they were discussing. They looked up with a start at her entrance, Barry uncomfortably, but Priscilla put on a sorrowful

THE SECRET OF TAMSWORTH FOREST

expression and squeezed out a couple of tears. Then she said in a hollow voice, "Sue, I know. Poor old you."

"You know what?" enquired Sue warily.

"That you're not my sister," continued Priscilla.

Sue gave a strained laugh. "Does that matter?" adding, "I'm still your cousin."

"But of course it does," replied Priscilla, looking stricken. "It means you won't come with us now."

"What on earth are you on about? Where won't I go?" Sue stared at her in surprise.

"To America of course." Priscilla tried to make her voice sound dramatic. "Mum and Dad are going to live there. We are all going in a few weeks."

Sue fell back, stunned. Her gaze flicked from her sister to Barry, who was biting his lip, and back to Priscilla again. "What about me? What did they say about me?" she asked. "They weren't going to leave me behind, surely?"

Priscilla had the grace to look embarrassed. "They...they...," she uttered and glanced imploringly at her brother for help, but did not get it, and then added, "they didn't think you were coming back home."

"Why would they think that?"

"Gran told them you had gone to live with Ruth."

Sue sank into a chair. Her legs would no longer hold her up. The blood drained from her face, making it look white and pinched. She could not believe she had been abandoned by the people she had thought of as her parents. Did they not care about her? Had all her heartache been in vain? She clenched her teeth and tightened her face muscles to keep herself from crying. "You will love America, Priscilla," she managed to say gruffly. "You will like it better than here. You've always hated Tamsworth Forest."

"I shall miss you, sis," said Priscilla. She went over to her side and put her arms round her shoulders. She dropped all her airs and graces and for once acted normally. "But you could still come to America with us, you know. I should like that."

Sue shook her head. She had not been back one day and already her mind was made up. "No. I shouldn't like America," she contradicted, "but please don't worry about me. I am going to try and get back to the other world and find my mother again."

Barry moved uncomfortably, not looking at all happy. "How are you going to do that? You know the path collapsed behind us."

Sue smiled. Thane suddenly made sense to her. A load was lifted from her shoulders and she said to Barry, "I have a strange feeling that things are not what they seem. All I can say is that I have had a chance to say goodbye to..." She broke off, as from the forest came the sound of a hunting horn. She looked towards her brother and sister. Barry was incredulous – Priscilla uneasy. After a few seconds the horn sounded again. Sue jumped to her feet and ran to the window. Twilight had descended over the trees. She caught a glimpse of White Hawk streaking across the lawns towards the forest in answer to the call. Sue could not restrain her cry of delight.

THE SECRET OF TAMSWORTH FOREST

"That was Thane's call. He has found an opening," she cried, and turned to the door. Barry sprang forward, catching hold of her before she disappeared. "You can't go, Sue. Not like this?"

"Yes I can, Barry. I'm not really wanted here – but I am in Therossa. I'm sorry, both of you, but I'm going. Say goodbye to everyone for me," and she broke free from his restraining grip and fled.

With sad eyes Priscilla saw her racing across the lawn towards the darkening forest. Then her heart almost stopped beating. She had not realised Barry had gone also until she saw him following in hot pursuit. She stood still for a moment then shrugged her shoulders. *He would not have liked America anyway*, she thought.

THE END

If you enjoyed
**THE SECRET OF
TAMSWORTH FOREST**
read more of how Sue tries to
integrate with the inhabitants of
Therossa and become the daughter
her mother expects, in the two
following books of the trilogy:

**Book 2:
THEROSSA**
Sue falls into the hands of
an underground tribe of people
and an evil Priest.

**Book 3:
THE CRYSTAL HORSE**
Priscilla is united with Sue and
Barry - but not in the way she
expected.

*To find out more about these books
and their publication dates visit the
Brighton NightWriters' website at:*
www.nightwriters.org.uk

Printed in Poland
by Amazon Fulfillment
Poland Sp. z o.o., Wrocław